CAPTIVE OF TALIONIS

TALIONIS SERIES
BOOK FOUR

C.J. MILACCI

Published by Journey Perspective Publishing

Philadelphia, PA, USA

ISBN: 978-1-958230-14-5 (ebook)

ISBN: 978-1-958230-15-2 (printed softcover)

ISBN: 978-1-958230-16-9 (printed hardback)

Cover design by Emilie Haney

Editing by Becca Wierwille

Proofreading by Chris Pearce

Typesetting by Journey Perspective Publishing

Find out more at www.cjmilacci.com

To my little sister, Ani.
You have shown me what it looks like for someone to rise above darkness, struggle, and pain, and become stronger as you courageously cling to Jesus and obey His leading. Although blood may not bind us biologically, God has woven our lives together in a way that amazes me. You are the sister I didn't even know I needed. The sister who has changed my life.
I love you, little goose!

CHARACTER & WORLD GLOSSARY

Bria: Main Character, captive of Talionis
Matthias Valarius: Love interest, son of Colonel Keenan Valarius, captive of Talionis
Nika: Bria's best friend, sentenced to death
Ari: Bria's close friend, fugitive of Talionis
Shane: Ari's boyfriend, soldier of Talionis, betrayed his friends when he thought Ari was dead
Bryson: Ari's brother, fugitive of Talionis
Cai: Bria's uncle and mentor who was taken by Laban after they escaped Talionis, former leader in Eryndale
Storm: the little girl Bria bonded with in Talionis and who she's desperate to protect
Kemena: Nika's older sister, now a captive in Talionis
Bria's Family
Elena: Bria's aunt, the woman who betrayed her to Talionis; Cai's wife
Josiah: Bria's dad
Lily: Bria's mom
Eli and Zeke: Bria's twin eight-year-old brothers
Ezri: Bria's brother who died when she was younger
New Recruits in Talionis

Strider Locke, aka Kiwi: a teen recruit brought in during the hunt for Bria and her friends, tech whiz

Arwen: a teen recruit brought in during the hunt for Bria and her friends, munitions expert

Ahkeesia, aka Keesia: a teen recruit brought in during the hunt for Bria and her friends

Quincy: a ten-year-old young recruit brought in during the hunt for Bria and her friends

Sam: a six-year-old young recruit brought in during the hunt for Bria and her friends

Jace: a nine-year-old young recruit brought in during the hunt for Bria and her friends

Penny: an eight-year-old young recruit brought in during the hunt for Bria and her friends

Asher: a teen recruit brought in during the hunt for Bria and her friends, leader of the Resistance in Talionis

Marci: a teen recruit brought in during the hunt for Bria and her friends, part of the Resistance

The Fearless Lady Crew

Catori: captain of The Fearless Lady

Davey: part of Catori's crew who helped Bria and her friends

Nate: Davey's brother who was also part of Catori's crew, but died standing against Talionis while helping Bria and her friends

Quwani: part of Catori's crew, but she was on leave when the crew helped Bria and her friends

Hosea: the man who brought Bria and her friends to Catori when they were on the run

Micah: Catori's husband who has been missing for years while he was held captive by Callypso, now reunited with Catori

Shep: Catori's well-trained dog

Talionis Soldiers & Personnel

Commander Demetrius Ark: Commander and leader of Talionis who is seeking revenge against his father, the Chancellor of Sitreea

Sergeant Laban Meritas: one of Ark's most trusted soldiers who hates Bria, drill instructor in Talionis

Lieutenant Colonel Keenan Valarius: Matthias's dad and a leader in Talionis

Staff Sergeant Andor Valarius: Matthias's uncle, senior Drill Instructor, Colonel Valarius's older brother

Sampta & Presida: sisters who oversee all of the uniform and clothing creation and design in Talionis, known as the tailors

Shay: Bria's neighbor from Derbe; after an injury in battle, she's been given cyborg parts and now has a hand that can morph into a gun, drones that fly around her wherever she goes, and several other enhancements; loyal to Talionis

Major Tay Vasco: Warfare Scenarios Instructor for Talionis

Elva Trill: Educational Instructor for Talionis, oversees all of Ark's propaganda

Corporal Emode: works with Major Vasco in Warfare Scenarios

Corporal Sidon: Talionis soldier who aids in training recruits

Corporal Homer: Talionis soldier who aids in training recruits

Private Rafael Cruz: former recruit of Talionis who is now a soldier

Sitreean Leaders

Antonio: Minister of Defense for Sitreea

Chancellor of Sitreea: Ark's father who refuses to acknowledge Ark's existence since Ark is his illegitimate son

Eryndale Scouts & Leaders

Essie: leader and founder of Eryndale; Cai's mom

Azarias: Cai's son; well respected scout in Eryndale who oversees various scout teams

Emmi DeFort: Malachi, Moses, Micah, and Jordyn's mom, well-respected woman in Eryndale

Kassre DeFort: Emmi's husband, a well-respected retired scout who took on a mission to fight against Talionis; met Bria and her friends when he rerouted *The Fearless Lady*

Levi: Azarias's six-year-old son

Malachi DeFort: Micah's older brother, Eryndale Scout, the Wild Dogs team leader

Moses DeFort: Micah's youngest brother, Eryndale Scout, part of the Wild Dogs team, most of his friends call him Retro

Jordyn DeFort: Moses and Malachi's adopted sister; she is one of the youngest scouts in Eryndale and she's excellent at navigation; part of the Wild Dogs team

Glacier: Eryndale Scout, part of the Wild Dogs team

Karyss: Eryndale Scout, part of the Wild Dogs team

Isaac: Eryndale Scout, Wild Dogs; he's also good with tech

Thaddeus: older scout, member of the S.O.C. and head of cartography in Eryndale

Wolf: Eryndale Scout

Lorenzo: older scout, excellent fighter, leader of the S.O.C.

Bill and Paul: Older brothers who live in Eryndale who lead a team of master craftsmen (Wade, Fred, and Joey)

Brandi: head of tech development in Eryndale

Gabe: a younger member of the C.A.E.

Reginald Finnigan: high-ranking official in the C.A.E.

Nalani: escaped from Talionis with Bria, but stayed behind on *The Fearless Lady* after almost drowning; now works with the medic teams from Eryndale

Other Enemies

Callypso: a believed myth and legend throughout the North American region, she's a Raider who destroys anyone who gets in her way; she calls those with her her pirates

The Raiders: a dangerous group to the west who stand for everything Eryndale is against

Main Locations

Talionis: The hidden city built on the ruins of what was once Philadelphia; the place responsible for kidnapping teens throughout the North American region and training them to become soldiers

Sitreea: a country across the ocean that believes Talionis is being used as a hidden intel gathering base and does not realize Demetrius Ark is using it to train soldiers for war

Eryndale: a refuge city built in the mountains that was established after the Demise of North America; it became a place that provided a home for those who did not have one, and the scouts from Eryndale help create new towns and villages for the survivors of the Demise

Derbe: Bria's hometown

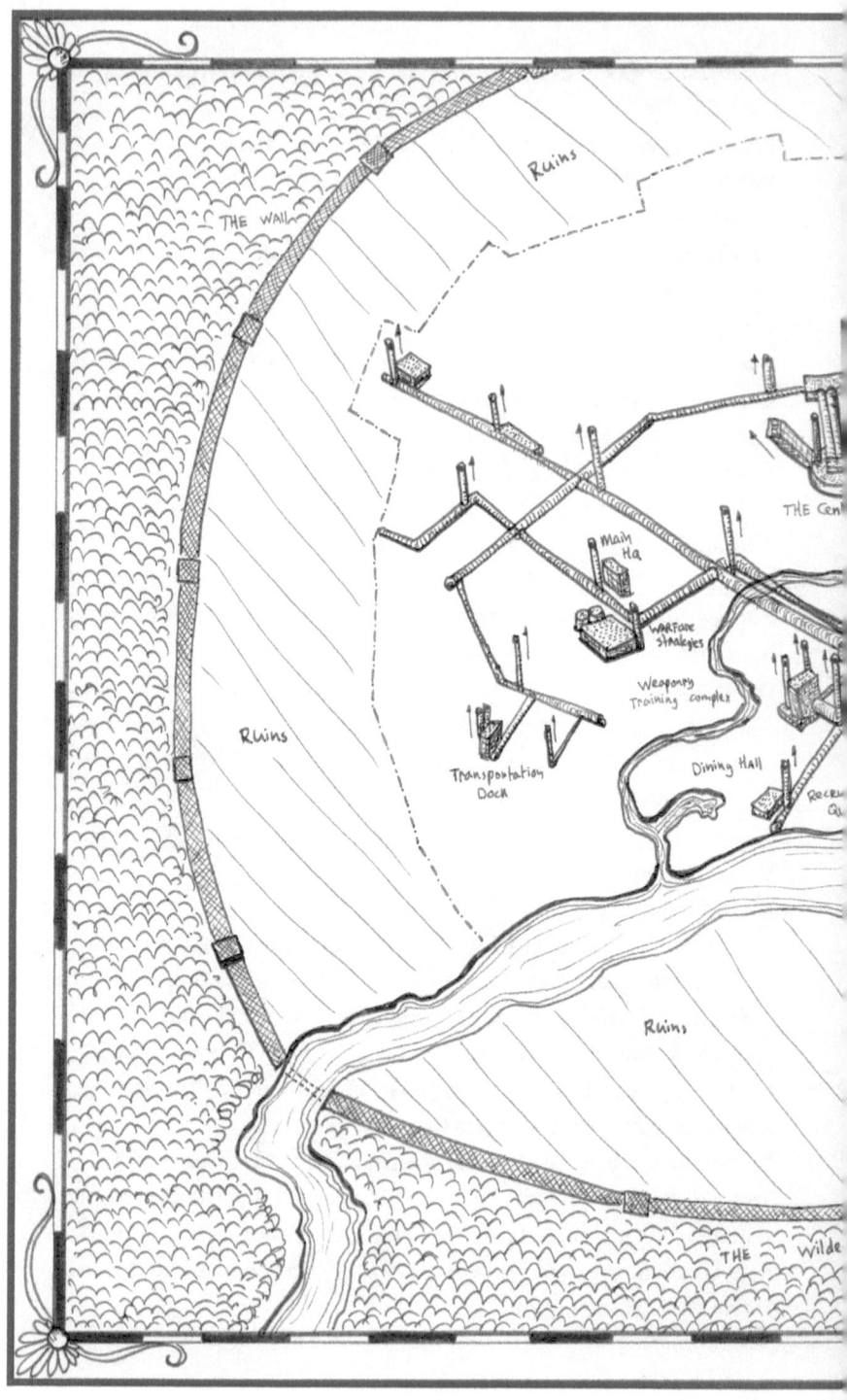

THE WALL

Ruins

Ruins

Ruins

Ruins

THE Cen

Main
Ha

WARfare
Strategies

Weaponry
Training complex

Transportation
Dock

Dining Hall

RECRU
Qu

THE Wilde

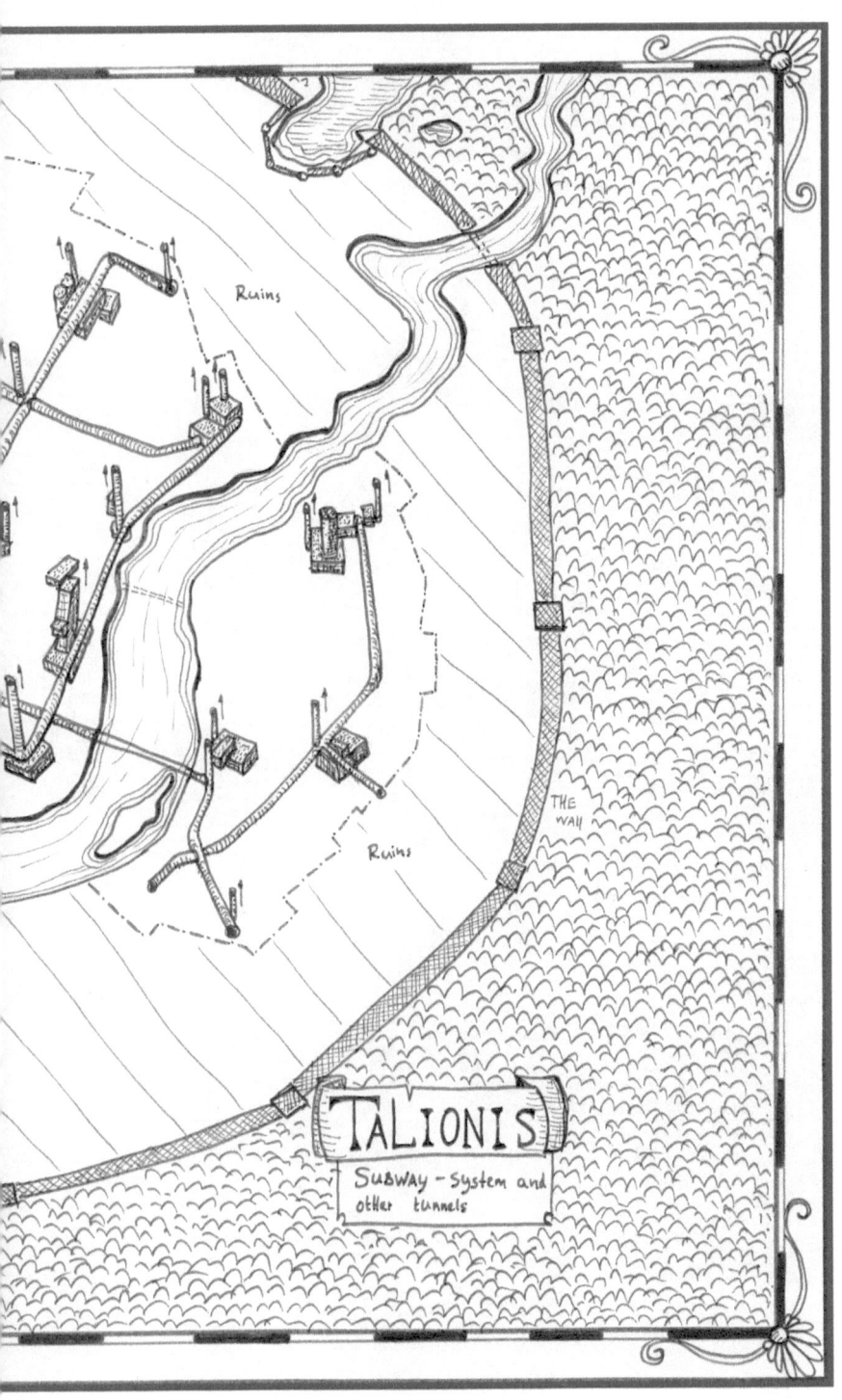

Ruins

Ruins

THE
WALL

TALIONIS

Subway - System and
other tunnels

THE CENTER

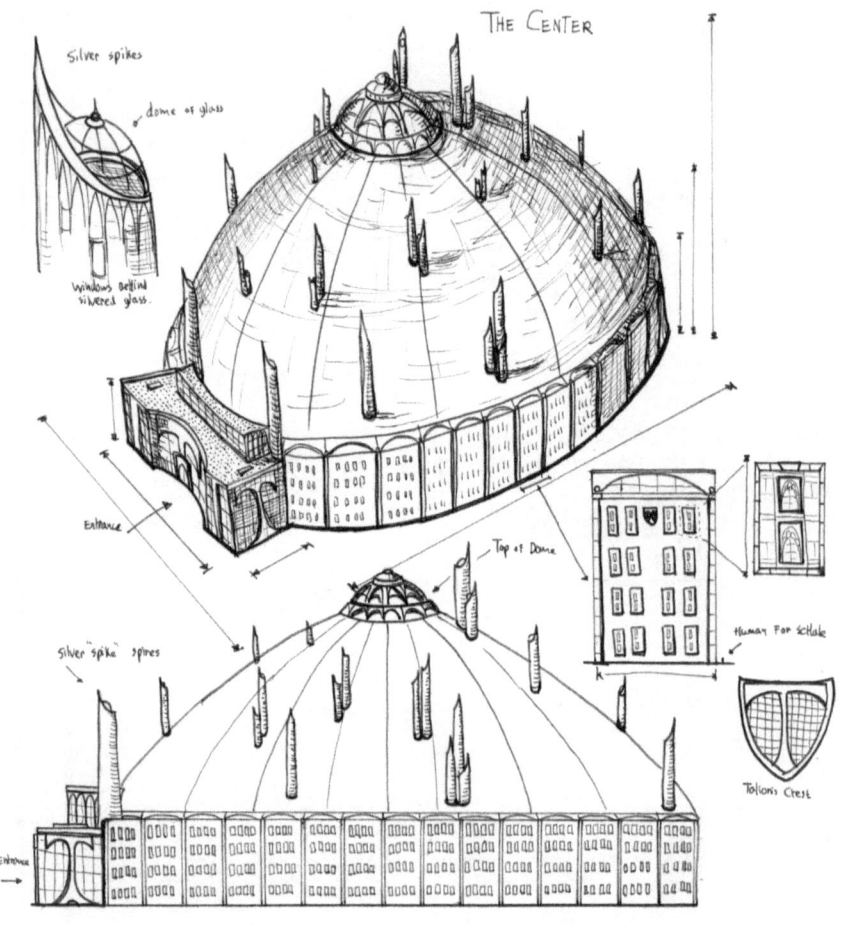

Silver spikes

dome of glass

Windows behind silvered glass.

Top of Dome

Silver "spike" spires

Entrance

Entrance

Human For scHale

Tolioris Crest

CHAPTER
ONE

There's nothing quite like the spewing of propaganda to remind me I'm back in Talionis.

The trial was yesterday, and today I begin my new role. Which includes a repeat of Elva Trill's lectures. I'm sandwiched between two soldiers as they escort me to Educational Training to start my day.

Not like Trill's propaganda ever worked on me before. But here I am, once again heading to her class.

The soldiers lead me past the Center. The mammoth structure is as stark and imposing as it's ever been. Its giant domed roof arches high enough to block the hot August sun, the silver spikes on top shooting even higher and casting ominous shadows on nearby buildings. On me. Like the building itself is reminding me I'm back in Demetrius Ark's clutches.

I shudder as we turn down the street leading away from the Center, pulling my mind back to the day. Away from the gleaming building that seems ready to swallow me up.

After this, I'm to report immediately to Major Vasco to assist him in running scenarios at the Warfare Strategies Building.

My stomach churns at the thought, but my face remains neutral as I march through the streets toward the ornate Educational Building. I tug at the scratchy collar of my gray jumpsuit.

Ark was true to his word. I look like every other laborer in Talionis and nothing like the recruits milling through the streets on the way to their various trainings.

The reality leaves me feeling out of place. Like I'm missing something.

Just as Ark wants.

I mount the steps to the Educational Building, and the female soldier on my right stops me from entering.

"Scan your access badge." She gives a pointed look at the innocuous pad to the left of the door.

I grab the access badge I was issued with my uniform from where it hangs on the lanyard around my neck and do as she commands.

"*Bria Averton, access to Educational Building recorded.*" The mechanical voice is overly loud this early in the morning.

A few nearby recruits eye me warily before slipping into the building ahead of me.

I move to follow them, but the female soldier blocks my way.

"You'll be required to scan your access badge upon entry to every building from this point forward," she says, eyes narrowed as she watches me. "This is a requirement for every laborer in Talionis. If your badge is not scanned, you are recorded absent from your duties and punished accordingly. Is that understood?"

"Yes, ma'am," I say through clenched teeth.

How am I imprisoned in this awful place again?

The woman finally allows me to pass, and I enter the familiar halls leading to Trill's classroom. The two soldiers remain outside. At least I won't have to deal with them on top of listening to Trill's noxious jabbering.

Recruits scurry past me in the hall, giving me a wide berth and flitting glances.

Most of them are unfamiliar to me, but they know who I am. Recognize my face. The soldiers probably captured them during the hunt for me and my friends after we escaped a little less than two months ago, and there's no way they would ever trust me.

I reach the entrance to Trill's classroom, inhale deeply. Enter.

A wave of memories washes over me, almost stealing the breath from my lungs.

I half expect to look over and see Nika rolling her eyes at something Ari is saying. Or to hear Ari's incessant babbling about a new discovery she made on her band.

But neither of my friends are here.

None of the faces around me are familiar.

I force my feet to move forward and take a seat near the back. Where I used to sit with my friends.

A lump forms in my throat, and I swallow it down. They may not be here with me, but they're both safe. Alive by some miracle.

Ari's safe outside of the walls of Talionis, with the crew of *The Fearless Lady* and the Eryndale Scouts.

She should have died.

She should have died because of *me*.

But she's alive, and it's a miracle. As much as I miss her, she's far better off than I am at the moment.

And Nika. My best friend.

I ache to see her for myself, to confirm with my own eyes that Sergeant Andor Valarius didn't execute my friend yesterday as Ark commanded. The note Sergeant Valarius passed me had my mom's handwriting on it, and Nika's. He said Cai, my mentor and uncle, asked him to tell me Nika was still alive.

Part of me worries it's all a trap. Ark's way of manipulating the situation. After all, I'm not even sure they kept Cai alive after they captured him.

But I can't bear the thought of Nika being gone.

The room fills as the rest of the recruits assigned to this morning's educational lecture enter. A lean, wiry guy with green eyes, dark brown hair and skin a shade darker than Matthias's slides into the seat next to me, a screen tucked under his arm. He nods at me, then whips out his screen and starts typing.

I subtly watch what he's doing. Streams of code crowd the screen, and his hands fly over the keyboard. The tip of his tongue pokes out of the side of his mouth as he concentrates, reminding me of my little brother Zeke, even though the guy next to me is probably ten years older than my twin eight-year-old brothers.

A fresh wave of homesickness washes over me.

Eli and Zeke might be safe in Eryndale, but it doesn't make me miss them any less.

A disturbance at the back of the other side of the room catches my attention. I crane my neck to see around the tall recruit in front of me.

Blood drains from my face.

Matthias stands at the back of the room, hands and feet shackled. Three soldiers surround him, as though he's a dangerous criminal. His eyes are downcast, shoulders stooped, and even from here I can tell his face is bruised and puffy.

I clench my hands into fists. Colonel Keenan Valarius isn't fit to be Matthias's father. Although he's the younger of the two Valarius brothers, he's the higher ranking officer. And he's ruthless.

Elva Trill waltzes into the room and begins the class. It's a repeat of a lecture I've heard before. Empty words about Talionis and the greatness of Commander Ark. Claims that all of the recruits will be part of the betterment of the region. Become people they could never have been on their own. An indoctrination routine to get every recruit in this room to believe lies of peace, when the true purpose of this place is to prepare them for war.

Matthias never looks up, and it's too painful to keep watching him. To see him so close and be unable to go to him. And the last thing I want to do is listen to a word Trill is saying.

So instead, I focus my attention on the kid next to me who is still furiously at work on his screen. The code is gone, and in its place, he has several files open. Files he probably shouldn't have access to as a recruit.

Despite everything going on, a smile twitches the corners of my mouth. This is the very type of thing Ari would do. Especially during an educational lecture.

I shift to get a better look without being too obvious. He has one file opened bigger than the rest. It's *his* file. The name next to his picture says Strider Locke, and as I watch, he adjusts his physical conditioning scores. Seconds later, he closes out of the file.

Yup. He and Ari would probably be friends.

Trill ends class, and the soldiers with Matthias practically drag him from the room. My gut clenches. I want to go after him, but with the way his father is watching him, it would be futile. Maybe after some time passes, I'll be able to check on him. The idea of waiting is far less appealing than racing after him, but it's safer for both of us.

The crowd of recruits swarms toward the door, and Strider joins them. I trail after him, letting my mind be distracted from Matthias by what I saw Strider doing on his screen.

There's no way I can trust the tech-savvy recruit yet, but maybe he could be an ally later. After all, recruits who are loyal to Talionis don't lie about their training scores.

CHAPTER

TWO

A new set of soldiers is waiting to escort me to Warfare Strategies when I exit the Educational Building. They bring me to a side entrance of a building I never wanted to enter again. Despite how good I was at navigating the scenarios.

Warfare strategy came easier to me than most of the recruits I trained with, but being good at something doesn't mean it comes without nightmares. Especially with how real the scenarios are.

I have to scan my access badge to register my entry to my required duty, but this time the soldiers who brought me to the building enter with me as well. They lead me down a hallway I've never been in and stop in front of a closed door.

Before anyone can knock, the door swings open. Major Tay Vasco's massive build fills the frame, his head almost scraping the top and his shoulders nearly touching either side. His dark, bald head glistens in the light. The man is like a black mountain. I forgot how intimidating he is face-to-face.

The soldiers and I instantly salute.

"At ease." Major Vasco's powerful, low voice sends nerves scattering through my stomach. "You two are dismissed. Averton, come with me."

The two soldiers exit the way we came, and Major Vasco leads me to a conference room three doors down from his office.

"Sit," he demands as he closes the door.

I obey, taking a seat facing the door and Major Vasco.

He crosses his arms over his chest, his face blank as he watches me. "I do not look forward to working with you. Is that clear?"

I shift in my seat. "Yes, sir."

A beat of silence follows as he stares at me. I do my best to meet his gaze without flinching.

Finally, he strides to the table and pulls out a chair across from me. He lays his hand flat on the table, and the lights dim. The walls aren't walls. They're screens.

And they're populating with recruit files. Hundreds of them.

"The Commander believes you should have time to study the files of the recruits you'll be working with. Understand their strengths and weaknesses." Major Vasco goes silent as though he's given a complete explanation, even though I'm still at a loss as to what I'm seeing.

I turn and focus on the screen directly behind me. Close enough that I can read the files on the recruits.

A gasp catches in my throat, desperate to escape and relay my horror.

The screen is filled with *children*. Some of them as young as five. As though my body needs to go closer to confirm what my eyes are seeing, I stand and approach the wall.

Dozens of little faces. Boys and girls. Kids.

I find Storm's face among them and press my lips together. She's no longer the youngest recruit in Talionis.

Blood pounds in my ears, and I whirl to face Major Vasco.

His gaze is already fixed on me.

"They're too young," the words fly out of my mouth. "They can't go through warfare scenario training."

Major Vasco stands slowly, eyes narrowing.

I probably shouldn't have said that. I've been in Talionis less than forty-eight hours. The lives of Storm and Matthias and Kemena are in danger if I speak out against *anything* Ark is doing.

But I don't regret a word.

"They're kids," I say, with a wave at the screen behind me.

"They would not be here if you didn't defy the Commander." His words cut through me. "It was never his intention to take children so young. But Storm has proven to be an excellent case study. Every recruit is useful and will be trained for the Commander's purposes," Major Vasco says, a warning in his tone. "And you will do as you are told. The Commander made the consequences for your disobedience clear. Did he not, Bria Averton?"

The words send ice through my veins. There's only one right answer to his question, even as defiance rises within me.

I drop my gaze from Major Vasco to keep him from seeing the anger raging through me. "Yes, he did, sir." Somehow the words sound calm.

"Very well." Major Vasco types a command on the table, and the screens shift to fifteen files instead of the hundred originally displayed. "For the next hour, you'll study these fifteen recruits in order to best test their strengths and weaknesses in the upcoming scenario you'll be observing."

He turns to leave.

"What's expected of me in the scenario preparation?" I ask.

"Nothing." He opens the door, then looks at me again. "I don't trust you, Averton. You'll study these recruits and observe the scenarios with them this afternoon. If you can prove to me that you have a use in the capacity of a Warfare Strategist, then my reports to the Commander will be favorable." He studies me. "I do not expect them to be favorable."

With that, he exits the room and slams the door shut.

I flinch, even as a cacophony of thoughts batter me like a rowboat in the ocean during a storm.

The recruit files on the walls are all for teens around my age. Maybe a year or two younger. Far too young to be facing battle, but old enough to make their own choices on whether they'll obey what Ark wants.

But the kids I saw. They're so young. Many younger than Storm. Others her age.

And I will *not* be part of preparing little kids to go to war.

God, what do I do? How do I protect Storm and the other kids?

There's no answer.

If I want to protect Storm, I have to do what Major Vasco ordered me to do. At least for now. But as I study the faces of the fifteen recruits on the walls, resolve strengthens my spine.

Even if I can't stop Demetrius Ark, I will *not* allow him to use kids in his plans.

I'll find a way to save these kids from the horrors Ark has planned for them.

The only question is, how?

Please, God. Help me find a way.

CHAPTER
THREE

Someone roughly shakes my shoulder, yanking me from my sleep.

"Get up." Sergeant Andor Valarius's voice in my ear jolts me fully awake.

"What's going on?" I ask.

"We need to go. Now."

"What happened?" I get out of bed and reach for my access badge.

"Leave that," he says.

"But if I don't scan in, I'll get in trouble." Which means Storm will get in trouble. And until I can get her out of Talionis, that's not an option.

"You won't be reporting for scheduled duties," he says. "Cai wants to see you."

The name of my mentor sends a jolt through me.

I scramble to throw on my boots.

Trusting Sergeant Valarius makes sense on some levels. However, it scares me to put my life in his hands. He has terrified me with his standoffish indifference and the scar that ripples across his cheek. He has yelled in my face. He has punished me in front of other recruits.

He's the reason I lost Ezri's necklace. The necklace I gave to Matthias aboard *The Fearless Lady* to let him know how much I care.

Sergeant Valarius is the one who delivered me to the Ruins months ago to serve out my punishment, which was really a death sentence.

But he's also the person who warned me when I returned.

The person who told me Nika is alive.

Contrary to whatever else I should do, I am eager to follow Sergeant Valarius to wherever Cai is.

I move toward the door.

"Wait." Sergeant Valarius stops me. "This way."

He enters my bathroom, and I stare after him.

Is this some weird dream? Why did he just go into my *bathroom?*

"Let's go, Averton," he hisses.

I rub my eyes and follow him. The bathroom is smaller than my cramped room with no exit points.

Either I'm dreaming, or Sergeant Valarius has lost his mind.

I step up to the doorway, and my jaw unhinges. The small wall between the toilet and shower is now a gaping hole, and Sergeant Valarius is halfway through it.

"What is this?" I ask.

He cranes his neck to scowl back at me. "Do you want to see Cai or not?"

I nod, words escaping me.

"Then let's go." He disappears into the dark opening.

I stare after him for a millisecond and then follow, my desperation to see my uncle spurring me forward, despite the risks.

I cross the threshold and enter a dark, dank space. Sergeant Valarius turns on a torch that illuminates a narrow tunnel, tracking downwards.

"Close the door." He shines the torch on a button to the left of the entryway.

I push it, and the entrance to my room vanishes.

Sergeant Valarius strides forward. I hurry to catch up, a thousand questions screaming for answers.

"Is Cai okay?" My whisper sounds loud in the silent corridor. "Did they hurt him?"

"They believe he's dead," Sergeant Valarius says.

"Is he back in the Ruins?"

He scowls at me. "Does it look like we're heading to the Ruins?"

I shrug, but doubt he sees it since he turns and picks up his pace.

My heart hammers in my chest. This passageway reminds me of the secret entrance to Ark's office through Colonel Valarius's office, which is higher up in the Main Headquarters Building where I've been imprisoned.

"Why is there a secret access point in my room?" I dare asking another question. "And how does Ark not know about it?"

He doesn't respond for so long I wonder if he'll ignore the questions entirely. The tunnel opens up, and he stops. We're on a platform of sorts. Off to the left are railway tracks.

I pinch myself. Nope. This isn't a dream. "What is this?"

"It used to be an underground train station before the Demise," he says. "We need to keep moving."

Something scurries to the left, and I jump.

"Plenty of rats down here." His voice holds a trace of humor.

I inch closer to him, hoping his intimidating presence can have as much of a negative effect on the rats as it does on the recruits who are under his training.

We weave down the corridor. Branches of this subway go in multiple directions.

"Does this cover the entire city?"

Sergeant Valarius glances over at me. "Perceptive. Yes, there are tunnels that link between here and multiple buildings of interest within the city. It's something Cai and I worked on when he was forced to be here to help establish Talionis. Ark had Cai create the secret passageway to his office and design hidden compartments throughout the city. It was the perfect cover for us to block off other access points to the underground tunnels. He even added in the access point right under Ark's nose through the cell you're in." He pauses, then we continue following the tracks deeper into the tunnel. "I thought it'd be worthwhile."

The way Sergeant Valarius says the word makes me wonder if he's angry at Cai for running and hiding out in the Ruins, but I don't ask. As it is, I'm shocked he shared as much as he just did.

Several minutes pass as we weave in and out of various branches of the subway's tunnel.

"Why are you doing this?" The question comes out too loud, and I clamp my mouth shut.

"Because I can't see another way to keep my brother and Demetrius Ark from getting away with what they're doing. So I'm listening to Cai, even if it goes against everything in me."

We stop at what looks like an old door.

Sergeant Valarius presses a code on a panel that seems old-fashioned compared to the rest of the technology within Talionis.

The door opens to reveal a small room. A table cluttered with maps and plans is pressed against the back wall, but it's the two sitting at the table that bring tears to my eyes.

Cai and Nika's older sister, Kemena, stop talking when the door opens.

"Bria." Cai stands. "I've missed you."

Kemena stands too, a smile on her face.

I gaze at them for a solid five seconds before rushing forward. I hug Cai first, then turn to Kemena, who pulls me into her arms before I can move to hug her.

Tears sting the back of my eyes.

I've only been in Talionis for five days, but it's been lonely. Nika and Ari aren't here. Matthias is under constant guard. And I haven't known where Kemena is working. So it's been days of trainings and wishing for someone I could talk to.

This is the first time I've been with people I can trust.

Kemena squeezes me tight, then pulls back. "Nika's alive." The words catch in her throat. She looks away, but not before I catch the glimmer of tears in her eyes.

"I know," I say. "But I didn't know how to find you to tell you." I spin to face Cai. "Can we talk to her? And . . . my mom?" The words hold the raw hope and desperation pulsing through me, but I don't know how to mask them with indifference. Not before two people who mean so much to me.

Cai gestures to the seats around the table. "Sit. We have much to talk about."

I open my mouth to ask again, but he gives a pointed look at the seat in front of me. I sit.

Cai focuses on Sergeant Valarius while Kemena joins me at the table. "Where's Matthias?"

I spin to face Sergeant Valarius at Matthias's name. My heart trips over itself at the possibility of talking to Matthias after days of him experiencing unknown torment.

Sergeant Valarius crosses his arms over his chest. "It's impossible to get to him. My brother has him under constant guard. It's a power move. One he'll tire of soon enough. But it means Matthias is currently unreachable."

My shoulders slouch, and Kemena squeezes my hand.

Cai frowns, but nods and joins us at the table. Sergeant Valarius slips into the shadows at the back of the room instead of sitting with us, which is fine with me.

It's clear Cai trusts the man, but I'd rather he leave me alone with my uncle and Kemena.

Cai's wise gaze finds mine. "As much as it pains me that you're back in this city, I'm glad to see you again, Bria."

"I'm glad to see you too." I hesitate. "So . . . can we talk to them? Nika and my mom?"

I sense Kemena holding her breath next to me as we wait for Cai's response.

He links his hands together on top of the table, his face serious. Too serious. I won't like his response.

"I'm afraid it's not that simple," he says.

"Then how do you know they're okay?" Kemena asks.

Cai looks between the two of us. "At our last communication, they were both well. But unfortunately, communicating with them is difficult and dangerous."

"Why?" I ask.

"We don't have any secure channels set up, so we've been using dead drops. It's hard to coordinate times to actually meet without potentially exposing one or both of our operations."

With a start, I realize there's no tech in the space other than the torch lights along the walls. "Can't you set up a secure channel? Get some screens to help you monitor what's going on in the city like you used to in the Ruins?"

Cai shakes his head. "We don't have anyone with the skills to set that up securely within the city."

"What did you mean by both of your operations?" Kemena asks. "What are you all doing?"

Cai gestures to the papers on the table. "Andor and I are working on reestablishing the tunnel system we covertly set up years ago. Hoping we can utilize it. And Lily and Nika have continued my work in the Ruins."

"What work?" Kemena asks.

Cai and I share a smile, then tell her how Cai used booby traps and skillfully timed attacks to terrorize soldiers entering the Ruins and those stationed at the guard towers on the Wall.

Cai's smile fades. "But the tech was compromised, so Lily had to go dark. She destroyed the tech stations I had set up out there, other than a basic radio scanner that gives her intel on any soldiers patrolling the Ruins." He releases a heavy sigh. "It's made everything harder for sure."

My mind skips back to watching Strider Locke messing with his tech during Educational Training. We need someone with his skills, but I don't know him, let alone if I can trust him.

"Can we get word to the scouts?" Kemena asks, eyes hopeful.

Cai shakes his head, his entire demeanor weighted. "It's too dangerous."

"Because of the leak," I say.

Cai nods. "We tried communicating directly with Azarias and Thaddeus, but the result was catastrophic."

"What do you mean?" I ask.

"The attack on the scout headquarters a few days ago . . . it was all my fault." He sounds ashamed, which is strange to hear from this man who I've only ever seen as confident, self-assured, and ready to defy any enemy to do what's right.

Ready to take my place and be captured himself to save me and my friends.

Even though it kills me to tell him the truth, I have to do it. He can't bear the weight of *my* failure.

"No, that was my fault," I say.

He shakes his head. "No, Bria. It wasn't."

"But Shay, she said that they found us because of what Ari did with the tech," I say. "That was because of me. I made Ari—"

"I know. We don't have time to go into all of this right now," he says. "But it wasn't merely what you and Ari did that caused the problem." He exhales slowly. "They found you and could track what you were doing because we were attempting to send intel to Azarias."

I shake my head, uncertain what to do with this information. I've blamed myself for what happened that day, and I still believe it's my fault. Not sure I'll ever be convinced otherwise. But my uncle saying he had a part to play in it makes me second-guess what I thought I knew about the events that transpired.

Kemena leans forward. "Well, if we can't communicate with Nika and Lily, then I want to go to the Ruins to see them."

"Yes," I say, latching onto the idea. "I could get us out—"

"No." Sergeant Valarius steps out of the shadows. "That's out of the question. You are both under increased security since you were captured days ago. Tonight is risky enough. Attempting to go to the Ruins would be suicide."

I open my mouth to argue, but Cai holds up his hand. "Andor is right. Now is not the time to attempt a trip to the Ruins." He looks between me and Kemena. "But this is not over. Ark hasn't won yet. Even though it may appear like hope is lost, it's not."

I absently straighten a paper near me. "It's hard to believe that when Ark has little kids mixed up in this now." I push the paper aside and face Cai. "Not just Storm. He's brought in *dozens* of little kids."

"It's true," Kemena says. "I've been shocked by how many I've seen."

Cai turns to Sergeant Valarius. "It's been a while since we discussed the youngest recruits. How many are there now?"

"Close to sixty," Sergeant Valarius says.

My stomach drops. "Even if we can't stop Ark, we have to help those kids. We can't let him use them as soldiers. Send them to war."

Cai places his hand on my shoulder. "I agree."

An idea sparks in my mind. "What if we smuggle them down here?"

Even as I say the words, Cai is shaking his head. "It's too dangerous for kids. Not to mention, it's hard enough to get supplies down here for me, let alone anyone else." He squeezes my shoulder. "But don't worry. We will think of something."

Thoughts of how much danger Storm and the other kids are in settle on my chest like a ten-ton boulder, making it hard to breathe.

How will we protect them?

"You two should get some rest." Cai stands. "You have long days ahead of you in the morning, and it's already late."

Kemena and I stand.

Cai turns to me. "I need you to do what you've done before in Talionis."

I blink. "What are you talking about?"

"Excel, Bria. Let Commander Ark believe you are doing all he wants you to do. It's necessary in order for us to continue with what we've been working on for these past several weeks."

"But I don't fully understand your plans and—"

"I know." He cuts me off. "In time, I'll share more. Tonight, I just need you to know that what you're doing here still has a purpose."

"I hope you can tell us more soon," Kemena says. "Because I want to find my sister and get out of here."

Cai's eyes light up. "I can see why Azarias cares about you."

Kemena steps back, shock written all over her face.

Cai gives her a gentle smile. "Although our communication allowed for Talionis to find the scout base, my son and I had a moment to reconnect. You were one of the first people he mentioned to me."

Kemena drops her gaze to her feet. "Okay."

Cai pulls a map of tunnels from the pile of papers on the table and hands it to me. "Andor and I have more to discuss. You can use this to get you and Kemena back to your rooms safely."

He gives me a brief overview of the map, showing me where Kemena needs to go and where my room is, with Kemena noting some landmarks she saw on the way down with Cai.

"Don't bring the map with you into your room," Sergeant Valarius says. "Hide it in the tunnel by the entrance. Your room is scheduled for regular searches."

"Will they discover the tunnel?" I ask.

"No," Cai and Sergeant Valarius say simultaneously.

Kemena and I share a look.

"The door only opens with a specific pattern typed into hidden buttons on your bathroom wall," Cai says. "It's one of the most secure entrances to the tunnel that we have since it's in the Main Headquarters Building." He nods to the map in my hands. "The back of the map will explain the combination so you can use it. But *only* use it when absolutely necessary."

"It's best for you to wait for me to bring you down here," Sergeant Valarius says. "I know when your room searches are scheduled and what your work schedule is. There are randomized fail-safes in place to keep you from doing anything Ark doesn't want."

"Okay, I get it," I say. "Only use the tunnels in an emergency."

Kemena and I say our goodbyes to Cai, then leave his safe room and enter the tunnels.

CHAPTER

FOUR

K emena and I navigate the tunnels easily enough. Both of our rooms are off one of the main underground tracks, which means we don't have to weave through the other smaller tunnels. Although I kind of want to explore them. The map Cai gave me is incredible. Detailed.

I wonder if Mom is responsible for this map as well. She was the one who created the map Ark had in his safe. The map that hid key towns for Eryndale and hid the refuge city itself.

"I know Andor and Cai don't want us to go to the Ruins," Kemena says, "but I *need* to see my sister. As soon as possible."

I step around a pile of crumbling concrete. "I want to see her too. And my mom." I have so many questions for her.

Kemena waves her hand to encompass the tunnel. "Could any of these tunnels get us to them?"

I study the map as we walk. "Doesn't look like it. According to this, there used to be an old drainage tunnel that would have crossed into the Ruins, but it's been closed off."

Kemena sighs.

"But . . ." I stop to look at the map more closely. "It looks like we could get *close* to the Ruins."

Kemena crowds next to me. "Show me."

I point to a tunnel that has a secret entrance near the old building I used to go through to get to the Ruins to train with Cai. "I used to cross into the Ruins through a hidden hole in the fence behind an old pre-Demise building that was around here." I tap the map where the building would be if we had an above-ground view of it.

Kemena bites her lip. "Do you think we could get to them?"

I shrug. "I mean, I think so. If the hole is still there."

I drop the map and focus on Kemena, an idea crystalizing. "Cai said it's not safe for the kids down here. But if we *can* get into the Ruins . . . what if we could smuggle the kids out there to Nika and my mom?" The words come faster. "It would be dangerous, but better than having them stuck down here with little supplies. Plus, my mom and Nika could keep an eye on them. And maybe we could set up a new secure tech site out there so they could get word to Azarias and the Wild Dogs? We might not be able to stop Ark, but we could at least save some kids."

Kemena's eyebrow arches. "That was a lot of words very fast."

My cheeks warm.

"But I like it." She puts her arm around my shoulders, and we start walking. "Especially if it gives me an excuse to see my baby sis."

The longing in her words echoes in my heart.

She drops her arm. "There will be a lot of logistics to figure out, but first things first. When do we try getting out to the Ruins?"

We round a slight bend in the tunnel. Kemena's exit is just ahead.

"In three days. By then, we'll have been here for over a week. Long enough that hopefully they're not monitoring us as much."

Kemena nods. "I want to get out there now, see for myself that Nika is okay. But we need to be smart about this."

We stop at the exit to Kemena's living quarters. She stares at the door that'll lead her into an abandoned basement two doors down from where she's staying.

"I hate that we're in this place, girl." She faces me. "But God can redeem even the darkest of times in our lives. Let's save as many kids as we can."

From what I know of their family, Nika and Kemena did not have an easy life growing up. And Kemena's parents didn't appreciate her for the ways she defied them by being so different from them. If she says God can redeem the dark times in our lives, she means it.

Since neither of us has HaloAct bands, it will be easier to slip away from our rooms at night. We agree to connect in two days to confirm our plan for meeting in the tunnels three nights from now.

Kemena gives me a hug. "I'm glad you're okay."

I hug her back. "Glad you're okay too."

It's hard to watch Kemena leave and then to go back to my room. After days of being alone, seeing Kemena and Cai has been like drinking a large glass of water when I was dying of thirst. I didn't realize how lonely I've been, and I don't relish returning to my cell of a room.

I stash the map under a rock to the left of my door, then push the button that opens the door into my room. I memorized the four-sequence pattern to reopen the door, so I can reenter the tunnel whenever I need to.

But I hate that I have to pretend like none of this exists. Do everything Ark wants.

The door slides back into place in my bathroom, all traces of it disappearing.

I practice the four-sequence pattern, locating each of the buttons etched into the wall, all but hidden from view. The door opens again.

Cai's secret entrances are a work of genius.

I stand there for five seconds, and the door slides shut again.

Cai and Sergeant Valarius are working on some plan to use the tunnels, but I don't dare hope it'll be enough to stop Ark. Even though the two men don't want me and Kemena sneaking out to the Ruins, I have peace about our plan. Something needs to be done to save the dozens of children held captive in this evil place. And I'm desperate to see my best friend and my mom again.

I kick off my boots and slip into bed.

A mix of thankfulness and anticipation weaves its way through me.

God, thank You for letting me see Kemena and Cai. And please help me and Kem save these kids.

CHAPTER

FIVE

Exhaustion pulses behind my eyes as I stand next to Major Vasco in the command center of the Warfare Strategies building, staring at the group of recruits running through one of the first scenarios I ever experienced.

A dozen soldiers are scattered around the room, following Major Vasco's commands, orchestrating every element of the scenarios, and monitoring the recruits' every move. But, like the other four times I've been here, I'm just here to observe and share my thoughts at the end. If today follows the same format as before, Major Vasco will send me to work on building a new scenario once I'm finished observing this one.

I rub my eyes, wishing the simple movement would expel my weariness.

The late-night meeting with Cai, Kemena, and Sergeant Valarius left my brain far too active by the time I got back to my bed. And I'm regretting the hours spent thinking of Kemena's and my plan to sneak to the Ruins two nights from now. All the possibilities for how we might save some kids. It's important to think through, but I shouldn't have sacrificed sleep.

I stifle a yawn and force myself to concentrate on the scenario, Cai's words whispering in my mind. *Excel, Bria.*

It's hard to want to excel, to pretend to be exactly who Ark wants me to be, all while knowing the horror the recruits are about to face in this scenario. Especially since there's a girl in there who's Storm's age. Her name's Quincy, according to the file I reviewed before the scenario began. And this is her first time through a scenario.

This team doesn't appear to want to detonate the explosive that will bring down the tower across from them any more than I wanted to. Quincy's shaking, arms wrapped around herself. I don't think she's hearing the conversation the rest of the group is having.

They're hesitant, uncertain, but there's one in the group who reminds them that this is what they have to do, that it's fake.

One by one, each of the recruits places their thumb on the device, signaling that they'll let it explode. Quincy hasn't moved from where she's huddled off to the side. One girl—Ahkeesia—goes over and gently brings her to the device and helps her put her thumb in place.

I glance to my side at Major Vasco. He stands still, arms clasped behind his back, as he watches the various screens zeroing in on different recruits' faces, monitoring their heart rates, blood pressure, and all of their vital signs.

I didn't realize they saw so much when we were in these scenarios, but I shouldn't be surprised. Why wouldn't they monitor us to this degree?

I almost want to smile as I think of how much Ari altered.

No wonder they were confused when they looked at her results and saw her ranking in places where she shouldn't have been ranking. The thought of my friend brings a bittersweet twinge to my heart.

The faces of the recruits go slack with horror as they witness the building in front of them explode, hear the screams. Quincy screams along with those in the building and covers her face.

My stomach roils. I wish I could stop her from living this experience.

I got sick from this scenario, not able to sustain the lunch I had eaten that was no more than gruel because I had been disobeying orders. And there was no way I was going to obey the orders in that scenario. Give my fingerprint over to allow the destruction to take place.

But I did. Not by my choice, but because Shane forced me. I felt so betrayed.

The betrayal then pales compared to the betrayal I feel now.

Shane is the reason I'm here. The reason Matthias is back under the cruel hand of his father. The reason Nika's hiding in the Ruins and Kemena is experiencing the horror of what it means to be under Talionis's rule.

Shane is the reason we're all here.

Yet Shane himself isn't experiencing any of those consequences. In the six days since we've been back, he's been lauded. Paraded as an example of Talionis's greatness, Ark's willingness to receive back those who were disloyal to him, who betrayed him. And Shane has let it happen.

Every time I see him or a clip of him, he's smiling, waving. Soaking in the admiration of every recruit. The praise of every soldier.

Major Vasco pushes buttons on the screen in front of us, and the scenario goes black for the recruits before switching to another one. They're putting the recruits through more scenarios during each session now, three or four—sometimes even five. Which is too much physically, mentally, and emotionally.

As the scenario shifts, I fix my attention on the screen following Quincy. Her eyes are haunted, face pale. She's ten and horrified.

And she's not the only child who's about to experience the nightmares found in warfare scenarios. My mind trails to the kids scattered around this city. Training. Learning to fight.

Even if I can smuggle them out of the city and into the Ruins, none of them will be the same after this.

Ark has stolen their childhoods, and he doesn't even care.

Blood pounds in my ears.

Cai's right. The answer is to excel in this city and attempt to gain some freedom as I do. Not that Ark will ever trust me again.

But if I can do enough to smuggle kids into the Ruins, to protect them from some of this horror, that will be worth it.

I just don't know how to pretend putting them through these scenarios is okay.

"Bring them out." Major Vasco's voice echoes in the room, snapping me back to the present.

I blink. I missed at least one scenario, maybe more.

"I want to split the group next time," Major Vasco says. "Put recruits Dan, Beckett, and Quincy together, but take the other four and place them in a group that's less advanced. They don't seem as ready to do what's necessary. Do you agree with the assessment, Averton?"

I start to nod, then stop. He included Quincy's name in the advanced group. That can't be right.

"You need to pay more attention."

My eyes snap to his.

His massive build towers over me, his dark bald head glistening under the artificial lighting.

I don't know why he does what he does or why he cares so much about the causes of Talionis, but the man is a genius.

This was a test, and he caught me unfocused.

He dismisses everyone else from the command center. "You're better than this, Averton, and we both know it."

I blink, not sure how to respond. This isn't exactly the *excelling* I was supposed to do.

But it's hard to even *pretend* to be committed to this place while watching a little girl go through scenarios.

A fire stirs in me, probably one that shouldn't stir, knowing the risks I'm taking with any sort of defiance, but I stare Major Vasco in the eye. "Well, maybe I'm a bit out of practice."

"You evade soldiers for weeks and yet you're out of practice in military strategy?" His brows draw together. "Interesting assessment. I give a report on you every time you're in here, and it would behoove you to actually help me with these scenarios. It's better for everyone, yourself included."

I want to spew back some angry retort, but something in me tells me to hold my peace, so I nod and give a salute. "If that's all, sir?"

"No," he says.

My hand falls back to my side. In the few times I've been here, after I observe a scenario with Major Vasco, I'm sent to work on building out a new scenario to hit some other target. He always dismisses me after we observe one set together, corrects me on the things that I need to be corrected on, tells his team what to do instead of what I just suggested, and overall seems to not be as happy with me in the room as he is when I'm leaving it. But he's under orders, same as I am.

"Today, you'll join me in the debrief. Commander Ark believes it is important for the recruits to see you are cooperating with Talionis. Apparently, he thinks it will help those who are feeling a bit . . ." He pauses. ". . . restless."

Words escape me, so I nod and follow him from the room.

The group huddled before us in the debrief zone seems weary. Haunted looks fill their eyes. Quincy isn't the only one who just experienced her first scenarios. The little girl is staring at the ground, tears flowing down her face, shoulders shaking.

A burst of compassion fills me, and I have to restrain myself from going to her and taking her in my arms.

I'll get you out of here. The promise screams to burst from my mouth as a comfort for the girl, but I bite it back.

Major Vasco does what he's done in every debrief I've ever experienced. He praises them for the things they've done well and instructs them on what they need to work on next. He speaks to each recruit directly, but the names barely register for me.

All I can do is stare at Quincy, hoping she'll look up and see the compassion in my eyes. The promise to fight for her freedom. But she keeps her gaze fixed on the floor.

When Major Vasco finishes, he turns to me. "Averton, your report."

The six older recruits watch me, but Quincy twists her fingers together.

I focus on the teens around my age. Three guys and three girls.

I want to give some smart retort, tell them to forget this training. Understand that what Talionis is doing is so much darker than what they think. Help them see that every scenario they go through is preparing them for war.

Not peace. Not the prosperity of a nation.

But anything I do will directly impact every one of these recruits. And Storm and Matthias. So I look each of them in the eye, then tell them what they need to improve and where they did well. I glance down at the nameplates and directly address each one by name.

I tell Quincy she was brave and that she should trust those she's working with, but she doesn't stop twisting her fingers together and she never looks at me.

To her, I'm as scary as Major Vasco. Just another person putting her through more nightmares than she dreamed possible.

When I come to the last guy, Asher, there's a hard look in his eyes as he glares at me. It takes me aback for an instant. Does he hate me because I'm working with Talionis? Or because I defied Commander Ark by escaping? I shake the questions away and address him. I need Major Vasco to believe I'm fully engaged in this.

"Your skills are impressive," I say, "and far better than you're letting on."

His eyes widen slightly. I've hit on something. He's brilliant. I can sense it in his movements when going from scenario to scenario, in the way he directs the recruits with him. He's strong and, according to his file, his physical conditioning training is going just fine.

But the defiance in his eyes tells me he is not happy to be part of this.

"What do you see in him?" Major Vasco asks, catching my attention.

The guy's nostrils flare.

"He's shortchanging his ability," I say, even though everything in me feels like I'm as much a betrayer as Shane is.

Still, I'm guessing that everything I'm seeing is something Major Vasco himself has noticed. And like everything in Talionis, this is probably a test.

I take a deep breath and report to Major Vasco. "He anticipates what's coming next and can strategize the movements of his entire team. He's doing some of it while in there, but not nearly as much as he probably can. Enough to get his team through, but not to excel."

Asher's jaw bunches as I talk.

Making an enemy of someone who hates Talionis is the last thing I want to do. Hopefully I'll be able to explain it to him one day.

Major Vasco gives a sharp nod. "Guess you were paying more attention in there than I thought. You're all dismissed. Get cleaned up, and then you can go to the mess hall for lunch."

The recruits file out. Ahkeesia guides Quincy out gently, and I'm glad the child has someone to comfort her. They remind me of Storm and me.

Asher pauses by me and whispers under his breath, "Traitor."

He leaves the room, but the twisting in my gut, the burning through my body, feels as though he just slapped me in the face.

I don't blame him.

This might be what I need to do, but I hate that once again I'm being praised by evil men and women.

CHAPTER
SIX

I lift a spoonful of gruel and let it plop back into the bowl. The stuff is as disgusting as my memory recalls. A reminder that I'm no longer a *favored recruit*. Just a laborer who's being punished for insubordination.

I shift in the small chair at the table in my room that's barely big enough to hold the tray and the food on it.

My knee smashes against the wall again, but I'm used to the pain from it. I haven't eaten a meal with another human since I arrived. I sigh.

So much is happening outside of these walls, outside of this place. There's so much I wish I could be doing. I think of the friends I've made within Eryndale. Moses and Jordyn. The Wild Dogs. I wish I could be running—and gliding mid-air—through territory with them in Skinter Suits, the brilliant single person transport technology Brandi, Eryndale's tech expert, created. Or working with Thaddeus and Azarias on creating a plan to sabotage Talionis. I'd even be happy to work with Gabe, the member of the C.A.E. who was sent with us from Eryndale on our mission to stop Talionis.

At least tomorrow night Kemena and I will sneak to the Ruins and hopefully find Nika and Mom. Then the four of us can work out a plan for rescuing the kids.

It's not enough to stop Ark, but at least it's something.

Kemena and I are supposed to meet tonight where she's scheduled to work at the tailors'. Somehow she convinced the eccentric women to assign me to laundry duty for my evening chores, which will give us a chance to covertly discuss how we'll get to the Ruins tomorrow night. Or at least to confirm our plan.

I stir the gruel, wishing I had something else to eat that had flavor. Not that I have much of an appetite, anyway. But I need to eat. I pick up a spoonful of the stuff, shove it in my mouth, and swallow.

It runs down my throat like mud.

There's beeping on the other side of my door, and I stand. It's probably Sergeant Valarius with my schedule for this afternoon.

The door opens and reveals the man on the other side. I freeze.

Colonel Keenan Valarius. Matthias's dad.

I squeeze my hands into fists at my sides and clench my jaw.

Every fiber of my being wants to rush this man and hurt him for the ways he's hurt Matthias. But I'll be the one that loses in the end. And not just me, but Matthias.

So I stand still, waiting to hear why Colonel Valarius has resigned himself to coming down here.

"The Commander wants to see you," he says. "Now."

He steps aside so I can leave the room ahead of him. I obey, grabbing my access badge from where it hangs by the door.

"What does he want me for?" I risk asking Colonel Valarius. I don't really want to converse with the man, but having him stare at my back as we walk down the hall toward the Commander's office feels like risking getting shot in the back at any second.

"You'll find out when you get there," Colonel Valarius says.

I want to snap at him, but doing so would be foolish. He's cruel, and he'll do whatever it takes to get ahead, to get what he wants. I keep my mouth shut and go where he tells me to.

Even though today only marks one week of being back here, it bothers me that I've heard nothing about attacks against the city.

Why hasn't anyone come? Why aren't the scouts trying to stop these people?

Kemena left a note for Azarias. Even Cai knew Azarias cares

about Kemena. I'm sure he's not happy that she's here now, away from him, unsafe. But no attacks have come.

No attempts to save us.

Nothing.

And the Wild Dogs and the crew of *The Fearless Lady* are all our friends. They would help if they could. Yet here we are, in the clutches of Demetrius Ark.

Each day that passes leaves me feeling a little more alone in this fight.

We march down the maze of hallways that I wish weren't so familiar. Maybe the reinforcements won't come from Eryndale. Callypso could be the one who comes in and saves the day.

I almost laugh at the idea.

The woman is an enigma. A terrifying enigma. Even the Raiders, a dangerous group to the west that stands for everything Eryndale is against, are afraid of her.

She's dangerous, untrustworthy. And yet, she's saved my life more than once.

The question I can't figure out an answer to is why? Why save us? Why help us at all?

It makes no sense to me, and it leaves me with a weird knot in the pit of my stomach.

The feeling intensifies as I try to figure out why Ark wants to see me. I haven't done anything against his orders. Yet.

I come to a stop in front of Commander Ark's office. Well, rather, Colonel Valarius's office.

Commander Ark's is through a series of secret passageways, perched above every other office in this building, strategically placed to see far more of the city than you can from any other place within Talionis.

Colonel Valarius unlocks his door with his key card. As I enter the office, unpleasant memories slap me in the face like rogue waves.

I stare at his desk as he goes over to release the lever that will open the bookshelves on the far wall to reveal the tunnel that leads to Ark's office.

I sat in front of that desk early on in my time in Talionis, when I thought maybe I could defy them by doing nothing, by being the worst recruit possible. I can still feel the burning sensation of the training bullet piercing my shoulder, still remember thinking I was dying.

I hear the scoffing laugh of Colonel Valarius as he tells me it wasn't real, but that next time I'd experience the pain of a real one if I wasn't doing exactly what they wanted.

They leverage everything.

They've leveraged Storm against me time and time again.

They've leveraged my care for others.

My desire to not die.

And now here I am, more bound to them than ever, forced to help recruits go through scenarios. To equip them to overcome the scenarios so Demetrius Ark can defeat his homeland of Sitreea and take it over, expand its borders, and rule as a king in another part of the world that I never care to see.

But they have Storm. They have Matthias. Kemena's in the city working for them. All of their lives are in danger if I don't do what they want.

Still, despite the fact that Cai told me to excel, all I want to do is openly defy Ark and his people.

"Get over here," Colonel Valarius says.

I obey and follow him through the dark, dank corridor that leads to Ark's office.

After a few silent and increasingly tense moments, we arrive at the door. I shift uncomfortably as I wait.

Over this past week, I've done what Demetrius Ark wanted, and I haven't seen him. So why am I being brought to him now?

Colonel Valarius raps against Ark's door.

We wait, and I shift again. What does Ark want? What is his play?

Whatever it is, I doubt I could prepare for it in the seconds I have before I face the man.

The door swings open, and Laban glares at me.

My breath catches in my throat. His golden eyes flash, and his nostrils flare, highlighting his misshapen nose, a result of one of our first interactions with one another.

I stare into his eyes and show a hint of the defiance I've tried to tamp down since I got here.

His lip curls into a snarl. "The Commander will see you now."

He stalks past me, roughly bumping me with his shoulder. I stand my ground as much as possible, but he still shifts me out of the way.

He's stronger than I am, as much as I hate to admit it.

"Bria, come in," Commander Ark's voice echoes from his office.

When I don't move to obey, Colonel Valarius pushes me through the doorway.

"Do you need me as well, sir?" Colonel Valarius asks.

"No." Ark waves a hand through the air. "You're dismissed."

Colonel Valarius leaves, and the door clicks shut.

From his desk, Ark waves his hand at a set of couches near screens that are currently dark. "Please, sit."

I hesitate, but then do as he commands.

Even though the couch is more comfortable than the hard chair in my room and my lumpy mattress, I can't relax.

"Give me one moment while I finish this up." He focuses on a screen in front of him.

Every second that ticks by is interminable. Which I'm sure is by design.

After a couple minutes, he rises from his desk chair and ambles over to where I'm sitting.

Without a word, he pushes a button on the screen, and the panels on the wall in front of me spring to life.

Recruits training through an obstacle course on one screen. Some going through a weaponry evaluation on another. A group in an Educational Training, listening to Trill drone on and on about the wonders of Talionis. Some are about to enter a Kill Zone. I clench my hands into fists. They're about to fall right into one of at least a half a dozen traps I see set.

Seconds later, several recruits go down as bullets fly from the soldiers hidden throughout the Kill Zone.

And then I see Storm, face set in determination. She climbs a wall much faster than I would have thought possible for a ten-year-old, outdoing several of the recruits who are older than her but clearly newer to the city.

Five recruits are in the pit, a large sandpit area in front of the Arena used for disciplinary measures, with a corporal. Laban arrives and yells at the recruits to do another rep of push-ups. He steps on the back of one recruit whose form is off.

And scattered throughout each scene are the young kids I'm desperate to rescue.

My nostrils flare, and I clench my jaw as my eyes flick from one screen to the next, my heart racing in my chest. So many of these recruits are about to die if Ark has his way. And I can't stop him.

The silence in the room is deafening as the recordings scream at me, *This is your fault. This is your fault.*

The words echo in my ears.

If I hadn't stolen Ark's stuff, how many of these kids wouldn't be here?

If I hadn't defied him, maybe he wouldn't have the forces he does now.

But if I hadn't, where would I be?

"You see, our numbers have grown," Ark's voice breaks through my tormented thoughts.

I don't respond. I focus on the screens, waiting to find out what he'll say next. What plan he has to leverage me.

"You seem to care a great deal about how recruits fare here. Especially the young ones." His voice is almost melodic in tone. "Although you escaped with only a handful, so maybe you don't care as much as you claim to. Leaving a child like Storm behind." He clicks his tongue.

I bury my hands into the fabric of the couch, clutching it until I'm afraid I'll tear it, but I don't respond.

He's baiting me.

My strongest move is to not react. At least not more than I am.

"But if you care so much," he continues, "then I want to make something clear to you." He sits on the couch directly in front of me. "Look in their faces, Bria."

He presses a button without looking at the screens. Each of the video feeds zooms in on individual recruits' faces, many of them young.

I see the pain of those in the sandpit, the fear of those running through scenarios, the determination of the ones in the obstacle course, and the horror of those who are getting shot in the Kill Zone.

Boys and girls, some no older than six or seven.

Storm, her young eyes somehow triumphant and sad at the same time as she hits the bell at the top of the wall she was climbing.

"Look at them, Bria. You know my plans more than I wish you did, but I'll just use that to my advantage. You know I want back what is rightfully mine. You know I want revenge for what my father has done. I'm confident you've read the files. Someone with your strategic mind would know it's necessary to have as much intel on their enemy as possible. You see that I will not allow anything to stop me."

He pauses, and I drag my gaze from the screens to look him in the eye.

"But I'm offering you this. Help me train these recruits. Make them soldiers who will survive the war you know is coming." He pauses. "Because however many of these kids go home is up to you."

Air wheezes out of my lungs at his words. He can't be putting the lives of all these recruits in my hands. But he is. He's making them *my* responsibility.

"Make them good enough, and they'll return to their families, to the lives of squalor you all seem to like so much. And I'll have what I want."

He leans forward, arms resting on his knees, hands linked. "But they have to be good enough. Every scenario they run through, there has to be perfection in their actions. Something you can teach them, I believe. And if you do, you save the lives of these people that you care about so deeply. If you don't, then they die." He shrugs his shoulder and leans back, but the movement is so calculated that I want to scream.

"Either way, I will get what I want from you." He pushes a button again, and all the screens become one image of Storm, standing at attention at the foot of the wall she just climbed, alongside other recruits, some close to her age, others several years older. "You claim to love this girl. Say you want to help her. Well then, you better help me. And stop being so preoccupied in your trainings with Major Vasco. I know you can do better, and I expect to see that. You've had a week to acclimate, Bria. Show me that your life, your ability, is worth me keeping you around. Otherwise, we'll have to come to some new arrangements. Understand?"

I give one quick nod.

He stands and smooths his hands down the front of his jacket. "Wonderful."

I stand as well.

"In order to help make sure you're at the top of your game, since you've had several weeks away from our training, you will be training with these recruits."

I turn and look at him sharply. "What? I've already done all this training."

"And it didn't seem to stick in the way we would have liked it to. So train with them again. Work hard, Bria. I expect you to be the best."

My stomach knots as a realization dawns on me.

He wants me to do this, not because he wants me in the best shape possible. He knows as well as I do that I'm physically conditioned, and that these past weeks of being out of Talionis haven't dulled my senses at all. If anything, I've grown stronger, quicker, more adept at reading a situation. Being on the run has a way of doing that to you.

He's doing this because he wants me to care. He wants me to care deeply.

Because every person I care about becomes something he can use against me.

"You're dismissed," he says. "Colonel Valarius should be at the end of the hall, waiting to take you back to your quarters. I want you to clean up and head to lunch with the other recruits."

"I already ate," I say.

"No, you didn't. I'm sure you have plenty of appetite. Based on what I've heard, the bowls you're sending back into the kitchen are still rather full. And we need your strength up, darling. Have lunch with Storm. I'm sure your time with her will be beneficial and motivational for both of you."

I swallow back bile, give a salute he expects, then turn on my heel and leave the room. At least I'll get to see Storm, even though it's dangerous.

CHAPTER
SEVEN

The sounds of the Dining Hall reach me before I open the doors.

The Recruits' Living Quarters are exactly as I remember. But this time, instead of walking into the Dining Hall to find my friends, I'm walking into a room of strangers. I fidget with the new HaloAct band Colonel Valarius issued me after my meeting with Ark.

The band is both familiar and strange. It's an upgraded model from what my friends and I wore when we were recruits. Along with several additional features, Colonel Valarius made sure to point out that the new bands have advanced tracking capabilities.

Which means I can't use Ari's work-around to reprogram the band and move about freely.

The thought leaves a bitter aftertaste as I reach for the doorknob to enter the Dining Hall. If I can't reprogram the band, how will Kemena and I get to the Ruins tomorrow night?

I give myself a subtle shake and open the door.

I don't want to eat, to prove Ark right, but my stomach growls, betraying me.

After grabbing a plate with a chicken salad sandwich and chips, I scan the room, looking for the puff of blond hair that will lead me to my young friend. As much as I know it's foolish to do exactly what

Ark expects and go find the girl I love like a sister, I can't stop myself. I've missed her, and I haven't been able to put my arms around her for weeks.

Other than when I stood before the High Council and Ark used her against me, every time I've seen her has been on screens. I spot her at the table that she and I would sit at with Cade and our friends.

A burst of emotions rushes through me at the thought of Cade. My brave friend who gave his life for me, who was stronger than I could ever hope to be on so many levels. Every room in this city holds so many memories.

I stuff the emotions aside and weave my way around tables and past recruits. Some of them look at me with curiosity, others seem to dislike me already.

I recognize a couple of recruits who I got through Kill Zones, some who I went through scenarios with, but most of the faces are unfamiliar. New recruits brought in through Ark's hunt for me and my friends.

Storm is chatting with a few of the recruits at her table, and then her eyes catch mine as I draw close.

"Bria!" She jumps from her seat and races toward me.

I quickly set my tray on the table an instant before she flings herself into my arms with so much force that I almost stumble backwards. I squeeze her tight.

For a long moment, I just hold her, resting my cheek against her fluffy blond hair.

"I missed you," she says.

"I missed you too."

She pulls away, grabs my hand, and tugs me toward the table. "I want to introduce you to my friends."

Three girls and two young boys sit at the table. I recognize Ahkeesia and Quincy from the warfare scenarios debriefing. Storm plops back into her seat and scoots over, then pats the spot next to her. It's a tight fit, but I squeeze in, because all I want to do is to be as close to this little girl as possible.

"This is Keesia," Storm points to Ahkeesia, who's the only other girl around my age at the table, and we nod to each other.

She's short, with chin-length light brown hair and dark brown eyes that hold a trace of uncertainty as she studies me. "Haven't seen you in here before." Her voice holds the same uncertainty. She recognizes me from Warfare Strategies.

"Bria's trustworthy," Storm says, placing a hand on Keesia. "Don't believe what everyone else says."

Keesia smiles at Storm, but the glance she gives me tells me she's not convinced. Not that I blame her. I would probably be unhappy if I were in her position.

Storm continues with her introductions. "That's Quincy."

The little girl barely makes eye contact with me before burrowing closer to Keesia.

"And that's Sam." Storm points to a boy around six or seven with straight black hair, olive skin, and brown almond-shaped eyes.

Sam doesn't glance up from the sandwich he's eating.

Storm introduces the other boy, Jace, who's probably nine, and a girl who's about eight named Penny.

I do my best to smile and enjoy the kids' banter as I pick at my sandwich. It's the tastiest food I've had in days, but I can barely stomach it.

There's something so normal about this. Sitting at this table. Hearing Storm's enthusiastic chatter. Listening to the hum of recruits talking in the crowded Dining Hall.

It's familiar and yet horrifically different.

This table is crowded with *kids*. The Dining Hall is full of faces I don't recognize, personalities I don't understand, backgrounds I have no clue about. People that are strangers and yet caught up in the same horrifying narrative I was in.

Ripped from their homes, their families, their loved ones. Forced to train, forced to become someone they never expected to be. Facing an enemy so different from the ones we grew up hearing about.

I take another bite of my sandwich, knowing I need to eat enough for whatever training I'll face this afternoon.

Storm hops up and goes over to whisper something to Penny. The two girls giggle, and the sound turns the sandwich in my mouth to sawdust.

"It's not right," Keesia whispers next to me. "They shouldn't be here."

I swallow. "Yeah. I can't believe there are so many kids."

Keesia shifts to face me more fully. "Storm talks about you. I told her she shouldn't trust you, and that is the one and only time I've ever seen her angry."

The thought of Storm angry is strange, but I stay silent, knowing Keesia is evaluating me.

"If you hurt her, I will do whatever it takes to bring you down," Keesia says, the intensity in her words confirming she means every single one.

I set my sandwich down. "Everything I do is to protect her."

We study each other for another moment, and then Storm is back. She leans against me for an instant before picking up her sandwich and starting a new conversation with Sam.

Keesia nods once, and somehow, I think we've come to an understanding of sorts.

I know nothing about Keesia, but anyone who would risk something for Storm seems like a possible ally.

My HaloAct band buzzes, another achingly familiar yet triggering element to have back in my life. I glance down to see a new schedule has been added to my band.

Ark is putting me through training similar to when I first arrived.

Early morning physical conditioning, weaponry training, even going through warfare scenarios myself again.

But there are still times when I'll be working with Major Vasco in meetings. I'll essentially be both a laborer working with the Warfare Strategies soldiers and a recruit.

In my gut, I know this is a setup. Every single element. Ark wants me to make friends, and at the same time, he wants me to make enemies. Those here who aren't happy with what's happening, who want to resist like Asher in the scenario the other day, they won't trust me. And Ark wants it that way.

I look around the table at Sam, Quincy, Jace, Penny, and finally Storm. I have to get them out of here. Whatever it takes.

Storm laugh at something Jace says, and my chest tightens.

Ark is watching her more than any of these other kids.

"Bria," Storm says, catching my attention. "Why are you here now?"

I loop an arm around her and pull her close. She rests her head against my shoulder.

"I get to eat with you now, my little squirrel."

She lifts her head up to wrinkle her nose at the nickname she despised before, but now doesn't seem quite as opposed to. Then she nestles her head against my shoulder again. "I'm glad."

I want to ask her a dozen questions, figure out how she's doing, find out what happened to Damara and how Storm was captured to begin with. But for now, I keep quiet and hold her against me.

The doors to the Dining Hall crash open, and Laban and Sergeant Valarius enter.

"Attention!" Laban shouts.

Every recruit in the hall jumps from their chair to stand at attention.

I do the same, mainly because I don't need Laban singling me out again. I can immediately assess the recruits who are unaccustomed to Talionis, the newest wave they've brought in. Their salutes aren't as stiff. Their posture not as straight.

And they don't have as haunted of a look in their eyes as some of the others who've gone through warfare scenarios.

Laban's raspy voice cuts through the air. "Time to head to your trainings. Line up, and get out of here."

CHAPTER
EIGHT

I n Eryndale, I was finally starting to enjoy my meals again, slow down enough to have conversations. Not feel like I had to eat in under five minutes so I could make sure I ingested the calories necessary for the physical exertion coming next.

But that's gone now.

I'm back in Talionis, and I'm back to training. I hate myself a little as I get up and clear my tray.

Part of me is almost *happy* to be heading to training.

My muscles itch to be exerted, and my brain needs a break from all the thinking this past week. This training will be brutal, whether it's Sergeant Valarius or Laban putting me through it. But I'm ready.

I give Storm another hug. She's taller than she was when I was here before, and I miss the weeks that we've been apart. Her body is stronger, her face more subdued. Less like a little girl, more like a little soldier.

An ache fills my chest. This is the transformation the other kids are about to undergo as well.

"Where are you heading?" I ask as the other kids join Storm.

The way they rally around her is both precious and heartbreaking.

She looks down at her HaloAct band to confirm. "I have a training with Instructor Trill."

"She's nice," Jace pipes up. "I like when she gives us cookies."

I bite my cheek to keep from quickly retorting that the woman is anything but nice and that all the kids should be careful. I'm being monitored—with the new band, it's probably to a higher degree than I'm aware of.

If only Ari were here. She would delight in figuring out how to get around the monitoring and advanced tracking capabilities of the new bands.

Strider Locke walks past and waves at the kids. They all smile and wave in return, but he barely notices as he resumes messing with his band. The seed of a thought plants itself in my mind, but I focus on Storm.

I get down on my knee and pretend to straighten her uniform so I can lean in close and whisper in her ear. "I love you, Storm. Be careful, okay? The things that people say here—they're not true."

Storm puts her hands on my shoulders, and her face turns serious. "I know."

I give a subtle nod to the kids chatting a few feet away, waiting for her. "They need to be careful too."

She gives me a solemn nod.

I hate putting any kind of pressure on her, but these kids trust her. And I trust Storm.

She's wise beyond her years. The problem is, she's being forced to do things a child should never have to do. I hug her again, then stand.

She leads the young group with her out a door in the opposite direction of the one I need to go through to get to the Physical Training Arena. I follow the recruits heading in that direction, wondering how I'll stack up against them.

Will today be circuit training or an obstacle course or something different entirely? Who knows what Sergeant Valarius and Laban have come up with in the past several weeks?

I roll my shoulders and bounce on the balls of my feet as I walk to loosen my body and prepare.

"Bria!"

The voice that calls my name makes my heart leap, then sends it sinking to the ground. I turn to find Shane marching toward me, dressed as a soldier, not a recruit, rifle slung across his back. Every stride perfect, hair shaved to a buzz cut.

I stand still as I try to determine what to say, what to do. I haven't talked to this guy since he betrayed me, betrayed my friends. All because he didn't believe us when we told him Ari was going to survive her injuries. He cares about her, but there's no excuse for his actions.

The High Council sentenced Nika to death because of him. As far as he knows, Nika's dead. And he needs to believe that still.

He stops in front of me. All at once, the humid summer air is suffocating.

"I need to get to training," I say.

His eyebrow lifts slightly. "I guess you'll show them a thing or two."

He smiles, but it dies quickly. Maybe because I'm frowning at him, arms crossed as I wait to see what he'll say next.

"I just . . ." He shifts, averting his gaze. "Look, I . . ."

"Shane, spit it out or let me walk away."

He hangs his head. "I'm sorry about Nika. I didn't know. I didn't think—"

"Stop." I cut him off. He didn't think. He didn't trust us. "Ari's alive, Shane. But because of you, Nika—" My voice cracks. It doesn't require any subterfuge to express the ache of sadness at the fact that my friend isn't with me right now. "She's not here." I draw in a shuddering breath. "I gotta go."

"Bria, I . . ."

I walk past him and ignore whatever else he has to say. I want to scream at him. Get into a fight with him. Express my anger, my hurt, my betrayal.

But I can't.

There's too much riding on me staying in line. Pretending to be who Ark wants me to be.

Cai's working on a plan in the tunnels beneath Talionis. Nika and

Mom are terrorizing soldiers in the Ruins. And Kemena and I will find a way to smuggle kids out of this city, even though the band on my arm tells me that's impossible now.

I jog the rest of the way to the Physical Training Arena and enter the cool interior of the building with a swarm of recruits whose uniforms indicate their different levels. Most of those here are beginners.

I remember the feeling of my first weeks in the Physical Training Arena. I built up to things, but it was so difficult, despite my athleticism from all the time I spent swimming in Derbe.

Everyone goes to their unit's holding area to await instruction. I stand in the doorway, suddenly at a loss for what to do. With my gray jumpsuit, I already stand out from the other recruits. Not knowing where to go next is only adding to the furtive glances being sent my way.

"Averton." Sergeant Valarius walks through the door. "Line up with Unit 2."

I obey. I'm more comfortable around Sergeant Valarius than I used to be, but I have no doubt he'll push me harder than everyone else here. For no other reason than to defer suspicion that he and I are aligned in any way.

The others in Unit 2 look at me with a side eye as I enter. When I was in a unit before, I wasn't close to everyone, but I was close to a few people. It's unique, that bond you get while you're training, fighting, working with one another, trying to make sense of where you are and what's happening.

As much as I hate Talionis and everything it stands for, I'm thankful for the bonds it forged for me with Nika, Ari, Cade, and Matthias. The thought of Matthias sends a sharp pang through my heart.

"Listen up," Sergeant Valarius says.

I glance around. Laban's not here. A swirl of relief fills me. I can't handle him along with everything else.

"I want Unit 1, Unit 4, and Unit 6 to head down and train with Corporal Saylano. The rest of you are with me. We'll be going through circuit training and identifying your areas of weakness." His gaze connects with mine. "For your sakes, try not to have very many of those."

I shift slightly. There's no room for error here.

I follow the rest of the recruits down the stairs and into the Physical Training Arena. I can't help but think about Nika, what it was like to train with her, to get stronger together. She pushed me harder, and I became better in physical conditioning than I ever would've without her. But she's not here to work with me, and Ari's not here to change my band.

As though on cue, my band chimes. I open it to find a holographic view of my training circuit through the Physical Training Arena. I'll work with the weights, then climb the wall, and go through an endurance test at the end.

All things I should be able to deal with.

Since most of them are new, I'll be expected to do far better than every recruit around me. In all reality, *I* expect myself to do better than all of them, as much as Sergeant Valarius and Commander Ark expect that of me.

I stretch, then head over to the weights.

A recruit steps in my path. "Why are you here?" Her words are sharp, and the way she looks down her nose at me makes me think of Shay. Although she's not as edgy as my former neighbor.

According to her nameplate, her name's Marci Morton. Maybe she's just cautious. She has every right to be.

"I'm forced to do this, same as you," I say.

She scoffs. "Doubtful." She crosses her arms over her chest. "I don't want to be here. None of us do. But you work with them, which makes you just as much my enemy as they are."

I glance around. "You better watch what you say, Marci. I don't know you, but your words will come back to haunt you if you say them too loud or in front of the wrong people."

She leans toward me. "Are you the *wrong people*?"

Before I can respond, Sergeant Valarius is there. "What's this? Get to work. Your training time has started, and I need to see movement from both of you. Now!" He screams the words.

A jolt zaps through me. It's like I'm a new recruit again.

I head over to the weight lifting unit I was aiming for, and Marci goes in the opposite direction. I almost call out to her, tell her I'm not one of the people she should be worried about, but I stop myself.

At some point, maybe I'll convince Marci she can trust me. If she so openly hates Talionis, she might be an ally down the road. But I need to keep a low profile. At least until I have a plan.

I lie down on the lifting unit, punch in the weight limit I want for the bar, then do my reps. Strider spots me, but we haven't spoken yet. This is the first time I've seen him without a screen, and he fidgets with a thread on his uniform as I go through my reps.

I start another round, and my muscles ache. Maybe I should have chosen a lower weight, especially since I doubt Strider could pull the weight off me in the event he needed to.

The idea almost makes me chuckle, and I look over, half expecting to see Nika there to share a joke with. But she's not there.

My band buzzes against my wrist. I've hit the amount of reps required for this circuit. I replace the bar on the rack and stand.

"Nice," Strider says.

I give him a half smile. "Thanks."

"I'm Kiwi."

My eyebrows rise. "Like the fruit?"

His bronze skin darkens into a blush. "Um, Strider Locke is my full name." He taps his nameplate. "But everyone calls me Kiwi."

He seems embarrassed by the nickname now, but I smile. "Nice to meet you, Kiwi."

"What are you doing here?" he asks. Same question as the girl a few minutes ago, but without the hostility.

I reach my hand out to shake his. "Well, first, I'm Bria."

"Yeah, Bria Averton," he says. "We sat next to each other in Educational Training the other day. Plus, everyone here knows who you are."

I withdraw my hand after he shakes it and glance around, as though looking to confirm this. No one else is paying attention to us. I look back at him. "What do you mean?"

"You're the reason most of us were taken," he says. "And now you're here."

I nod slowly. "Yeah, I guess I am."

"So, why are you here?" he asks again, his voice a little more urgent.

I sense a desire to know truth, not just a desire for information.

"They caught me."

"But are you a traitor to them, or an ally *for* them?" he asks. "Because ever since you've been back, we've been hearing different things. And your file is . . . confusing."

"I noticed you like poking around the back end of the system."

His eyes widen. "Uh . . ."

"My friend used to do that." I catch sight of a private heading our way. I motion for Kiwi to get down on the bench for his reps. "Work on your reps. I'll talk as you do it."

He nods, then sits on the bench.

His eyebrows shoot up as he takes in the weight limit I set the bars to, and he lowers the number sheepishly. "I'm not used to this kind of stuff."

I smirk. "It's all good. You get used to it."

The words sound reassuring, which wipes the smirk off my face.

He gets into position, and I make sure the bar is settled correctly before he pushes it into the air.

"So?" he says between labored breaths, after only five reps. "Why are you here? Who are you to them?"

I don't answer for a moment, then I say, "I'm their enemy."

"Then why do they talk about you like you're the poster child for being redeemed by the Commander?"

Kiwi's words send heat through me. "The *what*?"

"Well, Instructor Trill, Commander Ark"—he huffs out a breath —"all the holograms we're seeing at the end of our day talk about how vital our roles are in Talionis and in the North American region. How much what we're doing here will make a difference, and that if we fear that's untrue, we should just look at you." Sweat drips down his face, and he releases a labored breath as he pushes the bar up. "You were once an enemy of Commander Ark and Talionis, but now you're back." He settles the bar back on the hooks and sits up to look me in the eye. "And you're training again. You're working with Major

Vasco on Warfare Strategies. You're even going to Educational Training. You're part of Talionis." He swipes a hand over the sweat beading on his forehead. "They say you want to be here. That you changed your mind and realized Commander Ark's vision is better than you ever dreamed. Now you want to be a part of it."

I stare at him. I want to tell him the truth, which takes me aback. But the seed that planted in my mind earlier begins to sprout. If Kiwi is as skilled as Ari, maybe he could reprogram my band. Even help Cai set up secure tech servers in the underground tunnels and get encrypted coms set up for communication between Cai and Nika and Mom and the scouts.

But can I trust him?

He tilts his head, his face open. "Who are you, really? If not everything that they say you are."

"Um . . ." I fidget with my band, suddenly afraid it can monitor what I'm saying.

He leans toward me, eyes sparkling. "Don't worry about that. I have some special . . . filters in place." The conspiratorial wink he gives me is almost boyish.

And I find I believe him.

"Here." He reaches for my band and I let him, curious. He pushes a sequence of buttons on the band that takes less than five seconds, then releases my arm. "Now you've got a filter too."

Again, I believe him. "Ark doesn't want anyone who doesn't want to be here to trust me. So he's spreading lies. Making me untrustworthy to those I need to be allied with if there's any hope of stopping him." As soon as the words leave my mouth, I worry I was *too* honest.

But Kiwi thumps me on the back. "That's what I like to hear. Keesia said Storm trusts you. I think I should too." He gives me a toothy grin.

Our bands buzz, indicating our short rest between exercises is over.

Kiwi and I go through the rest of the circuit together. From free weights, to leg lifts, to utilizing more high-tech strengthening equipment, we stay partnered together. And each rep, each time Kiwi humbly listens as I correct his grip, or help him adjust his stance, every joke he cracks, even his mumbled comments about *adjusting things later*, all of it leaves me more inclined to trust him. Maybe even to consider taking the enormous risk of bringing him into Kemena's and my plans.

After all, with this band, there's no way we can enact our plan without tech help.

It's a huge risk.

My muscles burn as I drop into a squat with the weighted bar on my shoulders. I'm pushing my body harder than I have for over a week, and it feels good. Sweat drips down my back. I stand.

Kiwi applauds. "I'm impressed." He flexes a skinny arm. "I thought I was getting stronger, but you put me to shame."

I replace the bar in its slot. "You'll get there."

He leans closer. "I can at least make it *look* like I'm getting better." He gives me a cheeky grin, and I laugh.

There is no doubt in my mind that he and Ari would get along.

When it's time for me to climb the rock wall, I'm not sure if my muscles will be able to do it.

But I scale it faster than I used to. I'm doing well, far better than I should be.

And it's because the training they put us through works.

It worked to keep me from them, and it will work to do all Demetrius Ark wants it to do.

His words echo in my mind again. *However many of these kids come back home is up to you.*

The weight of it falls on me as I tap the buzzer at the top of the rock wall.

"Nice job, partner!" Kiwi cheers as I pass him while scaling back down the wall.

I muster up a smile that slips as soon as I'm out of his line of sight.

I have to excel. Be who Ark wants me to be. But while I'm doing so, I'll find a way to sneak kids out of this city.

The question is, can I trust Kiwi to help me do what I can't do on my own?

NINE

B y the time the training ends, I'm dripping with sweat, my muscles are burning, and my hair's sticking to my neck and scalp despite the air conditioned building. And I can't help but smile.

Sergeant Valarius put me through different trainings from others in the unit, I think to see where I'm at physically and to show them they can do more than they think they can.

I saw the looks on the faces of many of the new recruits, including Kiwi. They couldn't believe what Sergeant Valarius was making me do and the fact that I could actually do it. My band will register high levels for each of the things I've done today, from the obstacle course to the various maneuvers I had to go through for each of the different training sections, and it feels good to know I did well.

The feeling disappears. I almost wish I wasn't so good.

It's so similar to when I was first here, and yet I'm such a different person than I was then. I grab a towel to dry myself off and wipe the sweat from my neck and face.

"Well, I guess someone didn't forget her training." Laban's raspy voice behind me causes me to freeze.

I turn slowly. No one else is close, but people are around, so he can't do anything to me. As much as he would like to. The hatred in his eyes fills my bones.

"Can I help you, sir?" I ask through gritted teeth.

His lips curl into a sinister smile. "Guess you learned a little respect." He leans in close. "No one is safe that you care for, even if you do everything the Commander says."

My body goes cold, my sweat like chilled water pouring over me. "What are you talking about?"

"Every person here, every person you care about, is expendable for the Commander's cause. Especially someone like you, who did so much to try to stop it."

My heart hammers against my rib cage. "Why would you tell me that?"

"Because I want you to remember that you will never be forgiven for what you've done to the Commander."

My eyes narrow. "Why are you so loyal to that man? You know what he's planning."

His hand cracks across my cheek and whips my head to the right. I fight back a gasp of pain and slowly face him again.

"Don't try that with me," he says. "I'm loyal. Because of you and your treasonous acts, I've had to prove my loyalty to the Commander all over again. Years I've spent showing him I'm someone he can trust, and in the months of you being around, subverting others to bow to your whims and foolish ideas, I've had to prove my loyalty to the Commander. I won't do it again."

I let the burning sensation in my cheeks ground me as I stare into Laban's golden eyes that flash with hatred and something else. Something I can't define.

He didn't actually answer my question.

Laban crosses his arms over his chest and gives me a scrutinizing look. "What I can't understand is why the Commander would let your piddly little town stay standing. Derbe needs to burn, just like the other towns I went through searching for you."

I swallow back an angry retort, knowing it's what Laban wants. He'll do anything to goad me into a response that would jeopardize my position, as precarious as it is, and give him a reason to hurt me. To hurt those I care about.

An image of Storm flashes through my mind, and a fresh resolve fills me.

I won't do it. I won't react.

But as he turns and strides away, we both know he won something. Because his question is a mere echo of the one I can't answer.

Why would Commander Ark leave Derbe standing?

He destroyed the hometowns of my friends.

He's allowed Laban to run ruthlessly all over the North American region and hunt for me. He only ordered him to stop because Broche, the mercenary he hired to help search for me, told him there was no way he'd be able to track me if Laban kept burning up towns and villages.

But Derbe . . . he left standing. And Ark does nothing without a purpose.

I finish cleaning up and check my band to confirm I'm supposed to go to Warfare Strategies next.

Strange. My schedule's been updated to Educational Training instead. And my evening chores at the tailors' has been removed.

Unease fills me as I step outside. Why the change in my schedule?

And if I'm not going to the tailors' for chores tonight, how am I supposed to find Kemena and tell her about the new complication of my band?

———

As usual, Trill is late for class.

I don't recognize any of the recruits in this session, and despite constantly watching the door, Matthias doesn't make an appearance. I fidget with the edge of my sleeve. Even though I can't talk to him, seeing Matthias assures me he's okay. But I haven't seen him all day.

Five minutes later, Trill enters, perfectly dressed as always.

"We have a special treat today." Her voice ripples through the room as she stops in front of her podium. "I am beyond thrilled to present to you all the one and the only Demetrius Ark, Commander of this city, leader, and visionary." She applauds and others in the room do as well, although perhaps not as many as she'd like, based on the scowl on her face.

My gaze darts around the room. Where will Demetrius Ark come from?

Never in all my time in Talionis did he come to an Educational Training session. And anything unusual with Demetrius Ark scares me.

The screens around the room burst to life. He's not literally coming to the class, which eases some tension from my shoulders. I've already spent too much time with him today.

And I have a sick feeling that it's just the beginning.

Trill's eyes find mine as everyone in the room stands to honor Demetrius Ark, myself included. The smug expression curling her lips sets me on edge.

"Thank you for that welcome, Elva," Ark says, his poised, perfect expression hiding a calculating mind full of cruelty.

His enigmatic personality will draw the admiration of many in this room. They might not have believed Trill's lies before this, but more of them will listen to whatever she has to say after being in the presence of Demetrius Ark.

Something about him makes people want to follow him, even though he's not all he claims to be.

I shift so I don't have as clear of a line of sight to Elva Trill and her penetrating gaze. No wonder Shay and Trill get along.

They have the same calculating ability, the same desire to be someone who's recognized by leadership, no matter who that leadership might be. No matter the cost.

"Now onto business," Commander Ark says.

I clutch the back of my chair, rattled. I missed whatever long introduction he was giving to the recruits. My jaw clenches. Even though I hate listening to the man, it's important for me to know exactly what Ark is saying.

"Bria Averton, please come to the front of the room."

My name on his lips makes me feel like a piece of garbage. I hate that he knows my name. I hate that he uses it.

My hesitation is brief, but, based on the way his eyes sharpen as he watches me, he catches it.

A soldier behind me yanks me into the aisle then shoves me forward. I keep myself from stumbling and make my way to the front of the room.

Ark smiles as I come forward. "The rest of you may sit."

I stop next to Trill.

"Many of you have heard the name Bria Averton spoken. Some of you know how much pain she has caused me, and even some of you."

The empathy on his face makes me want to scream. This is not my fault. The pain caused is not because of anything I've done, but because of Demetrius Ark. And the pain he's causing is only beginning for these poor recruits. But I hold my tongue, waiting to hear why he's brought me up here.

Trill puts her arm around me. I want to throw it off. To slap her across the face. But I stay still.

"But she is not the traitor we've fought. Not anymore," Ark is saying.

My body tenses, every fiber of my being desperate to reject his statement. But Cai's words about excelling for now hold me in place.

"Today, we are restoring to Bria her rank as Elite Recruit, First Class."

I'm being praised, and it's all so that those who don't like what's happening in Talionis won't trust me as a possible ally. I clench my jaw so tight it hurts.

Ark goes on, addressing the recruits. "I understand that sometimes you might not understand what's happening, or why you have to do the things you have to do." He leans forward, his gaze imploring. "But please remember that I have a purpose for you. A purpose that will bring about great things, not only for yourselves, but for so many others."

The lie upon lie makes me want to be sick.

Keep it together, Bria. Keep it together.

A soldier comes forward and hands me a training rifle loaded with blanks like every other recruit has. I automatically take the weapon from his hands and sling it over my back. It settles with a comfortable familiarity, and I clutch the strap.

Commander Ark drones on about all the work I did to become an Elite Recruit and encourages the recruits in the room to fight for such a great honor.

I survey the recruits. Some look impressed, while others appear ready to throw something at me. The difference between the recruits who are like Shay and the recruits who are like me, even though they don't know it. And they would never believe it after this charade from Ark. Which is the whole point. This is just another opportunity for him to control the narrative of what people believe about me.

Because if they believe what Ark says, no one will help me when I try to overthrow him.

I clutch the rifle tighter. Will the little kids believe I want to help them?

None of them are in the room, although I'm sure word of this will spread quickly. Maybe Storm can help me convince the kids to trust me.

Either way, I have to act fast. The longer I wait, the more Ark's lies about me will spread.

Ark finishes his rant, and the silence snaps me back to the present.

"Thank you, sir," I say, not entirely sure if those words are appropriate or not.

His smile tells me I at least hit that one right.

"We will talk soon." With that threat, the video feed cuts off.

Trill applauds with so much gusto her hands must hurt. I bite my cheek to keep from snapping at her. She knows as well as I do that none of this praise is warranted.

I return to my seat and settle my rifle next to me as Trill dives into today's lecture.

The band on my wrist buzzes, and a notification comes up. *Elite Recruit Bria Averton, report to the tailors before dinner for uniform fitting.*

At least I can go to the tailors' this evening after all. Hopefully Kemena will still be there when I arrive.

I close out the message and adjust the band on my wrist. Even if Kemena *is* there, what will I tell her? This band is as good as being chained to a soldier twenty-four seven. I can't remove it without it alerting Ark, and I can't reprogram it using Ari's method since the tech's been upgraded.

The faces of the kids I ate lunch with parade through my mind. They're so little. I *have* to help them. There's no other option. At least not one that would allow me to live with myself.

CHAPTER
TEN

I arrive at the tailors' ten minutes early and put my rifle in the rack by the door. Sampta and Presidia do not allow any weapons beyond the threshold of their domain.

"That's new," Kemena says, coming out of the back room.

"Ark gave me my rank back." Saying the words makes it more real.

Kemena crosses her arms. "I heard. Sampta and Presidia have been working on your uniforms all day."

"You've been here all day?"

She nods. "I typically don't like to do what I'm told. But when I heard Ark was giving you back your rank and your evening chores here were canceled, I made myself extra useful to the sisters. I was hoping I'd be busy enough to stay until you arrived."

I glance toward the back. "I'm glad you're here." I hold up my band. "There's been a complication."

Kemena's lips press together. "Come with me."

I follow her to a small design room off of the laundry room.

Once we're inside, Kemena shuts the door. "This room doesn't have any cameras or surveillance. Can we still get out to the Ruins tomorrow night?" Her eyes search mine, and I hate that my next words will crush the hope I find there.

"Not with this." I lift my band and drop it back to my side, thankful for the *filter* Kiwi added earlier that, assumably, will keep this conversation private.

"I need to see my sister." Kemena runs her hand through her many braids. "And there are so many kids here. All day today, I've washed the smallest uniforms, and I promised myself we would do something to protect them. What are we going to do?"

I pace, avoiding the tables overflowing with fabric and design patterns. "There's one option. But it's risky."

"Everything we do in this place is risky, girl. Tell me what you're thinking."

I quickly outline how Ari used to help me and Nika reprogram our bands so we could travel through Talionis and into the Ruins without alerting anyone.

"Perfect. Just do that," Kemena says.

I shake my head. "I can't. These bands are new, and I don't know how to reprogram them." I hesitate.

"Spit it out, girl. We've got maybe five minutes until the sisters come looking for you."

I stop pacing. This idea is dangerous, but it's the only one I have. "There's a newer recruit who's like Ari with tech. I don't think he wants to be here, but I'm not sure we can trust him."

"What's his name?" Kemena asks.

"Strider Locke, but he goes by Kiwi."

Kemena's eyebrow quirks. "Kiwi? Like the fruit?"

"Yup."

She snorts. "Interesting." A line forms between her eyes. "Wait. What's his real name?"

"Strider Locke."

She stares up at the ceiling. "I've heard his name before. Some of the soldiers were talking about him. Saying his ranking doesn't fit with his normal performance."

"They told you that?"

"Girl, please. No. I was supposed to be cleaning in the Physical Training Arena, and they started talking. You'd think janitors are invisible, the way people talk in front of me."

I lean against a table. "Kiwi's changing his ranking. Ari used to do it too. She would adjust her trainings to fit with where Nika and I were ranking so she could be with us."

"Do you think Kiwi could help you reprogram your band so we could sneak out to the Ruins?"

I chew my lip. Bringing Kiwi into this will expose more than I'm comfortable with, but I don't see another option. Plus, he's already added a filter to my band. "Yeah. I think he can."

"Then it sounds like we need to ask for his help."

The door bursts open, and Sampta and Presidia bustle in.

"Ah, there you are!" Sampta exclaims. "We've been looking everywhere for you."

"I brought her in here so she'd be ready to be fitted for her uniforms," Kemena says.

Presidia pushes her glasses up higher. "Fine, fine. Let's get to it then. We certainly don't have all day."

"Right you are, sister." Sampta shoos Kemena out the door. "Finish with the laundry, and then you can go to dinner."

Kemena and I share a look as she leaves. I nod, even as my stomach twists.

Our only option is to trust Kiwi. The trouble is, if he's willing to defy Talionis, how willing will he be to trust me now that Ark's made a public display of restoring my position?

Sampta closes the door behind Kemena, then faces me with her sister.

Presidia wrinkles her nose. "What possible excuse could you have for the hideous condition this uniform's in?"

I shrug. "Well, it didn't look great to begin with."

Sampta puts her hand on her chest as though I personally offended her. "Excuse me? Not great?"

"They issued me an old uniform," I say.

"Everything we do is beautiful," Sampta huffs.

"Well, this hideous gray does nothing for anyone," Presidia says.

Sampta gives a curt nod. "True, sister, true."

As though they've choreographed the movement, both sisters step forward and push their glasses up on their noses.

"Elite Recruit again, we've been told."

I shift under their scrutiny. "That's what the Commander said."

"Fine, fine. And where's the old uniform she had?" Presidia asks.

Sampta shrugs. "Who knows, sister, who knows?"

"I believe it was destroyed," I say.

They both gasp.

"Although these aren't our best work, we expect them to be handled with care. No one is to destroy one of our uniforms without our prior command," Presidia says.

I gawk at them.

"Well, what's done is done," Sampta says with a flourish of her hand.

Presidia nods. "I suppose. We *have* improved the design, and the uniforms look different now than they did before, anyway."

"They don't look much different to me," I mutter.

Sampta's cheeks puff out, and her face reddens. "The audacity. Clearly you don't understand fashion or art."

I keep my mouth shut. They make me try on all five of the uniforms they prepared for me. All of them fit fine, but they insist on making slight adjustments until they're *perfect*.

They take my measurements, talking about how they hope they'll get to design something of value soon.

This reminds me of times I spent doing laundry duty with Nika and Ari and the women. They are always looking for ways to make the uniforms more beautiful.

"The outward appearance is what matters, after all," Sampta says.

The words catch my attention and pull me from my thoughts. "What do you mean?"

Presidia has pins in her mouth, so Sampta continues. "One thing we know is that the right outfit can change the world."

A laugh escapes, and both women freeze and glare at me.

"I just don't think that's true," I say, when it's clear that covering my laugh as a cough won't be enough for them.

Presidia removes the pins from her mouth. "Look at the Commander. He's changing the world. Do you think anyone would have even two thoughts about the man if he didn't look perfect all the time? And you. You look like a ragamuffin. Is *anyone* listening to you?"

I blink. "Uh, no, but I'm also—"

"My point." Presidia gestures at me with a pin. "What you wear, how you look, how you present yourself, it changes everything."

They go back to taking my measurements and entering them into a screen.

A verse that I read from Cai's Bible comes back to me. *Man looks on the outward appearance, but God looks at the heart.*

It's not until both of the women stand to stare at me again that I realize I said the words out loud. Great.

"Um. I mean . . . maybe people look at what others wear," I say, deciding I might as well interact with these women. "But I don't think that's what matters. At least not fully."

"Oh, do tell. Give us of your great wisdom," Sampta says with a dramatic wave of her hand.

I'm not sure *why* I continue, but the words flow. "It just seems like if you look good and people listen for that alone, it'll eventually fail if there's no substance. No real *reason* for them to listen."

Both women gape at me, but something in Sampta's eyes catches me. Like maybe she wants to hear what I have to say.

But then they laugh, gather their things, and make their way from the room.

"Your five new uniforms will be delivered to your room later this evening," Presidia calls over her shoulder as she heads back into the sewing room.

I nod my agreement, then leave the facility, my stomach growling. At least I can head to the Dining Hall for dinner.

I'm not sure why it matters to me what the women said, but it does. Part of me fears there's some truth to it, that people listen because of how you look and present yourself. But God chooses weakness sometimes, right?

And just because a man looks like he could win, looks like he could defeat everyone, looks like he has the charm, charisma, and beauty to change everyone's hearts, to make them believe his lies . . .

That doesn't mean that's what will happen. Does it?

———

Since the tailors haven't finished their adjustments, I'm still wearing my gray jumpsuit when I enter the Dining Hall. But the rifle on my back is enough of an indicator that I'm a recruit again.

I grab a tray with chicken, broccoli, and mashed potatoes and join Storm at her table. The kids from lunch are here, as well as Keesia. And Kiwi.

At the sight of Kiwi, my appetite vanishes.

I need to talk to him, but I'm not sure how to start the conversation. I mindlessly eat, barely paying attention as the kids chatter around me.

Kiwi catches me staring at him across the table, and his forehead wrinkles. I offer a weak smile and look down at my plate.

"Why do you have a rifle again?" Storm asks, halting the conversation.

All eyes zero in on me, and I set my forkful of chicken back on my plate.

"Um, they, uh." I clear my throat. "Ark gave me my rank back."

"So it's true?" Keesia asks. "You're an Elite Recruit again."

I nod.

"Is that why you were training with us earlier?" Kiwi asks.

"Yeah." I take a deep breath, my gaze fixed on Kiwi. "They want to pretend nothing happened."

Kiwi nods slowly.

"I don't like having a rifle," Storm says.

"I think it's cool," Jace argues.

The younger kids all start talking about why they do or don't like the guns, but Kiwi, Keesia, and I stay quiet.

I'm not sure what the two recruits near my age are thinking as we finish dinner. But I hope my cryptic words were enough to let them know I'm not okay with this. Especially since I can't risk outright saying I'm unhappy in the middle of the Dining Hall, surrounded by recruits who could report me in order to gain favor.

DURING DINNER KIWI MADE A COMMENT ABOUT HAVING NIGHTTIME CHORES cleaning in the Educational Building, so I'm crouched in a nearby alley, waiting for him to arrive.

Scaring him by jumping out when he walks by is probably the *wrong* way to start this conversation, but I can't figure out another option.

The humid warmth of the evening is broken up by a slight breeze, which is a welcome relief. Especially since I can't tell if I'm sweating because of the summer evening or because of the conversation I'm about to have with Kiwi.

After a few minutes, Kiwi comes into sight. He's whistling as he strides to the building for his chores, as though he doesn't have a care in the world.

I wait until he's only a few feet away before emerging from the shadows.

"Kiwi," I say.

"Ah!" He leaps backward, stumbling over his own feet and barely maintaining his footing.

"Sorry. It's me. Bria."

He clutches his heart. "Why you gotta sneak up on a guy like that?"

I offer an apologetic grin. "I need to talk to you."

His green eyes narrow, and he nods to the building. "I need to check in for my chores. Walk with me."

"It's a bit sens—"

"Inside will be better." He leads the way up the stairs.

I hesitate for a moment, then follow. If I can't trust him now, how will I trust him with what I'm about to ask?

Once we're inside, Kiwi opens the door to a small office I've never been in. He closes the door behind us.

"What are you planning?" He clicks the lock on the door. "And how can I help?"

I study him. When I decided to let him in on this, I never expected it to go this . . . easily.

"Along with my rifle, I got another upgrade, which you helped me with earlier." I hold up my band. "And I really need it to not track everything I'm doing. Can you help with that?"

"Of course I can help with that." He taps his own band. "This baby just tells them what I want it to now."

Yeah. He and Ari would be best friends. Or argue a ton. I'm not sure which, but there's a comfort in having someone around who gets tech.

"Can you show me how I can get it to mask my movements when I need it to?" I ask.

"Absolutely." Kiwi nods. "But first, tell me why."

Before I can protest, he continues.

"I'm not interested in staying here for whatever the soldiers have planned. And I'm not the only one who feels that way." He appraises me. "A resistance is forming. Growing stronger every day. We could all be a part of whatever you're planning."

The stark honesty from this guy I barely know leaves my jaw hanging open. "Why are you telling me all of this?"

"I don't believe you want to be here, and I think you could help us as much as we could help you."

I blow out a slow breath. "I need my band masked so I can get out to the Ruins."

Kiwi gasps. "What? Why would you want to go out there? Everyone—even the scariest of soldiers—is terrified of the Ruins."

I bite my lip. How much do I tell him? My pulse thrums in my throat. If I'm going to trust him enough to help me adjust my band, I might as well go all in. At this point, what I've already requested is enough to get me in trouble.

"I know why the soldiers are afraid of the Ruins." I pause. "But I'm *not* afraid. You don't have to be either. If I can get out there, I might have a way to help save some of the youngest kids." I stare at him, willing him to believe me.

His forehead smooths. "Okay. Then bring me with you."

"What?"

"If you're trying to save the kids, I'm in." He spreads out his arms.

"Whatever it takes. Plus, I can be your tech support. We could even get the Resistance involved." He gives me a massive grin.

I hold up my hand to stop this unexpected brainstorm. "We can't involve the Resistance. Not yet."

"Then at least bring me. Trust me, and I'll trust you."

My mind races with possibilities. Kiwi might be a solution to setting up secure tech in the Ruins for Mom and Nika *and* for Cai in the tunnels. We need someone with his expertise. But trusting him with everything . . . it's dangerous. Not to mention, he's not nearly as skilled in physical conditioning as me or Kemena. He could be a major liability for that reason alone—not even because he intentionally does anything.

He silently watches me, waiting for my response.

There's an openness to him, a stark honesty that's hard to fake.

And if I don't get his help, none of this matters.

God, please don't let trusting this guy be a mistake.

"Okay," I say. "If you can show me how to reprogram my band to mask my movements, we'll go tomorrow night."

"Sweet." He rubs his hands together. "This is gonna be epic."

He runs through the sequence I'll use to mask my band. It's a longer sequence of buttons and actions than what Ari showed me, but after a few times, I have the pattern down.

"Just be careful to only use this when necessary," he warns. "Preferably when you're supposed to be in one place for a while. They'll get suspicious and swap out your band for a new one otherwise." The way he won't meet my gaze tells me there's more to his story.

I nod my agreement.

"Oh!" He reaches for my arm again. "Use this sequence to cloak an entire room. It's like the filter I added for you, but it will mask everything being said in the room you're in. Not just your conversation."

"Nice." I focus as he shows me the sequence. "Why not just leave it on all the time?"

Kiwi's nose wrinkles. "If it's quiet too long in a room where they know there should be surveillance, they'll suspect something's up. Safer to only use this one as needed."

Again, I agree. Then practice the cloaking sequence to confirm I know it.

"You should get back to your chores," I say once I'm confident with the two sequences. "We've been in here too long as it is."

"First, how are we supposed to get into the Ruins without a transport?"

"I have my ways," I say, not ready to divulge all the information about the tunnels.

Kiwi nods. "Okay. Just tell me where and when to meet you."

"I need to work out a couple of details. I'll pass you the information tomorrow."

"Here." He types on his band for a few seconds, and a secure message comes through.

Top secret communication between Kiwi and Bria.

I raise an eyebrow. "Discreet."

"What? It's top secret. That in and of itself is discreet! Plus, once the messages are read, they'll disappear after sixty seconds."

I check my band. Sure enough, the message clears, but the channel remains open. "Okay. I'll send you a message tomorrow with the details."

With that, the two of us part ways.

CHAPTER
ELEVEN

I fidget with the band on my wrist. All day I was distracted in my trainings and in working in Warfare Strategies. It wasn't enough to get me sent to the sandpit, but my distraction didn't go unnoticed by Major Vasco and Sergeant Valarius. I'll have to be more diligent in the future.

But tonight will determine what the future entails.

Tonight, I'll finally get out to the Ruins. Confirm Mom and Nika are alive. And begin enacting a plan that will save the lives of little kids.

As long as Kiwi doesn't betray us.

Kemena was apprehensive when I told her Kiwi would be coming with us, but she agreed that his expertise would be invaluable. If we can trust him.

I leap up from my bed and pace the small space in my room as I mentally walk through the plan for tonight.

Everything is in place.

In less than an hour, I'll enter the tunnels beneath Talionis and meet up with Kemena. Kiwi will be waiting for us in the back of the Dining Hall in the Recruits' Living Quarters. Hopefully with the communication tech I asked him to gather.

As silly as it is, I haven't told him about the tunnels yet. Even though I'll be bringing him down into them in order for the three of us to get to the Ruins.

Using the tunnels like Kemena and I originally planned is probably a bad idea. But there wasn't time to change the plan. And it's still the safest option.

The only trouble is how much I'll be exposing to Kiwi tonight.

The tunnels. Nika and Mom in the Ruins. Even the fact that Kemena is in this with me. Everything Kiwi knows becomes a dangerous liability.

My band beeps. 2200 hours.

Time to go.

I shake out my hands, then program my band to mask my movements and monitor me in my room as though I'm sleeping.

I release a long breath and enter the bathroom. Doubts fling through my mind so fast I can barely cling to one long enough to assess if it's a strong enough reason to call off this plan.

Even as the thought of calling things off surfaces, so do images of the faces of the kids in this city. Several of whom I've gotten to know. Jace. Quincy. Sam. Storm.

The risk—no matter how great—is worth it.

I punch in the four-button code to open the secret panel in the bathroom. The wall opens. I enter the tunnels and retrieve the hidden map and torch as the wall slides back into place.

The walls leading from my room down into the wider subway tunnels feel closer than the last time I was in here. I pick up my pace.

Moments later, I enter the cavernous space of the old subway tunnels. My heart hammers in my chest, and I clutch the map tighter. Not that I'm using it. The path to where Kemena's waiting for me isn't complex. Even if it was, the map is imprinted on my mind. I studied it long into the night last night, confirming the route we'll take this evening.

But knowing the route doesn't make me feel the comfort I wish it did. I almost wish I was sneaking through the streets and back alleys of Talionis the way I used to when I went to the Ruins to train with Cai. At least that's familiar.

These tunnels are a new element. One more new thing on top of everything else.

Within ten minutes, I arrive at the location where Kemena and I are supposed to meet.

"You're early." Kemena steps out of the shadows of the passageway leading to the Lower Housing District.

I glance at my band. "Oh. Must have made better time than I expected."

"I'm nervous too," she says. "Let's go pick up Kiwi. Hopefully he's ready."

We head deeper into the tunnels beneath the heart of Talionis. The opposite direction from where we need to go. Kemena and I don't say much, and before long, we're at the tunnel that leads to a secret compartment in the Dining Hall.

I pause.

"Do you want me to get him?" Kemena asks.

I want to say yes, but shake my head. "No. He doesn't know about you. Or the tunnels. It's best if I get him."

"I'll wait here," she says.

I walk through the narrow tunnel and arrive at a wall. There's a small button to the side. Exactly where the map said it would be.

I push it, with a quick prayer that Kiwi is the only person waiting on the other side.

The wall shifts and slides out of the way.

Kiwi gasps. "What in the world . . ."

A glance behind him confirms the Dining Hall is empty. "Let's go."

I pull him into the tunnel with me and quickly close the door.

"What is this?" Kiwi asks.

"A tunnel system," I say. "Did you bring everything I asked you to?"

He nods distractedly as he presses his hands against the wall. "Nothing on the other side indicates this is even there. And nothing on my bands showed it."

"We need to go," I say. "The longer we're gone, the more dangerous this is."

Kiwi follows me down the tunnel and is startled once again when Kemena is waiting for us at the end of it.

I make quick introductions and then lead both of them through the underground system and toward the Ruins.

By the time we've gone as far as we could underground, Kemena and Kiwi seem comfortable with each other. Kemena's ease with him makes me feel better.

Having Kiwi as a part of what we're doing could make a huge difference.

"We have to travel the rest of the way above ground," I say. "This part is the most dangerous, but this area isn't typically patrolled as much. Still, stay as quiet as possible."

"Wait," Kiwi says, eyes glued on his band.

"Why are you using that?" I ask, my voice choked.

"It's fine," he says. "I have multiple security measures in place on this baby. I'm just scanning the area for any scheduled patrol units."

Kemena and I exchange a look, and she shrugs.

"We're good if we go now," Kiwi says.

My hand shakes slightly as I push the button that will lead us to the basement of an old factory on the outskirts of Talionis. I exit first and scan the area. It appears clear, but I miss the lenses Ari stole for us to use while we were on the run.

I wave for Kemena and Kiwi to exit, and the three of us enter the old basement.

I lead the way out of the basement, using the torch while I can. Once we exit the abandoned factory, we'll have to turn it off to prevent any nearby patrols from catching sight of the light.

Kemena is light on her feet, but Kiwi isn't quite as graceful. Still, we navigate the outer edges of Talionis undetected.

The old abandoned building hiding the entrance to the Ruins materializes in the darkness.

"Watch your step," I hiss as I climb the deteriorating staircase.

We carefully creep through the building, my shins aching in reminder of the many times I slammed them against debris and various pieces of furniture strewn through the old place. But this time, Kemena and I make our way to the back door without incident.

I can't say the same for Kiwi. Muffled groans and gasps come from him as he bumps his way through the building.

We exit into the small space between the house and the fence. It's the only way to get to this particular area, and the leaves and grass are more trampled down than they once were. My stomach twists.

Have the soldiers found this hole? Have they patched it?

I pull my sleeve over my hand and approach the ivy-covered fence, my hands prodding the hard material behind the leaves and foliage, looking for the opening.

My heart rate quickens when I can't find it.

"What are you looking for?" Kemena asks.

"The way in."

I keep going, my movements faster, my heart more panicked with each passing second.

My hand slips through, past the hardness into the open hole I've used time and time again.

It's been so long, I must have been looking in the wrong place. I release a relieved sigh, pull my hood over my hair, and then say, "Follow me."

Kemena pulls her hood up as well. "I better not get any bugs in my hair," she says under her breath as she follows me through the opening.

We emerge on the other side of the opening. I brush the leaves from myself and look back to see Kemena and Kiwi doing the same.

Kemena shudders. "I hate bugs."

"I understand." I try not to smile too widely, but she glares at me.

"Girl, watch it. I can tell you're laughing at me. Bugs are worth being scared about."

A small chuckle bursts from me, and she shakes her head.

Kiwi rubs his hands over his buzzed head. "That's crazy there's a hole into this place. How did you find it?"

I glance at the tree Cai was in the first time I used the entrance back into the Ruins. The entrance he told me about. "It's a long story."

"Now where to?" Kemena asks.

"Cai used to have sites in the Ruins. There's one in particular where I'm hoping we'll find Nika and my mom."

"Wait." Kiwi's head snaps up. "Nika, like the girl who the High Council sentenced to death? She's still alive?"

"She better be," Kemena says.

"I have so many questions," Kiwi says.

"We can talk as we go." Kemena waves her arm forward, the movement like a wispy shadow. "Lead the way. Carefully though, because, girl, it is dark out here, and I do not need to break an ankle."

A map of the Ruins forms in my mind as I walk, each step increasingly familiar.

I've been here so many times, raced through this place with Cai, worked with him to terrify soldiers, and learned to fight.

Cai's methods at first were odd, to say the least, but I can't deny that much of my abilities and my success as a recruit came from his unconventional training. I became stronger, better, because of him. And as dark and terrifying as this place is to every soldier in Talionis, somehow, I'm more comfortable here than I sometimes felt in Eryndale.

The constant barrage of questions from the leadership there, the lack of trust in me and my friends, and their lack of interest in doing what they needed to do to stop Talionis grated against me.

But here, even though vines and vegetation sprawl about, clutching twisted metal and parts of old vehicles, and trees and bushes burst through the rubble and debris of long-ago abandoned buildings, I'm at ease. The paths through the mess are forever imprinted on my mind. Paths that once appeared dangerous, hostile, but instead led me to hope. The courage to fight.

God, help me to find that hope and courage here again. Please.

As we pick our way over the jagged concrete teeth of ancient roads gnawing through the forest undergrowth, Kemena and I share more with Kiwi. Including our plan to use the tunnels to sneak kids out to the Ruins and to Mom and Nika.

"We'll have to go slowly," Kemena says. "But we're hoping we can get as many kids away from Ark as possible."

"It's a good plan," Kiwi says. "And I can help you make the kids disappear from the tech side."

We arrive at one of the first sites I ever went to with Cai, but it's dark and empty.

"Doesn't look like they're here," I say, disappointment swirling through my words.

"This place is a lot more impressive than I anticipated." Kiwi pokes his head deeper into the site.

Even in the dim moon lighting, it's clear Cai had it well stocked. I move to a bin where he kept torches. I remove one and turn it to the green light setting.

"Will they spot us with that?" Kemena asks.

"According to the flight manifest, no transports are scheduled to fly overhead tonight," Kiwi says as he digs through an old pile of tech. "I checked before we left."

Kemena lifts an eyebrow. "Well aren't you handy to have around."

Kiwi looks up with a cheeky grin. "Thank you."

For the first time since I brought him in, I'm happy to have Kiwi here.

"Plus, the soldiers rarely patrol the Ruins," I say. "And this light is harder to spot with infrared."

I hand Kemena and Kiwi each a torch.

Kiwi shines his torch over the old monitors and on the back wall of explosives. "Impressive that he has all this stuff out here."

"Cai could get just about anything he wanted while he was here," I say. "The soldiers are terrified of the Ruins because of him."

We go to two more sites, but find no indication of Nika or Mom being there. I glance at my band. We've been out for an hour already, and the longer we're out, the more dangerous it becomes.

"I know," Kemena says, as though I said the words out loud and didn't just think them. "But can we try a little longer? I need to see my sister. And every time we get somewhere and she's not there, I start believe she's nowhere."

Her voice catches, and my heart breaks. Because what if she's right? What if Nika is nowhere? What if she's gone?

If she's gone, she's not nowhere. The thought whispers through my mind.

If she's gone, she's in heaven. That's what my faith says. That's what I believe.

But God, I don't want her to be with You yet. I still need my friend.

And if she's gone, then where does that leave Mom?

"Okay," I say, shaken more by the thoughts than the threat of soldiers finding us. "There are two more sites that aren't too far from here. We can check the one to the east and then hike back toward the north to see if they're at the last one. But then we probably need to head back."

I sense more than see Kemena nod.

"If they're not out here, what will that mean for the kids?" Kiwi asks.

"We'll come back out and look until we find them." Even as I say the words, fears crowd my mind. If we can't find my mom and Nika, how can we sneak kids out here and expect them to be okay?

The Ruins aren't safe.

I lead them through the forest and we pass pre-Demise buildings that are crumbling and demolished. Some by Cai, some by the Demise.

We round a bend in a small path, and the river gushes in the distance.

"The site's just up here."

We hike closer to the river, then I lead them alongside of it and to the cave I know is waiting. Another one of Cai's many sites.

I push open the hidden doorway, and light spills out. I rush in, breath caught in my throat, barely daring to hope.

My eyes connect with Nika's.

She's pointing a gun at me.

As soon as she registers that I'm the intruder, the gun clatters to the floor, and she rushes toward me. Kemena walks in behind me as Nika's about to hug me.

Nika looks between both of us, then wraps her arms around us simultaneously, squeezing us into a hug. Tears press the backs of my eyes.

This is real, even though it feels like it shouldn't be. I am embracing my friend.

Her grip is powerful, and she's alive. She's okay.

"Bria?" Mom's voice to my right spins me out of Nika's grasp.

"Mom." The word is more like a sob than anything else.

I take a hesitant step toward her, almost unable to believe my eyes that she's standing in front of me, even though I knew she and Nika would be together.

Over ten months. I haven't seen Mom's face in over ten months. Lines crowd around her eyes, more than I remember. And new streaks of gray are woven throughout her hair.

But her eyes still hold the unconditional love I've always found there. Her face still softens in warmth and care as she looks at me.

My throat thickens. Is this a dream?

Mom closes the distance between us, and gazes at me in wonder. She traces her finger down my cheek. Just like she did the last time I saw her. On the anniversary of Ezri's death.

The day I was taken.

Her lips tremble, like she's remembering that day too. "What an answer to prayer. I never thought . . ." She squeezes her eyes shut, and my mom pulls me into her embrace and kisses my head.

My eyes burn, and I melt into her arms.

I've changed so much in the months since I've seen her, but somehow it's like nothing has changed. She's my mom. The best cartographer I've even known. The one who understood my pain over my brother's death better than anyone else. Who let me mourn, but also showed me how to keep living. Helped me dream of becoming a scout. Taught me everything I know about maps.

A skill she learned from Thaddeus in Eryndale. Where she was a scout. Where she's *still* respected.

As much as I know my mom, my time in Eryndale showed me there are many things I *don't* know.

She strokes my back, and I squeeze her tighter. Not wanting to lose her now that we've been reunited.

We have a lot to talk through, but for now, at least I get to be with her.

A *thump* behind me grabs my attention. I whirl out of Mom's arms.

Nika has Kiwi pinned to the ground.

"He's with us!" I say, rushing over.

"Oh. Sorry." Nika stands and offers her hand to Kiwi, but he doesn't notice.

He grabs his pack and sorts through it. "Hopefully everything's okay."

Nika's eyebrows raise. "What's he talking about?"

"Nika, Mom, meet Kiwi," I say.

Both Mom and Nika give quizzical looks at his name. Kiwi doesn't look up from where he's pulling tech from his pack and checking it over.

"His real name's Strider," Kemena chimes in.

Once Kiwi is satisfied that everything he brought is okay, he stands. "No one calls me Strider though. Just Kiwi." He shakes Mom's hand, then Nika's. "Nice to meet you both. It wasn't easy finding you."

"That's kinda the point," Nika mutters. She gives a pointed look at the tech, then turns to me. "Is he the male version of Ari?"

"Ari Willowpenn?" Kiwi asks reverently. "She's a legend in the tech circuit in Talionis. Mandeville always uses her as an example of how to be an exemplary tech recruit. Well, minus the whole sabotage and escaping thing."

"There's my answer." Nika crosses her arms. "Why exactly are we trusting this guy?"

"Nika," Kemena chides.

"What? It's a valid question," Nika says.

I hold up my arm with the band. "He's the only way we could get out here."

Mom puts her arm around my shoulders. "How about we all sit down?" She gestures to the mix of rickety furniture—a table with two chairs and a bench near an empty fireplace. "There's a lot to talk about."

"Actually, Kiwi is going to help reestablish a secure connection with the scouts," I say. "Can you show him what you have?"

Mom hesitates. "Everything was compromised. We haven't even been able to communicate much with Cai in the past few days."

"Oh, I can help with that too," Kiwi says. "He's the dude you were talking about in the tunnels, right?"

I nod.

"Great." Kiwi rubs his hands together. "I can get the setup started tonight, and if you can bring me to Cai, I can finish setting things up on his end."

"It needs to be completely secure," Nika says.

"It'll be safe," Kiwi says. "Promise. And if you can show me what you need for the outgoing com system, I'll get that established too."

We spend the next several minutes listening to Mom explain what communication they were using to connect to the scouts and listening to Kiwi give all the reasons he suspects it stopped being secure.

"You seriously found a male Ari," Nika mutters.

I bite back a laugh. "Sure seems like it." I approach where Kiwi's setting up his equipment. "We need to reestablish connection with Ari specifically. There's a potential leak within the scouts. Ari's someone we can trust."

Kiwi's mouth twists to the side, and he stares blankly for a moment. He nods. "Okay. From the little I know of Ari, I should be able to set up a roaming radio frequency code for her to find. Once she connects with it, it'll link with this com unit." He nods to the tech he was working on. "And the connection will be secure."

"How will she find the code?" Kemena asks.

Kiwi crawls under the desk cluttered with tech. "If I were her, I'd be connecting to various radio frequencies to see what I could find. I'll set up a looping message for her—something only she will understand. It'll be a code for her to input on her end. Once that happens, you'll be able to communicate with her." He pokes his head out to grin. "I'm even setting up a holographic com option so you can use that if you want." He ducks back under the desk and goes quiet other than the bumping and scraping of him setting everything up.

The four of us sit to wait while he works.

We catch them up on what's been happening in Talionis over the past week and how Ark gave me back my Elite Recruit ranking and is having me train again on top of working with Major Vasco on scenarios.

"How did you know we were out here?" Nika asks.

"Cai. He doesn't exactly know we decided to, uh, visit," I say.

Mom shakes her head gently. "I would be surprised if he gave you the go ahead to come out here. He's been strict about our communication protocols. But I'm glad you came."

I straighten. "Did you know about the secret tunnel system under Talionis? It's a whole network beneath the city."

Nika and my mom nod.

"The tunnels are how I got past the Wall," Mom says.

I twirl around in my chair to stare at her. "What? How?"

She smiles the knowing smile I've missed more than I realized. A lump forms in my throat.

"Nika told me you figured out I designed the map Demetrius Ark uses. You really are brilliant, you know that?" She tucks a curl behind my ear.

I give a half smile, but stay quiet so she'll continue.

"When I was working with Cai and Thaddeus to design the map, we discovered the tunnels beneath the city. At the time, we worked with Bill and Paul to ensure they would be hidden from Ark when Talionis was built. We hoped to stop Ark before he could build the city, but knew that would be a challenge. The tunnels were a safety measure we didn't want to need." She studies the empty fireplace. "Then Cai went missing. Elena didn't know everything Cai was doing. He loves his wife, but my sister can be . . . difficult. We thought it best if she didn't know all the details." She focuses on me again. "I had no idea she would allow Talionis to leverage her the way she did. Nika shared what you guys discovered." She squeezes her eyes shut. "I'm so sorry, Bria. I wish I'd known—"

"It's not your fault." I grab her hand. "But I don't understand. Cai said there wasn't a way out of the Ruins. If he knew about the tunnels, how come he didn't use them to escape long ago?"

"Cai didn't know about this tunnel. It's one I discovered when I was going over pre-Demise maps in Talionis after we lost you." Mom squeezes my hand. "Once I realized there was a way in, no one could stop me from using whatever means necessary to find you and get you out of here."

"If there's a tunnel, can we use it to escape?" Kemena asks.

Mom shakes her head. "Unfortunately, no. Soldiers discovered the tunnel after your escape. They collapsed it."

We go quiet, the only sound Kiwi muttering to himself as he works.

Nika and I share a long and understanding look. I have missed these silent communications with my friend.

Kemena clears her throat. "Okay, even if we can't get out of here yet, there's something else Bria and I want to discuss with you both."

"Yes," I jump in. "Ark has brought in dozens of little kids. Storm's age and younger. We have to get them out of the city."

"Bria," Mom says. "We can't use the tunnel. I wish it was an option—"

"No, I know." I stand and look between Mom and Nika. "Getting them back to their families now might not be an option, but we need to get them out of Talionis." I take a deep breath. "We want to bring them out here."

Nika blinks. "You want a bunch of little kids out in the Ruins?"

I lift my hands. "Safer out here with you than training to become soldiers. Plus, you guys have kept up Cai's work. The soldiers are still terrified of the Ruins."

"We want to smuggle kids out here, one or two at a time." Kemena nods toward Kiwi. "He's going to help us make them disappear from Talionis's database."

"Yup!" Kiwi chimes in. I didn't realize he was paying attention to this conversation. "I have a few ideas. Everything from completely erasing any information about them to making it look like they were eliminated." He pauses what he's doing. "I've been on the back end of their servers enough to see how often they eliminate recruits who aren't performing well."

The reminder of the lengths Ark will go to in order to get what he wants sends a chill over me.

"We know it's risky," I say. "But they're *kids*. Even if we can't stop Ark, we need to do whatever we can to save them."

Mom stands. "I agree. Nika has shown me several of Cai's sites. We can use those."

For the next ten minutes, we create the beginning of a plan. We'll start with one kid at first to see how it goes. In order to keep the kids safe, we agree to take it slow. As we talk through the options, it's clear Storm can't get out yet. She's too high profile because of me.

It's a reality I've known deep within my gut, but verbalizing it is painful.

"We'll figure out how to get her out, girl," Nika says.

"Done with this," Kiwi says, drawing our attention.

He walks Nika and Mom through how the com system will work. Then he looks between me and Nika. "What message should I set up for Ari to find? It's gotta be something only she'll be able to decode and, ideally, something others won't really notice if they stumble upon it."

Nika and I are silent for a moment.

Nika brightens. "Let's make it something to do with fishing."

I smirk, but Kiwi frowns. "Why?"

Nika and I share the story about how Ari hit Nika with a fish while we were aboard *The Fearless Lady*. By the time we're done, we're all laughing.

A few minutes later, Kiwi has the code set up.

He explains how Ari will need to decode the message in order to link to the com system he's set up. Once she does, a secure link will be established between her and Mom and Nika.

We prepare to leave once he's done. It's hard saying goodbye to my mom and best friend, but there's a comfort in knowing I'll see them again soon.

Next week, we start smuggling kids out to them.

Which means I need to do as well in my training as possible.

And we need to let Cai in on our new endeavor—and about Kiwi. I hope he's as on board with the plans as Mom and Nika are.

CHAPTER

THIRTEEN

I progress through the weaponry training course, my heart pounding in my chest.

This is a solo course, and everything I do, every move I make, is being evaluated. I've already taken more hits than I should have, and it's because I'm so distracted.

Thoughts of Matthias fill my mind. All I want to do is spend time with him, talk with him, let him hold me and tell me it'll be okay. Work with him to smuggle kids to the Ruins in just a few days. And it's overshadowing my abilities.

I shift to the knives on my belt as I prepare to enter the next stage of the course. At least in this part, I have the skills needed to dominate. As long as I can concentrate.

Which is only harder after hearing what Kiwi told me prior to entering my weaponry training for the day. I asked him to find more information about Matthias since I haven't seen him other than at a distance in Educational Training.

I hoped Kiwi would help me find a way to see Matthias. To actually talk to him. But he said there's no opportunity.

Not yet.

I pull two knives from my belt, then turn the corner into the room. As I hold the knives in my hands, I can't help but think of Cai.

The one who trained me in the Ruins. Who taught me how to hold a knife, to throw it, to make it stick in its target. The one who equipped me to be so much stronger than I thought I could be. The one who taught me about life and about God. The one who knows me and my fears and what I've gone through and has been there for me anyway.

My uncle wasn't thrilled when Kemena and I brought Kiwi to him two nights ago to set up a com system. I grip the knife tighter. At least he let Kiwi set things up. Now he and Nika and Mom can communicate more freely, and hopefully Ari will decode the message Kiwi is transmitting soon.

Things are coming together. We'll get kids out of here.

Although, Cai's concern that Nika and Mom won't be as free to terrorize soldiers in the Ruins if we do this still rings in my mind. He's right. I just don't know what to do about it.

A hologram springs to life in front of me, displaying an enemy combatant. I release both knives in my hands, and the combatant's hologram explodes, disappearing from my view.

I move forward, ducking behind a nearby wall so I can pull out another two knives. I probably shouldn't have released both at once, but my mind is everywhere *but* in this course.

Pull it together, Bria.

Everything we're about to do depends on me maintaining a status quo with the soldiers. If they're too focused on me, it could blow everything.

A noise above catches my attention.

I crouch into position, face the sound, and send a knife flying. A hologram bursts. Another hit.

There should be three more in this section. I need to stay alert.

I turn a corner, and two combatants rush me.

I send one knife soaring, then use the other to stab the hologram that's gotten within arm's reach. A pain pierces my side. A holographic knife stabbed me as well.

Sampta and Presidia must have upgraded the suits. The pain is worse than I remember.

I limp through the rest of the course and hit my final combatant.

The course ends, and I go to the screen to check my ranking. Not terrible, but it could be better. I need to work on my sharpshooting ability with the rifles, and my electro-fitted bow skills could use work. I also have points deducted for allowing the combatant close enough to stab me. Otherwise, my numbers in the knife segment are among the highest of the recruits on the board.

Corporal Sidon finds me and gives me the same news I just read for myself.

"I'd like to see you working more with the rifles and the electro-fitted bow," he says. "You're comfortable with the knives, but in reality, they're our least valuable weapon."

"A properly thrown knife can hit an enemy without a sound. Something a rifle can't do," I say. "The bow's quieter, but still there's something to be said for knives that can silence an enemy with nothing indicating you were there."

Corporal Sidon's eyebrows draw down. "Are you instructing here, or is that still my responsibility?"

I bow my head. "Apologies, sir. Tell me where you want me."

I spend the rest of my time in the range, rotating between the rifle and the electro-fitted bow. Corporal Sidon is right, which is irritating. I'm most comfortable with knives. They're like old friends on my belt, in my hands. I know how to handle them.

But gaining skill with the other weapons is important too. At least it is if I want them to believe I'm submitting to all they want me to do.

THE AIR IS THICK AND TENSE AS I LEAVE THE WEAPONRY TRAINING FACILITY and make my way to the Dining Hall for dinner. A palpable tension throbs just below the surface. An energy I've felt dozens of times before when I was in Talionis. One I never wanted to feel again.

The soldiers are awaiting the recruits in a Kill Zone.

I pick up my pace, hurrying toward the dining area with the swarm of recruits also headed in that direction. This is going to happen. I can't do anything, and yet every bit of me pulses with a need to stop what's about to happen.

To at least protect the youngest and most vulnerable recruits from what they're about to experience.

The bullets are training bullets. The maneuver meant to help us become who they want us to be. Soldiers who recognize Kill Zones and know how to avoid them or get through them safely, even when it appears there's no way to do so.

I've been through these many times. Beat them every time. But I've seen what it does, the trauma, the terror it brings to every recruit.

In the almost two weeks I've been here, I haven't experienced a Kill Zone. But now that I'm walking the same routes as the hundreds of recruits in the city, this is likely the first of many.

If I have to go through them, then I'll find a way to get as many through safely as I can. I pick up my pace until I'm just shy of a jog.

Kill Zones are terrifying, but there's always a way through, always an angle the soldiers forget to guard. A pathway, secret and hidden, that allows for the recruits to travel through safely.

The first wave of recruits enters. There's a small group of them, chatting, casual, completely unaware of what's about to happen.

"Wait!" I yell, waving my hands.

But the beauty of the evening is shattered as bullets rain down from the soldiers above. The rest of the recruits scream as several of the first wave drop to the ground in agony, holding various parts of their body.

Quincy is sobbing near the edge of a building, her entire body shaking as she watches. I've spent several meals with her since she and Storm are close friends, which means she won't be intimidated by my Elite Recruit uniform.

I jog over to her and guide her farther down the side of the building.

She stares at me, eyes wide with shock.

I crouch in front of her. "Quincy, it's okay. I'll get you out of here without getting hurt."

Her lip quivers. "No. I don't want to get in trouble. I don't want to get in trouble."

Anger swells within me. It's not right that a kid could be this afraid. That she would rather run through bullets than face the wrath of soldiers because she didn't.

From the scenarios she's gone through, to getting screamed at day in and day out by soldiers, to Kill Zones—she's already faced more horror in the short time she's been here than is right. Resolve stiffens my spine. *I'm gonna get you out of here, Quincy.* The silent promise eases some of my anger. But I still need to figure out how to get the girl to let me help her through the Kill Zone.

"Bria?" Storm's voice behind me causes both me and Quincy to turn. She gives a small, tense smile when she sees Quincy too.

Staccato gunfire rips through the air.

Storm presses her back against the building, her chest rising and falling. "Be careful running through there," she says, looking at both of us. "It hurts real bad if they hit you." Her gaze lowers. "I don't know if you can ever get through without them hitting you at least once."

Her words increase my anger. I wrap her into a fierce hug, a wave of protectiveness washing over me. I *will* get these girls through safely.

I pull back and look at Storm, then Quincy. "I can get us through."

Storm's eyes go wide. "Really? How?"

"You'll just have to trust me, okay, little squirrel?"

Her lips quiver with an attempted smile.

"But I don't want to get in trouble," Quincy says, voice trembling.

"You won't," I say. "I promise."

Quincy bites her lip, then nods. "Okay."

My heart melts. Quincy might be the same age as Storm, but she's more sensitive than my young friend. And Ark will destroy her if she stays much longer.

Three nights from now, Kemena and I are planning to bring a kid to the Ruins. And now I know which kid it will be. We're bringing Quincy.

A blast of gunfire, closer than it was before, crystalizes my focus.

I edge toward the corner of the building. "Let me get a look at what's going on, okay? You two stay here. Be careful."

The two girls crouch by the side of the building, and I take a quick look at the skyline. No soldiers are visible on this side of the building.

I open up my Halo Act band and scan the map to get a full gauge of the routes available, although I know them well. Still, I double-check to make sure I haven't forgotten about an alley or side street. Especially since it's been a while since I've traversed every alley and street in Talionis.

My pulse pounds, blood pumping.

It doesn't take me more than a few seconds before I see the pattern.

The soldiers have the recruits boxed in, as I expected, for anyone attempting to go straight through the Kill Zone or even from a slight angle. They know recruits will try to find shelter in the various alcoves. And as soon as one ducks in there for cover, they're shot.

I look up and discover snipers ribbing the tops of the buildings, camouflaged, but with rifles glinting in the setting sun. Going around them will be dangerous as well, because normally they set up sub-elements of the Kill Zone in order to keep recruits from completely circumventing it.

But they always leave a route because they want to know which recruits are smart enough to find it. Which ones will find a way to survive when it feels like death is screaming at every door, window, and opening into their lives.

It takes me a moment, but then I see it. The singular route through this place, at least the one I see first. In all reality, they may have created this with multiple hidden routes, but I only need one.

I back up until I'm facing the girls.

"Okay." I mentally race through the route I want to take. "I think I know what we can do. You ready?"

Both girls nod—Storm emphatically, Quincy a little hesitantly, but with more confidence than a few minutes ago.

"Good. I need you both to stay close to me and do exactly what I say. Don't hesitate. Okay?"

They nod again. Quincy lets out a quick, "Yes, ma'am," which sets me on edge. I ignore it.

Right now, there's no need to tell the girl I'm not a soldier. If anything, I need her to obey me as much as she would obey any other soldier in Talionis.

"There's a route through this Kill Zone that will keep us safe," I say.

"Are you sure?" Quincy's voice quivers.

"Yes," I say with more confidence than I feel.

Am I sure this isn't a trap? No. Am I sure Ark doesn't have some soldiers waiting at the end of the alley I'm about to take these girls through? No.

But I am sure it's our best option.

I reassure the girls as much as I can and lead them to the edge of the building we've been standing against.

"We'll stay as close to this building as we can," I say over my shoulder as I witness the terror before me. I force my attention to the two girls I can help. "There's an alley five yards down. Don't move more than a couple feet away from the building, all right? I want you to keep a hand on it at all times. There's a sniper right above us."

As soon as the words leave my mouth, I wish I could take them back. Quincy gasps, and Storm gives her a comforting pat on her shoulder, but her hand is shaking. These are *kids*, not recruits like me.

I press my hand into the rough wall, letting the texture ground me. "He won't see us as long as we stay close to the wall. We're in his blind spot."

"But what about ones on other buildings?" Quincy asks, her voice quivering even more than it was a moment ago.

"I don't think they'll see us." My lack of confidence bothers me, but the words seem to be enough to calm Quincy.

God, help me to be right.

Even if these girls get shot by someone else, it will be my fault because I'm the one who brought them to this point. And I can't bear the thought of either of them being hurt.

"All right, let's go," I say.

The longer we wait, the greater the chance the soldiers will shift to cover this spot.

We turn the corner of the building, and I lead the girls, my body crouched as low as possible. I run my hand against the wall to show them what I need them to do. I can keep my bearings and stay close to this wall, but I'm not sure the girls can.

I don't dare a glance behind me as my eyes scan the perimeter, constantly looking for any movement, any glint of a rifle that will tell me I'm putting them in danger.

My hand on the wall hits air. We've come to our alley.

I duck down it and wave the girls inside after me. I herd them in front of me. "Down the alley quickly."

At that, the two girls run, and I pick up my pace to match theirs, my eyes fixed on the horizon.

I pull my rifle around my shoulder, resting the gun in my hands. The bullets in it are useless blanks, not even training bullets. They'll do nothing to the soldiers. But somehow holding the gun, feeling like I have something to defend these kids, is enough to give me additional courage.

The door to the Dining Hall materializes as we follow the winding alley. The two girls pick up speed, and a small breath of relief fills me.

The grinding sound of boots on stone has me turn, lifting my rifle, the shred of relief vanishing into focus. There's no one at first. And then I see him.

A soldier.

"Get inside!" I scream at the girls.

I raise my rifle, pointing it at the man.

His lips twitch as he lifts two pistols. He knows as well as I do that my rifle can't do anything.

He widens the distance between the guns. Aiming for the girls.

I drop my rifle and charge him.

Confusion flashes on his face before he turns the pistols on me. But I'm on him. I use all of my training in hand-to-hand combat, everything I've learned from Matthias and Cai and the soldiers here in Talionis, to disarm the man. He's a younger soldier, probably a former recruit. A flash of recognition goes across his face, and the surprise vanishes as we grapple with one another.

I slam his hand against the wall, and he loosens his grip on the one pistol.

It clatters to the ground. He grunts.

I keep my hands clasped against his wrists. His knee crashes into the side of my thigh. Pain radiates through my leg, and my hands loosen enough for him to wrangle himself free. He puts both hands around the pistol he's still holding and points it at me.

"So you're the traitor," he says. His nameplate reads *Rafael Cruz*.

Breath tears out of me in ragged bursts as I wait to see what he'll do. I want to look behind me to confirm the girls made it into the Dining Hall. And I pray they aren't watching.

"You're one of the only ones who can find these, you know that?" His tone dips from smug and superior to almost impressed.

I shrug. "Don't know what you're talking about."

Rafael tilts his head, eyes narrow. "Yeah, right. You were legendary in my class. I was in the group that came in right after you left. I graduated quickly."

I shrug. "Okay. Should I be impressed?"

He gives me a small smirk. "Uh, yeah?"

I almost laugh at his outrageous confidence but sober quickly. This isn't someone from Eryndale or a friendly scout that I'm meeting in a village.

This is a kid who's been trained to become a killer. A soldier ready to do Ark's bidding. And he's currently pointing a gun at me.

I tense, waiting for the bullet.

But then the soldier dips his head at me. "You might want to be more careful next time."

I blink. "What do you mean?"

"Find better paths." The words are almost like some kind of code.

I blink at him.

He drops the gun, turns, and walks away.

I stand frozen.

He turns back. "Ah, I should probably grab that." He strides a few steps forward, picks up the pistol I wrestled from him, gives me a nod, and then, once again, heads on his way.

I stare after him, baffled, then shake myself out of my reverie, grab my rifle, and join the girls in the entry way outside of the Dining Hall.

They're both sitting inside. Heads pressed against the wall, chests heaving. But they have small, relieved smiles on their faces. They scramble to their feet when the door closes behind me.

Storm rushes over. "Did he hurt you?"

I shake my head. "No."

I'm as surprised at my answer as the girls seem to be.

"Let's go get some food." I put my arm around Storm, and Quincy stands to the side, looking a little uncertain.

I open my other arm toward her, and she rushes forward, wraps her little, scrawny arms around my body, and squeezes.

I freeze.

What if this display of affection puts Quincy on Ark's radar? Am I just putting her in danger by letting her close?

Her body trembles. She needs to know she's not alone. And we'll smuggle her out to the Ruins, out of Ark's reach.

I hug her back. She's a little girl and the beginnings of a young woman at the same time, and my throat burns.

I remember this age and how much I needed my mom. How is Quincy surviving? Her shoulders shudder beneath mine. I squeeze her one last time, then lead the two girls into the Dining Hall.

———

BRINGING A NINE-YEAR-OLD TO THE RUINS IS MORE CHALLENGING THAN I expected.

Kemena and Kiwi agreed to bring Quincy out to the Ruins first, and now we're guiding her through tunnels and encouraging her to not ask questions.

"Why are we down here?" Quincy asks. Again.

It's like going somewhere with Ari. She has a question about everything we're doing.

"Quincy," Kemena's voice is gentle but firm. "I already told you why, didn't I?"

"To get me somewhere safe?" she asks.

"Exactly. Now I need you to be quiet, because we're coming out of the tunnels soon, and then we can't talk at all. Okay?"

Quincy nods and says nothing, which is a small relief.

Tension radiates along every nerve ending in my body, and a thousand worst-case scenarios flood my mind.

Kiwi went ahead of us to the Ruins to check the systems he set up for Nika and Mom and to "eliminate" Quincy from the database.

Which means it's just me and Kemena with the girl right now. With no weapons or tech support on our end.

We come to the exit and pause at the door.

Kemena puts her hands on Quincy's shoulders. "Remember. We need to be extra quiet now, okay? It's super important."

Quincy nods solemnly. "Okay. What's gonna happen to my friends? Are they gonna be safe too?"

Kemena glances at me, but I stay quiet to let her respond to Quincy. "We will do our best to protect as many kids as we can."

"Will I get to go back to my mom and dad?"

Her questions echo Storm's before we escaped from Talionis. I look away from Kemena and Quincy. Despite everything I did to protect Storm and get her out of Talionis, I failed. She was recaptured, and I still don't know what happened to Damara, the woman who cared for Storm like she was her own daughter. Every time I try to bring it up, someone joins us or Storm starts another conversation.

God, help things to be different this time. Please.

I don't hear Kemena's reply to Quincy, but seconds later, she's holding the girl's hand and nodding for me to open the door.

After a deep breath, I push the button to open the secret exit from the tunnel. The basement of the abandoned factory is empty, and as we exit the building, there are no soldiers in sight.

Thankfully, Quincy stays quiet until we get to the fence separating us from the Ruins.

When I start to crawl through, she whimpers.

I stop. "What's wrong?"

"I don't like bugs." She crowds closer to Kemena.

"Me either, Quincy," Kemena whispers. "But I promise, this will be worth it. Plus, you'll get to meet my sister."

Quincy takes a deep breath and nods, which is enough for me to crawl through the opening. Moments later, Quincy and then Kemena appear.

We travel deeper into the Ruins and to the site where we found Nika and my mom last week, since that's where we agreed to meet tonight. They plan to bring the kids to a different site once we have more, but for now it's easier to remain with the communication equipment.

Kemena talks softly with Quincy as we hike, and it reminds me of how she was with Levi, Azarias's son. From what I saw, the boy loves her, and she loves him. I wonder if it's as hard for her to be away from him as it is for me to be away from Eli and Zeke. Hopefully the three boys are having fun, safe adventures in Eryndale. Just being kids, rather than experiencing horrors like Quincy and Storm and the other children in Talionis.

We arrive at the site, and Mom and Nika welcome Quincy.

The girl stays close to Kemena at first, but it's not long before Mom has convinced her to sit on a bed and have a glass of warm milk.

While Mom and Quincy get to know each other, I join Nika, Kemena, and Kiwi by the communication system.

Kiwi's grinning so wide, *my* face hurts looking at him.

"What are you so happy about?" I ask.

He strokes the communication panel. "Ari decoded my message. Responded saying the radio frequency linking system was an *impressive* bit of tech."

I give Nika a wide-eyed glance, then turn my attention back to Kiwi. "Good job." The realization that we've actually connected with Ari hits and relief floods through me. "Can we talk to her?"

"Nah. Not tonight." Kiwi's grin slips. "Which is a bummer because she thinks you or Nika figured out how to set up the looping message. Gonna have to clear that up."

I snort. "She has more faith in our abilities than she should."

"Seriously," Nika agrees.

Quincy giggles at something Mom says.

"Cai's not wrong," Nika says with glance back toward the bedroom.

"About what?" I ask.

"It being harder for Lily and me to do what we need to out here with kids around." Nika hands me a cup of tea. "But I can't imagine *not* smuggling as many kids out here as possible."

The four of us fall silent. Mom is whispering a story to Quincy as she pulls a cover over the girl.

"We need more help," Kemena says.

"But who can we trust?" I ask. "I want to bring Matthias in, but there's been no way for me to talk to him, let alone ask him to be involved in this."

Nika gives my arm a light squeeze. "Sorry, girl. That's tough."

I take a sip of tea to avoid exposing all of my emotions.

"We could bring in the Resistance," Kiwi says. "More are joining every day. Asher's always looking for ways to stop what Ark's doing."

I'm not at all surprised that the surly recruit I met in Warfare Strategies is a leader in the Resistance. I can still hear him whispering the word *traitor* to me after the debrief.

When Nika asks, Kiwi goes on to explain the ways the Resistance has been attempting to stop Ark so far. Everything from small acts of sabotage, like breaking tech equipment and removing firing pins from guns in the Weaponry Training Complex, to planting spies within the higher ranked recruits. Those who are pretending allegiance to Talionis in order to gather intelligence which they're passing onto the Resistance.

Kiwi spins his empty cup on the table. "We've even started doing micro hacks that the tech teams in Talionis won't notice to spread strategic intel to recruits' bands so we can prove to them Ark's lying. Mainly those we suspect aren't happy to be here." He grins. "I've headed up that part. Anyways, I'm sure Asher'd be on board for this. We've been looking for a way to smuggle kids out of the city for a while."

"I don't know," I say. "We need people we can trust enough to bring out here. Stay out here with the kids."

Kiwi's face turns serious. "I know. And there are a few I would trust with my life. Keesia's one of them. You know her. And Arwen, Marci, Asher . . . I could keep going."

"Maybe we should talk to them," Nika says. "We need help."

I set my mug on the desk. "Well, Marci and Asher don't like me much. But I do know Keesia."

"We could start with her," Kemena suggests.

Quincy falls asleep, and Mom joins us. Kemena updates her on what we've been discussing, and she agrees that help is a good idea.

As much as I wish the next person we involved was Matthias, it's not possible. We need help now, even though it's dangerous.

By the time Kiwi, Kemena, and I are ready to leave, the plan is in place to talk to Keesia and bring her to the Ruins. If she's willing, Kiwi will eliminate her like he did for Quincy, and she'll stay in the Ruins with Mom and Nika.

Part of me is jealous. I want to be out here, terrorizing soldiers and taking care of kids. But I'm too big of a pawn for Ark. And, like Nika pointed out, I have access to information that could help us in the bigger fight against Ark.

If I can uncover a way to actually use the information to take him down.

CHAPTER
FIFTEEN

I sit in my room with a screen propped up on my knees as I review notes for the new scenario I'm supposed to create. Major Vasco was given orders to let me run my own scenario, and as much as it sickens me to think of putting recruits through a training I created, I can't find another option. Not one that will allow me to maintain my position enough to continue hiding kids in the Ruins.

In the ten days since we brought Quincy to the Ruins, Kemena and I have smuggled four more kids out to Nika and Mom. They're kids Kiwi flagged as ones who are at an increased risk of punishment since they aren't taking to the trainings well.

Last night, Mom planned a surprise birthday party for me. The kids loved the celebration, and it was a nice diversion from the constant tension we're all under. Still, it's hard for me to believe I'm eighteen. I didn't even realize it was August 15th until she and Nika shouted happy birthday.

Plus there are more important things to focus on. Like how Mom and Nika need more help with five kids in the Ruins.

Until now, Kiwi hasn't been able to talk to Keesia. But he's coordinated a time to meet with her this week.

I'm not sure if I want her to say yes or no. Either way, having someone else involved is dangerous.

My screen beeps, drawing my attention to the building schematics on the device. I make a note on the scenario to ensure an alarm is tripped if the recruits enter the building through a first-story window.

Creating a scenario from beginning to end is a more intensive process than I anticipated. Everything must be accounted for. And, even though I'm supposed to be creating this extraction scenario on my own, I have no doubt Major Vasco knows every single element I need to consider and include. I'll fail if I miss anything.

I lean my head against the wall. Is there anything I can do to hinder what Major Vasco is doing with these scenarios? The more involved I am, the more I realize every scenario is linked to Ark's attack on Sitreea. I knew it before, but I see it so clearly now.

If we can't stop Ark, can I at least use the position I'm in to upset his plans?

Someone raps on my door. I set my screen aside, ready for whoever's about to enter. According to my band, my trainings for the day are done, and I'm supposed to spend the hour and a half until dinner working on the scenario. Maybe something else came up.

The door opens. My breath catches in my throat. Standing on the other side are Matthias and Sergeant Valarius.

I jump off my bed, and Matthias enters the room. Sergeant Valarius does not. "Make it quick," he says. "Your father will be livid if he finds out you're here."

Matthias's face shifts into a look of grim determination, but he nods, and Sergeant Valarius allows the door to shut.

I fall into Matthias's arms. He sucks in a sharp breath, and I pull back.

"Are you okay?" I ask, even though the answer is obvious.

He's *not* okay. But he's here.

He tugs me closer and wraps his arms around me. I gently hug him back, careful to not bump any of his injuries.

He inhales deeply as he rests his cheek on my head.

"I've missed you," he says.

"What are you doing here?" I want him here, but from what Kiwi said about how closely Matthias is being monitored, this isn't safe.

"I couldn't go another day without seeing you and making sure you're okay."

I pull back, but keep my arms linked around his waist. "I see you in Educational Training."

"Oh, that." He scoffs. "Come on. We both know that doesn't count." He gently twists one of my loose curls around his finger and smiles at me.

My heart fills.

"Tell me what's been happening." I step back to look him over.

A fresh bruise mars the side of his cheek. His hair is cropped short, and his face is cleanly shaven, like every other male recruit and cadet—the children of the Talionis soldiers and officials—in Talionis. Dark circles rim his bright blue eyes, but they still shine with affection as he looks at me.

"Well, you know, my dad and I are just catching up." He offers one of his smiles, but it doesn't reach his eyes.

Everything is probably ten times worse than I've imagined.

"Are you getting treated for your injuries?"

"My dad doesn't want me to, but Uncle Andor makes sure of it. And it's taken me begging him every day since we got here to wear the guy down, but at least he finally brought me to see you."

I smile, but it fades. "It's not safe, Matthias. You're not safe here. Ark watches me, and he—"

Matthias takes my face in his hands. "Seeing you is more important to me than risking Demetrius Ark's anger. His wrath toward me can't be any worse than my dad's."

I lean into his hand. "I wish you weren't going through all of this."

"I'm just glad to see you." He winks.

I step back and take his hand. "There's so much going on. So much I want you to be a part of."

He tilts his head. "What do you mean? I thought you were working with Major Vasco on scenarios. And I heard Ark gave you back your rank, so you're training again."

"Yes to all of that. But there's more."

I quickly outline all that's happened in the short time we've been back in Talionis, including a bit about how his uncle has been helping Cai. There's more to tell him than I thought, so I don't go into all the details I'd like to, but I tell him about Cai working in the tunnels, share how Nika's alive and in the Ruins with my mom, and explain how Kemena and I've been working with Kiwi to smuggle kids into the Ruins.

When I'm finished, Matthias looks more serious than I expected. "This is dangerous, Bria. If Ark finds out what you're doing, he'll kill you."

"I know it's dangerous. But I have to do something." I interlace our fingers. "I wish you could help me."

He offers a slight smile. "Me too. My dad's getting tired of . . . connecting . . . with me. And I'm supposed to start training again next week. We'll see each other more." He glances at the door. "Be careful, okay? We still have some time until Ark attacks Sitreea."

"We don't know that for sure."

"Yes, I do. I overheard my dad talking to Mandeville and Major Vasco. They're not planning the attack until late spring. Eight months from now. If we bide our time, maybe we'll find a hole in what Ark's doing." He shrugs. "Or the scouts will mount an attack."

His words and hesitation to act surprise me.

"I'm glad we have some time, but I can't sit by and wait, Matthias."

He rubs the back of his neck. "I know. Just, please, be careful. I can't lose you. Not like I lost my mom."

Memories of the conversations we've had about how his mom stood against Ark and then was killed by his dad wash over me. Matthias chose to follow in his mom's footsteps. He looked for ways to defy Talionis, like she did. Although not quite as loudly as her. Her faith in God became his faith in God, with Cai encouraging him along the way. Until Cai disappeared when he tried to escape.

Leaving Matthias even more alone.

He's lost a lot.

But that doesn't mean we should sit by and wait for someone else to act. He knows that. I think.

I don't know how to respond, so I step back into his embrace and let him hold me, the steady beat of his heart against my ear, the comfort of his strong arms around me.

I close my eyes and imagine we're standing aboard *The Fearless Lady*, sailing with Catori and Davey and Quwani and helping rescue those who have been terrorized by Talionis. Anywhere but here, trapped again in the clutches of Demetrius Ark. Matthias tormented by his awful father.

A knock sounds on the door, then Sergeant Valarius pokes his head into the room. "The loop I put on the video feed for these cameras expires in two minutes. Wrap things up."

Tears prick my eyes, but I blink them back. The last thing Matthias needs is for me to become some whimpering little girl who just wants to be with him. I need to be strong for him so he can continue to be strong. I rub my hand against the side of his head, feeling the bristles of his closely shaved hair.

"I wish things were different," I say.

"They will be soon," Matthias says.

He picks up my hand and kisses my knuckles. The thought of his quick kiss aboard *The Fearless Lady* less than four weeks ago brings warmth to my cheeks.

I wish he'd kiss me again, for real, but it seems like a bad time for that. Especially with his uncle standing in the doorway, waiting for us to wrap things up.

The chain of my necklace around his neck catches my eye. I reach over and brush it.

His lips curl into a soft smile. "You're with me. Even when we're not together."

"All right, we gotta go," Sergeant Valarius says.

I shoot the man a look, wishing I could yell at him for interrupting or beg him for more time. But at least he's helping us.

Matthias steps away.

He winks, smiles his Matthias smile, then disappears.

When the door closes, I miss him more than I did before he came to see me.

CHAPTER
SIXTEEN

It's hard to get through dinner without being completely preoccupied by my interaction with Matthias. He's more afraid than I expected. Probably because he's been so isolated by his father.

Once he and I can train and work together more, I'll find a way to get him involved in what Kemena, Kiwi, and I are doing. Having something else to focus on other than dreading every interaction with his father will help.

I go through the motions of eating and interacting with Storm and the others at the table, doing my best to stay engaged. Jace animatedly argues with Sam about who's stronger, and I can't help but wish Matthias were here, seeing how young and vulnerable these kids are. If he knew them, he'd understand that every risk I'm taking is worth it.

The door to the Dining Hall bangs open, and conversations cease. Sergeant Valarius enters and surveys the room. He spots me and heads over.

The closer he gets, the more the kids at the table cower. Sergeant Valarius has done things to help me and my friends, but he's still a soldier of Talionis. And he's terrifying to these kids.

I stand as he approaches.

"Come with me," he demands.

"I have chores—"

"I thought you were obeying orders now, recruit," he snaps.

I step away from the table. "Yes, sir."

I offer what I hope is an encouraging smile to the kids, then follow Sergeant Valarius out of the silent Dining Hall, the eyes of every recruit burning into me.

When we're outside, I risk asking, "Where are we going?"

"You've been summoned for a meeting," he says without so much as a glance back at me.

"A meeting?" The thought of a meeting with anyone makes my stomach turn. "With who?"

"Commander Ark, Colonel Valarius, Mandeville, Major Vasco, and Corporal Sidon. As well as a few other recruits and soldiers."

I knot my hands into fists at my sides, my shoulders tensing.

What does Ark want with me in this meeting? Does he know what I've been doing? Did he find out about my secret meeting with Matthias? Is Kiwi not as trustworthy as I hoped?

I've been betrayed before. Many times.

Maybe it happened again.

I do my best to wrangle my thoughts as I follow Sergeant Valarius through the streets of Talionis. We enter a building I haven't been in before and pass various offices and conference rooms. He stops in front of an open door, and waves me ahead of him. He enters after me, closing the door behind him.

The room inside has several people seated at a long conference table with Demetrius Ark at the head.

"Good, you've arrived." He gestures to an empty seat next to Major Vasco. "Please sit."

The only option is to obey, so I sit. My eyes dart around the room. Everyone Sergeant Valarius said would be here is. And so are Elva Trill and Shay.

Shay's robotic-type body is still something I'm getting used to, and the look in her eyes as she stares at me is one of indifference. Which scares me more than the hatred I see when I look into Laban's eyes.

Any part of this girl that I knew from my youth is gone. She's someone different. Something else entirely. She's a weapon of war, and all softness, all hope I had of her being any kind of ally has died.

She lost a hand that day when I faced her, Broche, and Laban right before arriving in Eryndale. But it's her screams for me to help her, to save her, to keep her from being at the mercy of Laban and Commander Ark after failing, that echo in my ear. As I look at her, I realize she died that day and became who they wanted her to be.

Her hand looks like a normal hand with a white glove on it, but beneath the glove, her hand can morph into a machine gun. At her command, dozens of drones will swarm around her and do her bidding. I can still picture the terrifying sight as I watched her fight the Eryndale Scouts.

Shane is also here, but he won't so much as look me in the eye. Emotions choke me. I don't know what to do with this guy who had been my friend but is now my enemy.

"Well, I believe everyone's here," Ark says. "Let's get down to business, shall we?"

Ark easily commands the attention of all those present. Everyone leans forward, poised, ready.

Even I feel like I need to be at attention.

Commander Ark goes through a variety of procedural issues, talking about the status of things with the recruits.

"Mandeville." He turns his attention to the man who heads up the technology division. "How are our recruits looking? Anyone who has the skills we need?"

Mandeville stands. "Some seem to have a little skill. However, no one is quite as adept as Recruit Willowpen was. Although Strider Locke is close."

At the sound of Ari's last name, Shane's head whips toward Mandeville. Ark's eyes zero in on Shane, but Mandeville doesn't appear to have noticed.

"I am still disappointed she's no longer with us," the short man continues. "Devastating to hear that she was cut down in the prime of her life, especially when she could have been such a great asset to all we need to do."

Shane looks like he's barely controlling his rage at the words. He must have told Commander Ark that Ari's dead, despite the fact that my friends and I insisted she was alive. If I was Shane and I loved someone the way he seemed to love Ari, I guess I probably would've been quick to claim she was dead. Especially if it kept her safe and away from the city.

Then again, Shane's doing everything Commander Ark wants, obeying his every whim. He and I are not at all alike.

Mandeville continues on, sharing the ability of various other recruits in the technology sector. Kiwi—or Strider, as Mandeville calls him—is one of the best. My heart hammers in my chest as Mandeville talks about one of my newest friends, but nothing he says indicates Kiwi's betrayed me.

After he's finished giving his report, Ark turns to Laban and Sergeant Valarius to ask for a report on their area of physical training.

Why am I in a room with all these people, listening to what they have to say, hearing their reports on various recruits? There's a point in it, but I can't figure out what it is.

Sergeant Valarius and Laban pull up their screens and quickly list all the recruits they believe have some promise and ability.

I recognize a few names from warfare scenarios and physical conditioning, but I don't know any of them well.

"And how is Bria looking?" Ark asks.

My breath catches in my lungs.

Laban's jaw clenches, but he doesn't respond.

Sergeant Valarius gives a curt nod. "She's been doing well, as we hoped."

"Excellent," Commander Ark says, his eyes locked on me and no one else. "I hope we continue to hear those good reports, Bria."

I swallow and nod.

"Major Vasco, report on the scenarios. How are they coming?" Ark asks, shifting everyone's focus from me.

Major Vasco reviews the report. Everything he reviews highlights an area of Sitreea that raises on a holographic map in front of us. I knew, even based on my recent working with Major Vasco, that we were doing all of this to further Ark's goals with Sitreea. But as I look at the map and better understand the country, the reality of how every one of our scenarios is going to impact the infrastructure and cause real problems hits me.

The strategy here is deeper than just a war. The way the scenarios, if done properly, could work would absolutely cripple the entire economy of Sitreea.

Ark won't stop there. He wants to expand the borders and create a country so much bigger than the one he's trying to take back.

Which means everything we're doing could change the course of how the rest of the world functions.

He may have told me that however many recruits come home is up to me. But there's no way to do all he's trying to do and save a single recruit.

"And Bria, have you provided the assistance Major Vasco needs?" Ark asks.

"I, um . . ." I clear my throat, unsure how to fill the silence that follows my non-answer.

"She has, sir," Major Vasco finally says. "We are beginning to better understand one another."

Ark nods his approval. Maybe I won't have to answer more of his questions.

At least none of the questions have anything to do with Kemena or the kids.

"Good," Ark says. He instructs Corporal Sidon to give his report, which includes notes about multiple misfires with his weapons.

He blames the younger recruits for mishandling the guns, but the sharp glint in Ark's eye tells me he suspects there's more going on. I need to tell Kiwi to encourage the Resistance to be careful. The last thing we need is Ark discovering the growing group of dissidents within the city. If he doesn't know already.

"Now," Ark says, grabbing my attention, "I'd like to review the materials that we've received back, thanks to Private Malton." He smiles at Shane. "We've reviewed much of what was taken." He tilts his head, studying me. "And I believe we have just about everything we need."

He knows the encrypted file is still missing.

I clamp my mouth shut and stare back at him, trying to keep my face as blank as possible as fears rise in me. Ari still has that file.

"We're thrilled Private Malton has brought us back the resources we needed." He bows his head and exhales slowly. "But the time we wasted was precious, and there must be an increased vigor in order to get back on our projected timeline."

There are nods and several instances of "yes, sir."

Ark lifts a hand, and the room goes quiet.

"I certainly hope we don't have a need to go beyond Talionis again in order to stop anyone else from hindering our work," he says. "We all know that could be incredibly detrimental to those we care about." Again his eyes find mine.

My entire body shakes. Does he know Ari's alive? Or is he referring to my family? To Derbe?

Ark continues talking, leaving me with my fears. But as the conversation moves on, a realization dawns.

Besides Ark, everyone else in the room seems to think Shane returned everything. And Ark doesn't want them to know about the missing file.

But the way he talks . . . he wants that file back.

What lengths will he go to?

Is Ari in danger?

Or the scouts, my friends, the city of Eryndale itself?

I don't think Ark fully understands the scope of Eryndale. It's been hidden, despite the leak there that's relaying information to Talionis. I can only think that person is trying to protect themselves, which is the reason Ark doesn't know more about the refuge city.

But what if he finds out?

What if he calls the troops to storm Eryndale? Destroy it?

What will happen to Eli and Zeke? Or my dad?

The meeting lasts far longer than I wish it did as they review additional plans. My mind wanders, fears choking me. With the way Ark is watching me tonight, I can't risk going to the Ruins or down into the tunnels to see Cai once the meeting ends. It's too dangerous.

But I desperately wish I could talk to someone I can trust. The fears clawing my mind will only have a stronger foothold the longer I'm alone with my thoughts.

"And that brings us to our final note," Commander Ark says. "Elva Trill."

She's not spoken until now, so I give her my attention.

"The next Sitreean delegation is set to arrive in five days' time," she says.

Ark growls deep in his throat. A look of impatience passes over his face, then disappears as quickly as a puff of breath on a cold day. "Make sure everything is in place to get the recruits into the bunkers in time. And I want nothing to go wrong. We're too close now. If there are any missteps, someone will pay."

His eyes go around the room, then stop on me once again. "And Bria, since we have brought you into this circle, you will join us when the delegation arrives."

"Excuse me, what?" Colonel Valarius sputters, half rising to his feet. "You can't be serious, sir. She's a liability. A huge liability."

"Oh, she knows the suffering that will happen to those she cares about if she doesn't comply. Right?"

I give a curt nod. "Yes, sir."

"Good. Now that we're all on the same page, everyone get some rest. The work before us won't be done on its own."

CHAPTER
SEVENTEEN

T throw a jab into the practice dummy's midsection, letting the stress from last night's meeting feed the power in my punch. I deliver a roundhouse kick to the dummy's head, return to fighting stance, duck, and drive an uppercut to its chin.

Sweat drips down my back, and my muscles burn. But the harder I fight, the less I have to think about last night.

A low whistle drifts from behind me. "Man, I taught you well."

I can't stop the smile that spreads itself across my face as I deliver one final right hook to the practice dummy. I wipe sweat off my face and turn to find Matthias leaning against another practice dummy, a massive smile on his face.

"Good to see you." He pushes off the dummy and comes over to me.

He takes my hand in his, and I startle at his open affection but don't let go. Warmth spreads through my chest. How is it that this guy can make me feel good, alive, even in a place like Talionis?

"I didn't expect to see you again so soon," I say.

He wiggles his eyebrows. "I convinced my dad it was time for me to train again."

I squeeze his hand and let go. "Doesn't seem like your dad can be convinced of much. Especially by you."

"Fair point." He winks. "But I can be subtle. My comments to Uncle Andor about how I'm afraid I'm falling behind other cadets helped, I think."

"Nice." I stretch. "I'm glad you're here." The admission heats my cheeks, but his smile is enough to make the vulnerability worth it.

"Ready to see if you're as good as me yet?" he asks, a sly smile curling his lips.

He releases the practice dummy from where it's locked on the floor and rolls it off the mat.

I rotate my shoulders. "I've put you on your back more than once. The student has become the master." I give an exaggerated bow.

"All right, Averton. Prove it." He winks and shifts into a fighting stance. "Let's go."

We begin sparring.

We each land blows and get the other one to fall on their back, and most of it is because we're laughing so hard.

Matthias makes way overexaggerated movements, wraps his arms around me to hug me rather than take me down, and then pretends we're dancing when he catches a right hook I send his way.

The stress of last night's meeting melts away with each passing second.

We're on a mat in the back corner where there are no cameras. The other recruits are busy doing their own training in different portions of the Physical Training Arena. So, we're pretty much alone. And I am having way too much fun.

We're trapped in Talionis.

Matthias is sporting bruises that are still yellow, purple, and green from a recent beating from his father. And we have no reason to be happy. Yet, when Matthias is around, I can't help but be happy.

I care about him differently than I care about anyone else. The reality of the thought sends a jolt through me. I throw a punch, not ready to fully analyze my feelings. He grabs my hand, twists and pulls me closer, steps behind me, planting his foot, and then pulls and sweeps me off my feet. I land on the ground in a huff.

I throw my leg and kick his legs out from under him. He falls a few feet away from me and laughs.

He shifts into a seated position, and I do the same.

The sea glass pendant Ezri gave me is on the outside of Matthias's shirt. He tucks it back in with a tenderness that makes my stomach flutter. "You going easy on me?"

"How else do you think you landed me on my back?"

Matthias laughs again, and I can't help but stare. His face is flushed, his eyes sparkling, and my heart leaps.

I've never fallen in love before.

I don't know all the emotions you experience, but I would spend every day of my life trying to get Matthias to smile the way he's smiling now. To be held in his arms when I'm sad. To spend my days laughing with him, enjoying life together.

He tugs me closer, and I rest my head on his shoulder.

"What's going on over here?" Sergeant Valarius's voice cuts through the air.

Matthias and I scramble to our feet. My heart races. I spin and salute Sergeant Valarius, since I have no idea what else I should do.

Matthias finds his voice before I do. "We were sparring. Exactly what our training dictates for this hour."

"Looked like a little more than that." Sergeant Valarius's voice holds a warning.

"Bria's band will show we've been sparring." Matthias's face holds a protectiveness while also a depth of caring that's different from anything he shows anyone else.

I'm falling in love with this guy, and without him saying a word, I know the feeling is mutual.

By the look on Sergeant Valarius's face, I'm not the only one who sees it.

Before I can decide what to do, Sergeant Valarius gestures toward me. "Commander Ark wants to see you."

"Yes, sir." I lightly brush Matthias's hand as I move to follow Sergeant Valarius.

All the lightness and fun of the past half hour evaporates, and a weight presses against my chest.

Why does the Commander want to see me again so soon?

"BRIA, THANK YOU FOR JOINING ME ON SUCH SHORT NOTICE," COMMANDER Ark says, as though I had any choice in the matter.

I do my best to not scoff and instead stay at attention while he wanders around the greenhouse, plucking flowers as though he's some average—not insane—man, who's looking for ways to make the world a more beautiful place.

"At ease," he says. "Enjoy the splendor of my greenhouse."

I drop my salute and take in the humid room bursting with a variety of flowers, trees, and winding paths with benches. Everything is perfectly situated and landscaped. Crafted to perfection.

The place is beautiful. I didn't even realize there was a greenhouse in the city.

Ark picks up a spray bottle and waters a light purple flower. "It must be hard, being separated from someone you care about."

The beauty in the space does nothing to ease the growing anxiety inching up my spine from being in this man's presence.

I nod slowly. "It's difficult to not be with those we love."

"And not merely love as friends or family, but as something more." He sets the bottle down. "Right?"

My hands shake. I fist them together, but don't respond.

"I had an interesting chat with Matthias and his father. Seems he has a necklace exactly like yours." He cuts a branch on a bonsai tree without looking at me. The snip sound crackles through the room.

I twitch, but still say nothing.

"In fact, I know that chain. I gave it to you." Another snip. "And the pendant from Ezri? That was very important to you."

My nerves dance, bounce, collide against each other. Every bit of my inner being shakes as I wait and watch him wander the room, cutting branches, adjusting plants. Making every element of the greenhouse look more beautiful, even as his words sink their evil darkness deeper into my heart and mind.

"Of course, you wouldn't part with something like that to a mere friend. Otherwise, we'd have found it on Nika."

Does he know Nika's still alive?

He can't.

I remain mute. Nothing I can say will make any of this less terrifying.

He sets his clippers aside and then pulls off his gardening gloves, revealing his clean and perfectly manicured hands. "Now, Colonel Valarius is still very unhappy with his son and the way he's acted."

He props his hip against a counter and casually tucks his hands into his pockets as though he has no care in the world. "I wouldn't want anything to happen to dear Matthias, especially knowing how you care for him."

My jaw quivers. I clamp it tighter, but the tremors in my chin make my entire head ache from being repressed.

"I want to make sure everything is done to keep the dear boy safe. Of course, now that I'm aware you two are so intimately connected and care so deeply for one another, I'll ensure you have additional training time together."

I squeeze my eyes shut. "Is that all, sir?" My voice shakes. When I open my eyes, the calculated smile on Ark's face is enough to send waves of ice through me.

"That's all." He stands straight and brushes his hands together. "Enjoy your training, Bria. Dismissed."

I salute, then turn on my heel to leave the room.

Ark knows about how much I care about Matthias. Fear sends its waves over me, drowning me. I should have known he would figure it out. He's too observant not to. But the way he spoke . . .

Catori's words to me about how the risks of loving Micah were worth it come back to me as I exit the humid warmth of the greenhouse and step outside into the equally humid summer day.

Part of my heart wants to believe her. Defy Ark. Continue to fall for Matthias and enjoy being with him.

But would Catori encourage me to do the same thing she did before if she knew all Ark could do to Matthias? Is the risk worth it?

Or will Matthias and I both pay a price so high it could shatter me, no matter what happens in Talionis?

When I round a bend, I almost run into a young recruit. After the boy moves on his way, a fresh horror consumes my mind.

If Ark found out about me and Matthias, how long until he figures out what Kemena and I are doing with the kids we're smuggling to the Ruins?

CHAPTER
EIGHTEEN

My mind is a jumbled mess by the time I arrive at Warfare Strategies fifteen minutes later. I don't know how I'm supposed to work with Major Vasco on any kind of strategy when I have images of Demetrius Ark hurting Matthias or discovering Nika and Mom in the Ruins or finding out that Kemena and I've been smuggling kids out to them.

I go through the motions of preparing another scenario. The room I work in is full of screens and tech I don't know how to use. But the holographic map table is relatively easy to work with and helpful in creating scenarios and troubleshooting issues.

I almost enjoy working with the maps. It reminds me of working with Mom before I was taken and spending time with Thaddeus while I was in Eryndale.

But every map I work with here will be used to send hundreds of teens and kids to their deaths, which leaves me disgusted.

I boot up the table, forcing my mind to focus on the work in front of me. Work I have to do in order to maintain my cover. That way, I can continue smuggling kids out of the city while I wait for someone to come up with a strategy that could defeat Ark. Or come up with a strategy myself.

Something has to be done to stop Ark before it's too late.

Tonight, Kemena and I are supposed to bring two kids out to the Ruins. Sisters. Maybe once we have the girls settled with my mom and Nika we can find out if there's been any news from Ari. Ever since Kiwi told us Ari was able to connect to the com system he set up, I've been anxious to talk to her.

I grab the screen with my instructions for building today's scenario, and a thought hits me. I'm building these scenarios from beginning to end. What if there was a way to subtly sabotage them? Create holes no one saw?

It might be enough to subvert Ark's plans if he manages to get so far as bringing the recruits to Sitreea.

I mindlessly scroll through the instructions as the idea grows in my mind.

It's not ideal. The best option would be to stop Ark before he leaves North American soil. But maybe it could destroy his plans if he gets to Sitreea.

I flick on the holographic map using the switch on the side of the table and study the neighboring country of DuPont for Ark's expansion. Today's scenario prep is intended to discover the best ways to infiltrate DuPont without causing the country to know they're being invaded. Ark wants to take over as peacefully as possible. As if anything he's done or is planning to do could be considered peaceful.

But what if I could set something up to alert the DuPont government? Is it possible?

I lean on the table and study the map. As I do, one thing becomes clear. If I want to sabotage the scenarios, I'll need help. I'll have to do something to the foundational elements. Otherwise, Major Vasco will figure out what I'm doing.

Maybe Kiwi can help. I can talk to him tonight. Possibly bring Ari into it as well, get her thoughts if she's able to communicate. I sigh. I'd love to actually talk with my friend, but so far we haven't been able to coordinate a time.

I give myself a subtle shake. For now, I need to concentrate on the work in front of me. At least it gives me something else to think about outside of my two recent interactions with Ark and his not-so-veiled threats.

Using my hand, I rotate the map, then zoom in on the walled capital city of Paris, where the scenario I'm supposed to be building will take place.

The door opens.

"Averton," Major Vasco says. "Time for your scenario."

I straighten and turn away from the table. "I thought I was building the scenario today, not managing it."

Major Vasco enters the room and shuts off the hologram. "How is it you so often forget the chain of command around here?"

I set the screen down. "Sorry, sir."

He studies me. "You won't be managing a scenario. You'll be going through one."

I bite my tongue and follow him from the room.

As I walk down the hall, I check my band. Sure enough, next on my schedule is a warfare scenario. Which wasn't there before my meeting with Ark.

The hair on the back of my neck rises. Whatever's about to happen is a test.

And I can't fail.

Hopefully the group I'm entering with is skilled enough at scenarios to work well with me. I need to excel. Prove I'm an excellent recruit. Hold the tenuous position I have so that work can be done to bring this evil city down.

Resolve fills me.

Even if these recruits are new, I can work with them. I've faced more scenarios than I can count. And I'm good at this. It's why Ark has me working with Major Vasco. Ark is trying to throw me off my game—first by revealing he knows I care for Matthias, and now by making me go through a scenario. But I won't let him get the better of me.

Major Vasco opens the door to a scenario staging room and motions for me to enter.

I obey, but only make it one step inside before I stop short.

Matthias and Storm are the only ones in the room.

CHAPTER
NINETEEN

Major Vasco slams the door shut behind me, confirming my fears.

They don't send only three people into a scenario, ever. Especially if one of those people is a child. But Ark is sending me into a scenario with the two people I care about most in Talionis.

Storm crawls close to me an instant before the room goes dark, preparing to send us into a scenario. I put my arm around her. She's a child. This whole time, Ark has known I care about her. That hasn't changed.

But now he knows about Matthias too.

Catori's words about the costs of loving Micah filter through my mind again. *It's worth it. Even though it hurts. Even though it's scary. It's worth it.*

I reach out and take Matthias's hand in the dark. He squeezes back with a strength that makes me wonder if he's as afraid of what's about to happen as I am.

Did Commander Ark speak to him as well?

Does Matthias know Ark's watching us?

Is he as aware as I am that this whole thing is a way to keep us in line, to remind us who's in power?

He must be.

A whistle sounds in the background as the ground beneath me shakes. The room brightens, and the familiarity of beginning a scenario sends its burst of adrenaline through me.

I release Matthias's hand as the room grows brighter and give Storm one more squeeze.

Another whistle pierces the air, then everything comes to light. We're on a platform at a train station.

People bustle around us, desperately trying to get on the next train to come into the station. Another loud whistle bursts, and in the distance, the train races forward at a shocking speed.

This will be my first train scenario.

"Did you get the orders?" Matthias asks, his words a breath in my ear.

I lean back slightly, allowing myself to feel the comfort of his strength behind me as I do a quick search of my pockets. "No."

He squeezes my shoulder, then searches his pockets. "I don't have anything either. Just a ticket fob." He holds up the small device.

Storm pulls her trembling hand out of the pocket of her jacket. "I have them."

"You and Bria"—she directs her words to Matthias—"are my caretakers. And it says we need to board the train and find a device to detonate a bomb that's on the railway bridge a hundred miles from here." She hesitates. "How will we get off the train before the bomb explodes?"

Storm hands me the paper, and I skim the contents confirming what she stated.

We are supposed to blow up a bridge so that the train careens into a ravine. I flip the paper over and find additional information.

"There's a package on the train to help us escape before the bridge." I blow out a slow breath and look between Storm and Matthias. "Everything has to be timed perfectly."

I focus on Matthias and see the understanding in his eyes even before I hand him the paper. We have one shot to get this right, or we'll fly to our deaths with everyone else aboard the train.

The explosives have already been set. Everything is ready to go. It just needs the detonation from us.

"This is almost too simple," Matthias mutters so only I can hear him. "Why is Storm here?"

I shrug, but the effort is almost too much with the weight of everything happening. With everything that's gone on in the last twenty-four hours, I feel like a train careening off the tracks.

It's like Ark knows that.

But Matthias is right. The task is too simple for the elaborate cover story that Matthias and I are married, caring for my little cousin, and have business in the Sitreean capital.

None of this makes sense.

An alarm blazes through the train station.

"Only eligible ticket holders are allowed to board the Express," an automated voice says. "You must have been approved by the Sitreean Minister of Defense in order to make the voyage to the capital city."

A woman to our left gasps, and the man with her slams his hand against the wall of the depot station. Panicked voices from others rise.

What has elicited such terror and fear from those on this train station platform?

The train whooshes into the station so quickly that my jacket whips and flaps behind me. My hair flutters about and then stills as the train brakes blow out.

From my time working on scenarios with Major Vasco, I've learned the Express is one of the fastest trains in Sitreea.

I catch sight of a screen nearby displaying news about local attacks spreading from a militia group that no one has tracked down. Disease is running rampant. Farms are dying because of a blight the Sitreean government believes the militia sowed. Everyone is fleeing to the capital to find refuge within the walls of the city. Hoping they might survive the attacks happening all around the country.

Everything clicks into place.

The attacks the news anchor is talking about are the simulated attacks of what Major Vasco and I have been preparing the recruits for. This is a likely scenario of what will happen if the attacks go according to plan.

Matthias grabs my hand. "This is one of the biggest cities in Sitreea." His eyes are fixed on the sign above the train door. "If everyone is fleeing from here, that means the attacks must be severe. Everything in Firenze is self-sufficient. There shouldn't be a need for them to rely on anything from the capital."

"They're not relying on anything. They're fleeing." I point to the screen, and Matthias frowns.

Then he nods to the train door, the ticket fob in his hand. The crowd pressing to enter the doors of the train is restrained by armed soldiers denying entrance to every person who doesn't have a ticket fob.

A young woman gets thrown aside, tears streaming down her face. "You have to let me go." She holds a baby in her arms. "Please, if we don't get on this train, my child will never survive."

A soldier backhands her across the mouth. "Only those who have proper documentation are permitted to board," the soldier says. "Next!"

Matthias ushers me and Storm forward, and he stays in front of us as he hands the brutal soldier the device with our tickets. The soldier scans it, reads something on the glasses he's wearing, then steps aside to allow us forward. "Proceed to the bunk room displayed on your ticket."

Matthias takes the device back, and a cabin number appears.

"Don't leave the room," the soldier says as we pass. "Every person who boards the train must remain in their cabin by order of the train marshal."

My heart skips a beat. Okay, so this won't be as easy as I thought.

Matthias inclines his head. "Yes, sir."

We board the train and walk down a long corridor, and it takes everything in me not to stop and stare.

Screens line the cars, and everything is ornately designed. Some screens display the countryside, but others show the news. Matthias guides us to our assigned cabin and scans the ticket fob. The door clicks open, and we enter.

The space is roomy, with two sets of bunk beds. I sit on a lower bunk and pat the space next to me.

Storm instantly joins me. Matthias shuts and locks the door to our cabin, pushing a nearby chair in front of it. He taps a screen on the wall, and a menu of restricted viewing options opens. Matthias ignores it and flicks off part of the ticket fob, exposing a magnetic data drive. He sets it on the side of the screen.

The menu flickers off, and a message appears.

Facial scan required.

Matthias stands directly in front of the screen, and there's a flash as it scans his face.

Security bypassed.

A new menu appears.

"All right." Matthias rubs his hands together. "Let's see what we can find out." He taps on the screen, opening a map of the train on one half and a map showing the train's route on the other.

I stand and study it with him. We're located near the back of the train, but, according to the map, the device is near the engine.

Matthias lets out a low whistle. "That's farther than I expected."

"Why would they put us here?" Storm asks. "If they could give us something that would let us see a map of the train, they should be able to get us placed in a room right near where the device is."

I'm both impressed by her reasoning and devastated by how well she's been trained.

"You're right," I say, before I can dwell too long on the innocence that's been stolen from my young friend. "It's like they don't want us to succeed." As I say the words, the reality of their truth rings through my mind.

My gut clenches, but I put my arm around her shoulders. "Let's figure out how to prove them wrong."

Matthias grins. "That's my girl." He winks at me, and Storm giggles.

"He likes you," she whispers in my ear.

My cheeks burn, but I whisper back to her, "I like him too."

We set about figuring out how to get from our room to the cabin where the device is located at the far end of the train. We'll pass through much of Sitreea, before crossing over the bridge that leads to the capital.

"This is a strategic bridge to destroy," Matthias says. "Most of the capital's supply chain for food comes from this area." He draws a circle with his finger around the southern portion of the map on the right side of the screen.

"Which means that by cutting off that supply chain, Ark will weaken the entire infrastructure of the city," I say. "Not to mention kill hundreds of people on this train."

Matthias's mouth pinches into a frown, and he rubs a hand over his buzzed head. "What do we do?"

"Maybe there's a passageway that's not visible to cameras or soldiers. Something used for maintenance?" I suggest.

"I don't think so." Matthias zooms the map out to show the entire train. "It's a train, so we're looking at a narrow and long structure, but this one is higher than other trains." He pinches in to zoom in on the higher portion of the train. "There's a storage compartment overhead that runs the entire length of the train."

"Can we get access to it?" I ask.

"Maybe."

Storm tilts her head. "What if I crawl out here?" She points to a narrow luggage access point for conveying suitcases from outside to inside the train without using the main doorways. The luggage is then brought to the appropriate cabin, leaving the access point clear. "Then I could climb up the ladder and enter the maintenance shaft to crawl to this hatch." She points to a hatch in one of the janitorial closet areas. "I could let you guys in that way."

"It's too dangerous," I say. "The speed of the train and the fact that the ladder is exposed—"

"I know, but I'm your little squirrel." She tucks her hand into mine. "I can do it."

She probably *can* do this, but the very idea of sending her on such a dangerous mission . . . I wrap my arms around her and squeeze tight, wishing I could shield her from everything she's experienced and will experience. But the reality is this isn't the first time I've been in a scenario with Storm where the only option for success required Storm to do something dangerous.

Which is intentional.

Anger and fear churn together in my gut.

Maybe Kemena and I were wrong. Maybe we could smuggle Storm out of Talionis. I can't bear to see her continue to go through the horrors Ark orchestrates.

I push the thought aside and focus on the map of the train. The longer I study it, the more I hate what I see. Storm is right. With how we've been positioned on this train, the opening she found is the only way forward.

We zoom the map in on the cramped luggage access point, and, with the limited size allowed for the luggage pieces in the cabins, it's clear Storm is the only one of us who will fit through the passage leading to the outdoor maintenance ladder.

The three of us spend the next fifteen minutes creating a basic plan.

Storm will shimmy through the luggage access point, climb up the outdoor ladder, and enter the maintenance shaft. From there, she'll crawl to the hatch above the utility closet that is three doors away from our bunk room and unlock the door so Matthias and I can join her.

Once we get inside, we'll use the maintenance shaft that runs the length of the train to get to the room that holds the detonator.

This is the first part of our plan, and it's riddled with holes and potential for failure.

None of this accounts for the massive risk Storm will have to take by climbing an outdoor ladder on a moving train. Or the potential of us being spotted by the cameras in the hallway. And we aren't even sure we'll be able to access the room that holds the detonator with the ticket fob we have.

"It would help if we had someone running our tech," I say.

"And if we had a couple of people who could cause a distraction while we're trying to get into the room with the device," Matthias adds. "The way this train was being patrolled by soldiers—someone is bound to notice us."

"I don't know much about tech," I say, "but I'm guessing we're facing potential security breaches even by crawling through the maintenance shaft."

Matthias nods. "But it's our only option. If I know Commander Ark and Major Vasco, this train and that bridge are exploding whether or not we get to the device."

"Then why would we have to do this?" Storm asks.

Matthias and I exchange a long look.

Storm huffs out a frustrated breath. "I know I'm younger than you, but I understand a lot," she says, arms crossed over her chest. "You can't treat me like a baby. I've been through things too. I know this isn't easy. But we have to work together and tell each other things."

Her speech and the stomping of her foot as she emphasizes the different words bring a smile to my face, which only makes her frown all the more.

"Bria," she says.

I school my features. "It's a test."

Storm nods. "I know. But why?"

"To get to me." The words are a whisper as they come out of my mouth, but they ring with truth. Ark is reminding me that every life I care about hangs in the balance unless I do exactly as he says.

But I've gotten around his commands before. I can do it again. I'm already doing it by sneaking kids into the Ruins.

Matthias removes the fob from the screen, and the original menu reappears. When he turns to face us, the glint of my necklace chain around his neck catches my eye.

"Let's go," I say, even as Ark's threats in the greenhouse crowd my thoughts.

Matthias moves the chair away from the door and peeks into the hall. "We're clear."

Storm slips through the opening. She moves quickly and quietly through the hall and disappears through the luggage access point.

I'm about to follow and head to the utility closet to wait for her to open the door when Matthias catches my hand.

"I don't think this is going to work," he says.

"Me either."

He leans his forehead against mine. "But let's do it together. Always together, okay?"

"I don't know."

He pulls back, looks me in the eye, and then gives me the softest kiss. I kiss him back like my life depends on it. Like it's the last time I'll ever be able to kiss him.

Because it feels like it *is*. Even though this is a scenario, caring about Matthias puts him in danger.

And in order to keep saving kids, I need Ark to think he's controlling me. Which means putting on a show of distance between me and Matthias. Even though this kiss is being displayed to every soldier in the command center in Warfare Strategies.

I pull back. "We should go."

He nods, but there's a question in his eyes. Like he knows I just decided to do something he won't like.

I hesitate, wondering if I should say something. Give him a hint about what I'm thinking.

A shot rings out.

CHAPTER
TWENTY

After the burst of the gun, my blood pounds in my ears, making any other sound impossible to hear.

No.

That was too fast, too soon.

There's no way anyone could have known we were about to exit and stop us that fast. Storm should have just opened the door to the janitorial closet.

Matthias beats me out the door.

Another *crack* of a rifle firing bursts through the sound in my ears.

My feet stay planted. I don't know what to do. Time seems to slow as everything around me falls apart.

Before I even exit the room, I know what I'll see.

Still, some small part of me almost dares to hope. Dares to believe that maybe, just maybe, I won't find what I think I'll find.

It's only seconds before I'm out the door, and the blood I see in the hallway drives the breath from my lungs as though someone punched me in the throat.

Soldiers shout at me in another language, gesturing for me to lift my hands and not take another step.

I ignore them. All I can see are the bodies of Matthias and Storm sprawled out on the train floor.

They weren't given this warning.

They were shot on sight.

And the soldiers were ready for them.

It was all a trap.

I drop to my knees as sobs wrack my body. It's not real. It's a simulation, a scenario meant to prepare recruits.

But Matthias and Storm's lifeless bodies in front of me, blood pooling around them—it's more than I can handle, fake or not.

No more gunfire. No more shouting of soldiers.

Once again, all I hear is the pounding of blood in my ears. I reach for Storm's limp hand and drop my head to Matthias's chest. The life in his vibrant blue eyes is gone.

Even as my mind screams *this isn't real,* my heart is torn in two. Unable to believe the logic.

A voice comes over the airway. A voice I know too well. "You have to be better than this, Bria. You have to be better than this." Ark is taunting me. "Only your best efforts for me will keep this from becoming a reality."

"I'll do better," I say, my voice wobbling far more than I wish it was. But tears don't fill my eyes.

I keep my head on Matthias' chest, desperately wishing for the rise and fall of his breath, to feel the strength of his arms around me.

A whooshing sound rushes over me, and behind my closed lids, I sense everything going black, the scenario ending.

We failed.

But we were supposed to fail.

Matthias gasps, and then his chest rises and falls.

Storm's crying nearby, but I'm frozen on Matthias. His arms wrap around me. Storm's hand squeezes mine. A sob breaks from my throat.

"It's okay, it was just a scenario," Matthias says.

I nod against his chest, then push away as the lights come on.

To him and Storm, it was just a scenario.

To me, it was a warning. If Ark thinks for one second I'm not in line with what he wants, the cost will be excruciatingly high.

Ark didn't have me shot. I didn't die. And that's how it would be in real life too. He would make sure I survived. No matter what, he would make sure I lived to see the result of my defiance.

Fear wars with anger inside of me as we leave the scenario. No matter how he threatens me, I can't let Ark win. I must keep fighting.

But by the time this nightmare ends, how much will I have lost?

God, please help me! The prayer screams through my soul, desperate. I don't want to give in. To be who Ark demands I become.

But I also don't want to lose Storm and Matthias.

―――

FEAR GRIPS ME AS I HEAD TO THE TUNNELS TO MEET KEMENA SOONER THAN we originally had scheduled for tonight. She responded almost instantly to the encrypted messages I sent to her screen earlier today asking to meet early. After the turmoil of the scenario, I need someone to talk to. Plus, I'm hoping she agrees with me that it's important to get Storm out of Talionis.

Maybe Matthias too. Although he'll be harder to smuggle out of the city, and it'll be much more evident if he's gone than it is with the kids.

Storm is different than the kids too. The thought whispers through my mind, but I shove it away, not ready to deal with the logic.

I navigate the tunnels without the map now, since I've taken the route through them multiple times over the past couple of weeks. But I almost wish I needed to pay more attention to where I'm going. Do something that allowed my mind to be diverted from the horrific image of Matthias and Storm lying dead in the hall of a train.

Fake or not, scenarios imprint themselves on me like lived experiences.

I near the agreed-upon meeting point and find Kemena waiting.

She closes the distance between us. "What's wrong?"

The two-word question is enough to unleash a rush of emotions and words. I recount everything from the meeting last night with Ark and his highest-ranking officials, to his threats in the greenhouse, and then the scenario with Storm and Matthias.

Kemena doesn't interrupt as the words gush out of my mouth.

When I finish, she pulls me into a fierce hug.

Tears burn the back of my eyes as I hug her back. "He's gonna win, Kem. Ark is going to win. We won't ever be able to stop him."

The words escape, the depth of my fears raw and exposed.

Kemena steps back, her face cast in shadows from the torch at our feet as she studies me. "I know it's hard to believe that God is still at work, but He is. We have to remember that."

"But Ark has more resources than us. He proved today that he'll do whatever it takes to make me be who he wants me to be." I pinch the bridge of my nose. "We have to at least get Storm out. Bring her to the Ruins."

Before I finish, Kemena's already shaking her head. "Sweetheart, that won't work. We've talked about this. If we want to get as many kids to the Ruins as possible, we have to start with those Ark isn't watching closely. The ones he won't miss." She gives me a sad smile. "Storm isn't one of those kids. You know that."

I rake my hand through my hair, desperation clawing at me. "But I can't lose her. Or Matthias. They're both in danger if Ark finds out what we've been up to."

Kemena gently grips both of my shoulders. "Bria. Everything we are doing comes at a high risk. We knew that from the start." Her eyes search mine. "Evil people will *always* attempt to keep us from what God has for us to do. Whether it's open threats like what you experienced today, or by attempting to manipulate us and our emotions. But we can't let them win. We must be brave. We must fight to do what's right, even when we're afraid." Her grip on my shoulders tightens. "Fear will not hold us captive."

Her words break past the clamoring noise of my day and rest in my heart. "This is hard."

Kemena nods. "It is. But you're not alone, okay? Ark just wants you to *feel* like you are." Her words are quiet but passionate. "What we're doing matters. We're protecting the most vulnerable from Ark.

Doing what others are unwilling to do because of fear. And we're not done yet."

The fear still lingers in my heart, but I take a deep breath. Kemena's right. Even though I'm terrified of what Ark is threatening to do, I don't want fear to hold me captive or keep me from what God has for me.

Please, God. Help Kemena to be right. Please be working in all of this mess.

My band buzzes with an encrypted message from Kiwi. He's waiting for us with the two girls. "All right. Let's go."

Kemena smiles, and the two of us head off at a brisk pace to meet up with Kiwi.

CHAPTER
TWENTY-ONE

A shrill whistle cuts through the air, and I sprint from the starting line.

Sergeant Valarius has me running a new obstacle course for physical training before any of the other recruits to demonstrate, as he said, *how it's done.*

Although after the late night in the Ruins getting the two sisters settled, I'm not sure I'll be as impressive today as Sergeant Valarius hopes.

I leap onto a balance beam and race across it. At the end, I jump off and grasp the handlebar of the monkey bar type area, except it's not multiple bars across where I can use both hands. This is a singular pole strung about thirty feet in length that I have to get across.

I hoist my legs up, link my feet and my ankles, then I shimmy myself down the bar.

The exhaustion from last night fades as I push my body to its limits. Kemena's words in the tunnels have stayed with me. Even though I'm still afraid of what Ark might do, I'll keep fighting.

Being with Mom and Nika last night helped as well. And Kiwi provided some levity as he joked with the little girls we brought out to the Ruins to help get them settled.

My hands burn as they slide one over the other and push my body forward, but I make quick progress. I get to the other side, jump to the ground, and run down a hill until I reach the next set of zigzagging balance beams.

I climb on the first one, race across, step up to the next level, which is three feet off the ground, and nearly sprint down the length of the board. When I get to the end, I leap off, thankful I didn't fall over the side into the sticky mud that surrounds the beams.

My heartbeat kicks in my chest, and I sprint toward the wall in front of me that has a rope hanging down the side. I grab the rope, its bristly roughness pressing into my hands, then scale the wall. This would have been nearly impossible when I first arrived as a recruit, but now it's almost easy.

This training is easy compared to what I went through for my training as an Elite Recruit, and sometimes it almost feels laughable that I'm doing this with recruits who've only been here a few weeks.

I get to the top of the wall, hear the screams of the drill sergeants as they yell for me to go faster. Even though I'm moving quicker than anyone else will run this course. At least anyone else in the unit they've placed me in for today's training.

These recruits are new and not ready for the intensity of working with those in Talionis.

But I can't stop myself from being a little pleased when I see the look of surprise on a drill instructor's face as I complete the next portion of the obstacle course much faster than he anticipated.

I'm doing what Cai asked me to do the one and only time I saw him. I'm excelling.

I drop, crawl under a string of lasers set up over a mud pit, jump to my feet, and come face-to-face with Sergeant Valarius.

I'm breathing hard, and I don't exactly know what to do. There are still several elements left to the obstacle course, and he's stopping me before I can get to them.

"Come with me," he says.

Mud drips from my uniform, my muscles burn, and my lungs are on fire from the exertion. But I shouldn't be done yet.

"Come with me, recruit." He enunciates each syllable, and the words send a chill through me.

I brush some of the mud off my uniform and follow him out of the Physical Training Arena.

"Where are we going?" I ask once we're outside.

"Commander Ark wants to see you."

I hesitate briefly, but Sergeant Valarius keeps walking, so I jog to catch up.

"He wants to see me right now? In the middle of one of my trainings?" And again less than twenty-four hours from the last time he saw me?

Sergeant Valarius doesn't even so much as blink in response.

"But look at me. I'm not presentable. Not for *the Commander*." The sarcasm dripping from my words is dangerous, but I can't stop it. And it's easier to deal with than the dread sticking to me more with each passing step than the mud clinging to my boots.

"He ordered your immediate presence," Sergeant Valarius says. "So, we're going to him now. Understood?"

I nod and fall into silence, my mind whirling as I follow him to the next set of buildings that will lead us to the Commander's office.

But Sergeant Valarius doesn't take me into the building that leads to Commander Ark's office. Instead, we turn and enter a different building.

"I thought you said we were going to see the Commander," I say.

Sergeant Valarius spears me with a look that says, *Keep quiet and follow me.* I shut my mouth and follow him down the hall.

We enter an empty conference room. The door on the far side from where I'm standing opens, and a private escorts Kemena in.

Kemena's eyes go wide with a questioning look. I subtly lift a shoulder. The only reasons I can think of for both of us being here are bad.

Does Ark know what we've been doing?

Last night was the first night we brought two kids out to the Ruins. Did Kiwi leave behind a trace?

Maybe I shouldn't have pushed to bring the five- and seven-year-olds out to the Ruins at the same time, but I couldn't bear the thought of the sisters being separated even for a short time. They've already been through too much. And they were so happy to be safe in the Ruins with Mom and Nika when we left last night.

Mere seconds pass before the third door in the room opens. Ark, Colonel Valarius, and several other soldiers enter, followed by Mandeville, who closes the door behind them.

No Kiwi.

Maybe this *isn't* about what we're doing in the Ruins.

But then why did Ark bring us here?

"Bria." Commander Ark looks me up and down, making me even more conscious of my muddy uniform. "I see you've been training." He turns to Sergeant Valarius. "How is she doing?"

"Fine, sir," he says.

I pinch my lips together, annoyed with myself for wanting to argue that I'm doing very well in physical conditioning. Not merely fine. It bothers me that I care at all.

"Kemena." Commander Ark looks at Kemena, who just crosses her arms and raises an eyebrow, as though daring him to address her more. A small smile curls his lips. "I've heard you've given our people a bit of trouble." He says this as though it's almost amusing to him.

Kemena still doesn't respond, but Ark's words surprise me. I didn't realize Kemena wasn't doing everything the soldiers demanded of her.

Commander Ark's smile doesn't slip. He gestures for everyone to have a seat at the table.

Kemena doesn't move at first, and a corporal I don't recognize shoves her in the back, pushing her into a nearby seat. She scowls but settles herself in, and I catch a glint of curiosity in her eyes.

I feel the same way.

Ark is acting as though he's pleased about something, which is never a good thing.

Seconds later, the door opens, and Matthias is brought in by a female soldier who almost looks familiar. Then I recognize her. She's a recruit who was training with me when I was here before, and now she's a soldier.

She eyes me with an edge of hostility.

"Matthias Valarius, as you requested," the girl says, saluting Ark, awe in her voice.

Ark tilts his head. "Thank you, Private."

Her cheeks blush.

"That will be all. Thank you." He repeats the praise, and she scurries from the room.

Colonel Valarius closes the door, pure hatred in his eyes as he glares at his son.

Matthias ignores him as he takes his seat and looks at me, the same question in his eyes as Kemena's. My pulse thrums in my throat, anxiety building.

I haven't seen Matthias since yesterday's scenario. My conversation with Kemena last night gave me far more courage than I feel at the moment as I wonder what Ark could want with the three of us.

It's like he knows whenever I decide to continue to defy him.

Commander Ark leans forward on the table. "Now that we're all here, we can begin."

Okay. This can't be about what we're doing in the Ruins. Kiwi isn't here, and if Ark knew we were smuggling kids out there, he'd know about Kiwi. Plus, Matthias hasn't been involved with the smuggling yet.

But knowing that's not the issue almost makes this worse.

"Begin what, exactly?" Kemena asks. I swallow a gasp at the lack of respect in her tone. It's not at all how her sister would handle this situation.

When we first arrived in Talionis, Nika told me to keep my head down and not do anything until we understood our enemy. Kemena has a far different approach.

The soldiers around the room tense, some even reaching for their weapons.

Kemena's approach is dangerous.

"You are a feisty one," Commander Ark says. "Other than your occasional compliance with Sampta and Presidia, no matter what's been done to you, no matter what punishments or threats we've given, nothing seems to impact you or give you the motivation to do as you're asked."

She snorts. "If it's an *ask*, then I don't have to do anything. You guys demand things around this place, and I ain't interested. You killed my sister, and you're destroying this region. The last thing I'm gonna do is what you want me to do."

A part of me cheers inwardly at Kemena's bravery in the face of such powerful people who can destroy her in an instant. But fear crushes my pleasure at witnessing Ark be defied. Kemena's risking his wrath, and, despite what I've told her, I don't think she fully understands the lengths Ark will go to in order to get what he wants.

"Well." Commander Ark steeples his fingers as he watches her. "Let's see how you feel after this meeting."

Dread builds in me like icy rain coating the roads in thick layers. If nothing else, the past forty-eight hours have taught me Ark is ready to make any threats he deems necessary to get what he wants.

And there's no doubt in my mind that he'll follow through.

The screens around the room come to life and reveal the outer perimeter of the wall surrounding Talionis.

At first, it appears as though it's just a live feed of the surrounding forest. Then there's movement. Small steps from some-body edging closer to the wall. As soon as I see the first person, the rest become easier to spot.

Dozens of camouflaged men and women creep toward the Wall.

Commander Ark zooms in on one man.

Azarias.

CHAPTER

TWENTY-TWO

"**N**ow, if you look here . . ." Ark draws out the word.

Kemena inhales sharply, and the grin on Ark's face tells me he expected it. Somehow he knows Azarias and Kemena care for one another.

And there's only one way he'd know. The leak among the scouts is close enough to Azarias to tell Ark.

Ark sighs. "There's something so special about a man caring so much for a woman, he's wiling to risk death to save her. Love is a powerful force." He shifts his focus. "Wouldn't you agree, Matthias?"

Matthias blinks and stares at Ark, keeping his face blank. His hand drifts up as though he's about to reach for my necklace, but then he stops himself.

Ark's cheek twitches. Then he faces the screens again.

I turn, drawn in despite the growing fear that I'm about to watch Ark murder Azarias and those with him.

The main screen shows an overview of everything that's happening, but smaller screens surrounding it zoom in on the faces of those attempting the rescue mission. I recognize my friends, members of the Wild Dogs, the scout team we trained with in Eryndale. Moses, Jordyn, Isaac, Malachi, Karyss, and Glacier. Quwani and Davey, from *The Fearless Lady* crew, are with them too. So is Thaddeus. Even

Gabe's assisting from the tree-line, where he's hunched with a com unit.

A scream builds in my throat as they creep closer to the wall. I want to tell them to turn back. Let them know it's a trap.

But even if I said the words, it wouldn't matter. They can't hear me. Don't know I'm watching.

Isaac pulls out a device that is likely what they plan to use to disengage the electrical current running through the wall. I doubt it will work.

"As you can see, your dear friends here are attempting what I can only imagine is a prison break. Their attempts to save you are admirable." Ark pauses. "However, from my understanding, no one approved this little escapade."

So many who I have trained with and worked with, now risking their lives to help me. And thinking they're doing it secretly.

But Commander Ark knew all along they were coming. Because of the leak.

He looks at Colonel Valarius. "Now."

Seconds later, the soldiers on the wall open fire at the scouts. Screams erupt from the scouts as they retreat into the woods. Azarias shouts unintelligible words, probably telling them to take cover.

The soldiers don't appear to be shooting to kill, but it's hard to know exactly what's happening and exactly what Ark ordered. My heart beats in my throat. Everything we feared is true.

Demetrius Ark has a contact in Eryndale, and that person is close enough to Azarias to know what he was planning and how to stop it.

Commander Ark set all of this up. Pulled me and Matthias from our different trainings and Kemena from whatever duty she was refusing to do to bring us all here to watch as our friends are shot at.

No bodies fall to the ground, which is something that I'm thankful for. I can barely breathe a prayer of thanks, because on the heels of it is a deep foreboding.

We are not safe, and the scouts will never get to us.

The feed continues to display images of the retreat, and I focus on the camera zoomed in on Azarias.

His face is twisted in anger, but his eyes hold fear.

He has to know that someone leaked this intel to Demetrius Ark. It's the only way they could have been so prepared for them attacking that portion of the Wall.

As I stare at him, I understand the feeling of not knowing how to protect someone you love. I didn't realize how much Kemena and Azarias cared for each other, but Kemena's hands are covering her mouth as she watches him. Her chin trembles. She squeezes her eyes shut and swallows hard.

The screens cut off.

Commander Ark turns and stares at Kemena until she looks at him. Fear for Azarias radiates off of her. And Commander Ark senses it as well. The man is so attuned to how people think and feel and act that I have no doubt he expected this reaction.

He's a master manipulator of emotions.

He stands and closes the distance between the two of them, then rests a hand on her shoulder. She jerks away, and his nostrils flare for an instant.

"Now, now," he says, his voice unnaturally calm. "I would think you would have a little more respect for me, knowing the power I hold."

"You have no power over me," Kemena says.

"And yet I know where Azarias sleeps at night. I know the cup he will drink out of tomorrow." The words are soft, yet sharp. "And I have the power to make it his last night of sleep, or his last drink on this earth." He rests his hands on the arms on either side of her chair and leans forward until his face is inches from hers.

She presses back into the chair, her chest rising and falling rapidly. But she doesn't blink as she stares this evil man in the eye.

"Do your duty, Kemena, and Azarias will live. Don't . . ." Ark shrugs. "He won't have time to prepare a pitiful attack like that again." He straightens and peers down at her. "Do we understand each other?"

She glares at him, and her jaw trembles again. I can't tell if it's from fear or anger.

"I understand you," she says.

He straightens. "Good. I'm glad we're on the same page now."

He looks around the room, focusing first on Matthias, then on me. "You two need to continue working hard. I could tell by your reactions that you have some friends in that group. Would hate to see what would happen to them if you failed to continue to work with me." He tilts his head. "Maybe we'll even bring some of them in."

He laughs at his own joke, and the soldiers in the room join him.

I clench my hands into fists until my nails bite into my palms. I don't know what to do to stop an evil like this.

But I will keep fighting to find a way.

THE MUD ON MY UNIFORM AND EXPOSED SKIN IS PARTIALLY HARDENED BY THE time Ark dismisses us from the impromptu meeting. My skin itches, and my body's weighed down both from the mud and the reality of what I just witnessed.

Ark instructs Kemena, Matthias, and I to leave through different exits, giving me no time to talk to either of them. Which might be for the best, considering I doubt I could mask my emotions right now, and I'd probably give away more than I intend.

As I exit the building, the mid-August heat wraps around me, suffocating in its embrace. All I want to do is wash off the mud and put on a dry uniform. Maybe sneak down to see Cai.

My HaloAct band buzzes.

I'm expected back at the Physical Training Arena immediately.

A timer counts down on my band. Three minutes. If I'm not back when it ends, I'll be in the sandpit. With Laban.

Ark isn't giving me a second to think. He's keeping me on edge, pushing me to my limits. He wants me to break.

I pivot and jog toward the arena. My band beeps out each second, pushing me faster. I round a corner, desperately wishing for a breeze, some relief from the heat. None comes. I dare a glance at my band.

One minute left.

I race down the street, weaving in and out of soldiers and pedestrians and earning several scowls along the way.

Keeping a low profile is important, but the one thing I don't need is time in the pit with Laban.

The last time I was sent to the pit, Laban delighted in pushing me to the point of breaking.

He'll do it again.

But I fear this time will be even worse.

The imposing structure of the training arena looms before me.

Beep. Beep. Beep.

The band chirps each second louder than the last. My thighs burn as I pump my arms and urge my body into a sprint.

Laban paces outside of the arena. Waiting. Ready to punish me.

I skid to a stop at the entrance of the arena as the alarm blares on my band.

Laban's golden eyes flash as he stalks toward me.

"I'm here," I say, my breathing labored. "I'm here."

He comes inches away from me. "I should send you to the pit. Beat some respect into you." His raspy voice grates over my already raw nerves.

I want to spit in his face. Or dare him to try to get me to respect him. But I force my face to remain neutral as I wait for him to decide what to do.

"Get inside, recruit!" Laban shouts, inches from my face.

"Sir, yes, sir!" I shout back.

I turn and run inside.

I should be happy Laban didn't send me to the pit. Thankful he's not forcing me to go through the humiliation of being pushed beyond my limits, losing my rifle, and having a record of pit time marked against me.

But I can only think one thing as I join a unit that's about to run the new obstacle course: *Why* did he let me go?

Yes, I arrived on time, but barely. Laban normally would count even a millisecond against me.

So why didn't he this time?

There's no answer I can find, and that alone has the monster of fear clawing at my mind as I start the obstacle course for the second time today.

CHAPTER

TWENTY-THREE

T he Sitreean delegation arrives tomorrow night, so tonight, Kemena, Kiwi, and I are heading to the Ruins without any kids. We need to brief Nika and Mom about what's been going on and get word to Ari. I wish Matthias could join us, but we haven't found a way to get to him. Yet.

Thankfully, Ark hasn't called me in for another meeting since he made us watch his soldiers thwart the scouts' attack. But Kemena's been far more pensive since the meeting.

The three of us pass the hollowed-out remains of a pre-Demise building as we head to the new site Mom and Nika are using. It's bigger than the first since they need space for the kids we keep bringing to them.

None of us says a word. We agreed to wait and do a full debrief with everyone in the Ruins, but the silence makes this trek harder.

I want to check in with Kemena and see how she's doing, which isn't really a debrief. But I also don't want to ask her something so personal in front of Kiwi.

We arrive at the site, and Mom and Nika welcome us in. The six kids are already asleep, and we crowd around the com system Kiwi transferred to this site. He sets up the encrypted connection, and a few moments later, a holograph of Ari fills the space.

"Bria!" Ari's face lights up when she sees me. "I've missed you!"

I smile in return. "I've missed you too. But I'm glad you're safe."

Ari's smile fades. "I'm so sorry about what Shane did. I never would have thought..."

"Girl, what he did is not your fault," Nika says.

"Not at all," I agree.

Ari shrugs. "I know. If he had waited just a little longer . . ." She shakes her head, wonder filling her eyes and replacing the sadness. "What Shane did broke my heart. But how God healed me, kept me from dying. That changed my life."

My eyes burn. "You believe." It's a statement, not a question. I can see the truth reflected in her face.

Still, Ari nods.

A deep thankfulness washes over me. When I thought Ari was going to die, it shook me. Because of my faith, I know where I'll go when I die. But I didn't have that assurance for Ari.

Now I do.

Thank You, God.

The conversation has shifted, so I wrangle my thoughts and focus on what Ari's saying.

"Once we realized you guys were captured, my brother and I knew we would have to be careful." Ari tucks a strand of blond hair behind her ear. "Most of the people here don't realize I've made a miraculous recovery. Thanks to Nalani, they think I'm dead and that Bryson left. We didn't want the leak to know we're still actively working against Ark. Only a small team knows the truth."

She and Kiwi get sidetracked discussing how Ari and Bryson are keeping themselves hidden. They start going back and forth on different tech ideas, which Nika and I immediately interrupt. Ari and Kiwi already seem like fast friends, even though they've only talked once before this.

Ari sobers. "But things didn't go well the other day. Azarias put together an off-the-books team to attempt a rescue mission."

"We know," Kemena says, her voice choked. "Is he okay?"

Ari nods. "Yeah. Everyone was okay, somehow. But they got in a lot of trouble once they returned to camp. Lorenzo was furious he wasn't looped in, but I think he was more concerned than anything." She scratches her arm. "We're all on edge because of this leak."

Kemena and I agree the leak is a concern. We brief everyone on what happened from our perspective. By the time we're done, a heavy silence descends.

I break it by sharing about my recent encounters with Ark.

"Wait." Nika puts her hands on her hips. "He sent for you *three times* in just a couple of days? He must really want you in line before the delegation arrives. I still can't believe he's going to let you be there for that."

"Me either," I agree. When we were last in Talionis, Ark was extremely careful to not allow a single recruit outside of the underground bunkers.

Kiwi looks up from where he's typing on a set of screens. "From what I've gathered, they're planning to up security all day tomorrow and the next day. Doesn't look like we'll be able to bring another kid out here until after that."

"That's probably okay," my mom says. "Nika and I have our hands full as it is. Any word on Keesia?"

Kiwi's nose wrinkles. "She said she's in. If we bring in the rest of the Resistance."

"That's a lot of people to involve," I say. "We can't be sure they're all trustworthy."

"True," Nika says. "But, girl, I am *tired*. Watching six kids who are getting more comfortable with us by the day is more exhausting than Elite Recruit training."

I raise my eyebrows at her. "I doubt that."

"Please. Don't even play like that," Nika says. "I would trade places with you in a second."

"Yeah, because being tormented by Ark through psychological warfare is a breeze." Sarcasm drips from my words.

Nika laughs. "Okay. You got me there. But seriously. Lily and I need help."

"We should bring the Resistance in," Kemena says. "With what Ark's planning, we need to do more than just smuggle kids out of the Ruins. And for that, we need help."

Her reasoning is sound, and I have to agree. "Okay. After the delegation leaves and security goes back to normal, we'll bring them in." I focus on Kiwi. "Can you make an introduction?"

He gives me a two-finger salute. "Yes, ma'am."

"We'll need more than the Resistance to bring Ark down," I say.

The others murmur their agreement.

"Cai is working on a strategy with the tunnels," Mom says. "He'll be ready to brief us soon."

"What about the scouts?" Nika asks. "I know there's a leak, but we could use their help."

Kemena shifts uncomfortably, but before she can offer any protests, Ari sighs.

"The Eryndale leadership is at a standstill," Ari says. "Azarias has been petitioning for more to be done. He even had Gabe on his side. But after yesterday . . ."

She leaves the sentence hanging.

Kemena's the first to break the silence. "Can you do me a favor, Ari?"

"Of course."

"Can you tell Azarias I'm okay? Carefully. Without anyone else knowing we've communicated." Kemena's serious expression emphasizes the intensity of her words, and I realize how much she cares for Cai's son.

Ari nods. "I will. Cai wants me to connect the two of them soon too. I'm just waiting for the heat from yesterday to cool off."

Nika loops her arm through her sister's and rests her head on her shoulder.

"There's another idea I had," I say, feeling a little bad for shifting the conversation, but needing to see if my thoughts have any merit. I look between Ari and Kiwi. "Can you help me sabotage the warfare scenarios?"

"What do you mean?" Kiwi asks.

I outline my fears of what will happen if we're unable to stop Ark before he brings recruits to Sitreea, and my plan for hiding things in the scenarios that could thwart Ark's ultimate goals.

"So you need code," Ari says. "I can definitely help with that. Kiwi, if we—"

"Hold up," Nika says, lifting her hands. "I do not want to hear tech speak right now. I'm too tired. You two can talk, and the rest of us will go have some tea. Then you can tell Bria what she needs to know."

"This will be really interesting," Ari says.

"Uh, no. It really won't." Nika comes over and puts her arm around my shoulders. "Girl, when have Bria or I ever understood what you were talking about with your tech?"

"You don't understand it?" Ari's eyes go wide.

Nika and I exchange a look.

"Sorry, Ari," I say. "But Kiwi knows how to dumb it down for me."

Ari shrugs and swivels her attention to Kiwi. She dives into several possibilities, and Nika, Kemena, Mom, and I head over to a table.

Kiwi and Ari troubleshoot ideas for over an hour while the rest of us talk through what's been happening. I share my fears about Matthias with Mom and Nika. They both encourage me to not let Ark win by pushing Matthias away. Which is easier said than done.

"He already knows you care about him." Mom rests her hand on top of mine. "From what I've learned about Demetrius Ark, you pushing Matthias away to trick Ark into thinking Matthias doesn't matter to you won't work."

She gives my hand a gentle squeeze. She's right. But *not* trying to protect Matthias feels unthinkable.

The conversation shifts and Nika talks about how it's been difficult to sabotage the soldiers with the kids being here. But Quincy apparently enjoys going with Nika on scouting missions and has a good eye for catching things. It's clear Nika's fond of the girl and happy to have her here. Despite her complaints about kids being exhausting.

By the time we leave, Kiwi and Ari have prepared a small device that, when connected, will enter code into the scenarios and allow me to adjust the elements I want to. Once the code is entered, the adjusted elements will be masked from anyone else who preps or manages the scenario.

As long as Major Vasco or any of his people don't notice what I've changed, this could prove to be a way for us to hinder Ark if the worst happens and he begins enacting his plan.

It's something, but it doesn't feel like enough.

CHAPTER

TWENTY-FOUR

O ne thing that hasn't changed since I was in Talionis last is that I still hate Technology Training. And I can't understand a word of what Mandeville is saying. He's droning on and on about some device, but the man can't use terminology anyone understands. At least not anyone who doesn't have an aptitude for tech.

Or maybe the bigger problem is that I'm exhausted from last night and disconcerted by the fact that I'm about to be paraded before the Sitreean delegation this evening. Something I'm not at all looking forward to.

I pinch the bridge of my nose and attempt to concentrate on what he's saying, but I'm as lost as the new recruits around me look. Which probably isn't great since I've been through this exact training before.

There are cadets in the room, preparing for when Mandeville tells everyone to break into groups to review today's lesson. Matthias is here, but he arrived right as Mandeville was starting class, so he's on the opposite side of the room.

Which is another reason I'm distracted.

Everything Ark has done over the past few days has been to make me fear being close to Matthias. And it's working.

But I don't *want* his fear tactics to work. I don't want to push Matthias away.

Seeing how distressed Kemena was last night about Azarias, knowing she kept him at a distance and regrets it now . . . I don't want that to be me.

I want to be with Matthias. Even though it's dangerous. Plus, Mom is right. Pushing Matthias away won't fool Ark into thinking I don't care about Matthias anymore.

Matthias catches me staring at him and gives me a subtle wink. My cheeks warm, but I smile.

"Break into groups," Mandeville says, clapping his hands.

I jolt. What exactly was he talking about at the end?

A group forms around me, and I'm relieved to see Kiwi among them.

He settles himself next to me. "Catch all of that? Or were you a bit . . . distracted?" The teasing lilt to his questions, along with his pointed glance at Matthias, has me elbowing him.

"Oof!" He grunts, then rubs his side. "What was that for?"

"You know." I give him a side eye. It strikes me that somewhere in these past couple of weeks, Kiwi has become a good friend. Like a brother.

A cadet I don't recognize comes over, but before she can sit with our group, Matthias is there.

"I'll take this one, Sorrella," he says with an engaging smile.

"Okay." Sorrella blushes, and a twinge of jealousy tightens my chest.

She doesn't even argue with him, and I can tell she likes him. Not that Matthias seems to notice. His gaze focuses on me as he carefully steps around the other recruits, grabs a chair, and squeezes himself into the space between me and Kiwi.

His shoulder brushes mine as he looks around the group, and I catch a whiff of the musky soap he uses. I want to lean into him and just be with him. But I keep myself from giving into the urge and pay attention to the introductions around the small circle.

Well, I *try* to.

It's hard to do with Matthias so close.

He nudges me with his shoulder. "You gonna introduce yourself? Or should I?" The warmth in his eyes steals my breath.

I clear my throat and tear my gaze away from him. "My name's Bria Averton."

"Elite First Class," says a guy whose nameplate reads Maverick. "We all heard about your promotion back to your old rank. Seriously impressive that you're at that level!"

"Is it though?" The girl across from me crosses her arms over her chest. "If she hadn't defied the Commander, she'd be ranking as a soldier by now. Like Corporal Shay."

The mention of my former neighbor sets me on edge. I haven't directly interacted with her since being back in Talionis, and I don't want to. But the fact that this recruit knows about and respects her tells me I need to keep my distance.

Maverick holds up his hands. "Hey. I'm just saying that from what I've heard about the level of training you have to complete to receive the level of Elite First Class—well, it's seriously impressive." He repeats his early phrase with a gigantic, contagious grin.

"Yup. It is." Matthias leans back and casually drapes his arm over the back of my chair.

A move everyone in our circle notices.

"Let's dive into an overview of today's lesson," Matthias says. He traces patterns on my back with his finger, sending goose bumps scattering across my skin.

If we were still in Eryndale . . .

But we're not.

I lean forward, breaking the contact. I won't completely push Matthias away, but I don't want to be foolish.

The group discusses the tech Mandeville taught on today. Tech I learned about before but never absorbed the knowledge.

And I won't absorb it today. Not with Matthias this close.

The rest of the class passes in a blur, and Mandeville interrupts everyone to dismiss the class right on time.

Matthias and I stand at the same time.

"Where are you headed?" he asks.

"Recruit Averton." Mandeville's voice rings through the air, stopping me from responding to Matthias. "Come with me."

"I'm supposed to—"

"Now." He jabs his finger at the watch on his wrist.

I've been on the wrong side of Mandeville's agitation before, and I don't want to be again. So, I give Matthias an apologetic smile and follow Mandeville from the room.

I trail after the short instructor down the maze of hallways of the Technical Operations Building until we reach a set of doors that require biometric scanning to enter.

The last time I was alone with Mandeville, it was because I was in trouble for being late to class. An offense he couldn't dare to let slide.

The man is punctual to a fault, always starting class precisely on time and ending it, even if he's in the middle of a sentence, exactly when class is supposed to end. He is the promptest person I have ever met. I think he might even question Ark if he required them to do something longer than the time stated on their schedule.

My mind drifts back to that moment when I was by myself, cleaning up after class, after receiving a sound thrashing from Mandeville's tongue. He was in his office, listening to a report, and it's when I first realized people we knew betrayed us.

It was the beginning of a journey that would lead me to discover my aunt's betrayal. That she worked with Talionis to give up names of teens to send them to this place. Teens I knew, like Shay, and my friend Jaxon, who was never brought in. And me.

Elena's betrayal still rings deep within me.

I never understood how forgiveness could be such a difficult task until I experienced such depths of betrayal. It's something I have to give to God over and over again in order to function without bitterness swallowing me whole. But I still haven't figured out how to forgive her, at least not in a way that allows me to trust her again.

Then again, forgiveness and trust aren't the same thing, I don't think. The fact that she's still in Eryndale, bound, yes, but free to speak her lies angers me.

How can she be in a place as safe as Eryndale when I'm forced to be here with a man who has murderous intent for every teen he's brought in?

It's unjust.

Mandeville clears his throat. He's standing outside of a secure area waiting for me to proceed him through the door.

"Any day now, Recruit Averton," he says with a quick gesture of his hand at the open doorway.

"What's going on?" I ask.

"There's something you need to see."

I shake away the thoughts swirling through my mind and precede Mandeville through the door.

The place is set up like a control room in a warfare scenario. Screens line the front of the room, higher than two stories, and dozens of men and women sit at desks watching the screens, all of them dizzily typing away.

It's like a higher-tech version of the command centers Eryndale Scouts use while in the field. A sense of foreboding wraps its thick tentacles around me.

"What am I doing here?" I ask.

"The Sitreean delegation arrives later tonight," Mandeville says. "Commander Ark requires you to be as prepared as possible to make a good impression on the delegates."

I stare at him blankly, and Mandeville gestures to the screen on the wall. "He wants you to recall all that is at stake."

The explanation is just as ambiguous. I study the screens. A series of transports travel quickly over forests and the ruins of pre-Demise cities. They're in the North American region, but I'm not sure where. There's no map showing where the transports are flying over, just images of the transports themselves and the view out their windows.

They slow, coming to an area I begin to recognize. A transport veers out and to the east, over an ocean. No. It's a bay. The bay I've gone swimming in over and over again.

The bay where I lost Ezri. Where he drowned because I needed to swim, even though I knew I wasn't supposed to.

The bay I swam in every chance I got to try to defeat my monsters —and failed every time.

The transports are surrounding Derbe.

I recognize the Lasson River from the video feed of one transport, and another is far above the town center of Derbe, using an advanced video technology that allows them to zoom in. I doubt those in Derbe even realize the transports are overhead. Waiting to destroy my hometown.

My family's not there, but what about Jaxon and Lencie? I don't know if they're still alive or if they've been hurt or what's happened to them since I've been gone for almost a year.

"What are you doing?" The words tremor in my throat.

I expected to find out Derbe was destroyed weeks ago, but Ark's preserved the town. It would have been easier to hear it was in ruins than to watch them preparing to attack.

How can I *witness* the destruction of the place I called home my entire life?

"The Commander will get what he wants by whatever means necessary," Mandeville says. "Tonight, he wants you to be on good behavior. Is that understood?"

The question pierces my ears, causing my breath to catch in my throat. I nod.

"They will remain in position surrounding Derbe for the next twenty-four hours," Mandeville says. "What happens to this hometown of yours is up to you. I recommend being on your very best behavior tonight for the dinner with the Sitreean delegation."

I nod, knowing I have no choice. Even without this threat, I planned to do everything Ark wanted tonight. But I can't help but wonder why he's going to such great lengths to ensure my obedience.

God, I don't know how to fight a man this evil. But show me a path forward. Show all of us what to do.

Mandeville dismisses me to find Sampta and Presidia so they can prepare me for the evening.

I almost groan outwardly, but keep it in. The last thing I want to do is listen to the two women exclaim over my lack of fashion and talk about the difficulty it takes for them to make me, in their words, "somewhat presentable."

But I obey.

It's my only option.

T he sisters prepare me in the same manner in which they've prepared me time and time again for other important events in Talionis.

But this time, there's an added flair to everything they're doing. Like they are excited for the delegation to arrive tonight. Which is strange. I don't understand Sampta and Presidia.

How are they who they are? Why are they doing everything the Commander tells them to do?

I'm instructed to bathe first. From experience, I know that if I'm not as clean as the women believe I should be before they do my hair and makeup and fit me for my gown, then they will bathe me themselves. An event I would like to avoid, if possible.

So, I spend extra time in the shower facilities to scrub every inch of myself clean. Part of it feels good, almost hurting myself with the sponge in my hand as I seek to wipe off all remnants of this day.

Everything is tainted by Ark and what he's doing. The threat's hanging over me.

Shouldn't it have been enough for him that I'm doing what he wants for Matthias and Storm? Does he really also need me on edge worrying about Derbe?

I dry myself off and almost laugh at the question that doesn't need an answer. Of course he wants me on edge like this. Of course he wants everything I care about hanging in the balance.

All because he wants to control me. He wants me to know that no matter what happens, I'm under his thumb, and I'll never be able to escape again.

At least so far he doesn't know about Mom and Nika and the kids we've smuggled to the Ruins. He doesn't know about the code Ari and Kiwi gave me to manipulate the scenarios. I don't think he even knows much about the Resistance, which is another point in their favor. I might be a prisoner here, but I refuse to be fully controlled and fully part of Ark's narrative.

I pull on the loose clothes the tailors left for me to wear for when they do my hair and makeup, more tense than I was a minute ago. I'm walking a dangerous line, and the slightest misstep will mean tragedy on some front.

But the risks have to be worth it. I can't be exactly who Ark wants me to be, because then I'll become someone I don't recognize. Someone willing to harm others just to keep myself safe. And I'll lose far more than I'll ever get back.

Fear will not hold us captive. Kemena's words ring through my heart.

I blow out a long breath and pause before exiting the bathroom to join Sampta and Presidia. *God, I don't want fear to control me. I want to be courageous and continue to find ways to defy Ark. But every time he threatens those I care about, it gets harder. Help me. Please. I can't do this alone.*

As soon as I exit, Sampta and Presidia set to work. First, they insist on adding highlights to my hair, despite my emphatic protests. Then they clean and paint my nails before going to work on my hair design and makeup. I barely recognize myself as they transform my face with makeup and twist my hair into braids in a fashion I could never do without Nika's help. I don't even know how I'll get this stuff out of my hair.

The women talk over my head as they work, as though I'm not even there.

"I hope we have enough time to get her in order so we can get ourselves ready," Presidia says.

Sampta nods emphatically. "Right so, sister. It is only right for the Talionis tailors to be in optimal beauty by the time they are seen by those in Sitreea."

"If only the Commander would allow our designs to be viewed by the Sitreean fashion department," Presidia says woefully. "I am confident our latest tech versions of uniforms that are both fashionable and technologically advanced would be all the rage."

I glance between the sisters. My uniforms aren't technologically advanced, which means there are new designs. And if there's tech involved, it will be one more way for Ark and his minions to see and control everything the recruits do. Everything *I* do.

"While fashionable is a bit of a stretch, sister," Sampta says with a sniff, "if we were free to make them the way we desire to design them, then everyone would know of our excellence."

It's like they don't realize all Ark is planning to do against Sitreea. They want to be known there, recognized, seen as valuable. But they know they can't share their uniform designs. I wonder what excuses Ark gave them, although I don't dare ask.

Still, I can't help but wonder what they actually know of Ark and his plans. They go on and on about Sitreea, the beauties of the country, and how lovely being in "proper company" will be when the delegations arrive.

"Why are you here?" I ask, no longer able to keep my curious thoughts to myself.

Sampta pauses pinning my hair up, and Presidia stares at me.

"What do you mean, child?" Presidia asks.

"Why are you in Talionis? Wouldn't your skills be better utilized in Sitreea?" I'm playing on the women's vanity, which might not be the best tactic, but I'm intrigued.

"Right so," Presidia mutters. "But we are here because we are needed here, and one day the Commander will allow our fashions to be seen and appreciated by far more than we ever could have found on our own." She says the words with passion, but there's the slightest catch in her voice.

"Didn't you come here a long time ago?" I ask. "I mean, look at this." I gesture down at the floor-length golden gown I'm wearing. It has a thin gossamer fabric around it that makes me appear to glow, and the fabric is lightweight while also looking thick and heavy. "This is amazing. Don't you think it's enough to impress those in Sitreea? Talionis has been here for how many years?"

"Fifteen," Sampta says without hesitation.

"And you've been here the whole time?" I ask.

"Well, yes . . ." Presidia's words trail off.

"I just wonder if Demetrius Ark is all you think he is," I say.

Presidia gasps. "Those are treasonous words, child. Bite your tongue."

I shrug. "Treason seems to be the theme of my life," I say, then regret it. I can't be this flippant. Not with all that's at stake. I need to save my risks for moments that can protect children or stop Ark. Not risk comments in front of some of Ark's most ardent supporters. "But, of course," I continue quickly, "my goal is to honor the Commander by helping him accomplish all he desires."

The women eye me shrewdly, but then look at each other and shrug off my words as they go back to work.

"Well, look at the beautiful work we have done," Presidia says, more to Sampta than to me.

But she's right. I'm beautifully attired in one of the most exquisite gowns I've ever seen, including the other gowns I've worn here.

Which brings to mind a question I should have thought to ask long before this. Why does Ark want the delegation to see me like *this?*

I'm sure I'll be briefed before the dinner, but I wish I had more time to understand my purpose in this evening.

My stomach clenches.

"A transport will be here to pick you up shortly," Presidia says. "Now, mind you do not sit until you absolutely must. We don't want the fabric to be at all wrinkled before you are seen by the entire delegation."

Presidia consults a screen. She gasps. "They'll be arriving shortly. Within the hour."

"Oh, sister," Sampta exclaims. "How will we ever be ready in time?"

"Well, we must go now," Presidia says. "If only the Commander hadn't required us to prepare this one. It would be very helpful if you knew how to do your own makeup and hair."

"I get by with my own hair daily," I mutter.

Presidia harrumphs and sails out the door with Sampta close behind her.

"Do not sit," they say in unison as they exit.

Part of me wants to, just to see the women's faces if I arrive at the dinner with a gown that has a single wrinkle in it. Thoughts of transports surrounding Derbe crowd my mind.

Choose your risks, Bria.

No, for tonight everything must be done exactly as I have been instructed, whether by Ark or by these women.

At least until I have a clearer understanding of why I'm being put in this position.

I study myself in the mirror, wishing there was someone else here to talk to, remembering when Nika and I were preparing together for dinners like this.

I'm happy she's safe in the Ruins, but selfishly, I wish she was here with me. Wish we could strategize how to navigate the evening before me.

But I'm alone tonight.

My band buzzes on the table where Sampta set it after insisting it be left behind so as not to *ruin my ensemble*. They had it cleared by Commander Ark. In fact, he himself insisted, according to the ladies.

No surprise. I doubt he wants the Sitreeans to know this kind of technology is being used to track recruits and prepare them for an attack against the very country Ark is saying he's protecting.

I inhale a deep breath, my chest tight. Then I make my way to the waiting transport.

It's time to meet those who have equipped Demetrius Ark with everything necessary to destroy countless lives. And they don't even know it.

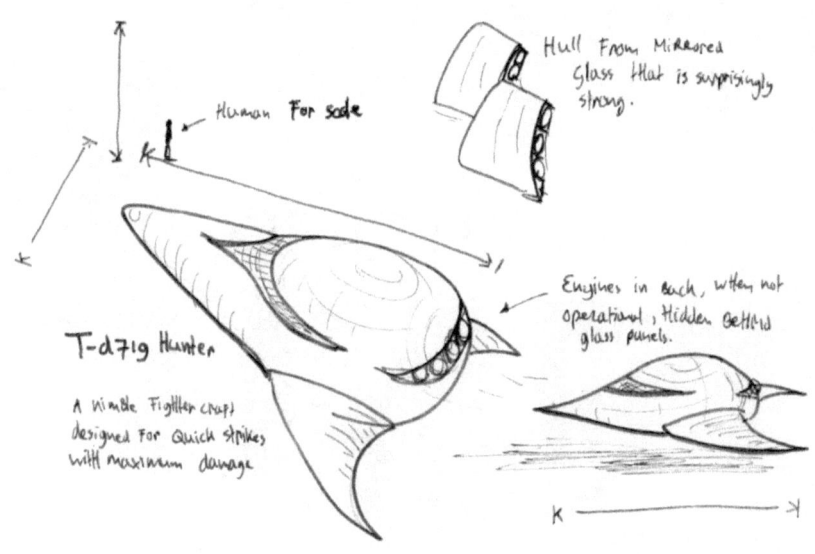

Human For scale

Hull From Mirrored Glass that is surprisingly strong.

T-d719 Hunter

A Nimble Fighter craft designed For Quick strikes with maximum damage

Engines in each, when not operational, Hidden behind glass panels.

K ——————— K

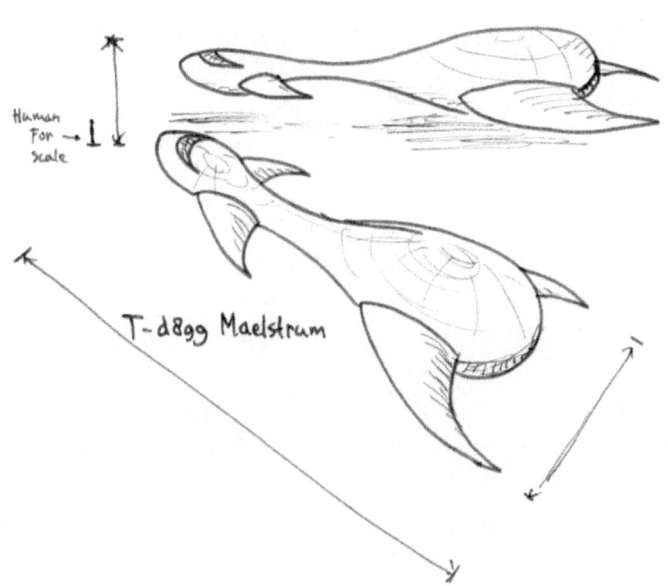

Human For scale

T-d8gg Maelstrum

Talionis Transport

CHAPTER
TWENTY-SIX

As I board the transport and choose a standing bay, my mind skitters to my first time I was dressed and prepared for a dinner with Demetrius Ark. Loaded into the fanciest transport I've ever seen, not unlike the one I'm in now. Prepared to meet the Commander whose hospitality we were to thank for our time in Talionis.

It was disconcerting how likable Demetrius Ark was, how he was somebody I almost wanted to impress with my skills, just like the other recruits.

That dinner was difficult, but I managed to be okay through it all.

The worst was the dinner after, where he invited a small, select group. Where I saw Matthias dressed so handsomely. Where Ark returned Ezri's necklace to me. The necklace I thought I'd lost forever.

When I first arrived in Talionis, Sergeant Valarius discovered I hadn't destroyed it along with everything else from my old life, so he forced a recruit to rip it off my neck.

Ark had the broken strap replaced with a gold chain. Returned it to me as though it was some extravagant gesture to show me he cared.

What it really revealed—what he *knew* it would reveal—is that he was aware of far more about me and my history than I originally understood. It was to keep me in check.

And it shot terror through me.

That night, I acted so rashly. I tried to save Storm, but my actions resulted in Cade's death.

That dinner changed everything for me, even though I didn't understand it at the time.

The transport descends on the roof of Ark's spacious compound where he hosts dinners.

I swallow hard, trying to shake off the memories that cling to me like wet seaweed. Right now, I'd rather be in the pit with Laban than going to a diplomatic dinner.

But maybe I'll learn something useful while I'm here.

I exit the transport to find Sergeant Valarius waiting for me, his face devoid of emotion.

He leads me down a hallway and toward the dining room.

"The delegation has arrived," he says. "You will be introduced by Commander Ark, and you are to reflect admiration for Talionis and encourage the delegation to believe all Commander Ark says. Is that understood?"

"Yes, sir," I say. "Is there anything else?"

"No." He opens the door before I can ask more questions.

I force myself to enter, feeling far less prepared than I wish I did.

Men and women I don't recognize fill the room, talking. Laughing. Several of Ark's most trusted advisors are here, including Elva Trill, Major Vasco, and Colonel Valarius. All of them are talking with various members of the Sitreean delegation, smiling to their faces despite the fact that they're planning to attack their country in a matter of months.

I walk away from the door but stay near the edges of the room, taking everything in.

Sampta and Presidia aren't here yet, and I suspect it's because the women are still getting themselves ready and blaming me for their tardiness.

I stop close to a drink table, and my breath catches in my throat.

Matthias is here, talking easily with members of the delegation.

He looks amazing. Perfect. His smile is full as he laughs at something a woman says. And that's when his eyes find mine. Catch me staring at him.

And that blazing smile is turned on me. I smile back. At least I have one ally in the room.

"Ah, Bria. You look lovely." Commander Ark's voice behind me stiffens my spine. "I'm glad you arrived. There are many I'd like you to meet here today."

I nod. "Of course, sir." My words are shockingly clear and measured, almost sounding like I'm happy to accommodate him. Which is a small miracle.

Ark leads me away from Matthias. Everything in me wants to be with him. To at least have the comfort of being near someone I can trust.

Focus, Bria.

I just need to get through this. And gain whatever intel I can in the process.

Ark brings me through the room, introducing me to members of the Sitreean delegation as a youth who they found who had no family and needed help. He goes on about how I've proven to be a wonderful asset here, aiding in the Sitreean defense effort. The narrative is sickening, because it sounds so *real*.

Every word he weaves masquerades as the truth, causing the guests to smile and warm toward me.

"Wonderful to hear," many of them say.

"Aye, Commander Ark, you are so kind. Always looking out for those who need a helping hand," an older man says.

Ark ducks his head in modest acceptance of the blatant lie. "I do love giving to others."

I almost laugh at the ridiculousness of the words, but stifle it with a soft cough.

All of them seem enamored with Demetrius Ark, even thrilled to have the opportunity to be in his presence and to witness firsthand all he's doing to protect Sitreea.

The lies make my skin crawl. These people have no clue that the man they so revere is preparing to destroy them.

But it's not my place to tell them. Not yet, anyway.

Even if I did, they wouldn't believe a word I said.

One man in particular differs from the others. He watches Ark with a look of almost uncertainty, like he's not clear on whether he trusts him, which makes me far more comfortable with this man than anyone else.

Ark brings me to a stop in front of the man. He's maybe a couple of years older than Ark, and his eyes hold a shrewd evaluation as he stares at me.

"Who is this, might I ask?" The man has a lilting accent, similar to Ark's.

"Antonio, may I present Bria." Ark gives a sweeping gesture to me. "She was alone and starving when we found her a few weeks ago. But she's now thriving in Talionis. Isn't that right?" Ark turns his penetrating gaze on me.

I incline my head, as I've done for every other introduction, but this time it's harder. Maybe it's because Antonio is watching me with a furrowed brow, as though he doesn't fully believe what Ark is saying.

"Yes, Commander." The rest of the words I've said to everyone else die in my throat. I don't want to tell Antonio I'm thrilled to be here. Or lie about how much I appreciate all the *gracious* Commander has done for me.

Antonio gives me a curt bow, clicking his heels together. "A pleasure to make your acquaintance, Bria."

Ark smiles, but the cunning in his eyes as he studies me tells me to mind my step. My lack of effusive praise was noticed. I need to be careful.

A server with a tray of glasses of sparkling cider approaches, and Antonio takes a glass for himself and passes one to me.

"Thank you." I take a sip of the cider. "What is it you do for Sitreea, sir?" I ask, hoping the change in conversation will shift the uncomfortable scrutiny away from me.

"Antonio is the head of the Department of Defense," Ark chimes in.

I take another sip of cider to hide my surprise. I didn't expect the man to have such a high rank. "A large responsibility," I finally manage.

Antonio smooths his mustache. "That it is. That it is. But having key defenses in place, like Talionis, allows my job to go more smoothly." The words are the right words, but the sharpness in the man's eyes as he inclines his head toward Ark catches me.

The two don't trust each other, but I can't understand their familiarity. Ark addresses everyone by their rank. The fact that he called Antonio just *Antonio* leaves me uneasy.

"We have been friends for many years," Ark says, as though he can read my mind.

I clasp the glass tighter, then force myself to loosen my grip before I shatter it. "Oh?"

"Yes," Antonio continues. "We were in the Academy together."

Ark chuckles. "Yes, those were the days." He claps a hand on Antonio's shoulder. "We swore to one another that no matter the rank we possessed, we'd always call each other by our first name."

Antonio offers a tight smile, and I wonder if he appreciates their childhood vow now. "True. Even when that name changes, eh?"

Ark's face flinches so briefly I almost wonder if I saw anything at all. But then he's the gracious host once again. "Well, I will let you enjoy mingling before dinner." He smiles broadly at Antonio and gestures toward the door. "It appears Sampta and Presidia have arrived. I'm sure you'll want to reconnect."

Now Antonio is the one who stiffens.

Or maybe I'm just imagining things.

This entire evening is like walking a balance beam over poisonous snakes. Words are spoken that clearly have deeper meanings, and I'm being suffocated between them. Even though I have no idea what's truly being said.

Antonio bows. "We'll speak in private later. *Demetrius.*" The way he says Commander Ark's name, almost forcefully, sets the already brewing tension between the two men even higher.

Yet they clasp one another's arms and part ways.

Is Demetrius not Ark's real name?

I watch Antonio as he does, indeed, make his way to Sampta and

Presidia. The sisters give a deep curtsy, giving deference to the man's rank. But it's the way Presidia's eyes never leave Antonio's that catches my attention.

"He's one to watch," Ark says, his voice low in my ear. "Childhood friendships do not always stand the test of time as one would hope."

A soldier approaches to tell Ark dinner is ready, but my pulse pounds so loudly in my ears I can barely make out the words.

Ark leaves my side to address the room, but all I can think is that Antonio might become an ally. If only I can find a way to communicate with him that won't tip off Ark.

CHAPTER
TWENTY-SEVEN

The crowd laughs at something Ark says, breaking through my fog. I've been staring at Antonio as he remains near Presidia and Sampta.

How will I ever get close enough to him to have any kind of conversation without Ark or one of his people catching on?

With the way Ark spoke to me, I almost wonder if he expects me to talk to Antonio. Which is an uncomfortable thought, since that's exactly what I want to do.

The doors of the dining room open, and the smell of the beef tips and gravy Ark's chefs have prepared wafts deeper into the room. The crowd moves in a wave toward the food.

"You look stunning." Matthias's voice catches me, and all thoughts of Antonio flee.

I turn. He's right at my elbow, gazing at me with open admiration.

"Hi," I say. "You look good yourself."

There are many reasons I should keep my distance from Matthias tonight. I'm sure Ark and Colonel Valarius will watch both of us closely. Not to mention the fact that I need to find out more about Antonio tonight and being around Matthias will be rather . . . distracting.

But as the crowd around us pushes us toward the door and Matthias places his hand on my elbow and guides me forward, I can't stop the skipping of my heartbeat. No words find their way to my mouth as he leads me to one of the long tables, and when he pulls out the seat for me, I sit. A glance around the room brings the sad realization that Antonio is sitting with Presidia and Sampta two tables away.

Talking to him tonight will be nearly impossible. Which is almost a relief, since I don't know what I would even say to the man.

Matthias settles himself next to me, pulling his chair in and much closer to mine than necessary. His shoulder brushes against mine, and he gives me the full force of his Matthias grin. Everything inside me melts, as powerless to stay frozen as an icicle before a raging fire. With the uncertainty of everything around me, I want to be close to Matthias.

To everyone here, Matthias is the picture of a perfectly dressed young soldier, attentive to anyone who talks to him, including the woman on his right, who engages him in conversation. When she realizes who Matthias is, her conversation veers toward his father, Colonel Valarius, and she gushes about how kind and generous the man is.

Matthias drops his hands into his lap and clenches them together, but that's the only sign he gives that he's uncomfortable with the woman's effusive praise of the man who takes every opportunity to harm him. He inclines his head and nods to the woman, allowing her to continue with her blabbering.

My shoulders tense, but not because I'm uncomfortable. I'm furious. This woman is a fool. So blinded by Colonel Valarius's smooth political talk that she can't see the hatred that glistens in his eyes every time he glances at his son.

I want to leap to my feet. Give the woman a piece of my mind. Make a scene that lets the entire delegation know of the evil lurking behind the masks of perfection their host and his soldiers wear.

But the transports surrounding Derbe and the danger such an action would put Storm and Matthias in hold me in check.

So, I do the only thing I can.

I carefully reach over and take Matthias's hands in mine. Half an ear listening to the woman talking to Matthias, and the other half failing to engage with the couple across from me who's asking me questions I can't find answers to.

I lightly clear my throat. "What is it you do for Sitreea?"

The simple question is enough to start them on a long and tedious conversation about finance.

One I don't pay an ounce of real attention to as Matthias's hands relax under mine.

He unlocks his hands from each other and grips mine with the one closer to me, interlacing our fingers.

It feels right, this support of one another in a place where we're in such danger.

I cling to his hand as tightly as he's clinging to mine.

Servants arrive with platters of food that they set on the tables before each person.

When our food arrives, Matthias still keeps my hand in his, as though letting go would break the lifeline he so desperately needs. And I understand.

But we need to eat and play our role here tonight as perfectly as possible.

The hair on the back of my neck rises. Someone's watching me. I look to the head table where Ark sits with a small smile on his face, eyebrow cocked. He says something to the person next to him, laughing at whatever joke was stated, but his eyes don't leave mine.

The warning radiates down the length of the table. Ark knows Matthias is a weak point for me. And Ark loves leveraging weak points.

I numbly take a bite of mashed potatoes, not tasting them before I swallow.

It's late when the Sitreean delegation prepares to leave.

Ark insisted I be around for the entire evening, not caring that my training has me up at the break of dawn or even earlier on some days.

Nor does it seem to matter that I've been stifling yawns for the past two hours. I think he might *like* how uncomfortable I am.

I push back my exhaustion and try to continue to be the perfect recruit he's expecting.

Matthias hasn't left my side since we found each other, and despite the risks, I've loved being close to him.

The delegation boards their transport to leave, and Commander Ark summons me. Matthias gives me a tight smile.

Moments later, I find myself in a room with Ark, Colonel Valarius, Laban, Major Vasco, and Mandeville. Sergeant Valarius enters.

"That went well," Commander Ark says. "Did you insert the device in the transport?" He directs the question to Sergeant Valarius.

"Yes, sir," Sergeant Valarius says, his face a stoic mask.

Something in me flips. He's doing what Ark wants.

Whatever device was just placed on that transport was one that Sergeant Valarius had every responsibility in placing there. Maybe he sabotaged it. The man is working with Cai. Then again, I have yet to see him defy one of Ark's orders. How much should I trust Sergeant Andor Valarius? Is he willing to do what it takes to stop Talionis?

Ark gestures to Mandeville. "Mandeville, would you please explain what we've placed on the transport heading back to Sitreea?"

"Of course, sir, that's why I'm here." He's the only person I know who can sound a little short and impatient with Commander Ark and get away with it.

He details how the device will, once in Sitreean airspace, allow him to pick up different elements of the transportation aircraft used in Sitreea, as well as the defensive measures they have in place.

Once Mandeville finishes, Ark elaborates on the ways in which the device Mandeville created will work.

Not only will Sitreea's entire aerial defense system be clearly outlined to Talionis's soldiers, but Ark will be able to cripple the defense at a moment's notice whenever we are ready to infiltrate the country.

According to Ark, every Sitreean transport will be marked by this device, creating its own fingerprint to identify it wherever it goes in the world. The device will also link with the communications in Sitreea and be what allows us to get a behind-the-curtain peek at everything they're doing.

My body runs hot and then cold. Each word he says is more terrifying than the last.

If Mandeville is monitoring a device with such capabilities, will entering the code Ari and Kiwi made me for the scenarios even matter?

"This device," Ark continues, "will be what gives us an edge we could never have had otherwise."

The grin he shares with the others twists my stomach into knots.

"Bria." His focus on me draws the attention of every other person in the room, and icy tentacles wrap themselves around every nerve in my body. "I do hope you and Major Vasco will work together to best utilize these new technologies."

I nod. "Of course, sir."

"Now." Commander Ark rises. "It has been a full and productive evening."

Laughter rings through the room, and again, I feel completely out of place. Why is Ark inviting me into this inner circle, allowing me to see everything he's allowing me to see?

The answer comes to me almost before I finish thinking the question.

He's taunting me.

He knows there's nothing I can do about this. Even if I was out of the picture, he would still get away with all he's doing.

Is there anything we can do that will make a dent in Ark's plans? Or are we fighting a losing battle?

CHAPTER
TWENTY-EIGHT

y alarm chirps, breaking into my sleep.

I rub my eyes and check my band. My physical conditioning training was moved up to the earliest time slot of the day. Another opportunity for Ark to remind me he's in control.

But he's not as in control of me as he thinks. The things he's planning, the lives he's going to take for his own gain—I won't stand by and do nothing.

And I'm not alone. In the next few days, I'll get Kiwi to introduce me to the Resistance. Something I'm more eager for than I was previously. I've seen the subtle forms of rebellion in the encrypted messages Kiwi sends to specific recruits debunking the Talionis propaganda. The frustration from Corporal Sidon over issues with his weapons, issues he can never trace to anyone. I've even heard whispers among some of the soldiers about recruits going missing right before their scheduled . . . elimination.

As unnerving as it is to bring in more people, we need all the help we can get. And the Resistance could provide that help.

I dress quickly, although the movements are harder than they should be.

Everything that happened last night is still more than I can process, but one thing is clear. Smuggling kids to the Ruins and sabotaging elements of scenarios isn't enough. I can't allow one transport full of recruits to leave Talionis, never to return to the American region again. I can't allow more people to be hurt by Demetrius Ark.

Resolve strengthens my body as I move to leave. The door is unlocked, as expected, since I am heading into a training. I strap my rifle to my back and exit the room, a light headache behind my eyes.

Probably the result of not enough sleep.

I arrive in the training arena and find a unit I haven't worked with before waiting—at least most of the unit. There's a gap for a recruit in the second row.

A girl straggles in, pulling on her one boot. Her hair sticks out in a variety of angles, and I can't help but quirk an eyebrow at her as she stumbles into the row and tucks her shoelace into her boot.

The girl is a mess.

When Laban enters, dread coats my mouth in a bitter flavor.

If I can tell this girl is ill prepared for training today, Laban smelled it as soon as he entered the room. Like a shark finding a wounded man in the water, Laban circles the unit, gaze fixed on the girl. His eyes are narrowed, golden slits that spark as though he's personally affronted at the girl's appearance and lack of preparedness.

He stops in front of her, then gives a flick of his gaze in my direction.

He'll push me. Try to break me.

I can't let him.

No matter what he does to this poor girl, I cannot let him break me. I remain stiff at attention, facing forward. But my heart pounds a rhythm that makes my blood throb, as though it wants to explode out of me, to act and protect this girl from Laban.

It's like this is my fault, which is wrong, but I can't quell the feeling rising inside of me. Whatever happens to this girl will be worse because I'm in this room.

A blind man would know Laban and I are enemies. Of course, after everything last night, Commander Ark would place me with him.

I almost wonder if the girl's alarm didn't go off on time, if even that was planned. If it was intentional, Ark expects something from me. But what?

"Recruit Arwen Baker."

"Yes, sir." Her voice catches.

"Is this any way to present yourself at training?"

"Um, n-no, sir," she stutters, terror in her eyes.

"You've been here for four weeks now. I expect better from you. You're going to the pit."

The mere mention of the pit makes her shake.

I bite my tongue until I taste the metallic flavor of blood.

"Unless, of course," Laban continues, his eyes flashing over to me, "another person wants to take your place, give you a chance to prove you can be an asset to Talionis."

"No. I-I'll go," Arwen says. "It's okay."

The courage in her voice, her willingness to do something that clearly terrifies her, causes me to relax my tenuous hold on my silence.

"I'll take her place," I blurt.

Laban's mouth curls into a wicked grin, and Arwen shakes her head.

"No, no, I'll take it. It's my punishment. I'm late. I'm not dressed properly." She moves out of line, her eyes desperate.

I step forward, more resolved to do exactly what Laban is baiting me to do. This girl doesn't deserve to be under his cruel treatment. If I don't step up, he'll treat her far worse than he would if I weren't in the room.

"No, you train. I can handle the pit." My eyes are locked on Laban's, and I don't notice Arwen anymore.

A cruel cunning gleams in his golden eyes. He grabs me by the shoulder and shoves me forward, but not before he hisses in my ear, "I've been waiting for this moment since you returned."

All traces of exhaustion from the night before evaporate from my body. I'll need to be in perfect condition in order to survive whatever is coming next with Laban.

But I'll do it.

I'll do it for Arwen. The punishment is harsher than it should be, all because I'm in the room. And I'll use every second I'm there to grow stronger. His punishment won't break me.

I double-time it to the sandpit, more so that I can't hear Laban shouting orders at the recruits left behind or feel his hand shoving me forward. I'd rather get there and get this over with.

I arrive at the pit to find another soldier there, focused on a screen.

She looks at me, her eyes widening in recognition. "Your rifle will need to be confiscated for the remainder of the day." She reaches for the weapon strapped to my back.

I hesitate. "Why? I haven't done anything wrong."

"All those who are sentenced to the sandpit for any kind of disciplinary measure must have their rifle removed."

"But I'm taking someone else's place." I shouldn't be arguing. This is how the pit works. But I don't want to have any appearance of non-compliance with Talionis. Not having my rifle will be a beacon to every soldier, recruit, and cadet, displaying my disobedience. For something I didn't even do. Maybe taking Arwen's place was a mistake.

"Then you take their place in this way as well," the soldier insists, reaching for my weapon.

I surrender it. I can't back down now. It would only cause more harm for Arwen and probably me on top of it. But surrendering the symbol of my favor in Talionis is harder than I would've expected.

But it's only for a short time.

I roll my shoulders and stretch a bit.

"Get in the pit," Laban screeches from behind me.

I do as he demands, turn, and salute.

"Sir, yes, sir," I say, every ounce of my training taking over, despite the headache that's pulsing harder than it was earlier.

I will give him no reason to say I haven't done exactly what he wanted. Plus, another soldier's here who will make sure this punishment goes according to the books.

"Corporal, you're dismissed," Laban shouts over his shoulder at the woman.

My stomach drops.

"Sir." She clears her throat. "It's my duty today to observe all pit training and punishment."

He stalks toward her until he's inches from her face. "I said *you are dismissed.*" He enunciates each word.

The corporal salutes him, turns on her heel, and leaves just shy of a run.

And with her goes any hope I have of leniency from Laban.

Not that I expect much from him to begin with.

"Burpees. Until I say stop," he demands.

I begin the exercise. My first ten aren't too bad. In fact, my body loosens up, and I enjoy the movement. But after forty, then fifty, then sixty-eight, it's like the sand is sucking me in, pulling me down.

"You're slowing down, Averton. Pick it up," Laban shouts in my face.

I do as he demands.

He turns on a nearby hose and sprays water into the pit, causing my feet to stick all the more as my boots get stuck. But I continue the burpees.

"Push-ups, now, on the ground, go, go, go!" He's in my face, screaming, his spit coating my cheek.

I obey, even as my loathing for this man forces me to push myself harder, to not allow him any sense of pleasure at my expense. I will be better. I will do exactly what he wants, and I will not break.

He, of all people, will not break me.

I force my thoughts to others, to people I care about, to my family. Matthias. I push harder, thinking of Nika. Of Kemena, who's willing to risk whatever it takes to help me save kids. Eli and Zeke, my parents. Cai, Ari, Kiwi. Catori and Micah. All of them filter through my mind, adding strength as I push harder.

After a while, my muscles weaken.

Breath scrapes through my lungs, sweat dripping down my back, my face, into my eyes. My muscles burn as I do another push-up. I don't even know how many it's been at this point. I lost count, somewhere around forty-five.

Then Laban's in my face, demanding sit-ups.

I flip onto my back and begin curling myself into the position.

At first, the new movement is okay, but I'm only twenty deep when it's fighting against me. My head pounds, the ache so bad I want to close my eyes.

I can't risk Laban's displeasure, but I'm unsure of how much longer I can do this. As I pull myself into another curl, my stomach cramps. I choke, sputter, turn, and vomit into the sandpit next to me.

"I did not say stop, recruit!" Laban shouts in my face.

Any soldier in Talionis would force a recruit to continue, even after being pushed so hard they threw up. And none more so than Laban Meritas. He's trained half of them, after all.

He turns on the hose again, drenching me. It soaks through my uniform to my skin. The warmth from the exercise evaporates as the icy water washes over me. It should be refreshing in the late-August heat. But it's cold. Too cold.

I shudder, but don't stop. I *can't* stop.

For minute after minute, until it feels like I've been here for hours, days.

I do my push-ups, crunches, burpees, and planks with shaking muscles ready to give out at any second, despite the intensity of my conditioning and training. The headache in the back of my eyes is blinding.

I moderate myself a little, but when Laban notices that I've slowed, he's in my face again, demanding a faster pace.

Sergeant Valarius arrives at some point, but my head hurts so badly I barely register his appearance.

"Averton was expected in weaponry training ten minutes ago," Sergeant Valarius says.

I finish the push-up I was doing, then drop into the sand.

The grittiness of the sand presses against my cheek, ingraining itself in my skin. I don't care. My chest rises and falls rapidly, my heart racing. The humid air wraps around my lungs like a thick blanket, making it nearly impossible to breathe.

I've been pushed before, pushed hard, made to be sick even, but this time feels different. Like my body might give out forever if I'm forced to continue a second longer.

"She's the one who chose to take a punishment for another recruit." Laban scoffs. "Her fault that she's missing a training the Commander demanded she be at."

"You know as well as I do that this has been long enough," Sergeant Valarius says.

Laban's nose twists into a sneer. "With a traitor like her, no punishment is ever long enough."

Part of me wonders who will win. The other part doesn't care. My eyes slide shut as my body quivers, both from the exertion and from the cold wetness of my uniform. Why am I so cold?

Laban grabs me by the back of my shirt and pulls me up. I don't resist or help. Let him do the hard work of getting me onto my feet. I need water, food, something to help my body function beyond this state of exhaustion and pain.

"Get to your next training, recruit."

"I need water," I rasp.

"You should have thought of that before inserting yourself into my disciplinary measures." Laban hisses in my face.

I stumble away from the pit. Maybe this is how they'll break me. By pushing my body so hard I can barely think, let alone stand and function.

Before I get to the weaponry training building, Sergeant Valarius materializes out of nowhere.

I blink, my eyes blurring, head swimming. Food. I need food. I don't think I ate much last night. Did I miss breakfast this morning?

Sergeant Valarius grabs my arm and pulls me away from the entrance of the building and into an alley.

"Eat this." He shoves a sandwich and a canteen of water at me.

I grab the canteen first, desperate for something to quell my thirst. I gulp it down greedily, choking myself.

He snatches the canteen away before I can guzzle the whole thing.

"Slow down. He pushed you too hard. And if you don't get your wits about you, you'll never survive the rest of your trainings today." He hands me back the canteen but doesn't let go at first. "Drink slowly. You know how to handle someone in this condition. Eat slowly. Get some strength, then get into your next training."

Sergeant Valarius disappears, and I almost wonder if he was even the one here.

How can he place such a dangerous device on the Sitreean Delegation's transport, and then less than twelve hours later, make sure I have enough food and sustenance to survive whatever training I have left for this day? Maybe he didn't actually do what Ark wanted. Even if he did, could it be for the same reason I'm trying to be a good Elite Recruit—to keep up a good front?

But none of my actions pose a threat to a country's national security.

My brain is in too much of a fog to make sense of the man.

For now, I'll eat his food, drink the water he provided, and then do what he said. Go back into my training.

If I don't collapse where I'm standing.

CHAPTER
TWENTY-NINE

The food helps my equilibrium, and the water clears my head a bit, although the headache behind my eyes remains. I'm supposed to go through a weaponry training track today with five other recruits. Most of them look green, if the way they're holding their weapons is any indication. But one of them catches my eye.

Arwen.

Her ponytail is cockeyed on her head with hair poking out from every angle, and she gnaws on her fingernail as she stares back at me.

She approaches. "I don't know why you did that, but thank you. I don't think I could have survived in the pit with Sergeant Meritas."

I start to nod, but the effort is enough to send my head swimming with pain. "It's fine." I sound terser than I mean to.

"You don't look so good," Arwen says hesitantly.

I rub my forehead. "We should get into our training before we end up in more trouble."

Arwen ducks her head sheepishly. That probably sounded like a slam. It wasn't intentional, but my head pounds too hard to rectify the situation.

The food didn't help nearly as much as I thought it would.

We pass through two sets of doors and into a range where other recruits are getting into position with their rifles. I reach for my weapon an instant before remembering it's not there. Corporal Sidon shakes his head at me and marks something on his screen. I don't have to see it to know I'll be starting training today at a deficit. The opposite of excelling as a recruit. Something I would care about more if my head wasn't throbbing.

Arwen shoots me several glances as she takes her own rifle from her back.

Bang! Bang-bang-bang!

The explosive sound of weapons being discharged echoes through the air, ringing in my ears. I haven't even put on protective ear coverings. I press my hands over my ears, but it doesn't help. The crack of the rifles sends shooting pain through my head. As though someone is pounding me with a hammer.

A wave of dizziness washes over me. I lean against a wall as blackness fills my vision.

"Um, sir?" Arwen's hesitant voice swells in the brief moment between guns firing.

Corporal Sidon strides over. "What is it, recruit?"

Through my blurring vision I see Arwen gesturing at me. "I don't think Recruit Averton is okay."

I want to argue, but that would require pushing myself away from the wall and trying to find words to speak. Both of which seem impossible.

"You look yellow, Averton." Corporal Sidon is directly in front of me now. "I don't need anyone being sick over my weapons."

The way the man talks about his guns as though they're his pride and joy has always struck me as strange.

"Go to the infirmary. Get something for whatever is going on." He waves a hand dismissively. "And try not to make a mess anywhere in my building."

"Yes, sir," I mumble.

I make my way from the building, bumping into walls and people on the way. A sluggish haze clings to me.

Pushing my body to its limit—far beyond its limit—is something I've done over and over again this past year.

The intense training as an Elite Recruit was worse than these past twenty-four hours of training.

So why would an hour, or however long it was, in the pit with Laban bring me to *this* point?

Did Sergeant Valarius lace the water I was drinking?

Would he do something like that? He's working with Cai, but I can't help the mistrust that's crept in after knowing how he aided Ark last night.

I exit the building, and the warmth of the day doesn't penetrate the growing cold deep within my bones. I shiver. The infirmary is a half mile from here.

I don't know how I'll make it five more *steps*. Let alone a half mile. *God, I don't feel good.*

I rest against the building and allow my eyes to drift close, one thought pulsing with every throb of pain behind my eyes. *I shouldn't feel like this.*

"Bria?" The sound of Kemena's voice is enough to make me crack one eye open. "Girl." She rushes to my side, and her arm comes around me.

"Hey," I say. Her face is blurry. Not a good sign.

"You need a medic." She gently navigates me away from the wall and leads me down the street.

Her steps are slow, probably from me putting so much weight on her. But each second that passes is worse than the one before.

We arrive at the infirmary, and Kemena demands a bed for me immediately. Even though she possesses no rank or title in the city, the nurse obeys.

I would too. Kemena isn't someone to mess with. Nika probably got her gumption from her sister. The thought would make me smile if it wasn't taking every ounce of my willpower to stay upright.

What feels like seconds later, I'm in a bed and surrounded by nurses and a medic. Their faces swim in and out of view, and their words sound distant.

I let my eyes drift shut, and as they close, I hear Kemena demanding answers. My chest warms as I succumb to unconsciousness. At least I'm not alone.

THIRTY

"Nerve agent . . . flushing her system . . . full recovery within eight to twelve hours . . ."

The disjointed phrases flutter through my mind, pulling me back to consciousness. I keep my eyes closed, not ready to be fully alert. And more than a little concerned by the phrases I do hear.

"How was she exposed to a *nerve agent?*" Kemena demands.

"Ma'am, I've told you more than I should have already—"

"Oh no. That is *not* how this is gonna go down." Kemena's voice is closer. A hand rests on my shoulder. "I want answers from you people. She could have *died!*"

The medic clears his throat.

I open my eyes.

"See." He points at me with the stylus in his hand. "She's already coming to."

Kemena glares at him for a long moment before turning her attention to me. She brushes my hair off my forehead, the gesture so maternal a longing for my mom wells up within me. Even though I just saw her two days ago. I think.

"Hey, girl. How you feeling?" Kemena's deep brown eyes hold concern and a fire that leaves me wondering how the poor medic survived being in her presence without succumbing to all of her demands.

I shift so I'm more in a seated position before responding. The headache is gone, and I'm no longer dizzy.

"I'm okay. How long was I out for?" I glance between Kemena and the medic.

The medic consults his screen. "Your friend brought you in three hours ago." His eyes find mine. "And it's a good thing she did. The nerve agent you ingested could have done long-term damage if you'd waited much longer."

My eyes widen. "Nerve agent? Ingested? What?" The questions fly from my mouth as my mind attempts to make sense of what he's saying.

He gives a furtive glance at Kemena, who settles herself onto the edge of my bed and gives him a look that says *just try to make me leave*. The poor medic seems done with the fight and turns back to me.

"Tell us what happened," Kemena says, her eyes pinned on the medic, who shrinks further into himself. "And we want the truth. None of the lies you be telling others about how this went down. Why did Bria get so sick?"

I glance at Kemena, thankful I have her here.

It makes sense that I was drugged. How else would I have ended up so completely messed up after the pit? But the fact that he's saying I ingested the drug is what's disturbing me, because the only person I ate or drank anything from today was Andor Valarius.

"Any day now," Kemena says, pulling me back to the present and to the medic, who's shifting nervously on his feet.

The man has faced soldiers, yet he looks nearly terrified of Kemena.

I'm still dazed from everything that's happened, and I couldn't insist upon answers the way she is.

The medic clears his throat. "I'm not sure what I'm at liberty—"

"I said we want the *truth*," Kemena interrupts, shaking her head. "And I don't really care what you're 'at liberty,'"—she puts quotes in the air around the words—"to discuss. Bria's life was in jeopardy.

You said yourself she got here just in time before any permanent damage was done. What happened to drug her and put her in that state? I need to know, and I need to know now. Sir."

The sir at the end seems comical, considering the fact I doubt Kemena cares about the man's authority.

He glances behind him at the door, then goes and shuts it.

Kemena crosses her arms over her chest and lifts an eyebrow at the man.

He clears his throat one more time, then pulls over a chair and settles into it.

"It doesn't make sense," he finally says. "She must have ingested the toxin somewhere in the past twenty-four hours, but no sooner than twelve hours ago."

I blink, almost shocked that this wasn't Sergeant Valarius's fault. I had pretty much given up the thought of trusting the man again. Yet here we are with the medic saying that it was impossible for the drink Sergeant Valarius just gave me to be what drugged me.

My mind clears.

It was *not* impossible for Demetrius Ark to drug me, however. Or any person at the party last night. And Sergeant Valarius *was* there. But I don't think it was him.

"What kind of drug was it?" Kemena asks.

"It's a drug that attacks your nervous system. About twelve to fifteen hours after it's been ingested, you'll begin feeling the effects." The words rush out of him like a confession. "First a light headache and drowsiness, then as you move forward, a blinding headache, until dizziness and vomiting begin. Once the person who took it passes out, it's only a matter of hours before the toxin can be stopped and the person treated. Otherwise, the dose could be fatal." He almost looks relieved once he's finished.

I stare at him. "Who did this to me?" I ask, knowing neither of them can give me an answer.

The medic looks almost frustrated, as though he wishes he had an answer. Like he's upset that this happened to me at all.

Which breaks my brain a little.

It doesn't help when people in Talionis seem to care. It confuses me more than anything. But the reality is, this man could be as much of a prisoner here as I am.

"I don't know," he says. "It's impossible for us to get a full understanding of what happened without finding out where the toxin originated from."

"What do you mean, where it originated from?" Kemena asks.

"Well . . ." He clears his throat again and shifts in his chair. "I've never seen a toxin like this in Talionis," he blurts out. "It appears to have come from a different location."

"Sitreea," I whisper as the certainty fills me.

But who from Sitreea would want me dead? It makes more sense to believe it was Demetrius Ark, or even Sergeant Valarius, than to think someone from the Sitreean delegation yesterday was attempting to murder me.

The medic leaves, and based on his candor, I assume there aren't any recording devices or cameras in this room, which might not be the best assumption. That entire thing could have been a major act. But part of me wants to assume I'm safe to communicate with Kemena.

"You look better than you did before," she says, taking my hand in hers. "You gave me quite a scare, girl."

I shake away my mental fuzziness and focus more on Kemena, after giving a quick glance around the room that further proves to me there aren't any cameras or devices in here. At least none that I can see. Still, I use the cloaking sequence Kiwi taught me just to be safe.

"How have you been doing with everything with Azarias?" I ask.

She snorts out a laugh. "Girl, I should be the one asking you how you're doing."

I offer a half-smile, but wait for her to respond. Despite going to the Ruins after Ark's threats toward Azarias, I haven't actually talked to Kemena about how it's impacted her.

She pinches the bridge of her nose and exhales slowly. "Being away from my duties is a risk. If Ark finds out, he'll ensure that his little minions hurt Azarias." She shakes her head. "But you know what? Azarias would want me here. And so, I'm going to honor that man by doing this, by being here right now, even if it terrifies me."

I look at her, unsure of what to say. "You and Azarias . . .?" I let the question hang in the air. We both know I'm trying to figure out if they ever admitted feelings to each other.

She grunts.

I wait for an answer.

"It was always complicated with us," she says. "I never wanted to fall for him, and I think he fought falling for me just as hard. Which was dumb. I'm amazing." She gives me a cheeky wink, and I chuckle.

"But he's a good man. A better man than any I've ever known." She breathes out a deep sigh. "And the more we worked together, the more I saw how determined he was to help me find my sister, the more I started to care about him." She gazes up at the ceiling before looking at me again. "And I wish I had told him that. God knows I wish I had told him that."

I watch her, understanding. It took a while for me to acknowledge my feelings for Matthias. It took me nearly losing him to tell him I cared. The time in that abandoned warehouse, telling him I cared about him, him taking me in his arms, pressing his forehead against mine, will forever be imprinted on my heart.

It feels like an eternity ago.

"It's hard to care when so much could go wrong," I say.

Kemena nods. "Yeah, girl. That's a true enough statement."

She leans over and rests her hand on my shin. "But you know what? Fear can force us to do things we will forever regret, because it can keep us from the action God is calling us to take. Then there are times when we can no longer take that action. And it all starts when we imagine everything depends on us. That all of the planning, all of the outcome is our responsibility. But the reality is, we can't control everything. And fear will keep us from all God has for us. I'm seeing that more and more clearly."

I sit silently for a long moment. "Ark sees every person I care about as leverage. I want Matthias close, but I'm so scared if I don't push him away, he'll end up hurt because of me."

"Girl, please. You will hurt that boy so much more if you push him away," she says. "He obviously loves you."

My breath leaves my lungs in a whoosh. I almost feel like I've been drugged again as I gawk at Kemena, trying to figure out what to say. No responses come to mind.

I just keep staring, blinking at her.

"It's dangerous," I say when Kemena doesn't rescue me by filling the silence.

"Yeah, there's danger in life every single day," she says. "That's something I'm learning more and more. But we can decide if that danger will push us to trust God more, or if that danger will keep us from all God has for us. Because those are our two options. Living in fear or embracing the fullness of what God has for us, despite the fear, despite the potential loss. Knowing that trusting Him and following His leading, wherever it may go, it's worth it. Even unto death."

I stare at this woman in front of me and hear truth in her words that I can't deny. And at the same time, a sort of desperation. A hope that she'll be able to live them out herself.

CHAPTER
THIRTY-ONE

I bolt upright in bed, drenched in sweat, heart pounding.

My breath comes in short bursts as I yank myself away from my nightmare. A nightmare I wasn't sure I'd escape from. When I close my eyes, I see it again.

Matthias shot. Not moving. Lying on the ground. Laban standing nearby.

The nightmare is terrifying because it was real.

Laban *did* shoot Matthias when we were running, trying to get to Eryndale. At the time, I didn't know they were training bullets.

I had just admitted to Matthias that I cared about him, and then he was gunned down before my very eyes.

I swing my legs out of bed, trying to shake the memory, but all that shakes are my hands.

The medic said the toxin is no longer a threat to my system, but a residual effect could be nightmares until my body has completely flushed it out. Since I felt *physically* okay for the rest of the day after leaving the infirmary, I didn't think much of it. Which seems to have been a mistake.

I go to the bathroom and get a cup of water. The cold liquid soothes my parched throat but doesn't wash away the memories of that day.

I hear screams, shots, the cries of soldiers and recruits going down.

Then the part that makes me almost hate myself is the memory of me ignoring Matthias and running after Storm.

I wanted to save Storm. To make sure she was okay. But she was in Laban's hands already, taken off in a transport.

Instead of checking on Matthias, I raced to save her.

Which was a completely impossible task.

What was I thinking?

I slam my fist into the sink, angry with myself and, at the same time, relieved the bullets that pounded Matthias's body were training bullets.

Still, memories continue to haunt me when I lie back down. I try not to think of the things I did wrong, but I can't stop myself.

I get up and pace the length of my room, wringing my hands together. The toxin-infused nightmare is the worst side effect of them all. I sink onto my bed and drop my head into my hands.

Maybe I can go see someone. I don't want to be alone. I check the time on my band and dismiss the idea. It's after 0200. Even if I went to see Kemena or Cai or Nika and Mom, I doubt any of them would be awake.

And the person I really want to see is Matthias.

I force myself to lie down again. Control my breathing. I need sleep. In just a few hours, I'm expected in Warfare Strategies. My task is to strategize plans for recruits going through a new set of scenarios using intel from the device Sergeant Valarius planted on the Sitreean transport. Since these scenarios are new, I can manipulate them more easily without others finding out. I need to be alert enough to use the code Kiwi and Ari gave me.

Thoughts of Ari ricochet me back to several weeks ago. My sleep-fogged brain viciously replays images of her, pale as death, life bleeding out of her. Like another nightmare, even though I'm not sleeping. Is this the toxin too?

Ari was shot with real bullets while helping me aid Callypso. A position we were in because I first asked her to help me get intel on what was happening with Storm and Cai. It doesn't matter that Cai says he had a part in the attack that day. At the moment, it all feels like my fault.

I grip my hands in my hair until my scalp screams in pain, but I don't relinquish the hold.

Over and over again, I have done things that have led to people dying and almost dying.

First Ezri, then Cade. And Ava. I couldn't save her. People tell me these things aren't really my fault. That I was a kid with Ezri. Cade made his decision. Ava's death is the result of the evil of Talionis.

But all I can see is my own culpability. That I am to blame, at least in part, for so many of these things.

I can't bear to think of losing someone else.

The clock on the wall reads 0230. The alarm on my band will go off in two and a half hours to wake me for my training.

God, help me! The desperate prayer rips from my heart. *I can't do this alone.*

I turn onto my side, curling into myself. New thoughts flood my mind.

Kemena, Kiwi, and I are making a difference and saving kids.

Ari, Nika, and Mom are searching for ways to bring together the scouts we can trust in an effort to mount an attack against Ark.

Kiwi will introduce me to the Resistance in the next few days so we can work with them to do more within the city.

Cai is working on a plan in the tunnels under the city.

And then there's Antonio, the Sitreean Minister of Defense. He might be someone we can trust. A resource who has enough power to actually stop Ark.

You're not alone. The thought is mine and yet outside of me at the same time.

I release a slow breath and close my eyes.

The fight isn't over. And there's still work to do.

I won't let my nightmares keep me from doing what's in front of me.

CHAPTER
THIRTY-TWO

T he small tech device filled with code that Kiwi gave me to manipulate scenarios weighs down my pocket like a boulder as I enter the room I'll be working in for the next two hours. I tap on the screen in front of me, and a map takes over the entire surface area of the table. The map of Sitreea and its neighboring countries. Every warfare scenario is designed to hit a different element of Sitreea, and now we're creating scenarios to attack the countries surrounding Ark's homeland so he can expand its borders.

Major Vasco enters, eyes fixed on me. He has no reason to trust me, and despite the fact that I've seen things in the plans we've made that he apparently missed, I don't think any of it's enough to garner trust between the two of us.

Which means finding a time to link the device in my pocket to this scenario will be much harder than I'd like it to be.

I stick my hands in my pockets, hoping it looks like a casual posture, and study the map, while also subtly hunting for an inconspicuous place to attach the magnetic device to the table. According to Kiwi, that's all that needs to happen for it to link, since this table is a tech hub for the scenario planning. Then I'll be able to manipulate the scenarios on my screen or when I'm alone in a room. My hands are slick with sweat.

"What are we looking at?" Major Vasco asks, his terse voice further proof he's watching every move I make.

I remove my hands from my pockets and wipe them on my pants. "You want invasion tactics for DuPont, right?"

He gives one curt nod. "Yes, as stated in your briefing, we need tactics to invade the eastern border. The country is in upheaval. Has been ever since the end of the War of Power. We can leverage that to our advantage."

I turn to him. "I didn't get any information on that."

"Then you didn't read your briefing fully."

"Well, I thought we were working on scenarios using the device Sergeant Valarius planted on the Sitreean transport," I say with a touch of defensiveness, since he's right. I *didn't* fully read my briefing. I've been too concerned about making sure I can link the device. "But I saw that the working class took down the monarchy within the first year of their rule."

"Oh, good. You read some of it." Major Vasco settles himself into a chair across the table from me. "So, with a kingdom in disarray, what are elements we can use to further fracture the current ruling party's hold on the country?" He speaks as though he's not talking about people or lives, but rather some pawn in a game.

My blood pressure rises. It's not right.

Yet, when I step back, I can see it the way he does. Analytically. As though I can dissect the entire thing and see where the holes could be. The problems within the country of DuPont on the border of Sitreea.

I slip my right hand back into my pocket and curl my fingers around the device. The more I can see this like Major Vasco, the better I'll be able to sabotage things without him realizing it.

I allow the analytics to filter through so I can more clearly see everything going on within the territory.

Military groups rioting. Citizens taking over the homes of those who were in power or who were wealthy and held positions of influence. Unrest in every corner of the region.

Unrest that could be leveraged and allow mere teenagers the

opportunity to take over a country if they are directed correctly and if their movements are strategic enough.

When I look up again, I find Major Vasco studying me. "You see it too," he says.

I nod, while carefully slipping the device from my pocket and concealing it in my fist.

"So, if we put recruits through a training, a simulation of DuPont, what would you say to do?"

I focus on the map and watch Major Vasco out of the side of my eye. I squeeze the device in my right hand and the button clicks. Then I rest my hands against the edge of the table, flattening my hand over the device.

My pulse pounds in my neck, but I lay out what I'm sure Major Vasco has already seen. "We need to make everything we do there look as though it's done by either the nobility that the citizens hate or by the citizens themselves. It depends on which area we're marking."

"Good. Continue," he demands.

The device under my hand vibrates softly. Which is exactly what Kiwi said it would do. "If we can hit this train disguised as citizens, and then attack this area as though we're nobility attempting to take back what was theirs"—I point to various places on the map with my left hand as I speak—"then it will cause the citizens of DuPont to believe that all of it has been orchestrated by enemies within their own country. No one will sense anything different. It will drive the country deeper into the chaos already stirring within its borders." Somehow the words make sense, despite my hyperawareness of the device still vibrating under my hand.

Major Vasco nods. "That was my thought as well." A hint of respect tinges his tone. The first I've heard since I've been back.

He points out another area of DuPont and talks through a scenario he's building.

The vibration stops. Everything has linked. I slip my hand from the table and drop the device back into my pocket.

I force myself to focus on Major Vasco's words and to keep my eyes locked on the map he's shifting to show the capital of DuPont.

Even though all I want to do is study Major Vasco to see if he noticed what I just did.

I sneak a glance at him. He's intent on drawing out an attack plan. I don't think he suspects anything.

A thrill of relief and excitement washes through me, and I suppress a smile. I did it.

Now I need to stay engaged in this prep for the next hour. Later, I'll find ways to sabotage the scenarios and prepare recruits to expose Ark. Without Ark or the recruits realizing that's what they're doing.

For the next hour, we strategize how we can break down DuPont from the inside out. The ways we can use the fractured country to divide itself further and be prepared for Ark's full invasion to take it over.

An invasion that each side might even welcome.

Ark will come in offering the nobility the help they've been desperate for and the citizens the power they long for. He'll give everyone what they want. None of them will realize that the country went into such dark turmoil because of the very man they'll be prepared to follow.

But it won't go according to his plan. Not if I can help it.

Again, a small thrill goes through me. I linked the device. We have backdoor access to the scenarios. If the worst happens and we can't stop Ark on North American soil, we'll stop him once he's in Sitreea.

CHAPTER

THIRTY-THREE

For the next two days, I work on the scenarios with Major Vasco with a renewed vigor. I begin to see ways I can subtly expose Ark's hand. Hopefully, when all the different attacks are happening simultaneously, it'll be enough to stop what he's doing.

Major Vasco seems pleased with my enthusiasm to work on the scenarios alongside him, and he even praises some of my recommended shifts. I can only hope and pray they're discreet enough to keep him from understanding what I'm trying to accomplish.

In the past forty-eight hours, I haven't had a chance to go to the Ruins or see Kemena. The focus of finding ways to attack Ark's plans has kept my mind occupied. But I'm excited when I receive an encrypted message from Kiwi to meet him between dinner and my nighttime chores.

It's finally time for me to be introduced to the Resistance.

There's been so much going on this week, the days have passed in a blur. Still, it's vital we involve the Resistance so we can continue our work of smuggling kids to the Ruins. And maybe we can join them in their careful sabotage within the city.

I follow the route Kiwi sent me and find myself in an area of Talionis with several pre-Demise buildings. The structures aren't as stable, and when I round a bend, I catch sight of a recruit ducking through a low hole in the wall of the building on the right.

Kiwi joins me. "Ready for this?"

I nod, even as confidence and uncertainty war within me. Nika and Mom need help in the Ruins, but Keesia will only work with us if we bring in the whole Resistance. Which is a lot of people to trust.

Kiwi claps his hands together. "Great. Let's do this."

"Wait." I hold out an arm to stop him from going forward. "What about my band?"

"Already taken care of." With that, he heads to the hole the recruit crawled through.

I glance around. No one's in sight. I follow Kiwi through the hole.

When I come up on the other side, hands instantly grab my arms. I'm pressed against the wall, but I don't fight.

My eyes adjust to the semidarkness, and I find a group of fifteen recruits crammed in the room. All of them stare at me with wide eyes and look like they're ready to tear me apart if I so much as breathe wrong. All of them except for Arwen and Kiwi.

"Averton." Asher steps into my view and doesn't tell the two recruits holding me against the wall to release their grip.

I stay still. "You're trying to stop Ark."

He comes closer until he's only inches from my face. "What we're doing here is none of your concern, Averton." He spews the words in my face.

"Come on, man," Kiwi says, trying to step between us. "I told you, we can trust her."

Asher squints at me, his face twisting in derision, and then he turns on his heel to face the other recruits. "What do you guys think? Do we trust her?" He gestures back toward me. "A turncoat, someone who's working alongside our enemies?"

Kiwi holds up his hands. "Dude. Are you seriously going to just believe the narrative Ark wants you to believe?"

Asher scowls at Kiwi. "She's not trustworthy."

Keesia steps forward hesitantly. "She's helping kids." She fidgets with the sleeve of her uniform. "I'm the reason Kiwi brought her here."

"She helped me," Arwen says, casting a appreciative smile in my direction. "She took my punishment in the pit."

Some of the other recruits look a little more ready to accept me. Even those holding me against the wall loosen their grip a bit.

But then I look back at Asher, who's clearly the one in charge. His face is still a hard, angry mask.

"Why I should I believe that?" He looks around the room. "The reason we haven't been caught is because we're careful. If nothing else, Bria Averton is a huge liability."

I straighten, which is enough movement to have the recruits restraining me tighten their grip once again. I ignore them as I focus on Asher. "This isn't about me. Kiwi and I have been smuggling kids to the Ruins, and we need help."

"Yeah," Kiwi jumps in. "We've gotten six kids out there so far. The soldiers think they've been eliminated, but they're safe. And we need more assets out there to help keep them safe."

Asher crosses his arms. "We have limited resources as it is. And she"—he jabs a finger at me—"is a liability."

My stomach drops. I didn't expect this to go this way.

"Well, I'm going to keep helping her," Kiwi's voice holds an annoyed twinge, which is unusual for him. "Who here wants to protect the youngest and weakest under Ark's cruel treatment?"

A few in the room raise their hands, including Arwen and Keesia, who keeps giving furtive glances at Asher.

Guess I'm not the only one who thought this would go differently.

"Fine," Asher says. "This is not a tyranny. Every person in the Resistance can make his or her own choice." He takes a moment to look at the four people who agreed to help me and Kiwi. "But don't say I didn't warn you that she's dangerous."

I push off the two recruits holding me. "I will do whatever it takes to bring down Demetrius Ark."

Asher scowls. "I don't trust you." He points at the hole I crawled through. "Get out."

I flinch, somewhere between shocked and insulted.

"I'll meet up with you tonight," Kiwi says.

I give a curt nod, then leave. A board slides into place as soon as I'm clear of the opening.

I blow out a long breath. At least four members of the Resistance are ready to help. And tonight, I'll meet up with Kiwi to figure out the logistics.

Still, I'm more disappointed than I expected to be that I won't be able to help the Resistance with the work they're doing in the city.

Kemena and I are working together for the tailors today, so hopefully I can let her know about the meeting with Kiwi tonight.

Uh-oh. The tailors.

I check my band and gasp. I'm already late for my chores with Sampta and Presidia. And it'll take me at least five minutes to get there from here. I take off at a run, ignoring the startled glances of soldiers, recruits, and workers as I race by them.

My rifle bumps a steady rhythm on my back as I swerve around people and buildings and toward the tailors'. Maybe Sampta and Presidia won't notice I'm late. They're not nearly as particular as Mandeville is about punctuality.

The building looms before me. I swipe an arm over my forehead to clear the sweat and slow my pace. No need to enter out of breath and give myself away.

I pass a sentry at the entrance who looks down her nose at me. She knows I'm late.

Which means Sampta and Presidia probably do as well.

I throw my shoulders back and head toward the main room the two sisters use. Might as well get the lecture over with. I open the door and stop short.

Sampta and Presidia are talking animatedly with Kemena. They don't even notice my entrance.

Kemena is facing the door, and she catches my eye. She darts a glance toward the laundry room, and I take it as my signal to head there.

I gently set my rifle on the gun rack by the door and move as quickly and quietly as possible to the room, picking up bits of the conversation. The two sisters are talking over each other as they exclaim about Kemena's brilliant idea. I almost pause to find out *what* her idea was, but that would make it clear I haven't been around for the past ten minutes.

So, I slip into the laundry room and begin my chores. Two minutes later, the three women enter.

Sampta sniffs. "You've made very little progress, recruit."

"More like *no* progress, sister," Presidia chimes in.

The women simultaneously cross their arms over their chests and tilt their chins into the air.

Before I can come up with a response that will appease them—and keep me from losing my rifle for being late—Kemena places a hand on each of their arms.

"She was likely as enraptured with our conversation as we were, ladies," Kemena says smoothly.

The sisters instantly relax.

"No doubt you are right, Kemena. No doubt," Presidia says.

My jaw almost drops. I've never seen *anyone* put the sisters at ease. Whatever Kemena said must have made an impression. Which only serves to increase my curiosity.

"Bria and I will have this work done in no time. Right, Bria?" Kemena says as she comes to stand next to me.

I nod, trying my best not to straight up ask what they were talking about.

"We should go work on the new design," Sampta says.

Presidia instantly agrees, and the two women turn to leave. They pause.

"Kemena, do you want to join us?" Presidia asks.

Now my jaw *does* drop open. I stare between Kemena and the tailors. What happened in that conversation?

Kemena shakes her head. "As much as I would love to, Bria and I have a lot of work to do here. Perhaps later we can continue our discussion and you can show me the new design?"

"Absolutely," Sampta and Presidia say together.

With that, they leave the room in an exhilarated frenzy.

I wait a full minute to be sure they're out of earshot, then turn to Kemena. "What was *that* about?"

She's folding clean uniforms. "Nothing, really. I just started engaging them in conversation about their designs because you were late. I figured you had a reason and thought the best solution would be to distract them."

I join her in sorting and folding the clean uniforms. "But they're so . . . excited. And they listened to you. They *never* do that."

Kemena chuckles. "I made up some ridiculous idea of creating a gown that used pre-Demise styles interwoven with tech so it glows in low light." She picks up another shirt. "It wasn't even my idea. While I was in Eryndale, Jordyn told me about a gown Catori was wearing the first time Jordyn saw her. It was the only thing I could think of."

I shake my head. "Guess it worked."

"It did." Kemena tosses a shirt at me. "But my question is, where were *you*?"

Even though Ari assured me the laundry room was safe from any tech, I still give a furtive glance around the room. Apparently Sampta and Presidia regularly insist on their space being cleared of any cameras or audio monitoring, since they don't want anyone else to discover their *secrets*. I'm not sure *why* Ark agreed to it, or if he even knows. To be safe, I enable to cloaking feature on my band as well.

I sigh and tell her about the meeting with the Resistance.

"At least a few of them are willing to help," Kemena says when I finish. "Maybe more will join over time."

"Maybe."

We lapse into silence. There's more I want to tell her, more to catch her up on with what I've been doing in Warfare Strategies, but I decide to wait until later. She'll meet me and Kiwi in the tunnels tonight, and it's safer discussing my scenario sabotage down there.

THIRTY-FOUR

I leave the tailors' and make my way to the Dining Hall for dinner. Working with Kemena was nice, but my mind swirls with everything that's happened.

In all my fears about bringing the Resistance into what we're doing, it never occurred to me they wouldn't want to be involved. How much have we inadvertently exposed by sharing just a snippet of what we're doing with Asher and the others who won't help us? Did we put the entire operation in the Ruins in danger?

I round a bend, head down, lost in thought.

"Ah, look at what we have here." Shay's voice grabs my attention and brings me to a halt.

The thought of being anywhere near my former neighbor makes me tired. Her clear alliance with Talionis, how she's given over to everything they want, is the last thing I want to deal with.

She stands several yards away. Her drones hover around her like a pack of dogs surrounding their leader. Her voice has an eerie, technical element to it, echoing with each word she says. As though it's being magnified through some technology.

A small group of young recruits cower in front of her, and I recognize Sam. Despite our best efforts to smuggle kids out of here, it takes time. We have to move slowly, but seeing them shaking in fear as they salute Shay—anger burns in me.

Her various cyborg parts glint in the setting sun, and she appears to be loving their fear. Just like Laban.

She turns to her drones and taps something on her wrist. Within seconds, every one of them has a gun aimed at one of the kids. She's taunting them with her ability to destroy them. And I won't stand for it.

I race forward and throw myself between the kids and Shay.

All the drones zero in on me at the threat to their master. I'm not holding my gun. Aiming a worthless weapon at this girl who has real weapons armed and ready to fire would be ludicrous. But I refuse to allow her to torment kids.

"Ah, Bria," she says. "Getting in the way, as usual." Her singsongy voice turns my stomach. "It's been a while since we've seen each other, old friend."

I glare at her. "We were never friends."

A muscle ticks in her cheek. "True enough. You were always getting into trouble by not listening when you needed to."

She turns to the kids as though this is a perfect opportunity to lecture on the merits of her superiority. "Bria is a cautionary tale, children." Her red hair billows behind her, unhindered by a hair tie. "We grew up together, you know. Arrived in Talionis together. Look at her now. Still a recruit, and I'm an elite soldier of this incredible city." She leans forward until she's eye level with Sam. "And you could be like me . . . or like her. Untrusted and a *traitor*."

The kids frantically look between the two of us.

"Let them go," I say. "They're late for dinner as it is."

Shay rolls her eyes. "What are you, little Miss Timekeeper? You're late as well, and it doesn't seem to be hurting you any. If you can be late, why shouldn't I keep these precious little ones from attending dinner on time?"

"Let them go," I repeat through gritted teeth.

"I don't want to," she responds. Something on her hand beeps, and she glances down. "But"—she sighs dramatically—"duty calls, so off with you, my little friends. And try not to get in my way again."

With that, she saunters away, her drones buzzing around her.

I lead the kids in the opposite direction and toward the Dining Hall, heart still pounding fear and anger. Sam slips his small hand into mine.

The gesture shocks me, but I hold his hand. At least he trusts me. A few of the other kids were eyeing me warily, but now that Sam's holding my hand, they seem more relaxed.

Once we're in the Dining Hall, I help the youngest kids get some food and settle at the table with Storm. She greets everyone cheerfully, but a question darkens her eyes. One she doesn't ask. Instead, she dives into a conversation about her favorite part of her day.

Keesia joins our table and offers me a smile. At least she's in this with me now. We'll get as many of these kids as possible to the Ruins. Protect them until we can get them away from Ark forever.

Storm laughs, and my stomach clenches. She knows we're smuggling kids to the Ruins—she's the reason the kids have trusted us enough to go with us.

If only I could get her out of here too.

I force myself to eat the meatloaf and potatoes the cooks made today, but it tastes as good to me as gruel.

KEMENA, KIWI, AND KEESIA ARE ALREADY IN THE TUNNELS WAITING WHEN I arrive, and I suddenly wish Matthias was here too. I miss him.

"Good, you're here," Kiwi says when I reach them. "Cai wants to see us."

"What? Why?" I ask. I'm happy to see Cai, but it's been weeks since we've met with him.

Kiwi shrugs. "I don't know. But we should go."

We silently weave our way through the tunnels until we come to a sealed door.

"Do you have the code?" I ask.

"No." Kiwi pulls out a screen, but before he can do anything with it, Sergeant Valarius emerges from the shadows.

Keesia yelps, eyes wide. I don't blame her.

"I do." Sergeant Valarius steps in front of the door and punches in the code.

As he's typing in the code, Kemena whispers to Keesia that Sergeant Valarius is trustworthy. Which I suppose is true, but I'm not ready to believe it fully. From the look on Keesia's face, she's not sure either.

The door opens, and Sergeant Valarius steps aside for us to enter.

I lead the way into the room and find it transformed from how it looked when I was here a month ago.

Kiwi has set up an entire control center. Screens line one wall, with a control panel table so big it crowds the space in front of the screens. Another smaller table is off to the side with papers filling it, same as the last time we were out here. The screens show various areas in Talionis.

"Wow," I say, turning to Kiwi. "How did you get all of this down here?"

"Sergeant Valarius helped," he says.

Cai turns from where he's standing over the control panel table. "I'm glad you're here. Andor has told me of several developments since the Sitreean delegation arrived, and I wanted to talk with all of you." His eyes narrow as he focuses on Keesia. "I don't believe we've met."

I quickly introduce Keesia and tell Cai about how she'll be helping Mom and Nika in the Ruins soon.

"We might need to postpone that." Cai turns back to the control panel before I can ask him why.

A moment later, Mom and Nika are facing us from the center of the screens.

After brief introductions and greetings, Cai quickly brings things back to order.

"Lily, can you please brief everyone on what Josiah, Kassre, and Hosea are working on?" Cai asks.

As soon as the question is out of Cai's mouth, my mind leaps back to when Thaddeus told me my dad—Josiah—, Hosea—the somewhat grouchy man who first introduced us to Catori—, and

Kassre—the husband of Emmi DeFort who housed us while we were in Eryndale—were working on a top secret mission. I'd forgotten about it.

"Of course." Mom offers a small smile before explaining how my dad, Kassre, Hosea, and Bill and Paul are working to break through one of the old tunnels near the river outside of the wall surrounding Talionis.

Apparently, a very small group is involved, but according to recent communication between Thaddeus and Cai, it's coming along. If all goes according to plan, they'll infiltrate the city through this tunnel and conduct a surprise attack. But they need more time to get everything in place.

My mind is swimming by the time Mom and Cai finish giving the overview.

"But why do we need to stop bringing kids to the Ruins?" I ask.

"Because I need Nika and Lily to disrupt everything the soldiers do in the Ruins. It's crucial in order for Josiah and Kassre to work undetected. If the soldiers are afraid of the Ruins and the threats there, they won't notice the work being done."

The explanation makes sense, but I don't like it. I share what happened today with Shay and the group of kids. "We can't let them stay and be tormented by people like her."

"I agree," Kemena says. "What if we do both? Keesia can go out to the Ruins to help with the kids as planned, and we could bring another recruit or two out there as well. Maybe the other members of the Resistance who are willing to help us."

Kiwi and Keesia look at each other.

"What?" I ask, dreading the answer already.

"Only Arwen is still willing to help," Kiwi says. "The others who originally said they would changed their minds after Asher talked to them once you left."

I scrub my hands over my face, exasperated. "Well, that's great."

"If you can get Keesia out here," Nika says, "that should help us for now. I don't like the idea of leaving kids in Talionis if we don't have to."

We discuss logistics of what Kiwi will need to do to eliminate Keesia from the servers.

"You should wait," Sergeant Valarius says. "Since the delegation was here a few days ago, no one will eliminate a recruit. Even though Sitreea doesn't know what Ark's doing here, Ark insists on no eliminations until at least a week after a visit. He gets more paranoid and doesn't want a single asset wasted."

The news is helpful but frustrating. I want to bring kids out to the Ruins tonight. Not wait a week.

But everyone agrees to play it safe for now.

Kemena clears her throat. "Speaking of the delegations visit . . ." She spears me with a pointed look.

I hesitate for an instant, then briefly share about the toxin poisoning and needing to be brought to the infirmary. Kemena fills in details I leave out. Like how life-threatening the entire event was.

By the time we're done, everyone else is staring at us in shock.

Cai's the first to recover. He focuses on Sergeant Valarius. "Can you determine who tried to poison her?"

Sergeant Valarius inclines his head. "I'll look into it."

Mom, Nika, and Kiwi caution me to be careful and check to make sure I'm feeling okay. The last thing I want to do is think about the poisoning. Not knowing who tried to kill me, or why, is unnerving.

I'm grateful when Cai shifts the conversation by asking me for an update on Warfare Strategies. At least I'm able to share one piece of good news.

Cai pushes his sleeves up, revealing his *Honor God* tattoo. Despite the turmoil of everything going on, the phrase comforts me.

"We're making good progress," he says. "I know not everything we've discussed tonight is what you all wanted to hear. But I'm proud of all of you." He looks first at Nika and Mom on the screens, then at those of us crammed in the room. "Evil people will always attempt to hold us back from what God has for us to do. We must be brave. We must be strong. We must fight, even when we are afraid. We must stand up and be counted among those who are willing to step in and do what others were unwilling to do because of fear." His gaze collides with mine. "And in it all, we must do it in God's timing. Not our own."

It always amazes me how Cai can read me. I don't want to wait. I want to act *tonight*. But he's right. Waiting is necessary.

For now.

CHAPTER
THIRTY-FIVE

Today I'm entering an obstacle course that's a hybrid of weaponry training and physical conditioning. The course will test us on both our weaponry skills and our ability to navigate the obstacle course. They've had some of these before. The first time I experienced one was in a physical conditioning training where hidden gunmen waited on edges of a field we had to race across. It was there that I realized my aptitude for getting through dangerous scenarios.

Every team that crossed the field suffered injury from the training bullets.

Every team except for mine.

I saw the way to go, and I got my entire team through. It ended up being a problem, because it proved to the soldiers that I was everything they had hoped I would be. A recruit with skill they could manipulate and use.

But that's also what allowed me to meet Cai. Because not long after, I got sentenced to the Ruins for still failing to comply with everything they wanted me to do.

I'm grouped with a team of five other recruits, and we're suited up to prepare for the obstacle course race. We're given weapons and equipped with everything we will need. Even our weapons have training bullets to act as a punishment for any of the soldiers who get shot.

At the end of the day, no one wins.

I stand to the back of my team and allow Asher to lead. After our encounter last week, it will take a miracle to get him to trust me.

He has an attitude the size of the entire city of Talionis and clearly doesn't want to be here. Yet he's strong, able-bodied, and, despite his attitude, he usually submits to what the soldiers demand of him. Probably because he doesn't want to bring any undue attention to himself or the Resistance.

Kiwi told me Asher grew up on a farm, and all he wants is to get back there. Apparently not a Resistance meeting goes by where Asher doesn't share at least one story about his family. And he encourages the members of the Resistance to share as well. Says it will help them remember what they're fighting for.

As frustrated as I am that he won't allow me to be part of the Resistance, I can't help but respect the guy a little.

"And you." Asher points at me. "Stay out of the way, and we won't have any problems."

I hold up my hands. "I don't have any issues with you."

He comes closer until we're inches apart. I want to push him away, give myself a little more space, but I don't.

"Well, I've got an issue with you," he growls. "You get out of this place only to come back? What kind of traitor are you? Working with them now to do something I know will destroy everyone here?"

I glance at the nearby soldier, Corporal Homer. He's eyeing us as though he's trying to decide if he should intervene.

"We're on the same side," I say, exasperated that nothing I've said or done has mattered. Even Kiwi and Arwen's endorsements of me haven't made a difference.

Asher's face contorts into a scowl. "Yeah, right. I'll never be on the same side as anyone who does a lick of stuff for this place."

I shrug. "Fine. But you know as well as I do that you'll get every kid on our team in trouble if you don't back off and do what they want. So suck up your issues and actually run this race and get these kids through. Okay?"

C.J. MILACCI

"Hey, we're not all kids," Kiwi says as he tries to get his vest on and drops one of his pistols.

Asher and I share a look that would almost move us from hostile enemies to friends, but he quickly backs off. He picks up Kiwi's pistol and shoves it at him.

Asher faces the group. "All right. I don't like her, but she's right. We gotta work together to get through this. You hear that?"

The four other recruits with us nod.

Other than Kiwi, I don't know the others, and they look young. Not more than fifteen years old. Kiwi, Asher, and I are definitely the oldest.

We take our place at the starting line along with the seven other teams racing.

"Listen up." Sergeant Valarius stands to the side, arms crossed over his broad chest, his taunt scar emphasizing his frown. "You'll be running through this course consecutively, but each team will be timed. The lowest ranking team will receive garbage duty tomorrow and will be stripped of their rifles. Understood?"

"Sir, yes, sir!" I chant with the rest of the recruits.

"Good. Teams will go through every five minutes. Team 1 will go first."

The team steps up.

"There are elements of physical conditioning where you will recognize parts of obstacle courses you've raced before, but there will be hostiles throughout." He paces in front of the teams. "The training arena has been redesigned to make different obstacles look like elements of towns and villages to better acclimate you to what it would be like to face enemy combatants in dangerous territory. No matter how strenuous the physical conditioning challenges you face, make sure there is always someone on guard to protect your team from hostiles."

"Team 1, prepare." He gives Team 1 fifteen minutes, then lifts a pistol in the air. "Three, two . . ." The pistol shoots off at one, and the team sprints forward.

I don't recognize anyone, but a tall black kid with gangly limbs and a serious face, has taken the lead. The team disappears around a bend. Not long afterward, we hear the staccato shooting of machine guns, the pop of rifle fire, and the screams of recruits taking cover.

They can't be that far away, and they're already hitting enemy combatants.

Team 2 takes off five minutes later.

Our team is next.

I put my hand on Asher's arm. "You'll have to trust me for this. These kids don't deserve to get hurt."

His nostrils flare, and he gives a pointed look at my hand. I drop it.

"I don't trust you," he says.

I tilt my head in acknowledgment and wait him out.

"But we'll work together on this. *Only* this. Understood?"

I nod once.

A glance at my band tells me we'll be starting in just a few minutes.

Matthias jogs over.

"Hey," he says. "Sorry I'm late. I got added to this team."

The focus I felt an instant ago vanishes. It's only been a week since I've seen him, but I've missed Matthias.

"Hey, man." Asher claps Matthias on the back. "Glad to have another one I can trust on my side." He gives me a sideways glare.

"Why do you trust him and not me?" I ask, feeling a bit like Nika as I ask so bluntly. I wish she was here with me now. She would not for a second put up with Asher and his frustrating ego and lack of understanding of what's actually going on.

Matthias steps between us. "Whoa, whoa. I can vouch for her. Bria's wonderful."

The way he says the words simultaneously makes my insides turn to mush and annoys me. Especially since Asher's eyes no longer hold open hostility as watches me.

Yes, I'm working with Major Vasco, but everything I've done since being captured has been with the ultimate goal of stopping Ark. And it bothers me that Asher might just believe Matthias at his word and not see all the work I've done, even though Kiwi and I *showed* him evidence of the kids we've saved.

I grit my teeth. "Let's get this over with."

We step up to the starting line and prepare to take off.

Sergeant Valarius counts down. The gun fires. I race forward.

Matthias is on my heels as we enter the course, like he's assigned himself as my personal bodyguard. He never gives me more than a few feet of distance, his gun at the ready.

When the first pops of fire begin, I flash back to my nightmare, to the moment Laban shot Matthias with training bullets.

Panic grips me.

"Why are you here?" I hiss at him. "Please go back. Get out of here."

He eyes me quizzically. "We both know I can't do that."

I swallow hard. "Just be careful."

I don't know if I can get through this course if Matthias is in it with me, and I need to protect these kids from getting shot.

We take cover by a building, Matthias pressed against my shoulder. I can't move because one kid is on my other side, and Asher, Kiwi, and the other two kids crowd on the other side of Matthias.

"All right," Asher says, taking charge. "We'll find places we can stay low and get through this. Only fire your weapons as necessary."

"Wait," I say before anyone obeys Asher's orders. "They always make the most obvious route the most dangerous."

The glare he gives me could give a laser a run for its money. "Whatever. We're listening to me for this round, got it?"

I stare him down. "I've been through these before." Maybe logical reasoning will work with the guy.

"So have I," he shoots back.

"Really? You've been through a hybrid of these two trainings?"

He ducks his head. "Well, not exactly."

"But I have, and she's gotten us through them," Matthias chimes in. "Bria can spy a way through just about any scenario."

Asher's head pops up. "Which I guess is why she works with Major Vasco to put us through scenarios now, huh?" The bite in his words is piercing.

I lock my jaw and breathe in and out. "Do you want my help in this or not?"

"I do," a young girl says. "My friend told me you got her through a Kill Zone a while ago. She's gone now."

"Quincy?" I ask.

The girl nods, her eyes sad. "I don't want to get shot again. It hurts." She lifts the sleeve of her uniform to show the mottled color of a healing bruise. Purples, yellows, and greens spread along her bicep. "If you can get us through without that, I'll follow you."

I grip my rifle to quell my rising anger. We can't get another kid to the Ruins for a few more days, but I wish I could bring this girl out tonight.

"Me too," a boy who can't be older than thirteen pipes up. "Tell us what to do."

Asher lets out a low growl. "Fine." He gestures to the edge of the building. "Get a glimpse of what's going on and tell us what you think we need to do."

I ease my way around the girl to my left and poke my head out ever so slightly to get a view of the course in front of us.

"We'll have to move any second," I say. "They'll be coming back this way, doing a sweep. That's what I would do, anyway."

Another grumpy harrumph from Asher, which I ignore.

"We'll want to stick to the edge and then cut to the center of the course once we hit the fake market they've set up." I face the group before me. "Follow my lead. Asher, lay down some cover for us so I can get these guys over to the market."

Asher gives me one nod. "All right." He comes up next to me. "On my count, you all run."

"Okay," I say.

Matthias squeezes my hand, and I squeeze back, even though I still wish he wasn't here. My nightmare of him dying is too fresh.

A nightmare induced by the nerve agent that almost killed me. I should probably tell Matthias about that, but now is definitely not the time.

"Okay, guys. You ready?" I make eye contact with each of the young recruits.

Kiwi gives me a grin and a small salute. "Let's get 'em." He unholsters his pistols. "Ready when you are."

"All right. On three," Asher says. "One, two, three." He pops up and fires rapidly at the areas where we've caught movement of soldiers.

I leap forward, leading the group behind me and knowing Matthias will make sure everyone else comes out after me.

I focus on the task at hand, my rifle at the ready, as I scan the area, leading the small band of recruits to the first building we need to get to. We arrive, and the quick glance behind me tells me no one has been hurt, despite the rapid gunfire.

"All right, let's move," I say.

I lead them through the fake town, shooting at the soldiers I catch glimpses of. Kiwi takes out a two in quick succession with some impressive shooting.

We come to the market, and seconds later, Asher is behind Matthias.

Matthias nods at me. "Ready when you are."

This time it's my turn to count the kids down, and then we're sprinting to the other side of the course, gunfire ricocheting around us.

I lay down fire along with Kiwi, Matthias, and Asher, not expecting the kids to do much of anything. I drop to the ground when I hit the wall I was aiming for and wave the kids in behind me. One, two, three, four. All the youngest ones are in, then Kiwi. Next comes Asher. Matthias is the one taking the rear this time.

He aims, fires at a soldier, and turns to run.

A training bullet hits him in the back.

He drops to the ground.

All the memories of when this happened before hit me as another training bullet, then another pummels Matthias's body.

He grunts, pulls in on himself. "Go," he says.

A surge of anger washes over me.

I jump to my feet, rip the machine gun from Asher's hands, and spray bullets at the soldiers hiding across the street. Some scream as I hit them. I grab Matthias and drag him to cover.

"Thanks," he gasps, pain written all over his features. His breaths come in short bursts. "That hurt." He rubs his ribs.

"How did you even get assigned to this?" I ask, exasperated. "There aren't any other cadets." I check him for blood, even though he was hit with training bullets.

"I missed you," he says.

Our eyes connect. "I missed you too," I admit. "But watching you get shot isn't exactly helping me at the moment."

He gives me a sheepish grin.

"If you two are done, we should move," Asher says.

Matthias limps along at first, but within fifteen minutes he's recovered from the hits he took. When we arrive at an obstacle riddled field, Asher starts leading us to the easiest path through. Which makes sense considering the lower-level conditioning of half of our team. But something is off. My nerve endings buzz, the hairs on the back of my neck standing up.

It's quiet. Too quiet.

Asher puts a boot on the balance beam for the first leg of the path he chose. A click to my right catches my ear.

Without thinking, I dive tackle Asher off the balance beam and to the ground. Gun fire erupts.

"Take cover!" Matthias yells as he and Kiwi shield the kids behind a short wall.

I roll off Asher.

"Thanks," he mumbles.

I nod, and the two of us army-crawl to where the others are waiting.

Without waiting for Asher's permission, I assess the course. Now that I know what I'm looking for, I easily spot the soldiers hidden throughout.

There's no easy path through. But there *is* a path. And I know how to get us safely across.

No one questions me as I instruct Asher, Kiwi, and Matthias to lay down cover while I lead the kids through the path I found. I quickly show the guys the soldiers' hiding spots, and point out the places where we'll pause within the course to regroup.

"I'll lay down cover so you guys can catch up to us," I say. "Ready?"

"Solid plan," Asher says. "Let's do it."

There's no time for questions, and thankfully no one asks any. The guys get into position, and I lead the kids into the course.

Everyone follows my lead, and we complete the rest of the obstacle course without further incident. Our team comes in as one of the high-scoring teams.

Asher pats me roughly on the shoulder. "Well, guess it worked out trusting you this time. Thanks for watching my back." He glances at Matthias, who's talking with Kiwi. "Maybe I misjudged you. Kiwi says your solid. And Matthias clearly trusts you."

"We've been through a lot together," I say. "And we're willing to take risks to do what's right." Although the risks are significantly harder for me to take when Matthias keeps getting shot in front of me.

I shove the image away and maintain eye contact with Asher. If there's any hope of stopping Ark, we'll need the help of the Resistance.

"One course isn't enough to convince me," he says. "But today was a good start."

CHAPTER
THIRTY-SIX

"Averton. The Commander wants to see you," the young female soldier says.

My arms are elbow deep in suds as I scrub a large soup crock. I blow a stray curl out of my face. "Now?"

She gives a single nod. "Immediately."

I shake my hands off into the sink full of soapy water, then dry them on my apron. Tilly, the head cook, is bustling about the other side of the kitchen, preparing for the lunch rush. I doubt she'll realize I left. Not that it matters if she does.

If Ark wants to see me, she won't stop me from leaving.

I remove my apron and follow the soldier from the kitchen and into the streets of Talionis. Now that it's mid-September, the air has cooled slightly with the approaching fall, and it's a welcome relief after the heat of the kitchen.

Soldiers rush past us, highlighting what I've noticed over the past two weeks. The daily activity has increased. Everyone moves in a hurried manner. As though preparations have ramped up.

Or maybe my anxiety about being called to *another* meeting with Ark is making me paranoid. That on top of the stress of Sergeant Valarius telling us to wait to bring Keesia out to the Ruins until he determines it's *safe* definitely has me on edge.

Two weeks is too long. Every minute we waste puts the kids in more danger. But in the meetings I've had with Mom, Nika, and Kemena, they've all agreed that it's better to wait than rush forward and regret it.

I follow the soldier through the streets and to the building that houses Ark's office. As we approach, I notice Kemena and Matthias being led over as well.

I tense.

Why did Ark call for all three of us?

Matthias and I performed well in the trainings we've done together, and Kemena and I haven't snuck out to the Ruins for a week.

We all arrive at the entrance at the same time.

Laban leads Kemena, and he gruffly dismisses the other two soldiers. "I'll take it from here."

His eyes snap to mine, and I stare back, willing myself not to glare, but unwilling to give him the satisfaction of seeing me stand down in front of him

He shoulders past me with enough force to knock me off-balance. Matthias's hand is there to steady me an instant later. Secure. Comforting.

Like home.

But I can't let myself be even a little at ease. We're about to go into a meeting with Ark, and he'll exploit any sign of weakness. I gently remove my arm from Matthias's grasp.

"Let's go," Laban says from the entrance of the building. He waves us forward impatiently.

The three of us climb the stairs, and Kemena nudges me lightly. I glance over to see her brow furrowed in question.

I give a light shrug, and she frowns. We both know meetings with Ark are dangerous. But why is Matthias here too? As much as I wish he could work with us to smuggle kids to the Ruins and on plans to bring Ark down, we haven't been able to involve him. The last time I asked Kiwi about it, he said Colonel Valarius's monitoring of his son has eased a bit.

We talked about bringing Matthias down into the tunnels soon, but nothing was settled.

I can't shake the feeling that Ark knows something about what we're doing.

I'm so lost in my thoughts that I almost run into Matthias where he's stopped in front of his dad's office.

His shoulders are tense as he stares stoically at the door while Laban knocks.

I stand close to Matthias, allowing my shoulder to brush his. He leans into me. The move is dangerous considering Ark has already used Matthias to threaten me, but I can't bear to see him face his father alone. Not if I can be there for him.

The door opens.

Colonel Valarius's eyes sweep over us, his lip curling in hatred as he gaze finds his son. "I'll bring them to the Commander," he says to Laban. "You're dismissed."

Laban salutes, then forcefully walks between me and Matthias as he leaves us to Colonel Valarius.

All of my swirling emotions come together into one. Anger. My body heats, and I clench my hands into fists, ready to grapple with Laban here and now.

Before I can act on my anger, Kemena gives me a light shove in the back to propel me through the door after Matthias.

I glare at Laban's back for one more instant, then trail after Matthias.

Colonel Valarius opens the secret passageway in his bookshelf that leads to Ark's office. Kemena gives a quick intake of breath, but otherwise hides her surprise at the elaborate entrance. Which is impressive. I couldn't hide my shock the first time I saw the secret entrance.

We move quickly through the passageway until we arrive at the door to Ark's office, which is open.

"Come in," he calls from inside.

The four of us enter to find Ark settled on a plush chair with Shane seated on the edge of a nearby couch. And no one else.

My heart skips a beat before taking off at a wild cadence. Why did Ark call a meeting with the four of us?

Did Shane betray *more* information to his beloved *Commander*?

Colonel Valarius moves to sit on a couch adjacent to Ark's, but Ark holds up a hand, forestalling him.

"We are no longer in need of your presence, Colonel. Thank you for bringing them."

Colonel Valarius stands back to his full height. "But—"

"That will be all, Colonel." Ark's voice holds a sharp warning.

Colonel Valarius clicks his heels together, salutes, then exits the room, each step more like the stomping of a petulant child. He slams the door shut behind him.

Ark gestures to the three couches in a semicircle in front of his chair. "Please, make yourselves comfortable."

Kemena and I sit on the couch farthest from Shane. Matthias looks like he might squeeze in and join us for a second before he thinks better of it. He settles himself on the one vacant couch. I don't even glance at Shane.

He betrayed us and now he's willingly working with Demetrius Ark. It's sickening.

I only hope he doesn't further harm our cause in his attempts to get into Ark's good graces.

Ark leans forward, elbows on his knees, fingers steepled. "Now. We have some business to discuss."

It takes far more willpower than it should for me to not look wildly at Kemena and Matthias at Ark's words.

The way he's so still, so poised . . . he's like a snake coiled and ready to strike.

This is the first time I've seen him since the Sitreean Delegation visited a few weeks ago. The first time since finding out I was poisoned. I've been happy with the distance, but now that we're in the same room I almost want to ask him what he knows.

No one says anything. Ark takes the silence to stare at each of us, and the tension in the room builds, pulsing like another person sucking all the oxygen from the air.

His gaze stops on me, eyes calculating and face free of emotion.

All thoughts of the poisoning vanish. He expects me to know what he's referring to.

But I'm at a distinct disadvantage, because I have no clue what's going on. Which means I can't prepare a response that protects us. Nor can I manage the wild card of Shane.

The corner of Ark's mouth twitches. Everything is slipping out of my control. And he knows it.

"My soldiers recovered almost everything you stole from me." His dark gaze remains on me. "But it wasn't *everything*."

In a sudden rush, I realize what this is about.

Ark's encrypted files.

I stole everything from Ark's safe when we escaped, and we could determine what almost all of it was for. Most of the files were easy enough to read and understand.

Battle plans.

Surprise attacks.

Contacts Ark has ready to be deployed at a moment's notice, lying in wait under the Chancellor of Sitreea's nose.

An old journal that outlined the affair Ark's mother had with the Chancellor.

A key to the Sitreean Armory.

Everything Ark needed to attack Sitreea, take control, and expand its borders.

Nika, Ari, and I spent hours aboard *The Fearless Lady* reviewing all the contents of the safe, going over every piece of information.

But the one thing we hadn't been able to understand were the encrypted files. It never made sense to me that Ark would have files no one else could decipher locked in a safe within his office—a safe only he had access to.

Ari and Isaac are working on cracking the code and discovering what was within the pages, but they haven't.

Yet.

When Ari miraculously awoke after almost dying, she said she had an idea. A way to decrypt the files.

At the time, I was just overjoyed that she was alive when she was supposed to be dead.

Now I'm afraid for her life again.

"What do you mean, sir?" Shane asks. He's on the edge of his seat, back ramrod straight as he addresses Ark.

Ark swivels his gaze to him. "A couple files are missing. Files that are important to me personally. That no one else is to know about."

Blood pounds in my ears as he says each sentence, emphasizing the weight of his words.

"We don't know what you're talking about," I say, the words gushing from my mouth in a jumbled rush.

Smooth, Bria.

I dig my fingers into the edge of the couch, wishing it was hard instead of overly plush.

Ark chuckles. "Oh, I very much doubt that." He leans back in his chair and crosses one leg over the other. "I'm sure Ari would have been fascinated by these files. Probably wouldn't have let them out of her sight. Desperate to uncover their secrets."

Oh, no. What will he do to Ari?

"Ari's dead." Shane's words hold a bitter weight as they fall on the room.

For the first time since seeing him here, I look at him more fully. He's so tense he looks like he could snap at the slightest amount of pressure. His gaze remains fixed on Ark as his two words consume the room. The way his face becomes a stony mask reveals that the words cost him. Even if he doesn't want to show it.

"I know." Ark sighs. "Her technical capabilities are a great loss."

Even though I know my friend is alive and I talked to her a week ago, I have to keep myself from jumping to my feet and screaming at this evil man that Ari's *life* is what matters. Not the loss of her *technical ability*.

Shane's hands ball into fists at his sides, and for the first time since he betrayed us, I think he and I are feeling similar emotions.

"What's so important about those files?" Kemena asks, breaking her silence for the first time. She sounds more indignant than curious. "You got everything else, right? Who cares if you don't have one thing." She gestures out the window. "Seems like you have plenty to keep your *plans* moving forward."

Ark picks at an invisible piece of lint on his pant leg before answering. "As I said, the files were important to me personally." He stands abruptly. "But no matter. It appears they are as lost as dear Ari."

The callousness to his tone jerks through the room, and Shane flinches as though Ark slapped him.

"That will be all," Ark says.

The four of us get to our feet, but before we can move an inch toward the exit, he continues.

"As long as nothing about my files surfaces, I will leave the troops outside my walls alone." Ark tucks his hands into his pockets. "But if even a word of them is revealed, you can say goodbye to every single person you care about in the forest surrounding Talionis. Dismissed."

With that, he leaves the seating area and heads toward his desk.

The four of us hastily exit the room. Even Shane appears shaken. Like maybe he has at least considered believing us about Ari being alive.

No one says a word as we traverse the passageway. It's not safe to talk anywhere in this building, and we all know it.

Not to mention Shane is literally walking the secret hallway with us.

But my mind buzzes like a live wire sparking on the ground.

What if Ari's idea worked and she *did* discover a way to decode the files? She and Isaac could be on the verge of deciphering them. It hasn't come up in the couple of times I've talked with her, but now I'm desperate to know her status with them.

Knowing Ark felt this information was so important he needed to ensure no one else understood it makes me believe the intel could be vital. Something we could use to stop him.

His threat rings through my mind.

It's not information he needs to carry out his plans, but it is something he will kill to keep quiet.

As Matthias pushes the lever that leads back into his dad's office, I can't help but fear my friend's life was spared only to be crushed by Ark. Because if anyone can figure out what that file says, it's Ari.

I'll talk to her about it tonight.

CHAPTER
THIRTY-SEVEN

Kemena and I enter the site in the Ruins alone. Kiwi is on night duty cleaning the Technical Operations Building, and Sergeant Valarius still hasn't given us the go-ahead to bring Keesia to the Ruins. But I couldn't wait to talk to Nika and Ari about the files, and Kemena agreed to go with me.

Mom and Nika are by the com system, and they turn when we enter.

"Cai said you guys might come out here tonight," Nika says. "What's going on?"

"Is Ari available?" I ask. "We can tell all of you at the same time."

"I don't love the sound of that." Mom says. She types a message and hits send. "We weren't planning to talk to her tonight, so I don't know if she'll be free."

Kemena and I share a look.

"What happened?" Nika asks. "I know both of you too well, and I don't like either of those looks."

Before either Kemena or I can respond, Mom turns away from the screen. "Ari isn't available tonight. Gabe is running a mandatory meeting."

"Spill it," Nika says, crossing her arms over her chest.

"I made some tea." Mom gestures to the pot on a nearby table. "Let's sit."

We settle at the table, and Mom pours tea into mismatched cups.

I can sense Nika ready to ask what's going on again, so I jump in. "Has Ari said anything to you about the encrypted files she was working on?"

Nika quirks an eyebrow. "Yeah. She said she's making progress on them. Thinks she might be able to decrypt them."

My heart leaps into my throat, and Kemena and I tense.

"What?" Nika asks, looking from one of us to the other.

"Ark said that if anything comes out about those files, everyone is in danger," I say. "Which means we *do* need her to figure it out, but she needs to be careful about how and when she reveals any information that she uncovers. And she has to be careful who she tells. Not anyone other than those we explicitly trust."

"Bria's right," Kemena says. "The circle has to remain small. If so much as a word gets back to Ark that the file is not only still around, but becoming decrypted, many lives will be lost."

The words send a shudder through me. I take a sip of tea, willing the chamomile to have a calming effect.

"But the fact that he's so on edge about it, and threatening such a retaliatory move . . ." I run a hand through my curls, my fingers catching in a knot. "It means that file holds valuable information."

"Maybe information that could help us," Nika says.

I nod, and the four of us lapse into silence. The possibilities are both promising and terrifying.

"I'll make sure to communicate all of this with Ari as soon as possible." Mom breaks the silence. "As troubling as this is, I think you're right. The information must be valuable." She pushes her mug to the side. "On a happier note, when I talked to Ari earlier, she mentioned you guys helped Micah reunite with Catori." She looks between me and Nika, eyes full of pride.

"Because of Callypso." Shame stoops my shoulders with the admission.

"Still, those two were apart for so long. I heard their story when I was in Eryndale briefly after you were taken," she says. "It was enough to break my heart. I could tell Catori loved her husband just from how the DeFort family talked about her. Emmi and I understood each other almost instantly because we'd both mourned the loss of a son. But I'm glad her story ended differently than ours."

Thoughts of Ezri swarm over me, and my eyes burn with unshed tears.

Mom clasps her hands together and gazes into the fire. "Losing a son . . ." She pauses to bring her emotions under control. "It changes you in ways you aren't prepared for. I'm sure Micah hasn't returned to his family yet, because there's too much going on. From the little I heard about him, he would be the type of man who fights for what he believes is right, even if he's weak."

I nod. "He certainly seems that way."

Mom clears her throat, and I have to clear mine as well, to push away the thoughts of Ezri and focus on the tasks at hand.

Nika picks up the story. "Apparently Callypso was holding him as what began as a favor toward Catori's grandfather and continued as a way to provide some leverage. She knew we sailed with Catori, and she figured Micah could be a good bargaining tool. No one can understand why she gave him up, but there's something in Talionis she wants."

"She's as dangerous of an enemy as Demetrius Ark," I say.

There's something about her, something that doesn't sit right.

"We'll all be in trouble if she actually finds whatever she's looking for in Talionis." The words leave Kemena's mouth and settle with a weight around the room like a pressure bomb.

Once again, the reality that we're facing so many enemies, that we are fighting against so much, and with far fewer resources than we should have, weighs on me.

Nika shifts the conversation to the Resistance and asks if we've had any luck gaining more access to those against Talionis. I update them on my last interaction with Asher, which includes mention of Matthias.

Mom clasps my forearm. "Nika told me you had a guy who was special. I'd love to meet him."

My face heats. "Kiwi said we might be able to get him out here soon. If Matthias's dad keeps relaxing his security at night." I look at my band, desperate to move away from the topic of Matthias. I've wanted him to be a part of what I'm doing, but the thought of him meeting Mom is . . . intimidating. "We should go soon. But first, do you guys need anything out here?"

"Help," Nika says. "I'm telling you, these kids are exhausting."

"We have a ton of little siblings, Nika," Kemena says. "You know how to handle kids."

"Uh-uh." Nika shakes her head. "*You* know how to handle kids. I love them, but at more of a distance." She gives me a woeful look. "Girl, think they would notice if me and you switched places? I'd much rather be training."

I burst into laughter along with Kemena and Mom.

Nika gives an exaggerated pout. "At least bring someone out here to help us."

Kemena and I assure her that we'll bring Keesia out as soon as possible.

We all say our goodbyes.

By the time Kemena and I travel back through the tunnels and I arrive at my room, it's 0200 hours.

Training tomorrow will be rough, but the time with my mom and best friend was worth it. I smile again at the thought of Nika and me switching places, but the humor evaporates. Even though she's in the Ruins, none of us are safe. And we won't be until we stop Ark for good.

"Averton." Major Vasco's voice behind me spins me around.

"Yes, sir?" I keep my finger on the area of the map I was just studying so I don't lose my place.

His broad shoulders fill the doorway, and his smooth head is only a few inches from the top of the frame. We've been working together for weeks now, and I'm still surprised by his size and how intimidating the man is.

The brilliance of his mind is the only thing that's more intimidating. It's rare for me to find anything he hasn't already caught when building the scenarios. Outsmarting him will be a nearly impossible task.

But every time I have the chance to work on a scenario, I look for ways to use the back door Kiwi and Ari helped me install through the device Kiwi gave me. So far, it's been little things. An alarm not triggering when it should. Masking troop movements for a few important targets. Hiding evidence that would expose recruits being in a specific location. Things that will hopefully go unnoticed now, but be catastrophic later.

"Come with me," Major Vasco says.

"I wasn't finished with—"

He takes one step toward me and is in my face. "Do you give the orders around here, recruit?"

I swallow. "No, sir." By now, I should know not to argue when he issues an order.

"Then come. With. Me." He towers over me like a massive wave that's about to pull me under.

"Yes, sir." My voice sounds more controlled than expected, and I follow him from the room without my shaking knees giving out.

The hours I've spent with him can sometimes lure me into thinking we have an understanding. That we at least respect one another as equals in some ways. He's helped me hone my ability to strategize. It's like he's always working the muscle that is my mind, and sometimes I think he enjoys having someone to train who's catching onto things.

But as I follow him down the hallway, my pace increased because of his longer strides, I can't help but recognize we're not friends or acquaintances.

He's a soldier. And I'm his duty.

Not to mention, we're fundamentally opposed to one another. Major Tay Vasco is committed to Demetrius Ark.

I am not.

Major Vasco stops in front of a Warfare Scenario prep room.

My eyebrows draw together.

"You'll be entering the DuPont scenario you designed two days ago," Major Vasco says as the silent question lengthens between us.

I blink. "What? I thought I was—"

"Again," he cuts me off. "Who is giving the orders here, recruit?"

I straighten my shoulders and stare at a point on the wall behind Major Vasco. "You, sir."

"Try to remember that."

"Yes, sir!"

A beat of silence is enough to pull my gaze back to Major Vasco. He's staring at me, his dark eyes so shuttered I can't decipher a single one of his thoughts.

"You'll be entering several DuPont scenarios alone."

My forehead furrows, but I remain silent. Questioning him again isn't an option, even though it's unheard of to send a recruit into a scenario alone.

"This is for you to get a better feel for DuPont. Elements you designed in the scenario are strong, but something's missing. Walk through your scenario, and see if you can discover what it is."

He removes two small tech devices from his pocket. "This goes behind your ear." He passes me the first item, shaped to fit around the curve of the back of my ear.

I put it in place. "What does it do?"

"Everyone in DuPont speaks French. This is a translator. It will allow you to hear each word as though it's spoken in English." He passes me the second device, which is a patch so thin and small I'm afraid I'll drop it. "And this goes on your throat. It will translate each word you speak into French."

I put it on my throat and it melds into my skin. I scratch my skin to get it off, but can't find it. "How will I remove it?" I ask, panic clawing at my mind as my fingers claw at my throat. I don't want anything in Talionis embedded in my skin.

Major Vasco grips my hand to stop my frantic motions. "There's another device we use to remove it. This tech is incredibly valuable, and we do not want it damaged. Understood?"

I nod and open my mouth.

"All I hear when you speak is French, Recruit Averton. I do not speak French."

I clamp my mouth shut as Major Vasco steps aside and shoves open the door. He tilts his head for me to enter.

I do as he wants, but the back of my neck tingles in unease. Why are they putting me through a scenario alone? Is it really only for me to discover something I missed in the plans I put together?

Or is because Major Vasco knows I'm creating long-term issues within the scenarios?

DuPont is in such upheaval, I haven't found any easy ways to manipulate the scenarios. And I've *looked* for a way. There are just too many unknowns to consider. So what does Major Vasco think I'm missing?

The door slams shut behind me with a loud *clang*, and the room goes dark.

I've gone through more scenarios than I could count. But each time, I was with others. Whether I knew them or not, there have always been people around me when the darkness cloaks the room like a thick blanket. Voices from other recruits who couldn't stand feeling alone in the darkness. I went through many scenarios with Nika and Ari, their familiar presence comforting as we prepared to act as soldiers against unknown enemies.

Now, I'm alone.

My throat swells with the desire to scream. Or at least talk. To pretend I'm not the only person in this cavernous space. To act like others are about to walk into an unknown location with me. Help me against whatever enemy I'm about to face.

Although, according to Major Vasco, this isn't a scenario for me to defeat an enemy or accomplish some mission.

I'm supposed to find where I made a mistake.

The room rumbles, light edging the horizon. I brace myself as the shaking increases and the country of DuPont takes shape around me.

Even though I know this isn't real, that it's just a scenario, my heart beats erratically.

I'm alone.

Other than the soldiers who are observing me and every single thing I do throughout this scenario. The thought does nothing to comfort me.

Do not be afraid. The words to the verse I read what feels like a lifetime ago whisper through my mind. I want to experience peace at the thought, but I'm still ready to bolt at the slightest movement or noise.

God, help me. I'm not sure what else to pray. And I don't have more time. The capital city of DuPont looms before me, and crowds of people swarm the area.

I steel my resolve. It's time to navigate this scenario and find whatever it is Major Vasco expects me to find. And maybe I'll see something I can manipulate through the back door. Something Major Vasco won't notice.

I tuck a curl behind my ear, the strange tech device bulging beneath my fingers, and make my way toward Paris, the capital of DuPont.

***

STANDING AT ATTENTION IN FRONT OF MAJOR VASCO, I PREPARE TO RECEIVE his orders to give my report on the various scenarios I went through.

He studies me, his dark eyes drilling into me.

I spent the last several hours moving through five different regions of DuPont—from the capital city of Paris, to the areas of the country that border Sitreea, to the underground group of royalty who are conspiring to stop the citizens, and finally to the place where the citizens are holding illegal court trials to judge every royal they can find.

And sentencing many to death.

I was torn between the beauty of the country of DuPont and the gruesomeness of the different scenes I witnessed.

At first, being alone set me on edge. Every rustle of a tree, loud and unexpected laugh, and the jostling of people crowding around me in city streets made me more and more nervous.

But the longer I stayed in the scenarios, the more attuned I became to my surroundings, the less stressed I got.

And the more I saw.

"Did you see it?" Major Vasco asks.

I give a curt nod. "Yes, sir."

He sits at the table between us and gestures for me to do the same. Then he turns on the screen on the table, bringing up a holographic map of DuPont.

I settle into my chair and slide it closer to the table.

"Show me." His words are a sharp command.

For the next hour I highlight how various areas of DuPont are far more exposed than either side in the civil war realize.

"They're so focused on one another, they're missing key points of vulnerability," I say after going over a dozen examples.

Major Vasco sits back in his chair and crosses his arms over his broad chest. "Good. Knowing what you do, how do you recommend we prepare recruits for this type of attack?"

"We set up small groups to target these areas, posing as either citizens or royals, depending on their location," I say. Then I outline the types of attacks I would recommend.

The strategy comes easily to me, but as I go through each scenario, I include elements that could disrupt what Commander Ark is seeking to do. That could expose him, not just to DuPont, but to the other surrounding nations.

I subtly incorporate the elements of sabotage, carefully watching Major Vasco for any indication he's catching onto what I'm attempting to do.

But it's all wrapped up in solid strategy. Every maneuver I suggest is ninety-eight percent in Talionis's favor. It's the smallest of acts in the beginning of each scenario that I hope will be enough to expose Ark's attacks before he can do the damage he hopes to.

And those are the things I'll embed into the scenarios through the back door.

"Well done, recruit. You did better than I anticipated." Major Vasco stands, and I follow his lead. "This will please the Commander."

My throat tightens as words desperately try to escape about how I don't care to ever please the Commander. But I keep my mouth shut and wait.

"That will be all."

I salute. "Yes, sir."

I turn and leave the room, fighting the smile attempting to take over my face. This will work. With the tech from Kiwi, I can use the position Ark has placed me in to expose him to the nations he's attempting to deceive.

My first goal is still to stop him from taking a single teen from Talionis to the countries on the other side of the world. But if he does, the recruits will be prepared to unwittingly sabotage their Commander.

And maybe that will be enough to bring them back home.

CHAPTER

THIRTY-NINE

"Unit 1, Group 3, ready for entry into Scenario 24," I say, standing in the command center of the Warfare Strategies Building.

This is the fifth set of recruits I've sent through a Warfare Scenario today.

Watching the recruits, their reactions, their facial expressions, everything that they face as they go through the scenarios. Seeing their heart rates spike and their blood pressures rise. Witnessing the raw fear in their eyes on the screens that display the close-up images of their faces.

All of it overwhelms me on so many levels.

I'm the reason for their fear this time. I'm the reason they're facing all they're facing. It doesn't matter how many scenarios I've operated; I hate it every time.

Soldiers are observing me, of course, watching my every move, but I'm in control of these scenarios.

In the three days since my time in the DuPont scenarios, I've operated scenarios for other recruits every day. And the soldiers aren't catching what I'm doing. Which feels like a small victory.

I stand at the control station monitoring all that's happening within the scenario, making sure the various elements are unfolding correctly. The response time of the police in this area of Sitreea. The ways this scenario is designed to disrupt the entire town. The fallout of the municipal building being bombed.

My fingers hover over the keys in front of me, ready to press the buttons that will initiate various reactions and put the recruits into different compromising situations. But what the soldiers around me don't know is that I've given the recruits orders that will trigger the police on the other side of the border from Sitreea. Everything the recruits are doing will cause far more problems for Demetrius Ark than anyone in this room realizes.

And it's because I created a scenario that looks great, even functions well as the recruits are going through it, but that triggers alarms and protocols within the bordering country.

God, let them not see it. The same prayer I've prayed every time I've put recruits through my scenarios whispers through me. But for the fifth time today, no one seems to notice codes I've inputted that will keep the recruits from triggering the alarms they would trigger if this happened in real life.

"Attention on deck."

The abrupt command whips me into focus, and I jerk away from the controls to see why everyone is coming to attention in the middle of a scenario.

Commander Demetrius Ark strolls into the room. "At ease. I'm only here to observe. Continue as you were." His voice thrums through the room, and my heart pitches.

He *never* observes scenarios from the command center.

Nerves flutter through me. I've spent the past few weeks getting in a position with the soldiers here that makes them think we're on the same side.

Demetrius Ark, however, is not someone who would ever believe I'm doing what I'm doing for the good of Talionis.

My hands shake, and I squeeze them into fists, pulling them to my side to keep them out of view.

What do I do? What do I do?

The question chants through my mind.

The only logical answer is to continue as I was and hope beyond hope that by doing so, I won't be causing a bigger issue.

Maybe Ark will go anywhere in this big space other than to me. Multiple control panels are situated around the room, but I'm running the scenario. I know before he's even at my side that Demetrius Ark is in this room because of me. He's planning to observe.

To test me.

The recruits on the screens are making their way through the northern edge of the town in the mountains.

There needs to be an attack against the recruits, just to keep everyone from realizing what I'm actually doing. I key in the code to trigger the alert at the soldiers' base a quarter of a mile away from the recruits. An alert that probably would have gone out much sooner than now.

Demetrius Ark stands next to me, his presence like a thick layer of smoke. Life-threatening and disorienting.

I sense his eyes shift from me to the screen in front of me. But I remain focused. Watch the recruits, make notes on my screen, and enter data as it's relayed to me.

I talk to the others in the room and continue to function as a lead on this scenario, even as I will myself to not shake, not show any hint that I'm afraid of being in this man's presence.

"You have learned to master this fairly well," Commander Ark says, his voice low enough that I don't think anyone else in the room hears it besides me.

"Thank you, sir," I say, sounding more distant than I expected, which gives me a little hope that I'm coming across as a diligent and maybe even indifferent soldier.

"I'm glad to see you're feeling better. Medical conditions like the one you experienced can be deadly."

Although he whispers the words, they resound in my ears like thunder. Ark knows about the poisoning.

I want to spin around and demand answers from him. Tell him to share everything he knows. But it won't do any good. Ark *wants* a reaction from me. Plus, the medic said the toxin originated in Sitreea. Ark wasn't the one who poisoned me.

But I have no doubt he's involved in some way.

I force out a slow breath and maintain a vigilant observation of the scenario. Several minutes pass and my heart returns to a steady rhythm.

"I climbed this mountain as a young cadet," Ark says.

I glance at him out of the corner of my eye, wondering why he's giving me this insight into himself.

"Oh?" I say, not sure what else to add to the word.

He gives a small nod, and I break my gaze away from the screen to look at him.

"I was one of the most advanced cadets in the Academy," he says, his voice low as he relives his memory. "We were on a training exercise on this mountain, and I saved the entire squadron of cadets I was leading. And defeated the group we were against."

"Impressive," I say.

He inclines his head. "Thank you. I know giving me a compliment is not one of your favorite pastimes."

I keep my face neutral.

He clasps his hands behind his back and watches the recruits fighting soldiers, some successfully defeating them, others falling. It's not long before the scenario goes dark. The recruits failed the attack on the base of soldiers outside of the town.

Commander Ark frowns. "Bring them out of the scenario."

I push the buttons on my screen that release the recruits from entering the next scenario we had on the docket for them.

The others in the room busy themselves with preparing the debrief files for the soldiers who will talk to the seven recruits who were in the scenario. Commander Ark again focuses on me.

"I thought what I was doing would be enough to win my father's affection." Ark studies me so intently I don't breathe. "But it wasn't enough." His face compresses into a look somewhere between anger and pain. "Nothing was ever enough."

The words are so low, so quiet I almost wonder if he meant to say them aloud at all.

"I moved ahead in my training that day," he says. "Became one of the youngest cadets to achieve my rank. My spiritual mentor at the time was very pleased with my success. But it was not enough to change my father."

His words cause me to come up short. What does he mean by spiritual mentor? I bite my tongue to keep from straight-up asking him.

What does Demetrius know about God, about spirituality? The man lives fully for himself, almost as though he himself is a god more than anything else. But I don't ask the question. I wait for him to continue, wondering what else he'll relay in this strange conversation we're having amidst the flurry of activity around us.

The screens shift along the wall in front of us to monitor the recruits being removed from the staging room and brought to their debrief center.

Major Vasco is one of the soldiers to debrief them, as usual.

I pull my attention back to Commander Ark.

"I met my father for the first time a week after that event," he says. "My mother had died right after I entered the Academy, and my father was the only family I had left. I thought my position would be enough to win his favor. But he wanted nothing to do with me." His lip curls. "He called my mother a nothing, a mistake. And that was the day I knew he would pay for throwing me away."

For an instant, I see a hurt, broken young boy. A mere teenager, younger than me, trying to figure out how to function in a world where his mother is gone and his father wants nothing to do with him.

My mind flashes to Shane and the hurt and pain he's experienced that's led him to make decisions that have hurt so many. So similar to Ark.

And yet the decisions each of them have made, though even understandable in some part, are not excusable.

"But why would you hurt so many people just to get back at him?" The question flows from my lips unbidden, and I want to clamp my hand over my mouth to pull it back in.

Commander Ark's eyebrows rise, and a wry smirk fills his face. "I have known pain, and it has made me the man I am today. What I'm doing for you, for every recruit I have brought into Talionis, is better than you will ever be able to understand until you achieve the greatness I have prepared for you."

He says the words with such a profound sincerity it's clear he believes every single one of them. Which is why he can move recruits to believe them as well.

"Choice is part of becoming great," I say. "You can't make someone great by forcing them to do what you want. None of this is about us." The words are flowing now. I should shut up, but I can't stop myself. "People follow leaders they trust. You cannot last forever by spreading sheer fear and hurting others."

He leans against the console, looking relaxed as he observes me. "And yet here you are, doing everything I want you to do, Bria. Tell me. Is it really impossible to bend people to our will?" He inclines his head toward the screen without looking at it. "You just sent over half a dozen recruits into a scenario you designed. You're training them to fight the way *you* want them to. You're controlling them. Through my techniques, sure. Yet you are the one managing every one of their moves. They enter the scenario you tell them to. They do the work you prepare for them. Tell me, are you not controlling each of their destinies alongside me?"

Bile rises in my throat as I look into the eyes of this man who is so self-deceived that he believes what he's doing is good and will create greatness in recruits. And he's woven me into what he wants.

No. He hasn't. I'm fighting against him. He just doesn't see it yet.

Still, his words remain with me long after he leaves.

Oh, God, help me. Help me stop him. And help me to not lose myself along the way.

CHAPTER
FORTY

My time for the day in Warfare Strategies ends not long after my encounter with Commander Ark.

In other circumstances, I could almost pity the man. But what he's become, the choices he's made that have defined not only his life, but countless other lives . . . I cannot condone his actions, despite the fact that he may have chosen to do them because of fear and pain in his youth.

Whatever spiritual mentor he had back then, I can't imagine the man or woman is happy with him now. If they even know what he's become.

I leave the staging room and gather my gear. I grab my rifle from the rack, sling it over my shoulder, and head out into the cool fall air.

Leaves rattle at my feet.

There's an hour until dinner, and everyone is finishing up their chores and duties for the day, except for those who have nighttime watches and duty.

I enter an area with other recruits.

Asher isn't far away, and Kiwi's next to him. Keesia and two others make up the group of five.

Kiwi glances back at me and waves. "Hey, Bria."

Asher stiffens at the sound of my name and turns to face me. "Averton."

Guess he still isn't convinced I'm trustworthy. At least Keesia is planning to go out to the Ruins as soon as we can get her out there. Maybe others in the Resistance will join us, even if their leader isn't ready to do so.

A streak of movement in a building up and to the left catches my attention. I hesitate. The group of recruits stops when Asher and Kiwi pause to stare at me.

"Hold on," I say.

I quickly take in where we're at. There are snipers ahead, preparing for a Kill Zone.

A few of the recruits farther ahead of us walk right into it, and shots begin firing.

"Get back," I shout.

I quickly sprint to the right and duck around a corner, waiting for the others to follow. Kiwi urges them to listen to me, and Keesia agrees with him.

"She's helped others get through these," Keesia says. "We can trust her."

Asher growls under his breath. "Fine."

The group joins me.

"I've never seen anyone get through a Kill Zone without getting hit," Asher says, the challenge in his eyes clear.

"Bria does all the time," Kiwi chimes in. He claps a hand on my shoulder. "And she'll help us this time. Right, Bria?"

I nod. "Of course."

Kiwi's right. I don't remember the last time I entered a Kill Zone and failed. I always see the way through. Find Ark's hole in the midst of the many ways he's looking to trap recruits. It's one of his favorite tests, and it's a test I always ace.

Maybe this is my chance to prove my usefulness to Asher.

I look through a gap in the buildings to the Kill Zone. Recruits are on the ground, others limping along. Every single person is in pain. And the volley of fire from the buildings is nonstop.

"There are more of them this time," I say.

"If you can get us through this," Asher says, "maybe I'll let you come to the next meeting."

The challenge in his eyes that says he doesn't believe I can do it pushes against my pride, even as I wonder why this Kill Zone feels different. Not quite right.

"I'll get you through," I promise, the words strong, despite my sudden fear that maybe I won't be able to this time.

"Then lead the way." Asher waves me forward.

Okay, Bria, think.

I shift down the alley a little more. A sharp *crack* sounds ahead of me. The training bullet hits the dust at my feet. I leap back.

"This alley isn't safe," I say, scrambling away.

"You think?" Asher says.

I guide the group back in the direction we came from, desperate to get out of the alley as quickly as possible and away from the trap lurking within.

"Follow me." I take five steps, the others close behind me.

A new flurry of activity and gunfire erupts.

The alley we're trying to escape becomes a death trap. Bullets rain down on us. The first one to hit me pierces my left thigh. The next hits my upper arm.

"It was a trap," Asher says, his voice thick with pain and distrust. "Find cover if you can."

Each of the recruits with me falls, clutching different body parts.

Everyone scurries to take cover, but no one escapes unscathed.

Asher's right. There's no way through this Kill Zone.

I duck into an alcove and tenderly pull up the sleeves on my uniform to find welts forming on my arms.

This whole thing was a trap from beginning to end. A place for recruits to experience pain. To be on edge. To not believe there's ever a safe way through.

It was Ark's way of telling me I can never stop him. He's rigged everything in Talionis. The Kill Zones only have ways out if he lets them.

The scenarios can only be safe for recruits if he wants to give them a false sense of security.

Everything in this city is under his control.

As the gunfire dies down, one thought surfaces. After this, will I be able to convince Asher he can trust me? Or will he think I led them into the trap?

CHAPTER
FORTY-ONE

I ease my uniform sleeves over the welts on my arms, grimacing as they agitate the bruised skin. I've been shot with training bullets more than once, but this is the first time I've had over a dozen welts to show for it.

Not unlike what happened to Matthias in the last course we went through. The memory sends a pang through me.

It's been days since I've seen Matthias, since we've talked. I miss his smile, his wink, his incessant need to make *me* smile, even on the darkest of days.

My band buzzes. My Educational Training requirement for the week begins in ten minutes.

I shove on my boots and prepare to endure one of Instructor Elva Trill's educational lessons without scoffing. I open the door to my cell and jog down the hallway.

I have seven minutes to get to a building that's a ten-minute walk from me, but it shouldn't matter. Elva Trill is rarely on time, and even if she is, she's usually too busy talking about herself or the Commander to notice when a recruit straggles in a few minutes late. Since this is a morning class, my guess is the woman won't be on time.

Still, I jog to be safe. I can't afford to lose my rifle.

Ark doesn't play fair. The Kill Zone yesterday is proof enough of that. But at least with my rifle, most soldiers, recruits, and cadets give me a little respect. Plus, I appreciate the better food the rifle gives me access to, as opposed to the gruel dished out for any recruit who loses his or her weapon.

I cut through the streets and make my way to the Educational Building. When I turn a corner, my rifle bumps against a welt on the back of my thigh. I suck in a sharp breath and jog up the stairs to the Educational Building.

A glance at my band confirms I've made up time, and I enter the building a minute early.

When I step into the room, I stop short.

Elva Trill is already at the front of the class, talking with a soldier.

And not just any soldier. She's conversing with Shay.

Why is Shay here for Educational Training? I slip into a seat two rows from the back. I'll find out the answer soon enough, but I doubt I'll like it.

A bell chimes to indicate the start of the class, and everyone stops talking. Their furtive glances at Shay continue.

Shay looks around the room, measuring every person she sees and finding them wanting. The drones that are forever around her hover by the wall several feet behind her, as though waiting for her signal to join her at her side or attack someone. Red lasers point from what seem to be their eyes, and a low hum emits from them that I can hear even from my place at the back of the room.

Shay and Trill act like the best of friends, which doesn't surprise me. Elva Trill was one of the main reasons Shay began to believe all the lies of Talionis.

At the beginning, she was as afraid of being here as I was. Maybe even more so. But after one Educational Training session and some of Elva Trill's cookies, Shay transformed into the perfect soldier of Talionis.

"We will begin on time today," Elva Trill says, "because we have a special guest."

Shay's eyes collide with mine.

Elva Trill introduces Shay as a soldier who is brave, a warrior who has fought in battle and come out stronger as a result of her allegiance to the Commander.

Shay's eyes don't leave mine, and I don't so much as blink.

Tomorrow is September 25th. The Anniversary of Ezri's death, and exactly a year since the day we were taken. In my heart, I want to ask her how she could let herself become this. The Watchers chose her because of her difficult home life. Picked her because she was one Ark could mold. Plus, Shay was always willing to throw someone else aside in order to get what she wanted.

Elva Trill gestures to Shay, and the movement is enough to break Shay's eye contact with me. Her red hair—the one thing left of herself—swirls around her shoulders.

I remember her standing on the beach, what feels like a lifetime ago even though it was just a year, calling me to shore so I could help my family prepare for the Festival because my aunt had sent her. My aunt Elena, who is a Watcher for Talionis. A traitor who betrayed me to send me here.

My aunt, who was someone Shay looked up to, cared about, and trusted.

No wonder the two of them were so taken in by Talionis. They both care more about themselves than anyone else.

Shay's face remains stoic, that of a soldier. Her one eye is equipped with technology. As she scanned the room, she was probably scanning everyone's bands.

"I was once like you," Shay says. "I grew up in a home miles from here. I believed the life I lived was the only one I would ever live, but I was wrong."

I clamp my hands into fists, my nails digging into my palms as she talks about Derbe as though it was dark and evil, and about Talionis as though it's good.

Elva Trill wipes her eyes a few times at Shay's elaborate speech, and recruits in the room soften as Shay shares about how she was once ignored and abandoned. But here, she has found her place. Her purpose. Her destiny.

Several in the room lean forward in their seats. The person they looked at earlier as though she was a monster is becoming more human to them, more relatable. Even someone to admire. I see it in their looks, their physical reaction toward her.

Smiles curl ever so subtly across Shay's and Trill's mouths. They see it too. They're feeding on the pain that many of these kids have faced. But there are others here who haven't experienced the same pain.

Recently, my friends and I discovered that most if not every recruit Demetrius Ark kidnapped in the first wave of extractions was a recruit who had been through something traumatic. A recruit whose past pain could help mold them to become all Demetrius Ark wanted them to be.

But now, there are many recruits who have lived a different life.

Who know pain, yes, but who also know there is a better life than the one Talionis offers.

My gaze flicks around the room. Keesia's arms are crossed over her chest, a frown on her face, her brow furrowed. Arwen sits next to her, her nose wrinkling as Shay talks.

Even Asher's here. The blatant hatred on his face almost makes me smirk. One day, hopefully, the two of us can push aside our differences and become friends, work together. Asher is someone I could trust to help me when things go down.

Shay brings her speech to an end, and many of the recruits erupt in applause. A female recruit around my age stands, clapping so hard her hands must hurt. Others join her, until most of the recruits are standing, except for me and a few others.

Shay's eyes lock on mine, and the glare she gives me sends a chill down my spine.

Trill dismisses the class, and I leave to head to physical conditioning. But I can't get Shay's face out of my mind.

CHAPTER

FORTY-TWO

"Averton, with me." Sergeant Valarius's voice interrupts me as I'm about to sit for the first break I've had in two weeks.

I bite back my immediate question of *why*. I was counting on this opportunity to rest before going out to the Ruins with Keesia tonight.

Sergeant Valarius gestures for me to follow him out of the break room, and I do so. He leads me into the city and I wrap my jacket tighter around my shoulders.

Wind whips past me as we make our way down streets and past various training centers.

"Where are we going?" I ask.

Sergeant Valarius doesn't answer, and I bite my tongue to keep from asking again. If the man doesn't feel like telling me, there is nothing I can ask that will get him to say what's going on. As we exit the outer limits of Talionis and head down a side street, the area takes on a familiar clearness.

I blink.

Is Sergeant Valarius taking me to the old church?

My heartbeat kicks up for a second at the thought, and before I can process what that would mean, he stops.

"Head to the church," he says.

"Why?"

He crosses his thick arms over his chest, and the scar on his face bunches as he glowers at me. "Do you really want to question a direct order, recruit?"

"No, sir." I salute and walk down the path toward the chapel. I dare a glance back and find Sergeant Valarius looking around. He checks his own band, then marches back toward the city.

Is Cai waiting for me in the church?

No. If Cai wanted to see me, he'd have Sergeant Valarius bring me to him through the tunnels.

So why am I walking toward the church?

The church where Matthias begged me to trust him.

The church where I felt peace in a different way than ever before as I looked at the old stained glass window of a cross with doors flung open on either side.

The church where so many memories of Matthias wait for me.

My heart rises to my throat. What could Sergeant Valarius want me to see or do here? Before I enter, I reset my band to keep it from monitoring me.

No matter the reason Sergeant Valarius brought me here, I don't want Ark's tech tainting the church.

The questions and emotions swarm through my mind as I enter the old building. It's broken down and full of the debris of a lost era. But a comforting warmth winds through me as I walk inside.

It's dark, and I pause a second to allow my eyes to adjust to the dim lighting. I remember the path through well, even though I've only been here a couple of times. Each of those times was so memorable, so worth imprinting in my mind that I don't think I could ever forget them, even if I wanted to.

I squint through the darkness and make my way down the old aisle through the building. And then, it's brighter. The curtains are flung open to reveal the stained glass window, and light filters through. It's not the same vibrant light as the first time I was here, because the sun isn't hitting the stained glass the way it does late in the day as the sun sets.

But I barely notice the stained glass.

Matthias stands from a broken bench with a grin. "Hi, Bria."

"Hi." My heart skips a beat as I take in his handsome features. His face isn't as hollowed out as it was before, and he looks stronger, as though his father's beatings haven't been as regular.

Likely, Colonel Valarius has found reasons to keep himself more occupied than when we first arrived.

I look away from Matthias's handsome face to take in the picnic blanket, candles, and food set out in front of him on the old wooden floor.

He gestures to it. "I heard you had a break, so I pulled some strings." With each word, he steps closer. "Since our trainings haven't coordinated lately, I had to take matters into my own hands." He takes my hand in his.

"It's beautiful." I squeeze his hand. "But it's the middle of the day. Someone will find out, which we both know is dangerous."

"This whole situation is scary." His eyes search mine as shadows dance across his face from the flickering candlelight. "And we don't know what tomorrow will hold. But Bria." His hand comes up to cup my cheek, his calluses rough but his touch gentle. "I want every second I can have with you. No matter what the risk, no matter the cost."

With each word, I can't help but fall a little more for him. My eyes drift close, and I press my face against his hand, lean into his strength.

He steps forward and pulls me into his arms.

I don't resist. Even though the rational part of my mind is telling me this is a bad idea, I let him pull me closer. Let him shelter me against his strong chest. And I wrap my arms around him.

"I've missed you," I admit. My voice is partially muffled against his chest.

His arms squeeze tighter. He rests his cheek against the top of my head. "From the little I've heard from Kiwi, you've been busy." He pulls back to look me in the eye. "And taking some big risks. He said something happened at the last delegation dinner . . ."

As much as I don't want to taint the beauty of this moment, I have to tell Matthias what happened. My heart stutters in my chest like it does whenever I think of the incident.

I look away from his intense gaze. "Someone from Sitreea tried to poison me."

"What?" The word is sharp and almost frantic. Matthias's hands frame my face, guiding my gaze back to him. "Are you okay?"

"Yeah, I'm fine."

His eyes search mine as though looking for any hint that I'm not telling him everything.

I rest my hand on top of his. "I wasn't okay at first. But Kemena got me to the medic in time. He flushed the toxin from my system." The words don't sound nearly as panicky as my twisted insides feel at remembering what happened.

Matthias's fingers tremble beneath mine. I pull his hand away from my cheek and hold it in both of my hands. "I really am okay now."

He swallows hard. "Why would someone from Sitreea want you . . . dead?"

"I don't know." I bite my lip. "Ark knows about it. I'm sure he had something to do with it." I straighten my shoulders. "But let's focus on something else. I want to enjoy this picnic. Not talk about . . . that."

A line forms between his brows. "Be careful, okay?"

I wink. "I'm always careful."

He smiles, but his eyes remain serious. "I don't want to lose you." He shifts and nods to the food. "I made lunch."

Relieved he's allowing the change in conversation, I raise an eyebrow. "You made lunch?"

His face scrunches as he shrugs. "Well . . . I may have had a little help."

I grin back at him. "I doubt Tilly let you walk out of her kitchen with it."

He wiggles his eyebrows and takes my hand as he leads me toward the picnic he laid out.

"We've been apart for too long. You're forgetting how charming I can be," he says with a huge grin.

I shake my head, but I can't deny that Matthias can be charming. He animatedly lays out all the food he's procured for us, and I can't help but smile at his enthusiasm. But I don't care about a word he's saying about the food. I just want to be with him.

We sit close to each other on the blanket, and I listen to him talk about his trainings and new recruit friends he's made. We look at the stained glass together and spend the next hour in each other's presence, acting as though these past weeks and months of running, of being captured and held in this awful place haven't even existed.

I could almost pretend we're in Eryndale, taking time by ourselves between trainings with the scouts.

But we're not.

Tonight, I head back into the Ruins with Keesia. Every minute we're in Talionis, Matthias and I are under increased scrutiny.

I shift to face him more fully. "I want you to be part of what Kemena and I are doing." I go into detail about the kids we've smuggled out to the Ruins, how we've had to pause for the past few weeks but that we'll start bringing out more as soon as we get Keesia out there tonight. Then I share about the tunnels and tell him how Kiwi's been trying to find a way to get him involved.

When I finish, Matthias rubs a hand over his head and lets out a low whistle. "Wow. You're doing more than I realized. I thought maybe you were getting involved with Asher and the Resistance, but this is beyond even what they're doing." He pauses. "This is really dangerous. If Ark finds out—"

"We're careful," I say, then force myself to be quiet while he takes in everything I told him.

He picks at crumbs on the blanket. "I want to help. But . . ." He sighs. "I'm not gonna lie. I'm scared." He looks at me. "I don't want what happened to my mom to happen to you."

I take his hand, suddenly understanding his hesitancy. Memories flood my mind of conversations we've had about his mom. She was one of the few people brave enough to speak against what Ark was doing, and she paid the price. So did Matthias. His father murdered her just to prove his allegiance to Ark.

"I don't know what will happen," I say. "But I know I have to do something."

He nods. "My dad is relaxing his hold on me, so I can help soon. Just give me a few more days to make sure he's not watching me as much."

"Of course." My band buzzes, a reminder that my next training begins soon. I start to stand. "I should go."

Matthias takes my hand and pulls me back down next to him, putting his arm around me. I could resist, but I don't want to. I drop my head to his shoulder.

"Just two more minutes." He kisses the top of my head. "You're in good shape. You can get to your next training in time."

I shift so I can roll my eyes at him, but the grin that sweeps across my face is wide enough to undo any pretend annoyance.

Matthias tilts his head to look me in the eye, and I catch the instant he sees my grin. A spark lights in his eyes. He winks, then he leans in close. He's going to kiss me.

The kiss is soft, sweet, and short, but it's enough to make pulling away from him to go to my training almost unbearable.

He stands with me, and I gesture at the food, even as my cheeks warm at his closeness. "Sorry I can't help you clean up."

He shrugs. "Nah, every minute I'm here will give me longer to think about you." He tucks a curl behind my ear. "Plus, my dad's in meetings all day so Uncle Andor helped set up a longer break in my schedule."

"You think of everything, don't you?"

He smirks. "You know it. I'll walk you out." He takes my hand in his, threads it through his arm, and holds me close to him as we stroll through the chapel.

He guides me with ease past the old debris and areas that are more cluttered, then he stops me right before the door. Before any eyes might glimpse us. He holds my face in his hands again, rubbing his thumbs against my cheeks.

"Be careful out there," he says.

I look at him and let the care I have for him shine on my face. The recklessness of caring about Matthias makes me feel almost invincible.

"You too," I say.

He places his hands on my shoulders and gently presses a kiss to my forehead, then reluctantly releases me. I leave the church and jog toward the physical conditioning training I have next, feeling like my head is in the clouds.

The risks he took to be with me are astronomical. But I'm thankful he did. I dare a glance back, slowing my pace. Matthias is leaning out the door, watching me.

He lifts his hand in a wave, the smile on his face so vibrant that I can see his blue eyes shining from here. I wave back, then glance at the time on my band as I reset it back to normal. My eyes widen. I need to pick up my speed if I want to get to physical conditioning in time. I turn on my heel and sprint away, back to the heart of Talionis and all the trainings in front of me.

Even as I run back into the life I'm forced to live, I can't help the ridiculous smile that crosses my face. Matthias Valarius is the best guy I know, and the fact that he cares about me, even with all the risks involved, melts my heart.

CHAPTER
FORTY-THREE

I'm nearly through my physical conditioning training when Sergeant Valarius stops my circuit and calls me over.

"Not bad today," he says.

I raise my eyebrow. Considering how preoccupied I've been since eating lunch with Matthias an hour ago, his compliment is surprising, to say the least. "Thank you, sir."

He doesn't acknowledge my response. "We have a situation. I'll require your presence later."

"Just tell me where you need me, sir." A thousand questions dance through my mind. Is this something he's doing for Ark? Or for Cai?

"You'll hear from me," he says. "Now, get back to your training."

The reality that the man is a double agent—and so good at both roles—makes things difficult in moments like this.

As soon as my physical conditioning finishes, I find a new encrypted message on my band. Most likely from Kiwi confirming details for bringing Keesia to the Ruins tonight.

I enter an alley without cameras and open the band to read the message. It's from Sergeant Valarius. I stare at it.

Why would he send me a message this way?

I open the message.

Cancel original plans. Go see Cai at 2300 hours.

He's included codes to get me past the various doors and information about secret passages to find where Cai's located.

At the bottom of all the information is a final message from Sergeant Valarius. *You will not have access to this information again until 2300 hours. If you do not arrive by 2330 hours, all of this information will be erased. Press this button to confirm and accept these terms within the next thirty seconds or this message will be permanently deleted.*

It takes all of my energy to concentrate on my trainings for the rest of the day. All I can think about is the information Sergeant Valarius gave me.

Why does Cai need to see me? And why am I supposed to cancel the plan to bring Keesia to the Ruins? Or is it just that *I'm* not supposed to go?

I miss a shot in weaponry training, and the soldier monitoring me yells at me to focus. I fire five accurate shots at the various targets in the range.

Kiwi's in this training with me, so when it ends, I message him to meet me outside. Once we're in a back alley, I tell him about Sergeant Valarius's cryptic message.

"He hasn't said anything to me," Kiwi says. "We've already prepped Jace to leave tonight with Keesia. He's only six. The longer he stays here, the more likely he'll say something to someone he shouldn't. Plus, I've already prepped all the back-end data for the two of them to be eliminated from Talionis tonight."

I blow out a breath. "You're right. Can you and Kemena get Jace and Keesia out there as planned?"

"Course we can," Kiwi says. "Will you let Kemena know, or do you want me to?"

I check my band. "Can you? I have to get to my next training."

Kiwi gives me a two-finger salute. "On it."

I leave the alley to go to Warfare Strategies, hoping I'll be able to focus.

At least Kiwi and Kemena can smuggle Jace and Keesia to the Ruins as scheduled. The only trouble will be if there's a reason the entire plan for tonight was supposed to be canceled.

IT'S STRANGE GOING THE *OPPOSITE* DIRECTION IN THE TUNNELS THAN I originally planned. Especially knowing Kemena and the others are probably heading through them and on the path to the Ruins right now.

But if Cai wants to see me, it must be important.

Before long, I arrive at the locked door leading to Cai's underground site. This is a different entrance than the one I've used before, so I check my band, then type in the code Sergeant Valarius sent.

The door opens with a soft click, and I step over the threshold and into a dark tunnel leading to a lit area several yards away.

I'm only a few feet inside when voices drift through to me.

"This is dangerous, Cai."

Matthias.

Cai must have called him here too.

"It is. But Matthias," Cai's voice fills the room, "you must choose what *you* will do. Bria's decisions are her own. She's looking for ways to fight. To eventually take down Demetrius Ark."

I pause. The pinprick of guilt for eavesdropping is swallowed up by my intense curiosity to know what they're saying about *me*.

"But someone already tried to poison her. And if she's caught, Ark will not show mercy," Matthias says.

"Again, her choices are her own," Cai repeats, enunciating each syllable. "Bria knows the risks. She knows all that's at stake. I know you want to protect her, but you need to respect the decisions she's making. And you have to make your own decisions about what you'll do."

Matthias releases a frustrated sigh. "But I care about her." His distressed voice slices through me.

"I know you do," Cai says. "But more important than Bria is your choice to do what God sets before you to do. No other person can do the things God's calling you to do, at least not in the way He is setting them before you. You must take hold of your calling, son, and not live in fear."

There's a ragged sigh, and Matthias doesn't respond.

"I know it's been hard," Cai says. "I know you've witnessed unimaginable things. I know everything you're facing has brought up old pain and old wounds, and the easiest thing to do would be to run and hide." Cai pauses, and there's a weight to it. "But there is a time where you will need to stand up and speak, and not be silent out of fear."

"Speaking is what got my mom killed," Matthias says, his voice thick with pain. More than I've heard out of him before.

It makes me want to burst into the room and take him in my arms, but I remain still.

Cai's silent for a moment. "God gave your mother a chance to speak, Matthias. He did not promise her life would be spared. We all knew the risks she was taking, your mother probably more clearly than anyone else. The last thing she wanted was to leave you. But she also wanted to stand against evil, and hoped that by doing so, it would give you a chance to one day live free of the darkness that is Demetrius Ark and Talionis."

There's a choked sob. "I miss her."

"I know." Cai's voice is soft, understanding.

"And Bria's like my mom in so many ways," Matthias says. "I didn't think I could be with a woman like my mom, that I could care so deeply for someone who would risk so much again. But I can't imagine anyone for me but Bria."

My stomach flips.

"Bria's a fighter," Cai says. "She won't stand by when there's such injustice. You know that about her."

"Yes, but maybe if we just waited, someone else—"

"Matthias." Cai cuts him off.

Matthias sighs, waiting for the reprimand I'm sure he knows is coming.

"I understand that silence seems to be the best answer. But it's not." Cai's voice is gentle, softer than I've maybe ever heard it, except for the time he listened as I bore my heart to him and shared how my younger brother died because of me. "Yes, salvation will arise for the people of God. But if it doesn't come with you being part of it, I fear you may bear a far greater pain than you would with whatever loss that may come from you standing up and acting when you have the chance."

"My dad is only treating me okay because I'm pretending to be who he wants me to be," Matthias says. "Are you telling me I should let myself get beaten because I'm actively saying and doing things against Ark and Talionis?"

"No," Cai says. "What I'm saying is that you are in an incredibly unique position. And one day, that position will breed opportunity that only you can take hold of. It will allow you to stand in a way you alone can stand, to speak in a way you alone can speak in. What you do and how you prepare for that moment, Matthias, will define your life. God has put you here for such a time as this. There are times to be silent, and there are times to speak. A time to wait and a time to act. And my son, you need to prepare to speak and to not fear taking action."

In the silence that follows as Matthias takes in Cai's words, I want to peek around the corner, but fear giving away my position. I've intruded on an incredibly private conversation, but now I see Matthias in a new way.

I've believed his faith to be strong, and I still think it is, but all of us face different struggles. Mine is with the need to actively attempt to save all those around me by protecting them, finding a safe way through, and keeping them from getting hurt. And taking the blame every time I can't protect someone. But it seems like Matthias needs to learn how to speak against evil, how to stand against it more actively than he has before.

I think back to our time in Eryndale, remembering the times when Azarias spoke so passionately. He did what Cai was saying Matthias needs to do and rallied others to stand and fight against evil.

Matthias is a supporter, but maybe his cheerful demeanor is a cover to hide a deep-seated fear. His fears are similar to mine, yet different. He's seen people die. Even his mother was killed for standing against the evil of Talionis.

No wonder he's afraid.

But will he stand when the time comes?

"Bria will be here any minute," Cai says, snapping me back to the present.

I move into action, creeping back to the door and waiting a minute so they don't realize I've been here listening. Then I walk forward with a firm step to announce my presence.

When I enter the room, Matthias is wiping his face. I offer him a small smile, even as I see him in a different light. He's not perfect, or even ready for what we're facing. Neither am I.

Somehow that imperfection makes me care about him more. I want to see him become all he was created to be, all God is calling him to be.

I face Cai. A smile softens his face, and his eyes hold a knowing look. I blush. Cai knew I was listening that whole time. He didn't call me out. He let me hear it.

Why?

I approach him, and he gives me a hug, brief and a little brusque, just like usual.

"Did Kemena and Kiwi go to the Ruins tonight?" Cai asks.

I nod. "Since Kiwi didn't hear from Sergeant Valarius, we decided it was best. He already had everything in place to have Jace and Keesia disappear tonight."

"Fine," Cai says. "Nika and Lily were eager to have some help. Especially Nika." He smiles wryly, but it vanishes quickly. "But I'm afraid things are changing."

"What do you mean?" Matthias asks.

Cai turns on screens displaying various areas of Talionis. Soldiers are everywhere, despite the late hour. "As you can see, there's increased activity. And Azarias said Ari's noticed some strange anomalies as well."

I tear my gaze away from the soldiers milling through the streets. "What do you think it means?"

"That's the problem," Cai says. "We're not sure."

"Is Ark changing his timeline?" Matthias asks.

Cai inclines his head. "Perhaps. But we've seen increased activity around the Technical Operations Building in particular." He types a command, and the Technical Operations Building takes over the screens, showing various angles and locations inside the building.

There are people everywhere.

"If it's tech, why didn't you bring Kiwi in?" I ask.

"Because we don't want to tip our hand that we suspect anything," Cai says. "And Kiwi likes to . . . explore. You two are in unique positions, and I need you to use those positions to gain as much intel as possible. But be careful. I suspect you'll both be tested in the days to come."

The somber words settle over the room, and the three of us view the screens in silence for a few moments.

Matthias is the first to break the silence. "Have you heard anything from the scouts? Are they preparing to attack?"

"They're confident there's a mole on the outside, someone within their ranks, but have no idea who it is." Cai's voice is somber. "They have units surrounding Talionis in key locations, but we're afraid even that information has been compromised by whoever the mole is."

Images of the different people I've worked with in Eryndale flash through my mind, but it's hard to imagine any of them betraying the city they care about.

Eryndale is a refuge, not a place of horror like Talionis. Yet, someone is allowing their connections in the refuge city to equip Ark to do far more damage than he could do on his own.

We spend the next thirty minutes talking about the placement of the scout units and the tactical advantages of each location for when the time comes for an attack. Cai shares details about the tunnels with Matthias and the plan my dad, Hosea, and Kassre are working on to break through a tunnel from the outside to bring in trusted scouts.

Cai turns to me. "I spoke to Andor about your poisoning."

Any word I could imagine saying dies in my throat.

"What did he learn?" Matthias asks, somehow managing to keep the fear in his eyes from tinting his words.

"Unfortunately, nothing," Cai says. "He spoke to the medic, but there was no way of determining what exactly delivered the toxin to your system. The only thing the medic's sure of is that you ingested it during the dinner with the Sitreean delegation."

My brow furrows. "Was it something I ate or something I drank?"

"It could have been either," Cai says.

"I ate and drank during the dinner too," Matthias says. "Nothing happened to me."

"From what Andor could tell, no one besides Bria was exposed to the toxin." Cai's words ring through the room in the silence that follows.

Matthias scrubs his hands over his face.

"So I was targeted," I say the words I'm sure we're all thinking. "Probably by Ark." I release a frustrated sigh. "How are we going to stop him?" I ask the question that gnaws at my mind. The one I can never find an answer to, even though I'm desperate for one.

"First, we need to know exactly when the deployment to Sitreea is scheduled to take place," Cai says. "I need you two to discover what you can."

Matthias gives one curt nod, and I feel his anxiety rising.

"We need to do something within the city as well," I say. "Eryndale's attack is necessary, but unless we rise up from within at the same time . . ." I shrug. "Talionis is too strong. They need to feel themselves fragmenting."

Cai leans against the desk. "I agree. Eventually, we'll involve the Resistance in Talionis. But not yet. We need more intel first, and more of a plan." He hesitates. "We also might need to slow or pause bringing kids out to the Ruins."

"Why?" I cross my arms over my chest. "We've been paused for weeks. We can't stop again. Getting them to safety is at least *something* we can do."

"I know," Cai says. "But if they're more closely monitoring their tech, I'm afraid of Kiwi's hacking being compromised."

He wouldn't appreciate hearing that, but I can't deny that Cai might have a point.

"We'll discuss it more soon," Cai says. "But you both should get back to your rooms. It's getting late, and I don't want anyone missing you."

I still have more questions, but a glance at my band tells me it's after 0100 hours. Cai's right. We both need sleep.

"Matthias," Cai says as we're preparing to leave.

Matthias looks at him. "Yeah?"

"Remember what I said."

Matthias inhales deeply, straightens his shoulders, and nods. "I will. Well, I'll try."

I sense his internal struggle, wish I could hug him and tell him I'll help him. Promise him that standing against evil was worth it, no matter the cost.

The problem is, I still wonder how much this stand will cost, and if I'll truly believe it'll be worth it in the end.

CHAPTER
FORTY-FOUR

An alert shows on my band with an order to leave my current training and head to Warfare Strategies. I put the electro-fitted bow I was working with for my weaponry evaluation on the counter and approach the nearest soldier—a specialist who doesn't like me very much.

I show her the alert on my band. "I'm being called to Warfare Strategies."

"I have eyes." She yanks my hand toward her to get a better look, then gives me one curt nod. "You're dismissed." She shoves my hand back at me.

I keep myself from frowning and leave the room.

Several of the soldiers have come to respect me at least a little for my skills, but others still see me as the traitor to their Commander who left Talionis, exposed much of what Ark was doing, and left them needing to regain the territory they lost because of my actions.

The specialist is one of the latter.

I weave my way through the streets, passing buildings, soldiers, and recruits, and soon find myself at the entry to Warfare Strategies.

Corporal Emode is there. She and I rarely interact, and when we do it's not pleasant. She shoves her round, black glasses further up her nose.

"We've been waiting," she says, her short stature not at all hindering her massive attitude. "Come with me."

She leads me with her staccato steps down the hall.

"What's going on?" I ask.

She whips around to glare at me. "You'll find out when you find out. I can't believe I'm reduced to walking someone down the hall like a babysitter. So below my rank."

She passes a private and snaps her fingers at the guy who isn't much older than me.

"Why weren't you the one they asked to do this?" She shakes her head. "Stupid. Absolutely stupid."

Her grumbling continues down the hall, all the way to a staging area. She stops at the door, keys in a code to unlock it, and gestures for me to enter.

"There you go," she says.

I hesitate, and she scowls deeper, which propels me through the door. Seven recruits are waiting in the room, Asher and Kiwi among them, and they're all at attention.

Kiwi's here, which is comforting. It means he and Kemena weren't caught last night.

Major Vasco stands in front of them.

"Good. Averton's here," Major Vasco says.

I salute, then move to the at-ease position when he gives me the clear.

"How may I assist you, sir?" The question's a standard one between the two of us, since it's what I ask every time I enter this building.

"You'll be entering this scenario with Team 1 to battle Team 2. It's a way we're testing how your strategy will work."

My blood ices in my veins, and it takes every muscle in my face to not react to Major Vasco's words.

"What do you mean, sir?" I ask.

"The Commander wants you entering the scenario this time rather than operating it from the booth," Major Vasco says. "He believes it will allow us to see more clearly the benefits of your proposals and the possible pitfalls."

"But, sir, you observe every one of my scenarios," I say, knowing I'm edging into arguing.

Major Vasco rests his hand on the pistol strapped to his hip. "Are you arguing with me, recruit?" he asks, his voice harder than I've heard in weeks. "The Commander has ordered this scenario to happen in this way. You'll enter with Team 1, as I said." He motions to three of the recruits I don't know. "The other four will be going as Team 2. Between the two groups, you will have varying factors. Both of you will hold to the same objectives."

I know the scenario well, since I helped map it out. Every scenario I've created, I've had a hand in running. Typically they run others when I'm on different trainings and in different duties around the city. I've set up safeguards for every scenario to hide what I've done in the event Major Vasco sends recruits through one when I'm not here.

But this scenario is one where I've taken the most risk, since it's one I designed from the beginning.

And it's like Commander Ark knows it.

I join the three recruits who are going into the scenario with me.

They are all in Unit 17, which is one I haven't worked with much. It's a unit from the extraction that happened right after I escaped. They're further ahead than others, but behind where I would've been with my friends.

Major Vasco gives the same speech I've given to other recruits who have gone through this scenario. I know everything he's about to say, yet this time, I need to be hyper-focused.

All I can think about are the ways the scenario could fall apart once I'm inside. The back door Kiwi created is supposed to keep everything I've manipulated hidden. But I know what *should* happen. What if I unintentionally expose something I did while I'm in there?

The thought throws me back to how I felt when I was new in Talionis and experiencing warfare scenarios for the first time.

A glance at the other recruits in the room shows me I'm by far the most nervous. Which is ridiculous. I've not only been through more scenarios than any of them, I've created them, helped design every one that is being utilized. Not to mention, I've been personally trained in warfare strategy by Major Vasco.

Yet this is different.

I strain my attention to Major Vasco, knowing that I need to hear exactly how he talks to these recruits and prepares them for entry. It's strange to have two separate groups going in at the same time.

"This will be a battle for top rank in warfare scenarios," he says, arms crossed over his broad chest as he assesses both groups. "You seven, eight with Recruit Averton, are the best we have seen in scenarios. You know how to react to the various conditions we put you in, both elemental and strategic, and you have succeeded in more scenarios than anyone else. This is one of our more difficult runs, and we want to ensure it is flawless before anything else happens with your teams."

I clamp my jaw so tightly it's giving me a headache, but I refuse to give in to my fears. I'll do the best I can and hope that Major Vasco doesn't discover how I've messed with these scenarios after this one ends.

"There are two ways this scenario can be accomplished," Major Vasco continues. "Your teams will be going through them with the objective of retrieving this woman." He presses a button, and an image of Alexa Strationi appears on the screen.

I know her name, her face, more about her than anyone else in this room besides Major Vasco, but I wait and listen as he details it for the recruits.

"Alexa Strationi is a high-up liaison between Sitreea's government and the country of Mabence. She and the Chancellor of Sitreea rarely see eye to eye, and we believe we can convince her to be an asset."

I blink. He's telling these recruits far more than I've ever told any recruits in a scenario briefing.

"You are to enter the diplomatic building here and retrieve this woman without triggering any alarms. She has silent alarm triggers within her office, and guards are patrolling the entire consulate. If at any point she believes she is under threat or being taken for nefarious reasons, she will alert a guard or trigger an alarm. Your job is to ensure this does not happen." Major Vasco looks between Kiwi and the girl to my right.

"Strider and Zadie, you're both excellent in technological elements. You may choose to attempt to disable alarms in this building, but I will warn you that the technological advances in this particular consulate are beyond what you have worked with so far. Proceed with caution."

He lays out a map of the consulate building and the entry points available to us. "Team 1 will begin in the surrounding forest and will need to make their way to the consulate from there, avoiding various patrols and guards along the way. Team 2, you will begin from the outskirts of a small town and need to make your way to the consulate from there." He activates the route highlights on the map, our team's in blue, Team 2's in red.

There's a moment of silence as everyone studies the map.

"Again, this is a test and a race. You do not have the luxury of time." He annunciates each word with an emphatic pressure that increases my anxiety. "View the opposing team as your enemy at all times. Is that understood?"

"Sir, yes, sir," we chant together, even as my heart skips a beat.

When I designed this scenario and sabotaged various elements, I never expected them to run it with two teams. The likelihood of what I've done being exposed is dangerously high.

CHAPTER

FORTY-FIVE

T he teams separate, and Major Vasco leads my unit to a staging room. I'm formally introduced to my three team-mates, Hawthorne, Fin, and Zadie.

I introduce myself. Hawthorne and Fin give me wary glances, but Zadie seems almost happy to meet me.

"I've heard a lot about you," she says.

I study her before responding. She has creamy white skin, jet black hair, and she's incredibly fit. No doubt she's on track to becoming an Elite Recruit.

"Okay," I finally say.

It's a terrible response, but I'm not sure what to say. I'm not sure if she likes what she knows or what version of me she thinks she knows. The one striving to do everything the soldiers of Talionis want, or the one who has defied them, escaped, and is here against her will.

Major Vasco slams the door shut, and the room goes black.

"This part always gets me hype," Hawthorne says.

"The scenarios used to freak me out," Zadie says. "But not anymore. There's something exciting about seeing what I can do in these things. I didn't realize strategy was such a skill set of mine until Talionis, and it's exciting to get to use it."

Are these recruits as good at strategy as I am?

It's the area where I've excelled consistently in Talionis from the beginning, and it's something I've done better than every other recruit I've met. Something other recruits have come to rely on me for, friends and acquaintances alike.

But here I am with three other recruits who claim to be excellent at strategy, and we're facing a team of four recruits that includes Asher and Kiwi, who are also excellent at these warfare scenarios.

What does that mean?

Maybe I don't have the level of skills needed to defeat Talionis as I once believed. I swallow back the uncomfortable thought and focus on the scenario we're facing.

Our team will travel down from the forest. We'll encounter multiple checkpoints heading into more populated areas, and we will likely need to pass through a few body scanners as well.

I keep my thoughts to myself and listen as Hawthorne asks similar questions to the ones dancing through my head.

Unlike these three, I've experienced this scenario—at least watched recruits go through it. But I listen as Hawthorne outlines a path I've seen recruits use successfully in the past.

The room rumbles in the middle of Hawthorne's sentence, and light breaks through as trees form around us.

"Here we go," he says as the forest comes to life.

We're in a small alcove that's hidden from the nearby road, and I look at Hawthorne to find he's staring at me, his brown eyes shuttered.

"You're a bit of a legend here," he says, not moving toward the road yet.

The other two nod in agreement.

"Yeah," Zadie says. "Every time we beat a scenario, we're told that Bria Averton did it faster and better than we did, with fewer casualties."

I look between the three of them, unsure how to respond. I don't know if the soldiers told them the truth and I really did better than they did, or if it was simply a way to motivate the recruits to do better by using me as an example.

"I don't like losing," Fin says, speaking to me for the first time. Although narrowed as he assesses me, his green-gray eyes stand out against his light brown skin. "And I've heard what you did to the Commander's plans, how you escaped and caused so many problems for him and his soldiers. But I have to admit, I'm curious to see how you get us through this."

"Hawthorne's route should work." I focus on what I know I can navigate in this minefield of a conversation. "I've operated the scenario before."

Hawthorne's eyebrows shoot up. "Handled as in managed the scenario with Major Vasco?"

I nod.

"Then why are you going through with us?" Hawthorne asks.

"I don't know," I answer honestly, even as I realize these recruits are very much patriots of Talionis.

"All right, then let's go. We've wasted enough time," Zadie says.

We gather the packs stored in a bush nearby with the various items we'll need for the scenario, then double-time it through the woods to the nearby road. We stay in the trees for a while, then emerge past the first checkpoint.

Zadie glances at her band. "We're making decent time, but we'll want to move faster whenever we can. This is a race, after all, and I, for one, did not come to lose."

Hawthorne grunts his agreement, and we pick up our pace. There aren't any issues as we travel the road, which is to be expected. It's early morning, and there are few people out at this time of day.

After another mile, the consulate looms in the distance. We've been given security badges to get us into the building to provide the least amount of disturbance possible at our entry. It will also allow us to get to Alexa much quicker. And the badges will be a way to gain her trust. At least, that's the theory we're operating under.

We smooth our hair and straighten the collars of our uniforms as we put on our ID badges. Then we make our way to the consulate, coming in for the morning shift of guard duty. We easily get past the body scan and front desk and into the deeper recesses of the building.

"Alexa's office is on the top floor," I say.

"The best way to access it is by elevator," Hawthorne says.

I nod. "Yes, but we should take the stairs."

"That's thirty flights," Fin says.

Hawthorne tilts his head as though trying to assess if my idea is worth his time. "No, she's right. The stairs are gonna have less security, fewer cameras. They won't be monitored, because who's going to climb that many levels?"

"But time is of the essence," Zadie argues, siding with Fin. "And I can disable the cameras and security."

"But if I know Asher," Hawthorne says, spitting out his name as though it's a curse word, "his team will find a way to use the elevator as an ambush against us."

I blink, not having considered that thought.

"Our best option will be what Bria said," Hawthorne says. "We'll take the stairs at least halfway up, then reevaluate."

Fin and Zadie nod, though they don't look pleased about the idea of climbing so many flights of stairs.

We're only on the fifth floor when an alarm triggers. My gut seizes. That was faster than I expected.

Panic and stress fill the next four minutes. The scenario we were supposed to complete falls apart before our eyes. We fail before we've begun.

As soldiers are rallying us together and dragging us to holding cells to be questioned, I catch a glimpse around a corner. Asher's arm encircles Alexa's shoulders as he ushers her out of the building to safety.

Somehow, he found a way through. Which means not only did we lose to the other team, we also tripped some kind of alarm, potentially exposing a way I manipulated the scenario. If it did, then at best it will diminish my abilities as a strategist. At worst, my loyalty and compliance with orders will be questioned.

No matter what, I've failed on multiple levels today, and that will be completely unacceptable.

MAJOR VASCO BRINGS BOTH TEAMS INTO THE SAME DEBRIEF ROOM AND begins by praising Asher's team. He goes on and on about how they succeeded in not only getting Alexa out, but also in providing distractions and decoys that ended with us being captured.

He spears me with a dark glare, then turns his attention to the others in the room. The rest of my team. He criticizes them for their questions and lack of decisiveness. And then he details how they inadvertently triggered alarms throughout the entire process.

I stand there, ready for the full force of his ridicule, but he doesn't look at me again. Instead, he lays into the other three on my team and talks about all the ways they failed in comparison to Asher and his team.

My heart hammers in my throat with each passing second, and tension rises from the recruits on either side of me. They're unhappy with their performance, and the ridicule from Major Vasco is only making it worse.

Major Vasco fixes his attention on me. "And *you*." The disappointment in his tone catches me by surprise. "You know this scenario better than anyone here. You've put recruits through it. How could you fail so catastrophically?"

I blink, uncertain what to say to the man as I stand at attention, my muscles tightening and my brain overloading with what might happen next.

"Your skills have deteriorated, Averton," he says, and the words snap at my pride. "You're excellent at bringing recruits through your scenarios, but accomplishing anything yourself seems to be a struggle now. I'm sure the Commander will agree that you should participate in additional scenarios moving forward."

"Yes, sir," I say, knowing it's the only proper response. The thought of entering additional scenarios sends my head spinning.

They haven't caught the ways I sabotaged the scenario, but that doesn't mean they won't next time.

Major Vasco paces before my team. "This time, you'll keep your rifles. But if you fail like that again, there will be consequences everyone in Talionis will observe. Understood?"

"Sir, yes, sir," all four of us say at once.

The anger radiating from Hawthorne, Fin, and Zadie leaves me uneasy.

"You're all dismissed," Major Vasco says.

I'm halfway out of the building when a private catches me.

"Major Vasco wants to see you," she says.

"I just saw him."

She shrugs a shoulder. "I have orders to bring you back to him."

I swallow a sigh, but follow her back down the hall and toward Major Vasco's office. It's rare that I meet him in here, other than the few times we've gone through different scenario strategies together.

When we enter his office, he doesn't look up from the paperwork on his desk. "That will be all, private," he says, dismissing the girl.

She salutes, even though he's not looking, then leaves. When the door closes behind her, his head comes up.

"I've already sent word to the Commander about your failure today," he says. "He is not pleased, Bria."

I don't know what to say, so I remain quiet, wondering where this is going.

"You were given some of the very best recruits to work with in that scenario. Why did it fail?"

I race through it in my mind, wondering what exactly went wrong. Why we ended up in the situation we did. How Asher and his team ended up winning. And all at once, a thought occurs to me.

"We were sabotaged, sir," I say.

His eyebrows lift, but otherwise, his face remains impassive. "Sabotaged. Interesting excuse."

"Not an excuse, sir," I say, my mind flipping through the scenario at rapid speed. My eyes dart back and forth as I think through what I just experienced, all of it crystalizing. "I know that scenario like the back of my hand."

"As well you should," Major Vasco agrees. "Which makes your failure even more disastrous."

"Right. But I wouldn't have failed had it not been sabotaged." I repeat the word, feeling more certain about the reality than I did a moment ago.

Major Vasco nods once. "Well, you might be right."

My eyes widen.

"In fact, I know you're right."

"Sir?"

"The Commander wanted to see how you'd survive if a member of your team was a mole for the other team."

Relief pools in my gut, even as questions rise.

"What do you mean?" I ask. "That was a setup?"

Major Vasco nods. "He wanted you to experience what it's like to be betrayed by someone you trusted, someone you thought was working with you."

My nostrils flare, and I school my features into a mask before I do something I'll regret later. The narrowing of Major Vasco's eyes tells me he caught my annoyance.

"How am I supposed to train recruits if the Commander is constantly testing me?" My voice still holds the irritation flaming within me.

Major Vasco stands from his desk, his presence a powerful force in the room. "You know as well as I do, Averton, that you have set yourself up to be tested every step of the way here."

I duck my head. "Yes, sir."

He comes around his desk and leans on it. "You failed. Learn how to catch things before they go wrong."

"Who was the mole?" I ask.

Major Vasco shakes his head. "You don't get the answer to that question. Figure it out for yourself. If you can't, you're of no use to the Commander's plan."

The words cause my breath to catch in my throat. "Is that a threat?"

"I'm sure you know the answer to that question."

I clench my jaw.

Nothing I do is safe in this place. Even when I'm pretending to be who the Commander wants me to be, he's putting people in my way to cause me to make mistakes.

At the end of the day, as much as Commander Ark might want to use my brain for his purposes, he wants me to fail even more. And he'll do whatever it takes to ensure that happens so that I have to watch while he has the victory.

I leave Warfare Strategies after the conversation with Major Vasco, my heart and mind in turmoil.

God, how is it that the evilest people I've ever known are the ones who always seem to succeed? It's not fair.

How am I supposed to defeat them when they're constantly changing the rules? How am I supposed to stop them when I can't figure out how to be craftier than they are?

I blindly make my way down the street, following paths I know well, wondering if I'll ever be able to leave the confines of this city and discover a life that doesn't include Demetrius Ark.

CHAPTER
FORTY-SIX

I head to the tailors at a faster clip than usual, eager to see Kemena. Between the conversation four nights ago with Cai and the Warfare Scenario trap a few days ago, I need to talk to someone safe, but the past few days have been so jam-packed, there hasn't been time.

After the Warfare Scenario trap, I spent every spare minute between trainings reviewing the scenario. Before long, it was clear Zadie was the double agent who betrayed our team. Her tech skills gave her a unique edge, allowing her to subtly send intel to Asher's team throughout the scenario. When I rewatch the footage, it also becomes evident that she delayed our progress a few times unnecessarily—from claiming we needed to wait for a patrol to pass when there wasn't a patrol, to stopping to tie her shoe. Which wasn't untied.

I brought all of my findings to Major Vasco a few days ago. He barely acknowledged them, but I haven't lost my position working in Warfare Strategies. Which means I passed Ark's test.

When I arrive at the tailors, Kemena's already there, and the sisters are nowhere to be seen.

I leave my rifle by the door and quickly go over to my friend. She embraces me.

"This is for you," she says, passing me thick rubber gloves that look big enough to cover my entire forearm as well as my hand. "Sampta and Presidia want us to work on laundering in a new way." She lifts an eyebrow, a deep frown on her face.

"Why?" I hesitantly take the gloves from Kemena. "I mean, there are machines." I gesture toward the washers and dryers lining the back wall of the room. "They do all the work for us."

Kemena snorts out a derisive laugh. "I told them that."

"You did?" I smirk. "And how did they like that?"

"Well . . ." She shrugs. "They didn't seem particularly fond of me pointing it out."

I chuckle before my original question pushes to the surface. "So, why do they want us to change what we're doing?"

"They're incorporating additional tech into the uniforms now."

I scowl. "Okay . . ."

"Apparently, Mandeville is concerned about the abrasive detergents we've been using."

"What are we supposed to do about that?" I ask. "Make new soap?"

She nods to a massive bucket in the corner, brimming with liquid. "Yep."

I groan. I've made soap with my mom before. Although it wasn't complicated, it was never one of my favorite projects.

Plus, focusing on a new task will make having any real conversation with Kemena that much harder.

She pats me on the shoulder as she heads toward the bucket. "Sorry, girl, but our job is getting more complicated by the day."

"Well, I'm happy I get to do it with you," I say.

Kemena might be Nika's older sister, but with the time I'm spending with her, she's beginning to feel like my older sister too.

She grins as she shoves her hands into thick rubber gloves. "Me too. Better than anything else I'm doing in this place."

I nod as we make our way to the bucket on the other side of the room. She talks me through the ways we'll make the soap and what the sisters are expecting us to do. Because of the new tech elements, they've added several additional ingredients. By the time Kemena's done explaining everything we'll be doing, it's clear this is an entirely different type of *soap making* than anything I've done before.

We begin the process, which is far more intensive than even Kemena's instructions had me believing. I've got my sleeves rolled up and the rubber gloves pulled past my elbows, and I remove lye from one bucket and carefully measure it into the concoction Kemena is mixing.

As we work, Kemena gives me a brief overview of what happened four nights ago when she and Kiwi brought Keesia and Jace to the Ruins. They were almost caught going from the tunnels to the Ruins because of increased patrols. Thankfully, Kiwi realized a new patrol was scheduled before they left the basement, but it was close. Too close.

After she finishes, I tell her about the conversation with Cai and his fears that we might have to pause bringing kids out to the Ruins.

Kemena slowly stirs the liquid in the bucket. "I don't like it, but I think he's right."

I pour more lye into her bucket. "I know. Something is going on. Earlier today—"

Sampta and Presidia burst into the room. "Bria!"

"Yeah?" I almost choke on the word. Did they hear what we were talking about?

"Come with us at once," Sampta says.

"I'm not finished." I lift the measuring cup in my hand higher for them to see.

Presidia shakes her head vigorously. "No more of this work for you today. The Commander has informed us that you'll be joining him for dinner tonight."

The sisters look overjoyed at the prospect of preparing me for a meal with the Commander, but the words send a jolt through me. The last dinner I had in the Commander's quarters, I was poisoned. I drop the measuring cup back into the bucket at my feet before the others notice the liquid sloshing out because of my shaking hands.

"But my chores are—"

"Not important," Presidia cuts me off.

"Kemena, dear, you'll need to finish this up, but we'll send a couple more recruits your way," Sampta says.

I almost gawk at her use of the term "dear" when referring to Kemena.

"I would love if Bria could help me finish," Kemena says, and I sense her protective nature trying to shield me from an unwanted experience.

But if the Commander wants me to join him for dinner, there's absolutely nothing Kemena or I can do to keep that from happening.

Sampta and Presidia are explaining that very thing to Kemena. I swallow back my panic, and stand and strip off my gloves. I hesitate.

"I could save us some time and use the gown I used when the last—"

"Oh my heavens," Sampta exclaims. She turns to her sister. "Does she not understand that a new gown must be worn every time she sees the Commander in such a capacity?"

Presidia is shaking her head. "Sadly, no, sister. She's completely devoid of the profound wisdom we possess."

I blink.

"Come, come, Bria. We have much to do." Sampta looks me up and down, her nose wrinkling. "And I can see you've done nothing to help us."

I almost ask what I possibly could have done that would have aided them in all of their excessive preparations for me to see the Commander, but bite my tongue. They lead me from the back room, and I give a last wide-eyed glance at Kemena.

She waves and says, "I'll see you soon, Bria," in a way that is simple, noncommittal, and wouldn't arouse any suspicion.

But I sense the promise in her words and can't stop the relief that comes with them. She'll be waiting for me in the tunnels tonight.

Sampta and Presidia take me to a side room off of their work-space. It's a massive dressing area. They have me bathe to clean off from the grime of the day, and then, after I've dressed in a simple outfit, they set to work preparing me.

"I never received an official invitation from the Commander. Are you sure he wants me at dinner tonight?" I ask as I wince through Sampta braiding a small portion of my hair.

"Are we sure?" Presidia scoffs. "Of course we're sure. We would never misinterpret one of the Commander's orders."

"But he didn't say anything to me," I argue.

"Well, perhaps he hasn't had time." Sampta yanks my hair tighter, and I breathe in a sharp hiss. "The Commander is terribly busy."

"Who else is going?" I ask.

Presidia pulls an elaborate black and gold gown out of a walk-in closet. "A few other recruits—we've already prepared them."

I open my mouth to ask who they are, but Sampta jumps in before I can say a word. "And, of course, Colonel Valarius and Major Vasco. Other soldiers as well, I'm sure."

"And I've heard there's a small group coming from Sitreea," Presidia says. There's a warmth in her tone, and I wonder if the group includes Antonio.

I suddenly become more interested in this evening. He's the Sitreean Minister of Defense, and I don't think he trusts Ark.

If we could convince those in Sitreea to believe what's really happening here, then perhaps we could defeat Talionis faster than we've hoped.

Assuming whoever tried to poison me at the last delegation dinner doesn't try again. The thought sends a tremor through me that has Sampta jerking my head back into position.

There are so many unknowns, so many factors, but I endure the preparation process, listening to Sampta and Presidia exclaim over their handiwork and how they always surprise themselves at the ability they have to transform me into someone worth being in the Commander's presence.

They don't seem to realize they're insulting me.

Eventually, I'm brought to a transport waiting zone to be ready once the vehicle arrives.

I'm only there for a few minutes before one of the Commander's elaborate transports descends, and I'm ushered aboard by one of his servants. Seconds later, we soar over the city. It's not long before we land on top of the Commander's suite for dinner.

When I arrive, servants are bustling about everywhere, and there's a tense atmosphere in the air that does nothing to ease my nerves.

"Ah, Bria." Commander Ark's voice behind me causes me to jump slightly.

I pivot to face him, a task that's harder to do in the heels I'm wearing. When I stumble, his hand is there to catch me. I still in his grasp, desperately wanting to pull my arm away.

He gives my elbow a gentle squeeze, as though he knows I hate every second of what's happening. I salute, using the opportunity to reclaim my arm.

Something flashes in his eyes, but he allows the motion.

"Hello, sir," I say.

"At ease, recruit," he replies.

I drop my arms back into position at my sides, then think better of that and link them behind my back, not wanting him to have any opportunity to take hold of me again.

"Sampta and Presidia did a fine job preparing you for this evening." Commander Ark gives an approving nod.

Before I can find a response, the door opens behind me, and Commander Ark's eyes light up.

I turn to look, unable to stop myself.

Storm walks in.

CHAPTER
FORTY-SEVEN

"Ah, dear little one," Commander Ark says, approaching her, his broad shoulder blocking me from her view.

I stand frozen as my mind races. Why would he have Storm here, dressed in a lavender gown, hair done, makeup causing her young face to look far too old?

She snaps to attention, her arms bunching the fabric of the gown she's wearing at the sleeves.

"Hello, sir," she says, her voice small and wavering as she gives the Commander the same greeting I did.

"No formalities necessary tonight. I don't want to see another salute, okay?" Ark says the words with a smile, but they hold a deeper threat.

"Yes, sir." Her voice wobbles again.

This isn't something she's done before, and Ark seems to delight in the fact that she doesn't know how to handle herself. The man is insufferable. Evil. I move out from behind Commander Ark and into Storm's line of sight. Her face brightens when she sees me.

"Bria." She takes a step toward me but stops herself, looking at Commander Ark.

"Oh, go see your friend, child," he says.

Storm hesitates a second longer, and Ark's face flashes an impatient look. "I said you can go to her," he repeats, his demeanor cracking.

Storm rushes to my side. I give her a hug that's hindered by the fitted sleeves of both our gowns.

She steps away, and I focus on her for an instant, ignoring Demetrius Ark looming nearby, watching the entire interaction, studying both of us as though we're specimens in his lab.

"You look gorgeous," I say to her. "And so old."

She gives me a small smile. Her beautiful puff of blond hair has been pulled into dozens of small braids and swept up into a thick bun on top of her head.

She leans close to me. "It hurt when they did my hair." She frowns. "And those ladies are weird."

I smile at her, unable to stop myself from giving her a small nod. "Yes, getting ready for a special dinner is always an adventure."

Her eyes widen, and she nods.

I take her hand in mine and face the Commander. "What are we doing here?"

The question slips out, unbidden. Storm's hand tightens in mine as though she knows it wasn't the right question to ask the Commander of Talionis.

But Ark's lips curl into a smile, as though he's pleased that I asked. "I do appreciate that about you, Bria." He tucks his hand into his pocket. "You're always ready to ask the hard questions. Even when there's a risk."

His eyes flicker to Storm. I tug her a little closer.

"You're here because we have a small delegation arriving from Sitreea, and I wanted them to meet some of those we've helped."

"I thought it was important to keep all recruits hidden during visits from Sitreean delegations." I almost bite my tongue once the words are out of my mouth. Why am I pushing any limits with Storm next to me?

Ark tilts his head. "It is. Which is why the recruits are in bunkers tonight, as usual. But after the last visit, several members of the delegation inquired about you. It quickly became apparent that we needed to allow some of them to see our . . . humanitarian efforts to aid some of the poor, helpless youth we've discovered near Talionis."

A sarcastic retort swells in my throat, but I swallow it back as Storm's hand quivers in mine.

Ark's gaze shifts between me and Storm. "I expect the very best behavior from both of you tonight."

"Yes, sir," Storm says before I can find the words.

He gestures for us to enter the dining room. "The others will be arriving shortly. Go, have some hors d'oeuvres. You must be hungry."

The words are a taunt. He knows about the poisoning. Probably orchestrated the entire thing. And now he's waiting to see how I'll respond. My heart beats so hard my entire body seems to pulse.

But I won't let him see my fear. I incline my head, keeping my eyes locked on his. "That sounds lovely. I'm famished."

Storm and I enter the hall and find a small party. A few soldiers are around the room, and Sergeant Valarius is among the ranks. His brow furrows when he sees me, and then Storm. But he doesn't break away from his position at the edge of the room, observing everything. He's still dressed in his standard uniform, and there's a rifle on his back. He must be on duty tonight.

Which is strange. No soldiers were on duty during the last delegation's visit. Perhaps Ark is showing his hand in a different way this evening.

At first, I don't eat or drink anything. The very thought of food makes me sick. Ark's sharp gaze finds mine. He arches an eyebrow as a waiter passes by with a tray of hors d'oeuvres. Without taking time to note what the food is, I grab one from the proffered tray and pop it in my mouth. It tastes like sand, but I swallow it down.

Ark gives an almost imperceptible nod before returning to his conversation with Major Vasco.

If I wake up with a headache tomorrow morning, at least this time I'll know to head right to the infirmary for treatment.

Storm and I spend the next half hour talking in cryptic words. Even she, as young as she is, understands we can't speak freely.

The Sitreean delegation arrives fifteen minutes before the scheduled dinner time, and everyone in the room stops their conversations. Storm and I have stayed to ourselves, even avoiding others in the room who we know, like Major Vasco, Colonel Valarius, and a few of the recruits. An easy task for me since Zadie, Hawthorne, and Fin are among the recruits tonight, and they want nothing to do with me.

Based on how comfortable they seem to be with her, it doesn't appear Hawthorne and Fin are aware Zadie sabotaged us in the scenario.

I catch her staring at me for the third time tonight. She looks away as soon as I stare back. Something about her demeanor strikes me as off. Like she's pretending to be someone she's not. Which I guess she is.

Tonight, none of us are recruits. We're all part of Ark's *humanitarian* efforts in the North American region.

I shake away the thought that maybe Zadie isn't as committed to Talionis as Hawthorne and Fin, and turn my attention to the Sitreeans entering the room.

My feet ache from being in these heels for even thirty minutes, and I long to sit, but I wait for the introductions that come when the delegation arrives.

Among them is the man I was hoping would be here. Antonio. He greets those in the room, then breaks away from a conversation with two others from the delegation and strides toward me and Storm.

"Bria, am I right?" he asks, hand extended.

I release Storm's hand and take his. He ducks his head toward it in a soft bow before releasing it.

"Yes. Nice to see you again, sir," I say.

"Call me Antonio. Please. And who is this lovely young lady?" He turns to Storm and offers her the same hand-bowing gesture he offered me.

"Storm," she says.

He introduces himself, then looks at me again. "I take it she was another one Demetrius took in to help her when she had no one else?"

I sense Storm's gaze on me and glance down to see her brow furrowed, but she's too smart to contradict what the man is saying.

"It would seem so," I say.

His eyes sharpen. "May I escort you into the dining room?" he asks, offering me his arm.

"Thank you, sir." I take his arm.

I grasp Storm's hand in my free hand, and Antonio leads us into the dining room.

He angles his head slightly toward mine, his voice low. "I would like to better understand how you came to be here."

My heart skips a beat. "I thought the Commander already told you my . . . story."

He pats my hand where it rests against his elbow. "Sit with me tonight, and perhaps you can share more."

"As you wish, sir."

Thoughts of another potential poisoning flutter away as hope stirs within me. This could be my chance. An opportunity to carefully weave things into this conversation that will give Antonio information he needs to stop what Ark is doing.

Tonight's delegation is comprised of some of the higher-ranking officials from Sitreea that were here before. It's merely a dinner party, apparently to celebrate Ark's birthday. He invited them purposefully, invited me and Storm and the five other recruits as well.

Matthias is missing this time, and as much as I want him safe, I wish he was here, wish he could be part of the cryptic conversation I'm about to have with a delegate from Sitreea.

There are high risks. If I share more than I should, if I expose something I shouldn't, it could mean the little girl next to me will be in far greater danger than she was before this evening. But if I can share the right information with this man in such a way that he'll believe it, connect the dots on his own, understand the reality of all that's going on, then perhaps we'll be able to devise a plan that stops Demetrius Ark.

There are about thirty-five people at the three tables, with others surrounding the room on guard. The display of military power surprises me, and I'm confident Commander Ark is doing it for a reason. The problem is, I'm not sure what that reason is.

As I sit next to Antonio, I push it from my mind.

We are halfway through the salad portion of the meal, and I'm doing little more than pushing the lettuce, tomatoes, and dressing around on my plate.

Antonio turns from his conversation with the older gentleman from Sitreea on his right and studies me.

"How do you find Talionis?" he asks.

I take a sip of water before responding. "It's different from what I'm used to."

"I can imagine," he says. "Do you enjoy the change?"

"I've learned a great deal here," I say. "But I miss home."

"Why don't you go back then?" He tilts his head, eyes narrowing. "I thought you were orphaned."

I lick my lips. This is the moment I either confirm Ark's lies or begin to unravel them, to share truth. Ark's far enough away from us that he won't hear, and I'm not wearing my band so he can't monitor me that way. Still, I need to tread carefully.

"Not entirely," I say.

His fork pauses halfway to his mouth, and he gives me a weighted glance before taking the bite of food. He chews slowly. "Some in Sitreea wonder about Talionis. Have questions."

"Understandable, sir," I say. "Questions about a secret military city are only natural. I'm surprised so many in Sitreea know about it."

I'm saying more than I should, but I allow the unspoken questions to come through.

"Indeed," he says. "Few know about it, and half of those who do are very pleased with what Demetrius is doing here. Others wonder if perhaps his years as a Special Forces operative have made him too reckless for an assignment that is merely gathering intel for the safety and security of Sitreea."

Each word he says seems to hold seventeen words behind it, as though he's attempting to tell me that not everyone believes Demetrius Ark is who he says he is.

"Sometimes safety is an illusion," I say. "Dark forces can rise up from where we least expect."

"Indeed. Which is why many are pleased Demetrius is so diligently looking out for Sitreea's best interests." He takes another bite of his salad, finishing it, then pushes his plate aside. He angles himself toward me. After a quick glance around the room, his eyes find mine again. "He persuaded someone very dear to me to be part of his operation here. I wonder at times . . ." He pauses, clears his throat. "I wonder at times if she actually had a choice in the matter, and if perhaps all she's doing now is for different reasons than those in Sitreea understand."

My mind latches on to the possibility that he's referring to Presidia. I force myself to take a bite of my salad, spearing a cherry tomato and popping it into my mouth. *God, how do I answer him? How do I tell him something without telling him?*

I swallow. "Perhaps there is more to her story."

His eyes narrow. "There's often more to every person's story, isn't there?"

"Yes," I say slowly. "And sometimes the darker parts of our stories are difficult—even impossible—to speak of."

Antonio nods and doesn't have a chance to respond as the servants clear our plates and bring out the main dish.

I barely notice the short ribs, garlic mashed potatoes, and roasted broccolini in front of me. The meat falls apart when I touch it with my fork, tender, perfectly cooked. But the expertise of Ark's chef is lost on me.

Antonio doesn't talk with me again throughout the evening. He engages with other people, but occasionally he studies me. Did I reveal more than I should've? I don't know if I can trust him.

But of every person I've met from the Sitreean delegation, he's the one person I think might suspect more is going on in Talionis than what's been presented.

Ark parades Storm and me before every person in the delegation at some point throughout the evening, and Major Vasco and Colonel Valarius do the same with the other recruits.

By the time the evening is over, I'm exhausted, having played the facade Ark wanted me to with everyone except Antonio.

God, please help me to have done the right thing.

CHAPTER
FORTY-EIGHT

ONE MONTH LATER

"Time!" Sergeant Valarius shouts, his voice thundering through the training section.

I'm with Unit 23 going through circuit training. There are rumors of a big event coming up that will impact all the recruits and soldiers, but no one knows what it is. The lack of knowledge hasn't kept any of the recruits from talking about it, though.

Every person I worked with today brought it up. Asked if I knew anything. Didn't believe me when I said *no*.

The only benefit of the annoying questioning is that it pushed me to work harder than usual through the circuit. I check my band as I make my way over to the watercooler and confirm my suspicions. I beat almost all of my previous records today. My muscles burn, and sweat drips from my hair and down my back, but the exercise felt good.

Even the excessive questions from the other recruits weren't so bad.

For the first time this month, I was able to push aside my fears that I exposed far more than I should've to Antonio.

After Ark's birthday dinner, Kemena met me in the tunnels as promised. Once she confirmed I hadn't been poisoned again, I told her about the dinner and my interaction with Antonio. She was more nervous about it than I anticipated. Which didn't help my own fears.

But so far, none of our fears have come to pass.

Nothing seems to be happening.

Because of the increase in patrols, we can't sneak more kids out to the Ruins. Barely been able to visit ourselves. Neither Matthias or I have found out anything else about the timeline for the deployment to Sitreea. According to Kiwi, even the Resistance has gone quiet over the past couple weeks after a close call with one of their spies within the higher ranked recruits.

Everything's at a standstill. Which is probably more of the reason for my annoyance with the recruits' questions.

I reach the watercooler at the same time as Arwen. She hesitates.

"Go ahead." I nod to the cooler.

"Thanks," she murmurs before grabbing a paper cup and filling it. She steps aside but doesn't leave with her water.

Instead, she sips it, eyeing me while I get mine. I don't look at her, even as I feel her trying to decide if she'll say what's on her mind. More than likely, she wants to know details about this mysterious upcoming event. At this point, I want to know more too.

With the amount of buzz surrounding the event, I doubt it's just a rumor. My suspicion is that it'll be some type of evaluation.

I take a long gulp of water and return Arwen's gaze. She's friendly and she's thanked me at least four times for taking her place in the pit, but we haven't interacted much in the past couple weeks. Right now, she's watching me with a clear question in her eyes.

When she doesn't say anything for several seconds, I sit on a bench a few feet away from the watercooler. Arwen joins me a moment later.

"How have you survived here for so long?" The question is little more than a whisper, but the sincerity in her words, the need for an answer, catches at me.

I take another long sip of water, trying to figure out how to respond.

She tucks a wisp of brown hair that fell out of her ponytail behind her ear. "I've pretended for most of my life so I could survive. Gotten to be pretty good at reading the signs that someone else is faking it." She states everything in a matter-of-fact manner, her gaze on the recruits and soldiers in the area.

No one's paying us any attention.

"We should probably talk about this somewhere else." It would be a lot easier if she asked me about the upcoming *event*.

Although I have to admit I appreciate her candor.

She shifts to face me better. "Nowhere in this place is truly safe for a conversation. Besides . . ." She gazes down at her hands, which are twisting her now empty paper cup into a mushy ball. "Even though the others might not know how to trust you, I think you're our best bet at getting out of this place."

There's a terrifying hope in her words—one that's heavier than the weights I just bench-pressed.

"Someone will see through me sooner than later," I say, shocked as I voice my fears to this girl who's nearly a stranger.

She looks at me again. "I don't think so. You do everything they want. You've kept your rank since you've returned. Rarely without your rifle." Her cheeks redden, probably because she's remembering how I lost my rifle for her when I took her place in the pit.

"But I see it." Her dark blue eyes search mine. "I see the times they push you too hard. Watch how your body tenses when you don't want to obey an order. And I see how you risk so much to help anyone around you, even if you don't know them. You took my place in the pit when you'd never even *seen* me before. People don't do that." She pauses. "Plus, Kiwi told me a little more about what you've been doing. We need you to be part of what we're doing."

Her words both comfort me and put me on high alert. Could Arwen *really* be the only one noticing those things? I doubt it.

Ark is far too cunning to miss any of it. I can't imagine he's watching me *all* the time, but still. I need to be more careful.

Both of our bands chime with an alert to head to our next training. I stand, and Arwen follows.

"You didn't answer my question," she says. "How have you survived here so long?"

Other recruits are coming closer now, but I feel compelled to answer her. "I'm not alone." As the words leave my mouth, I realize how true they are.

Last time I was here, I didn't believe God could ever want me. Now, because of Cade and so many others, I've learned how much God loves me. I might not have Nika and Ari with me every day, but they're alive when both of them should be dead.

Kemena and I work together regularly, and we've saved kids from Ark's cruel training. And in doing so, we've been able to spend time with Nika and Mom. Even talk to Ari.

Kiwi has become a trusted ally.

Cai's working in the tunnels under the city, and he's not giving up on taking down Ark.

Matthias and I have grown closer, despite Ark's attempts to tear us apart.

Yes, the evil around me has been pervasive. It's seemed to infiltrate everything.

But the battle isn't over.

Even though I'm nervous about talking to Antonio and worried about the increased activity by the soldiers, I'm not fighting alone.

And on the hardest days, when I can't see any of my friends or loved ones, God has still been with me. Given me the courage to continue fighting.

Arwen and I make our way from the building along with the crowd of recruits.

"Where are you heading next?" I ask once we're outside.

She nods to the left. "Educational Training."

I wince. "Sorry to hear that."

The words bring a smile to her lips. "Me too."

I point in the opposite direction. "I have to check in with Major Vasco. See you around."

Before I can walk away, she puts a hand on my arm. "Thank you for fighting."

The words are simple. Sincere. And leave me completely unsure how to respond.

Her hand falls away. "I'll talk to Asher. We need your help." She pivots and strides away at a pace just short of a jog, and I watch her for a moment.

Maybe things are finally looking up.

CHAPTER
FORTY-NINE

I knock on the door to Major Vasco's office, feeling lighter than I have in days. Being back in Talionis has brought many fears and anxieties to the forefront. There's constantly something to worry about, a new challenge. But the short conversation with Arwen helped put things back in perspective.

And hopefully she'll put in a good enough word with Asher to help me get involved with the Resistance. Between that, the scouts planning an attack, the work in the Ruins and tunnels, and my cryptic conversation with Antonio, maybe there's a chance we can stop Ark once and for all.

We just need a little time.

Muffled murmurs come from within Major Vasco's office, but no one has responded to my knock, so I rap my fist against the closed door again. A scraping sound as though a chair is moving away from a desk cuts through the air, then heavy footfalls.

The door opens, and Major Vasco towers over me.

I snap to attention. "Reporting for duty, sir."

"You're late."

I keep myself from checking the time on my band and stay at attention. "I didn't realize the time, sir. It won't happen again."

Major Vasco enters his office, and I follow.

The lightness from moments ago vanishes.

Something's off. I can't be more than three minutes late, and normally Major Vasco is fine as long as I arrive within five minutes of my scheduled time with him. Unlike Mandeville, Major Vasco doesn't demand everything start on the very second it's scheduled.

Major Vasco's shoulders are taut, and he glares at me as he sits behind his desk. No one else is here, so he must have been using a com device to communicate with someone prior to my arrival.

Maybe that's what's put him so on edge.

Whatever it is, I don't want to do anything else to set him off.

"Close the door," he demands.

I obey, then approach his desk.

He studies me, his dark eyes giving nothing away. I force myself to maintain eye contact, even though I want to look everywhere else in the room but at him.

"We've had a change in plans." His face remains impassive. "We'll be increasing the number of scenarios recruits enter and preparing them to endure longer and more intense days. They'll also have increased work with physical conditioning and weaponry training, combining the two to best train the recruits."

Every word he says adds a question to my mind, but I refrain from asking.

He crosses his arms over his chest, his muscles bulging. "Recruits will rise earlier and stay up later than they have before. You along with them."

I swallow back my immediate question of *how* we're expected to endure more than what we've already been facing. There's not a night at dinner where I don't see at least three recruits nodding off, unable to keep their eyes open because of the intensity of their trainings from the day.

The bigger question in all of this is *why*.

Major Vasco tilts his head. "Do you know why this is, Recruit Averton?"

I suppress a shudder. It's like the man can read my mind.

"No, sir." I can hear the questions swirling in the two words.

"It's because you all need to be ready for the biggest evaluation any recruit has ever faced."

This must be what the recruits were talking about this morning during physical conditioning.

Major Vasco doesn't continue, so I clear my throat. "What's the evaluation?"

"In three weeks' time, recruits and cadets will face off against the soldiers of Talionis in the Center. It will be a game of sorts, with every team competing to win."

I wait for him to say more, but he appears satisfied with his explanation. "It doesn't seem more intense than previous evaluations."

Major Vasco unfolds his arms and leans forward. "The Commander will be pleased to hear you say that. His goal is for the event to appear simple. Straightforward for recruits, cadets, and soldiers alike."

Unease whispers its familiar haunting song in my ear. "But there's more at stake in this evaluation."

A glint of approval appears in Major Vasco's eyes. He blinks, and it's gone. "I've taught you well." He types commands on his screen, then displays a countdown.

I can't take my eyes from the red numbers ticking off on the screen, even though I don't know what they mean.

1,091.34.27
1,091.34.26
1,091.34.25

"The entire game is a test. It will allow the Commander to evaluate all of his resources and prepare for Day X."

I don't want to ask. Don't want to confirm the suspicions rising within me. But the words billow up, taking flight from my mouth before I can stop them. "What is Day X?"

Major Vasco gestures to the glowing red numbers of the clock. "Commander Ark insisted you guess."

So Commander Ark is the reason I'm hearing this. It shouldn't surprise me. Major Vasco rarely gives me more information than what he deems absolutely necessary for me to accomplish the scenarios I'm given for the day.

I force my attention to the numbers. The format is specific. And the last number is ticking off each second. Which would make the next number minutes, and the first number hours.

As though he can tell I'm putting the pieces together, Major Vasco types another command.

The numbers shift to reveal one number: *45 days.*

My pulse thrums in my throat as my brain makes the jump I don't want it to make. But as much as I might want to believe it's something else, there's only one explanation. "Is that the day the Commander plans to attack Sitreea?"

Major Vasco gives a curt nod. "Yes. He's moved up the timeline significantly." He pushes a button. The numbers disappear from the screen, but they remain embedded in my mind. "The Commander believes you knowing this will allow you to understand the weight of every action we take from this point forward."

"Yes, sir." My voice feels like it's coming from someone else.

Forty-five days is less than two months from now. Mid-December.

According to what Matthias told us a while ago, he overheard his dad say the attack wouldn't take place until the spring.

What changed his mind?

And why is he letting me know his plans?

Major Vasco briefs me on the scenarios we'll be putting recruits through today. They're all ones I'm familiar with. Ones where I've found ways to subvert Ark's agenda.

But the reality that within only a handful of weeks I'll be taken to Sitreea, along with every other recruit here . . . forced into war . . .

Subverting his agenda isn't enough.

We have to stop him.

But there are too many pieces that need to fall into place. Too much that needs to happen to topple a military power like the one Demetrius Ark has created.

Something pushed him to feel rushed, which could be to our advantage. But what?

Then again, Ark could have been planning to change the timeline for a while. The soldiers have been acting differently, which is why Cai brought me and Matthias in to talk to him.

Did someone from Sitreea say something at the dinner last month? But then why has Cai noticed an increase in soldiers around the tech building?

Does that mean something in tech has Ark worried? Maybe the device Sergeant Valarius planted on the Sitreean transport months ago is showing data Ark didn't foresee.

The thought is more troubling than comforting.

Dangerous animals only become more aggressive when they feel threatened.

God, what am I supposed to do?

I enter the war room for the scenarios and take my place at my console in the front. Major Vasco will oversee today's scenarios as well, so he takes the lift to the high platform that overlooks the entire room.

I rub my hands together, trying to center myself. Every fiber in me screams to leave. To run and find someone else to dump this information on. Cai. Mom and Nika. Kemena. Matthias. Even Asher or someone from the Resistance.

Anyone.

There's no way I can bear acting as though nothing is going on. Handle dealing with this information myself.

But if I leave and run to someone, I'll be playing right into Ark's hands. He *wants* me to act on the intel he's provided. Intel that may not even be accurate. He's looking for any moment I'll mess up and make a major mistake.

Which means I need to stay more focused on the tasks at hand than ever before.

I step up to the panels that will allow me to control the scenarios. "Go to staging room one."

The corporal managing the cameras on the main screen obeys the command.

My hands freeze over the console, and a tremor runs up and down my entire body.

The cameras in the staging rooms are equipped with night vision, allowing us a clear picture of every recruit awaiting entrance into the scenario.

And the first group I have to run through a scenario today includes Storm.

"What's the holdup, Averton?" Major Vasco asks.

I clear my throat. "Just reviewing the plans for today's scenarios, sir." The excuse is weak, and everyone in the room knows it.

"Start the scenario." Major Vasco's voice holds a thick cord of impatience. "If you can't, I'll move Emode into position to manage things today."

A female soldier nearby inhales sharply. She knows as well as I do that if Major Vasco acted on his threat, I would face severe consequences.

And Storm would be facing an intense scenario with someone who won't care how much it terrifies her.

Rather than responding, I enter the commands to send the recruits into the first of the four scenarios they'll be going through today.

The room lightens and the scenario appears. I clench my hands. Storm isn't the only young recruit in the group of seven entering the forest scenario. There are two others. Sam, one of the boys who sits with us at meals, and a girl I don't know who's probably around Storm's age.

The sight of the three kids about to fight like soldiers in a scenario I'm controlling is almost enough to make me vomit all over the controls.

"Young group today," a soldier behind me says. He sounds skeptical. Maybe even upset. But he doesn't question the situation.

My hands shake as I enter the commands that will place the go bag for the recruits in a hidden spot in the forest not far from where they're standing.

God, how do I get out of this? I can't be part of putting kids through scenarios!

Even as I pray the words, my heart thrums out a discordant rhythm. I don't have another choice. If I defy Major Vasco and remove this group from the scenario, I'll be in trouble. And the group will be punished as well.

There's no way I can win in this.

"It's okay, Sam." Storm's voice comes over the video feed as she talks to the boy, her hand on his shoulder and her face far too brave. "It's scary, but it's not real. We just have to do our job, and then it'll be done."

Sam sniffles, his face contorting as he tries to hold back tears. "I hate these things."

Storm nods, compassion and understanding far beyond her years softening her features. "Me too. But we can do it together, 'kay?"

My eyes burn as I watch.

The older recruits have left the younger ones off to the side, and they're strategizing how to move forward. I don't recognize anyone in this group other than Storm and Sam. Which means it's a newer batch of recruits.

Storm is probably the most experienced of everyone in the scenario, but the older teens aren't likely to give her the time of day.

She takes Sam's hand in hers, smiles at him, then leads him away from the group and right to where the go bag is. She's done this scenario before. She knows what she's about to face, unlike everyone else.

And she'll be the one to uncover the go bag. Probably have some time with it before the older teens who are engrossed in their plans realize what's happening.

I lean over my control panel so no one can get a clear visual of what I'm doing and input commands to add additional items to the go bag. Including child-sized bullet proof jackets.

Seconds later, Storm is at the bag and pulling it out. She and Sam and the other young girl dig through it for a few minutes before the older teens see what they found. It's long enough for the three kids to find and put on the bulletproof jackets.

Major Vasco grunts. He knows what I did. But he doesn't say a word. Not yet, anyway.

Providing the protective gear is a small thing. It's all I can do at the moment, but my ability to control certain elements of this scenario gives me a boost of courage. I can shield these kids, at least this time. Protect them from witnessing the extent of horrors normally faced in this set of scenarios.

Major Vasco is too brilliant not to notice at least some of my adjustments. But I don't care.

I might not be able to pull these kids from this, but if I can protect them at least a little, I will.

And even though it's risky, one reality becomes clear. We need to start smuggling kids out to the Ruins again.

THE FOUR SCENARIOS TAKE OVER FIVE HOURS FOR THE GROUP OF RECRUITS TO work through. I find ways to divert the kids and shield them from seeing the worst things. A rockslide prevents their view of another recruit getting shot. I shift a scenario to a new one seconds before a bullet can hit Sam. I redirect Storm's shot to hit a combatant's leg so the woman is injured rather than killed. Even killing someone in a scenario has an emotional impact. I'm sure she's felt it before, but I don't want Storm to know any more nightmares than she already does.

There's even a point when I add instructions to a scenario that hint that the older teens should leave the younger kids to keep watch while the older ones attack a garrison.

When the sequence of scenarios is complete, Major Vasco sends another soldier to debrief them.

"Averton, with me." Major Vasco takes the lift down and strides out of the room, expecting me to follow.

I wipe sweaty palms on my pants and leave the room, ignoring the open stares of several soldiers.

Major Vasco isn't the only one who knows I protected those kids.

I catch the eye of a female soldier who appears to be around Kemena's age. She doesn't have the same hardness in her eyes as some of the other soldiers in Talionis, and she almost seems to approve of my actions. Even though she's a soldier and not trustworthy, it's enough to bolster my courage.

Major Vasco waits for me by the open door to an empty debrief room. He gestures for me to enter, and I do so without question.

This won't be pleasant.

He closes the door with a soft *click*. Which is almost worse than if he'd slammed it.

He faces me. I clench my hands together in front of me. He studies at me for a long moment, his face impassive.

"You're too smart to believe you just adjusted that entire scenario without anyone in the command center realizing it." His low voice rumbles through the small room.

I open my mouth, but he raises a hand to cut me off.

"Do you think you're doing those kids any favors by not allowing them to fully experience the scenarios?"

It's a rhetorical question, but I respond anyway. "They're *kids*. They shouldn't have to face any scenario."

The words are treasonous according to all Demetrius Ark stands for, and Major Vasco and I both know it. But after hours of putting kids through scenarios, I can't stop myself from saying them.

Sam is no more than six. Storm and the other girl are only ten. They should be playing, making up silly games, annoying older siblings. Not entering scenarios where they have to fight for their lives.

Major Vasco studies me. "You know the Commander believes every person in Talionis can be a part of the great work he's doing."

God Himself must restrain me, because somehow, I stay silent, even though all I want to do is lash out at every word Major Vasco just spoke.

"You didn't do those kids any favors," Major Vasco continues. "You saw the countdown. Every single hour spent preparing for the battles to come will mean the difference between survival and death." He pounds his thick fist into his other hand. "The harder every second between now and then is for every recruit—especially the young ones—the more likely they'll discover how to endure against the enemy they're about to face."

Nausea roils over me for the second time today as Major Vasco's words rip me apart. He's right. If I can't prevent Demetrius Ark from taking all the recruits he's kidnapped and forcing them to fight for him against Sitreea, then my actions today will actually hinder those kids' chance of survival.

But not if I can smuggle them to the Ruins first.

CHAPTER

FIFTY

True to Major Vasco's words, all recruits—and cadets—are put through more scenarios and more intense trainings for longer hours every day. Kill Zones are also more prevalent. Recruits no longer walk anywhere without fear, often gripping their rifles as though preparing for an attack. Even though the guns don't hold so much as a training bullet.

In the three days since I talked to Major Vasco, I haven't had a chance to think, let alone share what I've learned with others. My trainings have been nonstop, and before I can say more than two words to anyone, a soldier approaches and pulls me away to something "more important."

I can't enter the tunnels at night because Sergeant Valarius warned me soldiers are assigned to check on me at different times throughout the night.

Sneaking into the tunnels brings way too much risk of exposure, despite the fact that I'm desperate to tell Cai what I've learned. Or at least get word to Kemena and Kiwi to smuggle as many kids to the Ruins as possible.

Matthias and I haven't even been in trainings together.

Ark is intentionally isolating me.

But each day, the intensity of the soldiers' focus on me has dissipated. There's too much for everyone to do. The soldiers, recruits, and cadets are all preparing for the Center Games. The rumors are that the winning side will receive an elaborate reward. And everyone knows Ark does not accept failure.

So, the entire city is concentrated on training to be the best they can be for the games. I'm not even sure all the soldiers know Ark is using this as a preparation for the attack on Sitreea. And that the attack is only six weeks away.

Forty-two days.

I change uniforms for the combined physical conditioning and weaponry training obstacle course. I'm alone in the prep space since I ran here from Warfare Strategies. Instead of managing the scenario today, I had to go through it. It was a brutal one, and I can still hear the screams of the three recruits who were caught in the burning building.

I shake my head, knowing that won't clear it, but wishing such a simple action could. Then I tug on a jacket and zip it up.

This is my last training before my chores for the day. Which will be with Kemena. I'm not sure how I got scheduled to work with her, but I'm thankful I'll finally be with a friendly face to share what I know. I can't spread the word, but she can.

I jog through the empty arena and head out the back door and to the outdoor area of the training facility. Dozens of recruits mill about, prepping for this course. From what I heard during lunch from other recruits, this course takes hours, and it's one of the most intense we've been through.

Then again, I was put through the Elite Recruit training, which few recruits have experienced. Ark expects me to excel.

"I'm so glad you're okay." Matthias's voice over my left shoulder sends my heart somersaulting.

I turn to face him, taking a quick inventory of what the soldiers around us are doing. All of them are prepping for the course, going over screens and talking to one another. No one is paying us any attention.

All I want to do is fall into his arms and cry. Tell him everything

I've learned and beg him to work with Kemena and Kiwi to get kids to the Ruins. Storm, if possible.

But we're too monitored out here, and I can't say a word of it.

"A lot's happened," I say, settling for the cryptic message.

"Matthias! Bria!" Storm's voice keeps Matthias from answering.

Which is probably for the best.

At this point, he wouldn't have to ask much before my resolve cracks and I say far more than I should.

Storm drags Sam with her. The boy looks like he's trying to be annoyed at her for pulling him over, but I catch the happy gleam in his eyes. Storm introduces Sam to Matthias.

Matthias gives me a weighted look that promises our conversation is not over. Then he stoops down and shakes Sam's hand.

Kiwi and Arwen join us, but before I can greet them a gunshot rings through the air, silencing conversations. Sam starts shaking, and Storm takes his hand. Matthias stays in his stooped position and whispers something to Sam I can't hear.

Sam gives him a small grin, and the boy's shaking slows a bit. Matthias takes Sam's free hand before standing.

My heart melts.

Laban strides onto a raised platform.

"Listen up," he shouts the words into the silence that followed the gunshot. "You've all heard about the upcoming games." He paces the platform, his eyes lighting on different recruits, cadets, and kids. "You know it's paramount you do well. But what you don't know is that today's training will determine what weapons you have to fight with."

None of us are clear on what the games will entail, but we know we'll be battling soldiers. Which means we'll be at a disadvantage. All of our training is from Talionis soldiers, and they know everything about us. Our strengths, our weaknesses, our skills.

They're likely to outmaneuver us at every opportunity.

And today is how they'll find ways to put us at an even greater disadvantage.

They're going to use this course to keep us from having the same amount of resources. Once again, we're being put in a position that's completely and utterly unfair. But that's how things work in Talionis.

I set my jaw and glare at Laban.

"You will be separated into teams," he continues. "Each team must successfully complete the four legs of this course." He nods to a three-person tech team working on a portable screen table.

Within seconds, a holographic projection of the course shoots into the air, high enough to be seen by the fifty or so recruits present. It's zoomed out, showing an image of all four legs, but none of the details are clear.

"All four sections of this course will hit on different aspects of your training." Laban points at the tech team, and the holograph zooms in on the first leg of the race. "Every element of your training must come together for you to complete this course with excellence." He stabs his finger at us. "Unless you want to face a punishment worse than pit time, failure is not an option."

He allows the threat in his words to linger.

Storm and Sam crowd closer to Matthias. Every recruit tenses like an electro-fitted bowstring pulled as taut as possible. To the point of breaking.

A satisfied smirk pulls at Laban's lips, and I want to rush the platform and punch it off his face.

He's *enjoying* the terror of every recruit. Feeding off it.

"You'll need weapons to successfully complete the course, and you'll pick them up prior to your team's entry." Laban points to a weaponry staging site similar to what we find when entering a weaponry-based course. "The first part of today's course will be a physical conditioning obstacle course. And you must run through with all of your weapons. If you drop a weapon at any point, you will no longer be able to utilize it for the remainder of the course."

Murmurs start. Most of the recruits haven't faced a combined course where we needed to carry our weapons through the physical conditioning portion. Typically, weapons can be set aside for that part. Elite Training forced me to do more while holding a weapon than I wish I knew how to do. But the rest of these recruits are facing a terrifying challenge.

"Did I say you could discuss this?" Laban's voice cracks like a stun-stick through the air.

Silence descends, with most recruits studying their feet to keep from gaining Laban's attention.

I stare at him. I wasn't talking, and I refuse to cower in front of a bully like Laban Meritas.

His golden eyes find mine, and he doesn't mask his hatred of me. "Next, you'll navigate through a town mock-up." The hologram shifts to a decently sized town. At least as big as the town center of Derbe, if not bigger. "This will combine your weaponry skills with your skills learned from warfare scenarios. Each team will receive an objective when they arrive at the town. It will vary for every team. This is to ensure no team can prepare in advance for what you're about to face." He prowls across the platform, his predatory gaze flitting through the ranks of recruits. "If you heard something from a friend who went through this course earlier, forget about it." He sniffs. "And report them. All the information you are receiving, all you are about to experience, is classified. Any knowledge shared with a recruit who hasn't gone through this training yet will result in severe punishment. Is that understood?"

"Sir, yes, sir!" everyone, including the kids, shouts.

"Good. The third leg is one you could experience at any point in the course." Laban nods to the tech team, and the hologram morphs into a Kill Zone. "An unexpected point of enemy contact will arise at some time during the race. Everyone's weapons will be operational with training ammunition. Assuming you can hold on to them through the physical conditioning portion, of course." He crosses his arms over his chest. "I expect many of you to fail." He gives a pointed look at several recruits, including Sam. "Your team must get through the Kill Zone without getting hit. If someone on your team is hit, not only will they be feeling that failure for the next few days, but the entire team will be forced to take on a fifteen-minute penalty."

Penalty Warning flashes over the holograph of the Kill Zone.

"No team has completed this course in under three hours, but make no mistake. Every single minute added to your time due to a penalty will be a minute you regret later."

"I've never gotten through a Kill Zone without getting hit," Arwen whispers to me. Even though her words are spoken softly, I hear the tremor of fear lacing each syllable.

I offer her a half smile, but don't respond. I can't promise to get her through since I don't even know if the two of us will be on the same team. Or if Ark's allowed for a way through this one or made it impossible to navigate safely.

Laban claps his hands together. "And finally, the fourth leg of the course."

The hologram morphs to show the interior of a building.

Are they putting teams through an actual scenario during this course? In all the time I've been in Talionis, I've only seen scenarios as part of an evaluation. Never as part of a physical conditioning obstacle course.

"As you can see, the course will include an indoor portion. Over the past week, part of the arena has been redesigned to be a tech warehouse. You must hack your way into the building using technology found throughout the course."

I glance at Matthias and find his eyes reflecting the same question I have. What is Laban talking about?

"There are various pieces of tech hidden throughout the course, including some stashed near the building." Laban shakes his head. "I didn't want to share that intel with you, but the Commander wants you to have every advantage possible before entering a course this intense."

Chills ripple over me. Of course Ark wants the recruits to think he's doing them a favor. He'll do everything he can to ingratiate himself with those he's planning to use as though they're no more than pawns in his game.

I drag my attention back to Laban.

"Using the tech you've gathered, you must gain entrance to the building, disable an alarm, and navigate to a room in the center of the building." The hologram shifts with each of Laban's words as the tech team illustrates what we'll face. "Once you gain access to the room, you'll enter a code that will appear on your bands. Every person on your team will have a piece of the code. You must enter it in the correct order into the system database. Once entered, it will plant a virus within the system. You'll then have five minutes to leave the building without getting caught."

The hologram plays out the simulation of the events, and I dread hearing what Laban will say next.

"After five minutes, it will be apparent the virus has been released, and you'll likely be captured and imprisoned." Again, he stalks across the platform, his footsteps heavy against the wood. "Teams that fail *will* be imprisoned for four hours and miss dinner as a punishment for failure." He stops his pacing. "And as you should be able to guess, prisoners cannot keep their weapons." He pauses. "Which means you will not have a single weapon available for your use in the upcoming Center Games."

The weight of his words lands on my chest like an anchor. My gaze drops to Storm and Sam.

How will these kids survive?

CHAPTER

FIFTY-ONE

L aban takes a screen from a man on the tech unit. "A few other details before you're divided into your teams." He doesn't look at the screen. "Each team is competing against the other teams in this course. You'll be going through in waves, but every team will be timed. Points will be awarded according to successful completion of each leg, time spent within the course, and number of enemy targets hit. The team with the lowest points will be assigned the worst duties and chores within the city, and their break times will be revoked for a week. You'll of course be required to complete your regular trainings every day without fail." He starts to bring the screen up, then pauses as though he remembered something.

I'm sure it's an act. Laban loves preying on fear.

"Oh, you're also free to sabotage other teams, steal their weapons, or cause a delay in their progress through any section of the course. Any team who successfully accomplishes any of these things will receive additional points." He raises the screen fully and types something into it.

I should be focused on strategizing my way through this course, but all I can think about is how I need to ensure Sam and Storm are protected through this mess.

Major Vasco's caution about them needing to understand the fierceness of things here so they can survive in Sitreea has echoed in my mind since we had the conversation. But I can only hope that somehow I end up on the same team as the two kids.

"Teams will be divided up differently this time," Laban says, yanking my attention back to the platform. He looks at me again, and my unease builds. "You'll be with those you are currently gathered around. You've chosen to stand next to your fellow recruits and cadets for a purpose, and we believe you will work best with them. So, your six person team will include the five people around you. You are as strong as your weakest teammate."

His eyes gleam as he stares at me.

I glare back at him, angry, and at the same time, almost . . . excited. He thinks having Storm and Sam on my team will be a weakness. But caring about two kids, even if it's to my detriment, is a strength.

It means I'm not a monster. Not like him.

I'll do everything in my power to protect Storm and Sam through each leg of this race.

Plus, Matthias will be in this with me.

Soldiers move through the crowd of recruits as those who want to be together stand closer to one another.

"Looks like we're with you guys," Kiwi says, his voice far more cheerful than seems right for what we're about to face.

Arwen gives a tentative grin, but her eyes dart around the various groups. I'm not sure if she's looking for someone or if she's sizing up our competition. Maybe she's not happy to be with little kids and is trying to find an out.

Her head swivels, and she catches me watching her. Before either of us can say anything, a soldier appears.

"Extend your bands." She doesn't look at any of us as her focus remains on the screen in her hands.

We all obey, and after a few seconds, my band buzzes.

Team 17 linked.

The words scroll across my band and the bands of my teammates. Matthias fidgets with his band, reminding me he's not as comfortable with the tech as the rest of us. Cadets only wear bands for specific events. Not all the time like recruits.

The soldier drags her gaze from her screen to look at us. "You'll be going through in the third wave of teams in thirty minutes." She extends a pack. "This is for any tech you collect throughout the course."

Kiwi snatches the pack and says, "Perfect," as the soldier leaves.

He slides the pack on his back. "So. What part of this thing are you most looking forward to?"

"You're not nervous?" I ask.

"Course I'm nervous!" Kiwi bounces on the balls of his feet. "But I find it's better to focus on the positive whenever I can. Plus, I got the tech side of things down, and I'm a pretty decent shot." He says the words without cockiness. Just confidence. Something I've come to expect from Kiwi. "I'm feeling pretty good about the Technical Operations Building at the end."

He crouches his tall, lanky frame until he's eye level with the kids. "You guys wanna help me find tech while we're going through this course? You're smaller than some of the other recruits." He drops his voice to a conspiratorial whisper. "I'm guessing that'll give us a sweet advantage in seeing tech they miss. What do ya say?"

Sam smiles at Kiwi and stands taller now that he has a job.

"We should get our weapons," Arwen says.

"Good call." Matthias offers her a grin that turns Arwen's face bright red.

And leaves me far more jealous than I should be.

I tamp the feeling down as our team gets in line for the weaponry staging site. There's no need to be jealous of Arwen, and I can't allow unnecessary emotions to cloud my judgment with what we're about to head into.

Matthias and Kiwi strike up a conversation about their favorite weapons and include the kids by making ridiculous jokes about how each of the weapons are used. It's enough to continue to ease the tension in Sam's and Storm's shoulders, but I'm still wound tight.

Arwen and I end up next to each other, and I pick up where Kiwi left off. "Are you feeling good about any section of this course?"

She twists a piece of light brown hair around her finger. "No?" She sighs. "The truth is, I'm best at blowing things up. Doesn't sound like we'll need that in this course or in helping the North American region." There's a trace of irony in her voice.

I gape at her. "Blowing things up?" It's a dumb repeat of what she said, but I can't help myself.

Arwen seems sweet, and I've had good interactions with her. She even offered to help get me involved in the Resistance a couple days ago—something I'm hoping actually happens.

I never would have pinned her as a munitions expert.

She ducks her head. "I just . . . understand explosives. From the basic ones to the more complex and technical ones. Some are really cool, others like the Apex Hunter are scary. But . . ." She lifts her shoulder, then drops it. "It's kinda a pointless skill." She lets out a mirthless laugh.

"No skill is pointless," I say, remembering all Cai taught me about explosives and how he used them in the Ruins to terrify soldiers.

Skills Nika and Mom are still using.

Not that I can tell Arwen about it at the moment.

It's our team's turn to enter the weaponry staging station, leaving no time for us to continue our conversation.

The room isn't overly large, and it's packed with weapons—even though over twenty recruits and cadets have already gone through and geared up for the course. Everything is weatherproof, so even if a recruit drops a gun into the muddy water beneath an obstacle it will be okay.

Although there are many weapons in the room, the options are limited. Electro-fitted bows, rifles, and handguns. No knives. Which makes sense. They can't exactly make throwing knives *safe*, but I wish I could have the comfort of the weapon strapped to my belt.

Instead, I strap on a belt holster and a shoulder holster for two pistols, loop an electro-fitted bow onto my back, grab a rifle, and put on a helmet. It's more weapons than I should carry through an intense course, but I want to have enough in case something happens to one of my teammate's weapons.

Once I'm geared up, I turn to find Storm trying to help Sam strap a pistol to his small waist. It's too big and clatters to the floor when Storm lets go.

Corporal Sidon glares at them, no doubt furious they've *hurt* one of his precious weapons. I scoop the gun off the floor, set it on a low shelf, take each kid by the hand, and lead them to the side of the room.

"All right, let's see what we can do for you guys, huh?" I ask, trying to sound cheery like Kiwi or Matthias. And utterly failing.

Storm sighs. "Nothing fits Sam."

"But I need a gun," Sam says. "I gotta protect myself."

My stomach twists at what this child is going through. We *really* need to get him out to the Ruins. Being with Nika and Mom would be so much better for him. Hopefully being with me now doesn't bring him more to Ark's attention, like my proximity to Storm has.

I do a quick search of the electro-fitted bows and find a small one. "How about this instead? We can strap it to your back so your hands are free."

"It's not a gun," Sam says.

"It's even better," Matthias chimes in, joining us. He claps his hand on Sam's shoulder. "I'll show you how to use it, okay, buddy?"

Sam's mouth twists to the side as he considers Matthias's offer. "Okay. I guess."

Matthias focuses on me. "Arwen and Kiwi are waiting for us outside."

I nod. A quick survey of Storm shows that she's already geared up with a pistol. Hopefully it's enough.

Then again, between me and Matthias, our team will have plenty of weapons. Matthias leads Sam out of the room ahead of me, and Storm and I almost laugh at the two rifles slung over his back and the two pistols holstered to his muscular body. A bulge at his ankle has me annoyed I didn't think to strap another gun to my ankle. At least he thought of it.

Arwen and Kiwi wave at us. They're off to the side, away from other teams, and the four of us approach them.

My mind zips through the information Laban gave us about the course. It's different from anything even I've experienced.

A glance at my band reveals a timer counting down until we're supposed to enter.

Fifteen minutes left.

I turn to Storm and Sam. "Have you guys done a lot of these courses?"

I know Storm's answer, but I include her in the question so Sam doesn't feel singled out. Storm nods, and Sam echoes the movement, his dark brown eyes big and full of fear.

I wish I could pick the kid up and race to the Ruins *now*.

Impossible daydream.

"Well, we'll help you this time, okay?" I say, with a glance at the other three members of the team.

"Of course we will," Matthias says with one of his big Matthias grins.

Kiwi and Arwen nod their agreement.

"I'm not going to lie," Kiwi says, "the courses are never my strong suit." He rubs a hand over his buzzed hair. "Then again, I haven't done one yet where I got to put my tech *and* sharpshooter skills to the test."

"Sharpshooter?" Matthias asks.

Kiwi ducks his head. "Yeah. Got the qualification last week."

"He's good," Arwen confirms. Her face blazes five shades redder than Kiwi's when Kiwi smiles at her.

Guess the girl just blushes any time a guy smiles at her. Which makes me feel a little dumb for being jealous earlier.

"The courses always remind me of Damara." Storm's voices cracks as she says the words, and I'm instantly focused on her.

I put my arm around her as I search for the best way to proceed. Since I found out Ark had Storm, I've wondered how she ended up back in Talionis. But I haven't known how to bring up the difficult topic, let alone ask her. Especially since there's been no sign of Damara, the woman who cared for Storm like she was her daughter.

When Shane failed to get Storm and Damara out of Talionis the day we escaped, we all hoped the two of them would be protected in the Ruins. That hope was shattered the day I saw a holograph of Ark with a terrified Storm while we were on the run.

The thoughts race through my mind faster than a speeding transport, but I can't find words to ask the questions clamoring in my heart.

"Who's Damara?" Arwen asks. "I haven't heard of her."

Storm's chin quivers for an instant before she pulls herself together like a strong little soldier. "She was someone who took care of me when I got here. She protected me."

There's a long pause. Storm needs the chance to share what happened to the woman she loved so dearly, who protected her against such evil people, risked her life for her. A quick glance at my band tells me we have ten more minutes before our team will be called to enter the course.

I gently squeeze her shoulder. "What happened, sweetie?"

"We ran out of supplies, and we couldn't find another site." The words gush out of Storm's mouth. "We had to find more food before we could go back into hiding. We were super careful, but when we were sneaking into the kitchen to get supplies, the soldiers found us. I tried to run, but then there was a shot. It was so loud." Her eyes hold a faraway look. "When I looked back, Damara was dead."

A sickening wave washes over me. I suspected Damara was killed, but hearing Storm say the words hits me hard.

Sam has moved closer to Matthias, his eyes wide and panicked. Anger replaces my sadness.

It's not right that kids should go through this kind of trauma.

Damara would have fought for these kids. The fiery Hispanic woman was strong. An inspiration.

Tears burn the back of my eyes. I can't believe she's gone.

Our team is called to prepare to enter the course.

I cup Storm's face with my hands, and she drags her gaze to me.

"I'm sorry you went through all of that, honey." My voice cracks. I swallow. "So sorry."

I want to give her promises that I'll protect her now and keep these things from happening, but those are promises I can't keep. And I don't want to lie to this girl.

"We'll get through this one day at a time, okay?" That's something I *can* promise, and I'm happy about it, even as I wonder what survival will look like.

She nods, and the ghost of a smile dances across her face.

We go to the starting line. A heaviness presses against my chest. Another friend, gone. How much will Ark steal from me before this is all over?

Storm slips her hand in mine. I breathe out a slow breath.

I need to focus all my attention on getting my team through this course.

The ravenous gleam in the eyes of the recruits on the other two teams entering the course with us sends my stomach into knots. To them, our team looks like an easy way to gain points—and favor. Something every recruit and cadet in Talionis is trained to fight for.

"Good luck in there," a guy on the team closest to us says, catching my attention.

Hawthorne. I haven't interacted with him since the scenario we went through, but from the little experience I have with him, I know he's ruthless. And loyal to Talionis.

I incline my head, but don't say a word.

"Always gotta watch out when there are kids involved, you know?" The words are simple, but the threat beneath them is clear.

The starting gunshot goes off. We sprint forward.

CHAPTER
FIFTY-TWO

O ut of the corner of my eye, I'm relieved to see Hawthorne's team ignore us in the race to get to the obstacle course first.

It's fifty yards away, but a quick inventory of our team shows me Sam's little legs will never keep up with us for the length of this course.

Matthias scoops the boy up and tells him to hold on while he runs. Sam's small, but I can't imagine Matthias will be able to keep up a fast pace with a six-year-old clinging to him.

But the relief on Sam's face is enough to keep me from questioning Matthias's actions. If he didn't do it, I probably would have.

We're a few paces behind the other two teams, with Hawthorne's in the lead. He waves his group through, shouting at them to move faster.

"We *will* be one of the best teams in this course," he shouts at each of them, as though the words are a self-fulfilling prophecy he's speaking over them.

He's dangerous.

It's something I should have known just from working with him once, but as I witness his intensity, see how he's ready to fight, to be the best, it's clear he's a soldier for Talionis. He's willing to do whatever it takes to win if it will mean pleasing Demetrius Ark.

We reach the wall we need to climb to enter the course. Arwen and Kiwi step forward to start climbing.

"Let them get two minutes ahead," I say.

"But two minutes could impact us," Arwen says. "By a lot."

"It's probably safer that way," Kiwi says. "I've never seen Hawthorne fight fair. With all that's at stake in this course, I doubt today will be any different."

Matthias drops Sam to the ground and looks him in the eye. "Okay, buddy. You've got this."

Sam scuffs his foot in the dirt. "I'm not very good at these."

Kiwi ruffles his hair. "Me neither, dude, me neither. But we got a killer team with us." He gives the rest of us a lopsided grin. "Let's say we show these people we're better than they think we are, huh? Me and you?" Kiwi thrusts out his hand to Sam.

The little boy looks at him, then at Matthias. Awe sparks in his eyes at the two older boys who are giving him so much attention. "Okay," he says, giving Kiwi a high five.

"Just take it one step at a time," Storm says. "That's what I did when I first got here. And you get better every time." Her voice is so confident, so reassuring,

Yet the words remind me of how long she's been here and how much she's had to endure to survive.

Sam's face sets in determination.

My band shows two and a half minutes have passed.

"All right, let's go," I say, taking on the role of team lead even though we never discussed it.

No one seems to mind.

"I'll take lead position, and Matthias can bring up the rear and make sure everyone gets through." I state the words but give Matthias a questioning look to make sure he's okay with this plan.

He nods, and I don't waste another second.

I grab the thick rope and start climbing.

In no time, I've scaled the wall, and I'm standing at the top waiting for the others to join me.

My stomach drops. At least a dozen obstacles are visible from here, twice as many as a normal course. And that's just what I can *see*. There are likely more around bends and hidden by other obstacles.

Hawthorne's team is already two obstacles deep, past the next wall we'll have to climb after scrambling down the other side of the one I'm standing on, and over one of the longest sets of monkey bars I've seen outside of Elite Training. They're approaching an A-frame cargo climb—a tall, A-shaped structure they'll have to climb up and over using only a cargo net for support.

After that, there are rope climbs, seven balance beams on a path to a mud pit with laser wires over top of it—

"What are you standing there for, recruits?" A soldier on the other side of the wall shouts up at us.

With a start, I realize the rest of my team is on top of the wall, staring out at the obstacles looming before us with me.

"This is a *race!*" His voice snaps over me like a whip.

"Let's go!" I say to my team. There's no use dreading what we're about to face. It'll be better to hit it head-on.

Even as I think the thought, I can't stop myself from glancing at Sam. How will we get him through this?

"We'll figure it out," Matthias says at my elbow.

The way he knows what I'm worrying about without me saying a word is a little unnerving.

I maneuver down the side of the wall, dropping to the ground when it's a few feet away. As I wait for the others to join me, I do a quick check of my weapons. Everything's secure.

Arwen is the next on the ground, followed by Storm, then Sam and Kiwi. Matthias drops down last.

"Make sure your weapons are secure," I say as I jog to the next wall.

The last thing I want is to draw the attention of the soldiers stationed throughout the course. At least not more than we already have. I scale the wall quickly. Too quickly.

The rest of my team is only a few feet off the ground, with Storm making the fastest progress. I catch Matthias's eye, and he winces.

Unless we can pick up the pace, we'll be one of the worst placed teams.

Which isn't acceptable.

The problem is figuring out how to motivate my team without sounding like the soldiers.

"You guys are doing great," I say. "Move as fast as you can."

Matthias snorts, and I fight back a grin. He knows this pace is killing me. Storm responds quickly and makes her way up at twice the speed of the others.

I help pull each person up, except for Matthias. His biceps bulge as he hoists himself the last of the way up the wall, and he catches me watching before I can turn away.

Get it together, Bria! Now is not the time to be impressed by a guy.

I distract myself by patting powder onto my hands for the monkey bars. The rest of my team follows suit.

"Be careful here," I say. "This is a long set, and there are small resting points throughout." I look Kiwi, Storm, Sam, and Arwen in the eye. "Stop and rest if you need to. But remember, the longer you stop, the harder it'll be to start again. Make sure your weapons are well secured, and do your best not to fall. It's a sure way to lose your weapon."

"And get covered in mud," Arwen adds, her nose wrinkling as she glances down at the mud thickened water nine feet beneath the bars.

"Yeah." I clap my hands together to get some of the excess power off. "Let's do this."

With that, I launch myself from the platform and grab the third bar down the line. It's not until I hear Kiwi shout a good-natured, "Show off!" that I realize I probably should have grabbed the closest bar.

Oh well.

The added weight of my weapons provides another layer of difficulty to the bars, and it's not long before sweat is dripping down my back, despite the cool day.

Since the monkey bars require everyone to do their best on their own, I push myself, moving faster than necessary considering the fact that I'll have to wait for my team on the other side.

I pause at the second resting point to gauge how everyone's doing. Storm and Sam almost appear to be having fun. Both of them are smiling, and they're not as far behind me as I expected.

Kiwi's next, and even from here, I can tell he's struggling. But it's the fear on Arwen's face that turns my stomach to lead. She's paused midway through the first batch of bars, her arms trembling.

"Don't stop, Arwen," Matthias calls from behind her. "It'll just make it harder."

I tense, half expecting her to let go and fall into the mud. But then she takes a shuddering breath and reaches for the next bar.

"That's it," Matthias says. "One at a time. Swing your whole body, and use that momentum to help your arms."

She does as he says.

"Yeah, there you go," Matthias says.

I release a breath I didn't know I was holding. At least she's moving. As long as she doesn't stop too long at any of the rest points, she should get through. Especially with Matthias encouraging her along the way.

I add more powder to my hands and take on the next set of bars. Storm and Sam aren't far behind, and I smile as they shout to each other about pretending to be monkeys.

At least Sam doesn't seem as terrified now.

"You two kids!" Corporal Emode shouts. "This isn't a game. Take it seriously, or face a penalty!"

It takes all the self-control I can muster not to drop from the bars and rush her. Instead, I clamber over the last set of bars, my arms burning, and wait at the end for my team.

Storm and Sam both wear somber expressions now, the fear returning in full to Sam's eyes as he shoots furtive glances at Corporal Emode.

He reaches for the next bar, but his attention is more on the short, angry soldier. His fingers miss the bar, and he yelps. His weapon jostles from his shoulder and falls into the mud below, where it's instantly swallowed up. Somehow, he continues to cling to the other bar with his right hand.

But he won't hold long.

Without taking time to think, I grab the bars I just left behind and race toward him. "Hold on, Sam! I'm coming!"

My rifle beats into my back as I move at a reckless pace over the bars.

I have to get to Sam.

He's so small. And he hasn't been trained. Not like the rest of us. If he falls from this height, he'll get hurt.

Seconds later, I'm at the bar he couldn't get a hold on. I release a hand and reach for him. "Grab my hand, okay?"

He doesn't move or look at me as he stares down at the mud. His little body quakes.

"Come on, Sam," I say, trying to keep the desperation from my voice. "Look at me."

"You can do it, Sam," Storm says. She's doing a dead hang from the bar directly behind him.

How long will she be able to hold on?

My own muscles burn as I hold the weight of my body and my weapons with one arm, the other stretching toward Sam.

Before I can tell Sam to reach for me again, Kiwi, Arwen, and Matthias are all shouting their encouragements. It's enough to bring the boy's attention up from the muddy water.

His eyes latch onto me, and I will him to reach for me as I stretch my fingers closer to him.

"Swing your body toward me, okay?" I say.

He nods and obeys. His fingers brush mine, but I can't latch on.

"Try again," Storm says.

Sweat drips into my eyes. *Please, God, help him. Help me.*

Sam's brow furrows in determination, then he swings for me again. This time, I grab hold of his hand. Using the momentum from his swing, I strain and pull him up.

"Grab the bar," I demand, my breathing labored.

Thankfully, he does.

"Follow me the rest of the way," I say. Before he can respond, I clamber over the bars and to the end point.

As soon as I arrive, I turn back to see Sam and Storm aren't far away. When Sam is only a couple of bars out, I reach for him, and he catapults himself at me. I stumble back against the railing as his arms and legs wrap around me. My weapons dig into my body as he clings to me, but I ignore the pain and hold him while we wait for the others to arrive.

His heart pounds so hard and fast, I can feel it.

The rest of our team arrives without further incident, and Matthias and Kiwi convince Sam to let me go so we can proceed forward through the course.

We scramble down the ladder and away from the monkey bars and jog to the A-frame cargo net climb.

Arwen comes up next to me right before we make it to the climb. "Nice job back there."

"It was too close." The words are difficult to squeeze out as my mind replays Sam dangling from the bars. Seeing his bow fall into the mud. Knowing it could have been him.

His bow.

I stumble, then regain my footing. "He lost his weapon."

Arwen and I exchange a meaningful look as we stop at the A-frame. The rest of the group arrives a second later. Now isn't the time to address the weapon issue, but dread coils in my gut. Whatever "games" are coming, Sam will be in far greater danger without a weapon.

Is there any way we can get him to the Ruins before then?

I climb the A-frame, using my legs as much as possible to give my arms a break, and focus on the task in front of me. There will be time to figure out how to help Sam later. Right now, I have a responsibility to get my team through this course safely.

The rest of the obstacles are difficult, but we get through with no issues. Even if we *are* going slower than I wish we were. At each obstacle, Matthias is at the back helping whoever is struggling the most, and I make sure each member of our team gets to the other side of every challenge intact.

By the time we come to the end of this leg of the course, we're all covered in mud and breathing heavy. But there's a sense of camaraderie.

Through an hour of navigating various obstacles, we've become a real team. It's almost surreal how quickly a bond can form when difficult things happen.

"Where next?" Matthias asks me after a soldier scans our bands to confirm we've successfully completed this leg of the course.

A shot fires not too far away and to the left. With a quick glance at my band to confirm, I nod in the direction of the shot. "That way. According to the map, the mock-up village should only be a couple hundred yards away. On the other side of the tree line."

"Lead the way," Arwen says.

With that, we head to the next leg of the race. Despite the camaraderie, I can't help but worry about how we'll do in the rankings at the end of this course.

CHAPTER
FIFTY-THREE

T he village comes into view as we jog at a pace everyone can sustain. A much slower pace than the one I *want* to be moving at.

"What's that?" Sam asks an instant before he's digging under a bush off to the side of the trail.

He tugs out a piece of tech that looks vaguely familiar, but that I can't place.

"Nice, little man!" Kiwi says, high-fiving Sam. He takes the pocket-sized tech gadget from the boy and puts it in his pack.

Sam grins at Kiwi, but it fades as staccato shots from the looming village fill the air.

There must be another team inside this leg of the race. Hopefully we don't end up in trouble as a result.

Without a word, our team starts jogging again. We arrive at the entrance of the village, where Corporal Sidon waits for us.

I snap to attention and sense the rest of my team do the same.

"At ease," Corporal Sidon says, appraising us—or, more likely, our weapons.

His sharp gaze zeroes in on Sam, and Corporal Sidon's nostrils flare. He doesn't say a word, but it's clear he's unhappy to see the boy lost his electro-fitted bow.

Sam crowds closer to Storm, and Corporal Sidon shifts his gaze to the rest of us.

"Since you were briefed by Sergeant Meritas, you know this is a combination of your weaponry skills and warfare scenario strategic ability." He spreads his legs shoulder-width apart and places his hands on his hips. "Those of you who have weapons"—he looks down his nose at Sam—"will be free to use them. But know this. If you use a weapon and hit a neutral or friendly target, or if you miss an enemy combatant, it is at the discretion of the officers as to whether or not you will retain the weapon to be used in the upcoming games. Is that understood?"

"Yes, sir!" we say the words simultaneously.

Corporal Sidon nods once. "Good." He focuses on Kiwi. "You've trained hard for this. Make me proud in there."

Kiwi shifts uncomfortably but mumbles, "Yes, sir."

Corporal Sidon flings his hand at the rest of us dismissively. "Half of your team can barely handle a weapon."

More shots go off in the town behind us, closer to the entrance than I'm comfortable with. At the sound, Corporal Sidon's eyes light up.

"Now, onto your objective." He pulls a small screen from his back pocket and scans it. "You'll be following the typical procedure for a retrieval scenario." He taps buttons on his screen, and our bands chime with the receipt of information. "There are three items in this village you must retrieve and bring to the extraction point indicated on the map I just sent to your bands."

I open the message as he talks and find a detailed map of the village we're about to enter. Three points are highlighted within the village, with our extraction point marked with an X. The items listed for retrieval are a map, an electronic key card, and a small, circular piece of tech.

Corporal Sidon continues his briefing. "We've provided you with the intel on *where* these items are, but make no mistake. This will not be a simple retrieval. The town is under enemy control, and you may face combatants at any point." He pauses to let his words sink in.

CAPTIVE OF TALIONIS 339

"There are other teams attempting to complete this portion of the course as we speak. They are not your allies."

Chills ripple over my skin, despite the warmth I felt moments ago from the exertion required from the course. What if Hawthorne's team is in there?

Corporal Sidon reiterates what Laban told us about how we're competing against other teams and that we're allowed to sabotage said teams. "It's encouraged, even," he concludes.

I'm confident Hawthorne is pushing his team to ruthlessness.

Hopefully they've finished this portion of the course and we can sneak through without any encounters. With them or any other team.

We're too easy of a target, even for teams who aren't as skilled.

"Your course time has been paused while you received this objective," Corporal Sidon says.

At least the past several minutes won't be counted against us, I guess.

He types a code into his screen that brings a red countdown up on the side we can see. "Your timer restarts in ten seconds. Good luck."

The countdown begins.

10, 9, 8 . . .

I pull my rifle into my hands and check the training ammunition. Loaded and ready.

7, 6, 5 . . .

A quick survey of my team tells me they all have their weapons ready . . . except for Sam.

4, 3 . . .

I swallow back my apprehension. I have to focus on what we're about to face. The rest of us have weapons. We'll protect our youngest teammate.

As 2 flashes on the screen, I lift my fist into the air.

1, 0.

I drop my fist, signaling for my team to follow me, and duck through the entrance into the village. I lift my rifle, ready to face enemy combatants, scanning the buildings for any sign of movement.

I pause a few feet down the path we need to take to provide cover, gun at the ready.

Arwen comes up next to me and hesitates.

"Get to the corner down this street and wait," I say without looking at her.

She obeys and leads the others to the corner, while I keep my gun trained on the opposite street, alert for signs of the enemy.

Matthias passes me last and taps my shoulder, signaling for me to follow.

We regroup with the rest of our team at the end of the street.

Kiwi's now in the front, looking through the scope of his sniper rifle. "No sign of the enemy."

I do a quick review of my band, even though I already mapped out the start of our route while waiting for Corporal Sidon. "According to the map, our first retrieval is a block away. Stay alert. The enemy could be anywhere."

I lead my team to three more alleys with no sign of the enemy, although the sound of gunfire is a constant percussion through the air.

We duck into a storefront where we're to retrieve the tech item. After a quick search, we find the building empty of other people, which makes me uneasy.

This is the first item on our list, sure. But why aren't we facing *any* opposition?

Arwen finds the tech and passes it to Kiwi, who adds it to his pack. Both of them appear more relaxed than when we first entered the village.

Storm and Sam also seem less stressed.

"Where next?" Matthias's voice is tight and his body tense as he holds his rifle, his eyes focused out a window and on the empty street.

He's ready for action. Expecting it.

The lack of enemy encounters may have caused the rest of our team to breathe easier, but Matthias and I have been through too much to assume we're in the clear.

A wave of gratitude that he's in this with me washes over me. At least I don't have to bear the stress of protecting the other four alone.

I do a quick review of the map on my band. "The map is only a few blocks away."

Matthias spares a glance my direction. "Lead the way."

I take position at the front door, and the others gather behind me. After confirming the path is clear with no signs of snipers, I slip out the door, head on a swivel, gun poised and ready.

Gunshots echo in the near distance. Another team must be pinned down.

Maybe that's why we're not facing any attacks.

"Down!" Kiwi barks the word, his voice unusually harsh.

I drop, grabbing Sam and pulling him down with me.

Kiwi's gun cracks as he releases two shots in quick succession.

With Sam tucked half under my body, I follow the direction Kiwi's gun is pointed in. A soldier falls to his knees on a rooftop that's a hundred yards away.

"We can move," Kiwi says. "He was alone."

I scramble to my feet, along with the others. "How did you even see him?"

Kiwi does a quick check of his rifle before replying. "Sniper status, remember?"

"Nice job, man," Matthias says.

I'm hyper-alert as I lead my team the last block to our next destination. How did I miss the lookout Kiwi saw? At least Kiwi didn't miss him.

The real question is, did he notify anyone else before Kiwi took him out?

We enter another empty building and retrieve the map.

Still too easy.

I shake off the sense of foreboding wrapping itself around me like seaweed clinging to my ankles.

"The last location is the farthest away," I say, taking a second to look at each member of my team. "It's close to the extraction point, but we'll need to move quickly, quietly, and be on the alert. We know the enemy is out there, even though we haven't had a full-on attack from them yet."

Sam, Storm, and Arwen look petrified at my words, but Kiwi and Matthias nod their agreement.

Seconds later, I lead the team out of the building and down an alley. We'll have to cross through the center of the town in order to quickly make it to our next location. Theoretically, it would be safer to take a roundabout loop, but my gut tells me that would be a trap. Especially for my team.

If I were operating a scenario like this—or a Kill Zone—I would have ambushes set up on what appeared to be the safest route. Hit teams when their guards are lowered.

We weave through streets and alleys, echoes of gunshots in the distance, but nothing in our path.

It's too easy.

I creep down the final alley that leads to the largest exposed portion before we make it to where the electronic key card is hidden. I put my fist in the air to halt my team's progress, drop to my knees, and peek around the corner.

Gunfire blasts through the air, but not at me. I press my back against the wall, hand out for my team to hold, and search for the team under fire.

Asher is trapped in the center of the village square. Training bullets ricochet off the dirt as he huddles under a short stone wall. A quick survey of the rest of the square tells me he's alone.

I pull back into the alley and face my team. "Asher's pinned down."

"Where's his team?" Matthias asks.

"He's probably acting as a decoy," Arwen says. "He's done it for his teams before."

Respect for the surly Resistance leader rises in me. A guy who's willing to take on such huge risks for those in his command is worth following. And he certainly hasn't gotten that example from anyone in Talionis.

"We should help him," Matthias says, reminding me of what a great guy *he* is.

Our eyes connect. We both know there's a risk in aiding a team when our objective says all other teams are to be viewed as enemies. But we can't leave Asher on his own.

I nod my agreement. "Arwen, can you stay with Storm and Sam? Wait here until we send you a message."

"Okay." She white-knuckles the rifle in her hands, then leads the kids deeper into the alley.

I give as reassuring of a smile as I can to Storm. She offers me a wavering one in return as she unholsters her pistol. The sight puts a sour taste in my mouth.

"Kiwi." I shift my focus to him. "Think you can provide cover for me and Matthias?"

He scans the building to our right. "Yeah. Give me a minute to get into position." He points to a window on the third floor. "I'll ping your bands to let you know when I'm ready."

I nod, and he slips into the building, leaving me alone with Matthias.

His gaze is trained on Asher. "Do we make a straight line for him?"

I assess the dozen enemy combatants around the square. They're grouped into three teams. One on the ground to the east. One midway up a building to the west. And the final team positioned out of our line of sight to the north.

We're outmanned and outgunned. But we have the element of surprise, assuming we can make our way to Asher without tipping our hand.

"Let's go at an angle." I point to an empty food stand a few yards to our left.

Matthias tracks the route with his eyes. "Good plan."

We go quiet, the only sound the gunshots yards away.

Our bands buzz with Kiwi's message.

All set.

"Ready?" Matthias asks.

"Yup." I send a quick message to Kiwi. *Moving now.*

His rifle cracks as he draws fire, and Matthias and I sprint to the empty food stall.

I shoot at the group of soldiers to the right. "Go!"

Matthias takes off for Asher as Kiwi and I cover him. He slides into place next to Asher, kicking up dust.

"Move!" Matthias shouts the word and begins firing at the soldiers.

Within seconds, I'm diving for cover next to the two guys.

"What are you doing?" Asher asks, a mix of skepticism and awe in his voice.

I take a shot at a soldier who's running at us. Direct hit. She goes down. "What does it look like? We're saving you."

Asher grunts. "Thanks."

"What are you doing here without your team?" Matthias asks, now holding a pistol in each hand and firing at the soldiers on the left while I shoot at the ones to the right.

"I was the decoy," he says, confirming Arwen's suspicions. "They got through. They're waiting for me at our extraction point. I got pinned down. And ran out of bullets right before you all showed up."

Matthias pulls a spare gun from his ankle holster and passes it to Asher.

"Kiwi has our six," I say. "We can get back to the alley we were in."

"Kiwi's a sick shot," Asher says, taking aim at a soldier in a building directly in front of us. "Just say the word, and I'm ready to run. Tired of this spot."

We're moving in three. I send the message to Kiwi.

"On me in three, two, one. Now!" I jump up and sprint to the food stand, firing my pistols in the general direction of the soldiers.

Matthias and Asher are right behind me as I press my back against the food stand and take cover.

Move. Kiwi's text comes through to our bands, and we don't hesitate.

Seconds later, the safety of the alley envelopes us.

A glance down the alley shows Arwen, Storm, and Sam are okay.

Asher and Matthias send out rapid-fire shots covering us, and Kiwi bursts out the side door of the building.

"We have to move now!" I say.

The four of us race down the alley to the other three, and they join us as I lead everyone through back alleys and side streets. We come to a mock-up of a bakery, and I shove the door open, confirm it's empty, and wave everyone in.

Once we're all inside, Kiwi takes up position at the door.

"That was some risk you took," Asher says. He eyes me and Matthias before extending his hand, first to me, then to Matthias. "I owe you."

"People are more important than winning a race," I say.

Asher stares at me, eyes narrowed as he processes my words. "I misjudged you."

"You did," I agree.

His eyebrows rise, and he almost smiles. "I need to get to my team." He passes Matthias his pistol.

Matthias shakes his head. "You keep it. I have a feeling you'll need it again."

"Thanks," Asher says. With that, he heads to the door. He claps Kiwi on the shoulder as he passes him and says something I can't hear.

Then he's gone.

"We should move too," I say. "The soldiers probably aren't far behind us."

As we find a different path to our final retrieval point, a sense of gratefulness fills me. Yes, we added additional time to our course results. And we did the opposite of what we were told to do to other teams.

But I may have finally found a way into the Resistance.

CHAPTER
FIFTY-FOUR

We complete our mission in the village without further incident, and Sam finds two more pieces of tech for Kiwi. The kid has taken his task seriously. And even if the stuff doesn't prove useful when we get to the final leg of the race, at least having something to do has kept him distracted.

I'm on alert, rifle reloaded and in my hands as I lead my team.

The map we're following to our final leg of the race has us traveling near the river, and the sound of it in the distance tickles my ears. At this time of year, there may not be ice on the edges of the water yet, but I'm sure it's icy cold. The last thing I want to do is enter the water, let alone make the kids jump in. But we haven't hit the Kill Zone portion of the race yet which makes me uneasy.

There's no chance we're getting to the Technical Operations Building without an unexpected point of enemy contact.

"Keep an eye out," I say.

The soldiers have set up twelve-foot-high blockades staggered throughout this portion of the course. Nothing is clearly visible, and I'm inclined to think some of the barriers are soundproof. Other than the river gurgling to our left, it's way too quiet.

We approach the only opening to a thick metal barrier that stretches in either direction. I hold up my fist, halting my team.

Matthias materializes next to me. "What's up?" His voice is low.

"Something's not right." I scan the top of the barrier, but there's no movement.

Still, I can't shake the feeling that the Kill Zone is on the other side of this wall.

According to the map, this barrier is the first of five built close together with openings scattered at different points on each. We have to weave our way through them before coming out on the other side, at which point the tech portion of the race will be a half mile away on the right.

"Do you hear anything?" I ask Matthias without looking at him, my eyes skipping to the different places I would hide if I was attempting to ambush someone.

"No." His voice is resigned and draws my focus. His blue eyes hold mine, and I know he feels the same weight of responsibility to get our team to safety as I do. "But we have to move. Trap or not, we have to finish the course."

I swallow hard. "I know." Taking a deep breath, I lead my team to the first opening. Before entering, I glance over my shoulder at the others. "Be ready for anything."

Each person nods. Matthias moves to the back of the group, taking his position next to Sam. Matthias gives me a thumbs-up, and I turn back to the opening.

Trust him. The thought whispers through my mind.

I square my shoulders and move through the opening.

We weave our way past the first three barriers. Sweat trickles down my back despite the crisp fall air. Something is coming. Every step we take without it hitting only increases my anxiety.

A muted shout pierces my ears as I reach the next barrier opening.

This is it.

The Kill Zone is on the other side of these barriers.

There's no doubt in my mind.

In seconds, we've arrived at the final barrier. The sounds of gunshots and yelling are clearer now.

I open and close my fist above my head three times to signal Matthias. Lift my gun. And charge through the final barrier opening.

There are bushes directly outside of the opening, providing unexpected cover. I crouch low behind them and take in the scene as my team falls in around me.

The soldiers have set up a forest, with trees, rocks, and massive boulders scattered between the river and the entrance to the Technical Operations Building. They've even wedged old walls and pieces of buildings in different places.

Soldiers are scattered throughout the area, some exposing their locations as they fire at a team attempting to make their way through the Kill Zone. The team returns fire, using a boulder as cover less than twenty yards from us.

Asher's team, which includes other members of the Resistance who I recognize like Marci and the guys who pinned me against the wall in the one and only meeting I attended.

It makes sense that they wouldn't be far ahead of us, but I didn't expect them to be in a Kill Zone *with* us.

"I'm counting fifteen soldiers," Kiwi says. He's two feet away from me, looking through the scope of his sniper rifle at the zone we're about to enter.

"Asher's team's close by," I say.

"Should we work with them to get through?" Matthias asks.

Before I can answer, Kiwi lets out a low whistle. "Well, this ain't good."

I look through the scope of my rifle. My stomach drops when I see who marches through the forest as though she owns it.

Shay.

Her six drones whirl about her, deflecting bullets before they can reach her. Every weaponized part of her body is on full display, from her machine gun arm where her hand used to be, to a pistol mounted from her left shoulder. She wields another pistol with her real hand. Her uniform has metal shields attached to it, adding additional protection.

"She's heading right for Asher's team." Kiwi's voice shakes with the words.

"They won't stand a chance," Arwen says, echoing my thoughts.

I scan the terrain, desperately looking for a solution. Shay's full attention is on Asher's team. If we can flank her and signal them, we might be able to get through this. Assuming we can take out her drones.

A crumbling wall near the river catches my eye. From what I can tell, there are no soldiers near it.

"We need to get to that wall," I say, pointing to the target. "But stay out of sight. We need the element of surprise."

Each member of my team—including the kids—agrees, and I army crawl toward the river. Within a minute, I reach the bank of the river. The wall is three yards away. If we stay on land, there's a huge chance we'll get spotted.

But if we swim . . .

The water rushes by a mere two feet away. Both beckoning me and promising me pain. The old monster I tried to fight in the water no longer threatens like it once did. The forgiveness I've experienced with God has changed things for me in more ways than I realized. But my relationship with water holds far too many terrible memories. Not just of Ezri anymore, but also of Ava's drowning and of almost losing Nalani.

A hand on my elbow captures my attention. Matthias is there.

"We going in?" he asks.

A glance back toward Shay tells me time's running short.

"Yes," I say, deciding in that moment. I shift to face the others. "Kiwi, you, Matthias, and I are going to swim to the other side of the wall. Arwen, Storm, and Sam." I look at the three of them. "Wait here for my signal. Do not move. Do not shoot. Don't let anyone know you're here. Got it?"

All three of them nod, but Arwen looks ready to argue. Thankfully, she doesn't voice her disagreement. We don't have time for an argument.

Kiwi, Matthias, and I slip into the river. It's shallow, and we crawl through the arctic water more than swim, keeping low so the bank shields us from view. My hands are cramping, and my uniform is soaked and chilling my entire body by the time we crawl back up the bank and take shelter near the wall.

"Kiwi, can you send a message to Asher?" I ask. "Let him know where we are?"

Matthias shakes his head. "They encrypted our bands for—"

"Done." Kiwi grabs his sniper rifle. "Ready when you are, boss."

If we were in any other situation, hearing Kiwi call me boss would make me chuckle. But Shay's deadly gaze is zeroed in on a team of recruits who have no hope of finishing this race without major penalties if we don't help them.

Matthias and I ready our weapons.

Asher's team looks in our direction.

I hold up three fingers and count them down, whispering the numbers to the guys with me. "Three, two, one. Fire!"

Kiwi picks off three soldiers in rapid succession, and Matthias and I fire at others. I hit one, then Shay's gaze finds mine.

Her red hair billows out behind her, and a smile curls her lips. She says something unintelligible from this distance, then she heads our way.

Bullets from the soldiers who haven't been hit kick up dirt near us and send pebbles flying from the wall we're hiding behind.

"Well, the distraction worked," Matthias says, pulling out his pistols and swinging his second empty rifle to his back. "What now?"

With the focus off of them, Asher and his team move deeper into the Kill Zone. A lump lodges in my throat. Was helping them a mistake? Will they just let us take the fall for them and complete the course faster?

I drag my attention back to Shay. She's closer now.

With startling clarity, I realize I've led Matthias and Kiwi into a perfect kill box. There's no way we're escaping here without getting shot. Which means a forty-five-minute penalty for our team. And that's assuming Shay doesn't find Arwen, Storm, and Sam.

I fire three shots, but her drones shield her.

Two drones drop to the ground. Shay pulls up short.

"Was that you, Kiwi?" I ask.

Before he can respond, I catch sight of Asher, perched in a tree, his gun aimed at Shay. He shoots and misses. Marci's on the ground and tosses him a new gun.

Shay turns, her arm-gun poised.

I jump to my feet and fire as quickly as I can. Matthias and Kiwi cover me. Another drone drops. Then another.

Shay's face contorts into an angry scowl. She whips back to face me and runs at me. I brace myself.

Staccato gunfire rings next to me.

Shay falls to the ground.

An eerie silence follows.

"We better move before more soldiers arrive," Matthias says.

"Yeah," I agree.

A breeze blows past, sending a chill through me as it further cools my wet uniform.

Matthias, Kiwi, and I hurdle the wall, and I call for Arwen and the kids. We jog into the forest, connecting with Asher and his team halfway through.

"Thanks for the assist. Again." He doesn't look at any of us as he says the words.

Matthias slaps him on the back. "Hey, we can't let the hard work we did saving your butt back in the village be for nothing, man."

Asher snorts.

"Thanks for not leaving us behind," I say.

The words bring Asher's sharp gaze to me. "Of course."

I think I offended him, but there's no time to apologize.

Our teams split to follow our individual routes. My team heads to the final leg of our race: the Technical Operations Building.

CHAPTER
FIFTY-FIVE

W e near the entrance to the redesigned portion of the training arena, and I bring the team to a halt behind an outcropping of bushes so we can assess the situation.

The soldiers have gone to great lengths to change the facade of the training arena. It *looks* like a tech building, with slick silver panels, an arch entryway leading up to the door, and large screens displaying the name of the building: Echelon Industries.

No guards patrol the outside.

Kiwi lets out a low whistle. "They really went all out."

"What do you see?" I ask.

He tugs out a piece of tech Sam or Storm found for him and puts it to his eye. "The archway is a full-body scanner. It'll pick up any weapons and send an alert to their guards. There's a data pad on the door, which probably requires a code and biometric identification. At least that's what I would require if I put it on a door. And . . ." He pauses, leaning forward as he cranes his neck to see a different angle of the entrance. "Yup. Just what I thought. There are sensor pads at the entry as well."

"For what?" Arwen asks.

Kiwi sits back on his heels and drops the tech he was looking through. "Probably as a fail-safe against the biometric identification.

The sensors will pick up the body mass of the person trying to gain entry and scan the footprint to confirm whoever is attempting entry really is who they say they are."

Sam's nose scrunches. "Why do they need a footprint?"

Kiwi ruffles his hair. "Because every person's footprint is unique."

Matthias and I exchange a weighted look. This is way more intense than I expected.

"And getting inside the building is only the first part." I adjust the empty rifle on my back, painfully aware that I'm not the only one low on ammo. We can't strong-arm our way in.

Storm sighs. "This feels impossible."

I keep my mouth shut so as not to instantly agree with her.

"No, not impossible." Kiwi rubs his hands together. "This is where the fun starts."

No wonder he and Ari get along so well whenever they talk.

"Tell me you got a plan," Matthias says. "Because I'm not seeing any options here."

Kiwi puts one hand on Sam's shoulder and the other on Storm's. "My friends here have hooked us up. They found a decent amount of tech during the course." He digs items out of his bulging pack. "And that's what'll get us through."

He lays out a half dozen pieces of tech, and Storm, Sam, and Arwen add a few more pieces. We gathered way more than I thought. Well, *they* gathered. I wasn't even on the lookout for tech. I was too concerned about getting everyone safely through every other portion of this course.

Kiwi points to a small square item. "All right, so this—"

I hold up my hand. "As much as I'd love to hear what each of these things are—"

"Sure you would," Matthias mutters with a smirk.

I roll my eyes at him and continue. "We're on a clock. Do you have a plan to get us into the building?"

Kiwi salutes with his characteristic two fingers. "Yes, ma'am. We have what we need to gain entry and disable the alarm. You're good with maps. Can you figure out our route once I get us inside?"

I nod. "Sure."

"Great." Kiwi hands out the tech to Arwen, Storm, and Sam. "You and Matthias work on that, and the rest of us will navigate this fun tech so we can get into the building. We'll signal you once we're ready to make entry."

I open my mouth to protest, wanting to take on the dangers of being close to the building myself. But the reality is I have no idea how to use any of the tech, and Kiwi's already scrambling toward the building and waving the other three to follow.

Dragging my gaze away from the group, I punch in the code on my band to open the map of the Echelon Industries building.

"You should go with them," I say to Matthias, keeping my focus on the map of the inside of the tech building.

"No, someone needs to have your back." Matthias's voice rasps slightly, much closer than I anticipated. "Plus, Kiwi clearly has a plan, and I'd get in the way."

"Mmm." The noncommittal sound comes out as I study the map. Not that there's much to study. The rooms are laid out in a simple grid pattern with one way through the building to the room we need. And one way out.

There's nothing for me to strategize until we're inside and I can take stock of the security force.

I shift to study the front of the Echelon Industries building and see the other four members of our team doing something near the arch.

Matthias takes my hand. "Bria." The desperate edge to his voice is enough to bring my eyes to him. "I need to tell you something."

"Matthias, now's probably not—"

"No." He presses his lips together. "I never get to see you." He squeezes my hand lightly. "With everything going on, all that might happen, now is what we have." He stares into my eyes, and I can't look away.

"They're probably monitoring us," I say, my voice low in an attempt to avoid any recording devices picking up my words. It's too risky to use the cloaking feature on my band in a course like this.

"I don't care." He drops his voice to match my cautious whisper.

He takes my hand and puts it over his heart. It's beating rapidly, despite the fact that we've been sitting here for a few minutes. "Every risk you take terrifies me. Because every time, I wonder if that's the risk that will take you away from me forever." He ducks his head, and his chest shudders beneath my hand as he takes a deep breath.

My heart pounds in my throat as I search for a way to respond.

Before I can come up with any words, he looks up, his piercing blue eyes capturing mine, more serious than I've ever seen them. "I love you, Bria. I've wanted to tell you that for a long time."

The words break over me like cool ocean water on a hot day. All the reasons his admission is dangerous, the possibility of Ark and Colonel Valarius knowing the depth of Matthias's feelings for me, the pain this moment could inflict later—all of it melts away.

I reach up and cup his cheek with my hand. Hope lights his eyes and takes my breath away. I bite my lip.

This is dangerous.

So dangerous.

But I take a deep breath. "I love you too." As the words leave my mouth, I know with a certainty that I *do* love Matthias.

The reality both thrills and terrifies me. Because admitting how I feel leaves me exposed. Vulnerable.

And in Talionis, being vulnerable could get me killed.

Matthias wraps his arms around me, and I hug him back and rest my head against his chest. For a few seconds, maybe I can just enjoy the fact that he loves me.

Our bands buzz, jerking me back to the reality of where we are and what's happening.

Kiwi and the others are ready for us.

I PUSH ASIDE THE MOMENT WITH MATTHIAS AND WORK WITH MY TEAM TO complete the tech portion of the course. Especially because if I let myself think about the foolishness of what Matthias and I admitted to each other in the middle of one of Ark's courses, I'll end up unable to actually *finish* the course. And there are others counting on me.

Although admitting we love each other was a dumb move, I can't keep the smile off my face. It's enough that Arwen and Storm have given me funny looks.

We arrive at the center room, and Arwen proves to be adept at solving puzzles. With her clarity of mind, we're able to enter the codes on each of our bands in the correct order into the system database and plant the virus.

I lead my team through the final path of the course and out of the Echelon Industries building just as an alarm sounds.

We cross the finish line of the race a few minutes later, and everyone high-fives each other, complimenting one another on various things done throughout the course.

Laban stalks toward us. Everything else fades to the background.

"You got through, but I can't imagine anyone's gonna be happy with your time." He sneers, his golden eyes locked on mine. "Elite Recruit." He spits on the ground at my feet. "Pathetic."

My insides tremble, and then there's a comforting hand on my arm as Matthias steadies me with his presence. Laban looks between the two of us, and I step away, letting Matthias's hand fall, keeping my face cold, even though it breaks my heart to do this to him. Especially after the moment we had together less than thirty minutes ago.

But I can't let Laban think Matthias is a weakness for me.

Although, if they monitored us in the course the way I suspect they did, he already knows.

"You said that if we worked well as a team, we'd receive points toward our overall score," I say, focusing on the problem at hand. "It's not just about the individual effort. The Commander wants to see that we can fight together for his cause, does he not?"

The scowl Laban gives me tells me he can't disagree with a word I said.

"Individual rankings are scored as well," he says. "And you should've done better."

I incline my head. "I could have, on my own. But the Commander designed this as a team course today, not an individual one. And I got my entire team through, even with some who are new to Talionis." I straighten. "I expect the Commander will be pleased with that."

Laban's nostrils flare. I can tell he wants to call me out for insubordination. Pummel me. Put me in my place. But other soldiers are nearby, and the reality that there are probably cameras and microphones picking up every conversation following the course, he won't dare to disagree with what I said. Especially since he and I both know it's exactly how the Commander feels.

He steps toward me, invading my space. He's fit, wiry, and even though he's not as big as Major Vasco or Sergeant Valarius, in a fight, he could easily outmaneuver me. Like he's done before.

But in this moment, I've won. And he knows it too.

"Watch your step, Averton," he says. "You don't want to make the mistake of thinking you've gotten the better of me."

"Never, sir," I say, keeping my voice steady. My anger will only provide him with an opportunity to put me in my place, and I refuse to give him the satisfaction.

He turns on his heel and strides away. There's a somberness to our group after his appearance.

"I really don't like him," Sam says.

"Me either," Storm agrees. She hesitates, a far-off look haunting her eyes.

"What's wrong?" I ask.

Storm blinks hard, as though trying to erase a nightmare. "He's the one who killed Damara."

Her words suck the air from my lungs. I hug Storm to myself, even as another reason to disdain Laban fills me.

God, don't let these people win. Please, God, don't let these people win.

My team and I weave through the crowd of recruits to discover our ranking in the course. I clench and unclench my hands as I walk. What if Laban's right and my individual ranking is too low?

"We did better in there than I expected," Matthias says, his voice low and by my ear.

I swallow hard. "Hopefully it was good enough."

Sam skips over and grabs Matthias's hand as we close the

distance to the ranking screen. My heart warms at the sight, pushing aside some of my unease after the conversation with Laban.

But the unease returns almost instantly. The ranking screen looms before us.

It's listed by team. Not individual.

After a moment, Kiwi points. "There we are! Right in the middle. Nice job, team!" He starts high-fiving each of us, going on and on about how great we are.

Several of those around us shoot him disapproving glances. No one celebrates ranking in the middle.

But Kiwi's antics bring smiles to Sam and Storm's faces, which is enough for me to want to hug him.

Not to mention, he's right. Being ranked in the middle *is* good for us. We'll be able to eat dinner, keep our rifles, and we won't be given additional chores throughout the city.

I exhale a slow breath. It could have been so much worse.

"I'm ready to help." Matthias's voice is so soft, I almost don't hear him at all above the cacophony of recruits around us.

I tilt my head to the side, searching his eyes. He nods, as though to confirm I heard him correctly, then gives a pointed look at Sam. I can't stop the smile that breaks across my face.

Matthias is ready to help me get kids out of the city.

CHAPTER
FIFTY-SIX

A burst of anticipation courses through me as I make my way to the tailors' to work with Kemena tonight. The course today was taxing, but my team ranked okay. At least we weren't in last place.

Still, with the rigorous amount of trainings I've had, coupled with the weight of knowledge that the attack on Sitreea is so soon, a heaviness shrouds me wherever I go. I rotate my shoulders, wishing I could shrug it off.

At least no one has changed my schedule to remove me from working with Kemena at the tailors'.

Although the room isn't supposed to have any recording devices, I enter the cloaking code Kiwi taught me into my band.

I enter to find Kemena folding the first load of wash, piles of dirty laundry everywhere.

"Wow. That's a lot of clothes," I say.

Kemena blows stray hair out of her face. "Yup. I came in early to get started. Figured the course today would impact work tonight." She sets the clean uniform aside and reaches for a pair of pants. "Sampta and Presidia are not at all okay with how their uniforms have been *mistreated*." She puts quotes in the air as she says the word and her nostrils flare.

"Oh, I can imagine." A washer beeps, and I unload it.

"Some of the uniforms have blood on them." She picks up a shirt speckled with dried blood. "They cared more about the clothing than the kid who was wearing it. I don't mind those ladies, but their priorities are massively screwed up."

My chest tightens. Kemena's right. The sisters' priorities *are* screwed up.

Once I've transferred the load to the dryer, I join Kemena in separating the outer uniforms from the undergarments. We start a few new loads of wash in the machines that line the wall at the back of the room. Once they're in, we turn our attention to the load finishing in the dryers and pull clothes out.

As we work, I quickly outline for Kemena what Major Vasco told me, my gaze constantly checking the door. My band may be cloaking the room, but it won't help us if someone walks in. With each word I speak, I fold the laundry more quickly and she slows, her eyes wide. When I finish, she's barely moving at all.

Kemena stares unseeing at the half-folded shirt in her hands. I feel lighter than I have since Major Vasco revealed Ark's timeline update to me. But now, Kemena bears the weight of all I shared. I should feel bad for dragging her into this, but mostly, I'm relieved to not be navigating it alone.

She gives a subtle shake of her head and begins folding clothes again at her normal pace. "We need to get word to Azarias. As soon as possible."

"I agree." A glance at the door assures me we're still alone. "Tonight. I'm going to the Ruins. And bringing Sam."

"I'm coming with you," she says with a finality that leaves no room for argument.

Not that I would argue. I *want* Kemena's help with this.

We lapse into silence.

Cai should know about these developments too, but I'm desperate to get Sam to safety. I'll have Mom and Nika send word to him once we're in the Ruins.

"How are things going between you and Matthias?"

"What?" My voice wobbles. *Smooth, Bria.*

Kemena gives me a side-eye as she scans a batch of folded uniforms so they can be sorted and delivered to the appropriate recruits. "What happened?"

My face heats. I swipe up another scanner and begin scanning before I respond. "Uh, you know." I'm not ready to process what happened between us in the course today.

Let alone try *talking* about it. Not with everything else going on.

Kemena snorts. "Great job not answering the question." She delivers a stack of clothes to a bin for *Unit 19 Females*.

As she returns to where I'm working, my mind scrambles for another topic. But all I can think about is Matthias telling me he loves me.

"He told you *what?*" Kemena stops dead in her tracks.

My eyes widen. "I said that out loud?"

She raises her eyebrow. "Mm-hmm."

I scrub my face with my hand, not sure *what* to say now.

"What did *you* say?" She leans her hip against the table. The tenderness in her eyes makes me want to respond.

"I told him the truth." My throat thickens.

"Which was?" Her voice is gentle. Encouraging.

"I love him too." The words rush out so fast it sounds more like one word than four.

She gives me a small smile. "And now you're wondering what you were thinking?"

Breath gushes from my lungs. "Yeah."

She comes over and pulls me into a hug. I hug her back, surprised when tears press the backs of my eyes. Must be more exhausted than I realized. Or the emotions of everything that's been happening are finally catching up to me.

She leans back and looks me in the eye. Her somberness catches my attention. Is she about to reprimand me? Tell me now isn't the time for this?

Her lips press together. "I'm a little jealous."

"What?"

She runs a hand through her braids. "You got a chance to tell him. Even with everything going on."

"You don't think it was too dangerous? Too much of a risk?"

"Love isn't safe. But it's worth it." She pauses. "I never thought I'd find a man I could respect. Let alone love. But I did." Another weighted pause. "And I never told him. Now, I'm not sure if I'll ever get the chance."

Azarias. I don't know how to respond, so I stay silent.

The washers beep, but Kemena doesn't move, so I don't either.

The silence lengthens, and I can't take it anymore. "I've lost so much already. People I love. Friends. Family. I'm . . . afraid." Saying the words brings a bit of relief but also highlights the depths of fear consuming my mind.

"I get that. But if you let it, fear will keep you from God's best for your life. Fear will make you build walls that don't let people in. It will tell you to push away those you love, because loving someone means losing them will hurt more. Fear will tell you to protect yourself when God tells you to trust *Him* to protect you and those you love." Kemena's deep brown eyes bore into mine, and I feel like she's talking not just to me, but to herself as well. "We're not called to fear, Bria. We believe in Jesus. We're called to courage, faith, and love. We are called to trust God and not ourselves." She squeezes my shoulder. "Let's both try to do that better."

"There's a lot to be afraid of," I say, even as her words ring through me and beckon me to listen. To live the kind of life she's talking about.

"There will always be something or someone to fear. Now, it's Demetrius Ark and all his plans. In a year, it might be someone else. The Bible says God has not given us a spirit of fear, but of power, love, and a sound mind." She drops her hand from my shoulder. "I don't always live that way. But whether I have one day left on this earth or many years, I want to *start* living that way."

We spend the rest of our time in the tailors' mostly in silence. I can't shake Kemena's words from my mind. Deep within my heart, I know she's right. God is calling me to courageously trust Him—not just with plans to take down Demetrius Ark, but also with those I love. Including Matthias.

If only that trust were easy.

But maybe that's why it's valuable. It's simple, but hard.

I SEND AN ENCRYPTED MESSAGE TO KIWI TO COORDINATE WITH MATTHIAS. We're getting Sam out of Talionis tonight.

At first, Kiwi replies that it's dangerous, but I don't take no for an answer.

So now, Sam, Matthias, Kemena, Kiwi, and I are in the tunnels beneath Talionis, heading to the Ruins.

Sam's happy to be with Kiwi and Matthias, despite his constant yawning. The poor kid is exhausted.

Navigating our way from the basement exit of the tunnels to the Ruins is difficult with five of us. But Kiwi's hacked into the soldiers' movements, so we avoid the extra patrols. It takes longer than usual, but we arrive at the site in the Ruins without being spotted.

I knock on the door, and an instant later, it swings open to reveal Nika with a gun.

Sam gasps, and Nika lowers the weapon.

"Sorry. Didn't realize you guys were coming out tonight," she says, stepping aside so we can enter. "We've had some close calls lately, so I'm on high alert."

"I understand." I lead the way inside.

Matthias comes in last, and Nika throws her arms around him. "Matthias! It's good to see you!"

"Uh, good to see you too." Matthias pats her awkwardly on the back, eyes wide. I think this is the first time Nika has ever hugged him, and he clearly doesn't know what to do with it.

The interaction brings a smile to my face despite the craziness of all that's happened. And the reason we're here.

Nika steps back and greets Kemena and Kiwi. Kiwi introduces Sam.

"Nice to meet you, Sam," Nika says.

"Where's my mom?" I ask.

Nika nods to the back of the site. "She's in the communication room talking to Ari."

"Good. We have a lot we need to share," I say.

Sam yawns again, his eyes heavy. Kemena takes him to the back room where the other kids are and settles him on an empty mat.

The rest of us join Mom in the communication room.

Ari gives Matthias as enthusiastic of a greeting as Nika. Then Matthias turns to Mom. The rest of us fall silent. I've wanted the two of them to meet for so long, but nerves flutter in my stomach. What if they don't like each other?

Matthias swallows hard and shoves his hand toward Mom.

"Hi, Mrs. Averton. I'm Matthias." His voice cracks.

Mom's face softens into a smile. "Call me Lily." She steps forward and embraces him.

At first, Matthias stays frozen, like he doesn't know what to do with the hug. But an instant later, he returns the embrace.

Mom steps back, keeping her hands on his shoulders. "Thank you for taking care of my girl."

"Always," Matthias says solemnly.

My face burns. It's like they're forgetting that I'm *right here*.

I'm about to interject so I can share about the updated timeline and shift the conversation away from me, but Mom turns back to Ari.

"You should tell them what you were telling me," Mom says.

Ari's eyes light up. "Oh, right! We did it."

"Did what?" Kemena asks as she enters the room.

"We cracked Ark's encryption. Now Isaac, Bryson, and I are working on decoding each of the files and what we're seeing already —these things hold way more intel than we expected. The process is time-consuming, but I'm working on an algorithm that will help us. It should be ready to run by the end of next week. At that point, we'll be able to decipher everything."

"That's awesome!" Kiwi says, not noticing how Matthias, Kemena, and I don't react.

Matthias takes my hand in his.

"Good job," Kemena finally says, a tightness to her words. "But you have to be careful who you tell about this."

Ari's nodding before Kemena even finishes her statement. "I know. Only a few people even know Isaac and I have been working on them. And besides you guys, we've only told Azarias, Bryson, Catori, and Micah that we cracked the code."

Cracking the code is vital, but Ark's warning about what will happen if a word of it is leaked rings in my mind. Another thing to worry about in the midst of everything going on.

"I know it's late, but is Azarias around?" Kemena asks.

Ari shakes her head. "No. He and the Wild Dogs are on a scouting mission tonight."

Kemena looks at me.

"What's going on?" Nika asks.

Matthias, Mom, and Ari are looking back and forth between me and Kemena with a mix of curiosity and concern.

"Ark moved up his timeline," I say. "The attack on Sitreea is set for forty-two days from now."

Silence descends for several long moments. Ari's the first to snap out of it, and she begins typing on a screen, her lips moving as she silently talks to herself.

"I overheard my father say something about the timing change to Major Vasco, but I didn't want to believe it was true," Matthias says, more to himself than anyone.

"That's months earlier than we were prepared for," Mom says.

"I know." I let go of Matthias's hand so I can pace. "And I don't trust that I have all the details. Ark uses information as a form of manipulation. For all I know, he could be telling me the timeline is moved up just to see what I do next."

"I don't think so," Kemena says. "There's been a major increase in activity all around the city. Ever since the last Sitreean delegation." She focuses on the hologram of Ari. "Which is why I really need to talk to Azarias."

After the conversation she and I had earlier this evening, I wonder if she has more she wants to say to the scout leader. But I keep the thoughts to myself.

Ari glances up from her screen. "He won't be back until morning." She scowls. "Everything has been tightened up out here. They won't let me hack into anything in Talionis—even though I'm pretty sure I know what I did wrong last time."

Her words bring me up short. "Ari. You almost *died* the last time you tried hacking into Talionis. I think *not* trying that again is probably a good idea."

"Yeah, but—"

"Bria's right," Nika says. "You don't know how scary that was for the rest of us, girl. We want you around. For after this whole mess is over."

Ari holds up her hands. "Fine. But if I could gain access to their servers, I could see what I can find out about this updated timeline."

"That's a good idea," Kiwi says, scooting up to a screen. "I could help—"

"Please don't. It's too risky." Even I can hear the pleading tone in my words. I don't think I'll ever get the image of Ari almost dying out of my mind.

"Okay, okay. I won't." She flicks her blond hair over her shoulder. "But what are we going to do? We still think there's a leak somewhere high up in Eryndale."

I want to ask her who exactly *we* is, but I don't get the chance as Mom jumps in.

"We have to take the risk and let the Eryndale leadership know." There's a finality to her tone that brooks no argument. It's a tone she rarely used with me and my brothers, but every time we heard it, we knew we were in trouble if we didn't obey. "There are enough in Eryndale who still stand for what's right, and they need to be mobilized. We have a short window to act. And we *must* act."

I've never seen my mom like this before. And somehow, I know this is the woman those in Eryndale respect. This is why it was such a big deal to them that I'm Lily's daughter.

Part of me is impressed. The other part feels like I've been left out of a secret for all my life. A secret I still don't fully understand. Which leaves me surprisingly frustrated.

We spend the next thirty minutes going over the details of what I know about the attack on Sitreea.

Ari takes notes on her screen, and when we're finished, she looks up. "Lily, do you want me to let them know we've been communicating with you?"

"Wait. No one out there knows Ari is communicating with you?" I ask.

Mom puts a hand on my arm, but keeps her attention fixed on Ari. "No. Same procedures as usual. Tell them you got word from Sergeant Valarius about it if you need to. Or even that you found a way to communicate with Bria. But keep me out of it for now." She turns to me. "We've kept information about our work in the Ruins very limited. We can't risk the wrong people finding out what we're doing. Especially now that more people know Ari's alive."

Before I can respond, Mom is addressing Ari again. "I need you to get word to my husband, Kassre, and Hosea. They think they have a longer time to work with Bill, Paul, and their guys to get their plan in place, but obviously, they don't.

"We need to let Cai know too," I say. "We opted to come here tonight with Sam."

Mom nods. "That's fine. We'll get word to him tonight." She looks between the four of us. "I thought we were holding off on bringing more kids out here. Why risk bringing Sam out tonight?"

"Bria and I decided it was necessary," Matthias says. "The trainings are ramping up, and Sam's young. And vulnerable. After his dinner, Kiwi and I got him into the tunnels, and Kiwi erased him from the servers."

"I'm glad you got him out," Mom says.

I focus on Ari and shift the conversation away from Sam. "When you brief the lead scouts on the updated timeline, tell them to prepare for an attack sooner rather than later. If they can pool their resources to be ready in thirty days, I might be able to come up with a plan to work with the Resistance here on a coordinated attack effort." I glance at my mom. "And maybe Dad and Kassre can be ready as well. We'll need all the help we can get. Ark will not go down without a fight."

CHAPTER
FIFTY-SEVEN

I hang another uniform on the long wall rack in the tailors' warehouse. These are the uniforms for the upcoming Center Games, and Sampta and Presidia have left me alone to hang each unit's uniforms in the appropriate section of the rack. Kemena was about to work with me, but they pulled her away for something else.

The games are tomorrow, and an underlying raw energy pulses through the city—with the recruits, cadets, and soldiers.

More rides on this than Ark has revealed to the recruits. But the soldiers clearly know more than the rest of us. My suspicion is that Ark's using the games as a test run to determine who he'll place where in the attack against Sitreea.

The attack that comes closer with every day.

I hang a smaller uniform on the rack. This one's for a kid. My stomach sours.

With the increased patrols and trainings at night, we haven't been able to smuggle more kids to the Ruins. As it is, Kiwi's afraid there's some suspicion after Sam's disappearance. Apparently, there have been more searches for him in the database than Kiwi's seen after any of the other kids we smuggled out of the city.

It's been five days since we were all in the Ruins, and none of us

—me, Matthias, Kemena, or Kiwi—have been able to get back to the Ruins or down into the tunnels to see Cai.

Each day that passes leaves me more on edge. More uncertain of what's going to happen. And Ark is watching me with an intensity that's borderline obsessive. He's observed every scenario I've run the past few days. This morning, I'm pretty sure he caught me trying to manipulate the scenario. I quickly reversed the code I entered so the silent alarm would be triggered.

The glimmer in Ark's eyes afterward, though . . . he knew. And he almost seemed pleased. Which freaks me out far more than I care to admit.

It's like he *wants* me to try to stop him. All so he can prove he's the more brilliant strategist and no one can stop him.

At the moment, I'm not sure anyone *can*. There have been no attacks from the Eryndale Scouts, at least not that I've heard. And the silence from them . . . what if they don't help? What then?

I shove a hanger into the sleeves of the next uniform with more force than necessary.

God, why can't You just make all this stop? The question twists through me, causing an ache deep in my chest.

From what I've read in my Bible, I know evil persists in this world because of sin. But to see the effects so close. To know an evil man will be responsible for so many deaths . . . and to not know how to stop it . . .

It leaves me feeling powerless.

I've seen God work miracles. Witnessed Him move powerfully. But I can't understand why He's so silent now.

I put hangers into a few uniforms, then grab the pile and take them to the rack.

The one positive of the days since the course is that Asher has welcomed me and Matthias into the Resistance. After seeing how we worked to help him—even at the risk to ourselves—he invited us to the next Resistance meeting. Which was last night.

Unfortunately, they have less of a plan than I hoped. Because of the increased patrols and trainings, they've been forced to stop their normal efforts. Especially after a close call with Marci when she tried to sabotage a set of weapons. She made it out, but the soldiers are looking for the person responsible for breaking into the weaponry.

The numbers were impressive, though. Over a hundred recruits are part of the Resistance. Ready to move. If they just knew how.

I stare at the piles of uniforms still waiting to be hung, and a deep weariness drapes over me like a cloak. I've been running and fighting and searching for a plan to stop Talionis for so long.

Will any of it even matter?

"Need any help?" Matthias is leaning in the doorway, hands in his pockets, watching me.

My cheeks warm. "How long have you been there?"

He pushes off the doorframe and strides into the room. "Long enough to witness you batter these poor uniforms with the way you're putting the hangers on." He wiggles his eyebrows. "What did they ever do to you? Sampta and Presidia will be outraged."

A smile teases my lips. "I'm sure they will be."

He takes my hand. "Wanna talk about it?"

"It's nothing new."

Since the course, Matthias has found any and every opportunity to join me in whatever I'm doing. If I didn't know any better, I'd think he was changing his personal schedule so he has an excuse to be with me. Maybe he is. He and Kiwi have become good friends, and Kiwi certainly has the skills to tweak a schedule without anyone finding out.

However Matthias is managing it, I'm glad he's around.

We've talked about a lot while training and doing chores together. Our hopes. Fears. Struggles. I've been using the cloaking feature on my band more than I probably should, but the risk is worth it.

He gives my hand a light squeeze before turning to the mound of uniforms that still need to be hung. "Let's get this done. Then we can go for a walk."

"I doubt we'll have time for that."

He smirks. "A guy can hope, can't he?"

We lapse into companionable silence and find a rhythm as we

work together to put uniforms on hangers and place them in their appropriate spots on the rack.

Matthias reaches past me to grab a hanger, and his short sleeve rides up enough to reveal a fresh bruise on his bicep.

I take his forearm in my hand and gently push the sleeve up further. I hiss through my teeth. The bruise is shaped like fingerprints. "Matthias. Who did this?" I ask the question even though I know the answer.

He gently pulls his arm out of my grasp and tugs the sleeve back over the bruise. "Dear old Dad." He doesn't look me in the eye, but I position myself so he can't keep working.

"Why?"

The one-word question brings his blue eyes to mine. "Does he need a reason?"

Anger pulses through me. I'm ready to march out of this room and find Colonel Valarius to give him a taste of his own medicine. "Why don't you stand up to him? You're one of the strongest people I know. You're the one who *taught* me how to fight!"

He almost smiles at that. "Ah. You finally admit I'm responsible for your impressive skills?"

I glare at him. "Matthias. I'm being serious."

He ducks his head. "Sometimes standing up to people comes at too high of a risk."

Some of my anger dissipates. But not all of it. I take his hand. "You lost your mom because she stood against what your dad and Ark are doing." I hesitate. "But she was right to do so. They're evil, and they need to be stopped."

He reaches past me to grab a uniform, dropping my hand. "I prefer subtle acts of rebellion. Especially if it'll keep those I love safe." His eyes flick to mine before he focuses again on the uniform he's hanging.

I follow his lead and pick up another uniform, more to distract myself from the fact that he dropped my hand than anything else. "You escaped Talionis, sabotaging the city in the process. Not exactly subtle."

He takes his uniform over to the rack and hangs it. "And you saw how they retaliated." He rubs the back of his neck. "Sentencing Nika to death. Allowing my dad to do whatever he wants to keep me in line." He swallows hard. "Threatening your life if I step out of line."

My eyes widen. That's new information to me. But not surprising.

With three big steps, he's in front of me again. "When it's time to act, when we have a solid plan, I will. But until then, I can't take the risk."

I search his eyes, feel the fear. Understand it. "Even if we can't ultimately defeat Ark, I want to be someone who stands against him. Speaks against what he's doing. Don't you?"

"We got extra help today, huh?" Kemena asks as she strides into the room. She eyes Matthias. "Somehow, you've been getting assigned here a lot lately. The sisters always seem surprised." Her tone is dry.

Matthias flashes her a grin, but it doesn't reach his eyes. "Lucky break for all of us."

"Sure." Kemena starts hanging uniforms, and Matthias appears relieved to drop our conversation.

With the three of us working together, it's not long before all the uniforms are hung and ready to be delivered to the recruits.

"Why do we need new uniforms for these games?" I mutter as I hang my last uniform.

"Because we've added some new tech elements," Sampta says as she and Presidia prance into the room.

I whirl to face them fully.

"What?" Matthias says.

I knew it was something they were working on, but I didn't expect it to be ready so soon.

Presidia pulls a uniform from the rack. "We have worked with Mandeville to make these uniforms unlike anything anyone has ever seen."

"Indeed," Sampta agrees. "The material is highly durable and almost impossible to tear. It can be used for a variety of situations, and there is now tracking woven into the fabric that allows for it to be found in the event that a recruit goes missing."

Great. Another way for them to monitor us besides just getting our vitals through our bands. What will that mean for the games?

Presidia opens the shirt to show the inside. "The lining is light but woven with a special combination of metals, allowing for increased protection against many weapons. It will also allow the wearer to carry more in their pack."

"How can clothes do that, exactly?" I ask, thankful that so far none of the tech they've mentioned monitors conversations.

"Every bit of this is infused with a new tech fiber that keeps the wearer from registering the full weight of their packs." Sampta's eyes shine behind her glasses as she talks. "It's a special technology Mandeville invented that helps absorb weight and increase the wearer's movements. It will allow you to move faster and jump higher."

"Impressive," Matthias says.

"Everything we do is impressive," Sampta harrumphs. "We have several new ideas as well. But this is all we could have ready in time for the games."

Presidia rehangs the uniform, and the sisters dismiss us.

Matthias and I part ways, but our conversation lingers in my mind. He never answered my question. When the time comes, will he be ready to stand against Ark? Even if the cost is high?

I grab my rifle from the case at the front of the Warfare Strategies Building and step out into the sunny afternoon. It's too bright and cheerful today. The weather should reflect the ominous feeling of the games that will take place hours from now.

Instead, it's beautiful. The sky is clear. The air crisp and cool. A perfect mid-November day.

I kick at a pile of dead leaves as I round a corner and make my way to lunch. This morning, I went through a scenario rather than running it, and my head's still clogged with the memories. I lost four people from my unit in the extraction exercise. Unacceptable.

But if we can't stop Ark, far more will be lost. Truly lost.

Distant sounds of gunfire echo through the air. A Kill Zone must be active in the eastern part of the city. Likely an attack on the recruits heading to lunch from physical conditioning.

I grip the strap of my rifle. It's full of training bullets, like all the recruits' rifles are now. Maybe I should go see if I can help any of the recruits with the Kill Zone. I look back in that direction but keep walking forward. Most likely, there are no routes through. Ark's been rigging everything since he increased his timeline.

But still . . .

I slam into someone and almost lose my footing.

Thick hands steady me. "Easy." Sergeant Valarius stands in front of me like a wall.

I bet he was just standing there and didn't say a word, even though he knew I was about to run into him.

I snap to attention. "I'm sorry, sir."

"At ease," he says. "This alley is currently secure, and I needed to get word to you."

My heart trips over itself, and I bite my tongue to keep from asking him what he's talking about. Andor Valarius isn't one to waste words. And he doesn't like to be rushed.

He scans the area behind me, then focuses on me. "I've been informed that the intel you provided isn't enough to act on."

I gape at him. "What?"

His dark and intimidating gaze lands on me. "They said they need more time. And they need additional intel to confirm the time-line you gave."

"Why can't you confirm it?" This can't be happening.

"I haven't heard anything of an updated timeline."

I wait for him to elaborate, but he doesn't.

"Major Vasco showed me a new attack date. Just a few days ago. Plus, everyone's been more on edge." Desperation tinges my voice. "We have to act as soon as possible."

Sergeant Valarius's face gives nothing away. "Nothing can be done unless we provide the scouts with additional intel."

He hesitates, as though trying to decide what else to tell me. I bite my cheek to keep from arguing. He's the messenger. Someone else made this call. Plus, I'll take any other information the man wants to give, even though I'm irritated.

"Be on guard with the games tonight," he says. "The soldiers are on edge. My brother made it clear in his briefing to all the soldiers this morning that there will be severe consequences if they are taken out by any recruits or cadets tonight. Which means they'll be placed on the front lines of Ark's attack when it happens. No one wants that."

With that, he turns on his heel and marches away. I have a dozen more questions. More I want to say. But it isn't safe to continue a conversation like the one we were having for too long, even in a secure alley.

The distant shots from the Kill Zone have stopped, so I continue to the Dining Hall for lunch, despite my lack of appetite. I need to eat, or I'll be a mess tonight for the games. But I can't believe Eryndale won't act on the intel I provided.

By the time they're finally *ready* to attack, it'll be too late.

But who's stonewalling this? Is it the leak? Or someone who's obtuse, like Reginald Finnigan?

I need to talk to Cai, but there's no opportunity between now and the games.

As I near the Dining Hall, I enter the swarm of recruits heading to lunch, my mind whirling. Sergeant Valarius may not have known about the updated timeline, but he knows more than he's telling me.

The question is, what exactly is he withholding? And how careful do I need to be around him until I find out?

Matthias and I have talked about his uncle, and Matthias trusts him. Said Andor has kept him from more than one beating from his father over the years.

So why won't Andor tell me more of what's going on?

CHAPTER
FIFTY-NINE

"The Commander wants to see you," Corporal Sidon says as I'm about to take a bite of my sandwich. "Now."

I've only been in the Dining Hall for five minutes, and I just sat down with my lunch. Storm gives me a worried look, and I smile at her as I stand. "Eat a good lunch, okay?"

She bites at her lip, clearly not hearing a word I said. I wish my connection with her didn't make it impossible for us to get her out like we did with the other kids.

Matthias gets her attention and starts chatting with her, which is enough of a distraction to ease some of the worry lines on her brow.

When I reach to pick up my sandwich to bring with me, Corporal Sidon gives a sharp shake of his head. "No time for that."

I cast a longing look at my abandoned lunch before following Corporal Sidon from the room. Tonight's games will require energy. Which means eating well until then.

An impossibility if I'm called into meetings with the Commander during meal time. Knowing Ark, the timing is intentional.

I set my jaw and trail after Corporal Sidon through Talionis and to the Technical Operations Building.

My eyebrows bunch together. "I thought you said the Commander wanted to see me."

Corporal Sidon opens the door to the building and gestures for me to enter. "He does. But the Commander is a busy man. He's finishing up a meeting with Mandeville, and he ordered you be brought here. No sense wasting time traveling between buildings."

"Could have let me finish my lunch then," I mutter under my breath as I pass Corporal Sidon.

His eyes narrow, but he doesn't respond.

We walk down a series of hallways, and he stops at a restricted access area of the building and keys in codes to open the door. The last time I was in this area was with Nika and Ari, early in our stay in Talionis. Ari hacked her way past the access point and made Nika and me keep watch while she dug into the secret servers.

It's how we discovered more about the Watchers. About my aunt's betrayal.

The memories wash over me, leaving me soaked with emotions I don't have time to deal with as Corporal Sidon stops in front of a door with biometric entry requirements.

He knocks.

I take a deep breath as the door swings open.

Mandeville stands in the entry, his hair askew as usual. "You're thirty seconds late, Corporal."

Corporal Sidon doesn't respond, but there's a tick in his jaw that gives away some of his irritation.

Mandeville looks past him at me. "Well, get in here. We don't have all day. Important event tonight. Every second counts."

I pass Corporal Sidon and enter the room. It's a high-tech office space, with screens covering the walls, a desk with a hologram in the center, and a half a dozen chairs surrounding it. Ark sits at the head of the table, studying me.

Mandeville slams the door, and Ark waves at a chair. "Take a seat, Bria."

I obey, and sit straight in the chair as I wait to find out what's going on. Worst-case scenarios should be flying through my mind. Possibilities for this meeting. But there's nothing.

I have no clue why Ark would want to see me and Mandeville.

Silence stretches. Mandeville shifts impatiently in his chair but remains silent. I guess he won't question the Commander's use of time like he does everyone else's.

As the seconds tick by, I turn my focus away from Commander Ark and to the hologram billowing up from the table. My breath catches in my throat. It's an image of Callypso and her pirates.

And she's looking right at the camera that captured her image. As though she *wanted* the picture taken. Her dirty blond metal-studded hair cascades over her shoulders, and her weapons are on full display. My heart trips over itself.

I haven't wanted to think of Callypso. To wonder about her end goal with Talionis. But now, she's staring me in the face.

"So, you recognize her," Ark's voice crackles through the air, drawing my attention for a split second before my gaze latches onto Callypso again.

I nod, even though it was a statement rather than a question. "Her name's Callypso." I'm not sure why I mention the detail to Ark.

"Mandeville, please share what we discussed."

"As you wish, Commander." Mandeville drums his fingers on the table. "We had a major breach to our system." Mandeville's eyes dart to Ark, who nods at him to continue.

Although I get the impression the head tech instructor doesn't want to share the intel with me.

"A hacker found a back door into some of our most secure servers —" Mandeville stands suddenly. "Sir, with all due respect, she shouldn't know any of this!"

Commander Ark's eyes narrow. "You're questioning my judgment?"

"N-no, sir." Mandeville sinks back into his chair.

Ark leans forward, hands clasped in front of him. "I gave you a month and a half to fix this. But until Bria entered, we had nowhere to start in our search for who breached the system. Now we have a name." His gaze flicks to me, then back to Mandeville. "Bria clearly isn't fond of the woman. I want her to understand what's happening so that she can . . . assist us."

My hands tremble in my lap, so I clasp them together. The timing lines up with the increased soldier activity around the tech building that Cai shared with me and Matthias. Was Callypso the cause?

"Continue," Ark commands.

Mandeville clears his throat. "The first breach was forty-three days ago. We thought we dealt with it, but over the past week, there have been a series of targeted attacks on very specific servers. They're searching for something, but we're unsure what."

I'm suddenly all the more concerned about Ari and Kiwi messing with the servers. We told them not to, but the two of them seem to think they're invincible when it comes to tech.

Mandeville shoves a hand through his hair, leaving spikes array in the wake. "So far, we think we've stopped them. There's only so much the hacker can do from a distance. But we fear these security breaches could cause additional problems to our, uh, timeline."

The intel is interesting, but I have no clue what I have to do with any of it. I turn a questioning look to Ark. "I'm not exactly great at tech."

Mandeville snorts. "There's a gross understatement."

I ignore him and continue. "What exactly are you hoping I can do?"

Ark steeples his fingers. "According to a reliable source, our dear Ari made a miraculous recovery after you all were taken. She and Bryson appear to be doing well."

Blood drains from my face, but I will my expression to remain neutral. "That's impossible. The medics told us she was going to die."

"As I said"—Ark shrugs—"apparently it was . . . miraculous." He practically spits the word, which leaves me with questions I can't entertain.

The far more important issue at hand is shielding Ari and Bryson from Demetrius Ark's hunt.

"Ari Willowpen was one of the best I've ever seen in technical capabilities," Mandeville says. "Although some of her endeavors to circumvent our security were sloppy, she was one of the only recruits clever enough to discover hidden intel we planted."

My stomach drops. No. If that's true, it means . . .

"We wanted you to discover the Watchers," Ark says smoothly. "Why do you think it was so simple for you, Ari, and Nika to enter this secure section of the building?"

I stare at him numbly. How much do they know? How much did we do that *wasn't* hidden? A sour taste fills my mouth. How much do they know about what Kiwi has done?

Ark waves a hand dismissively. "Now isn't the time to discuss the gross insubordination you all committed." A dark humor sparkles in his eyes. "Nika has already paid the price."

I squeeze my eyes shut and let the pain of missing my friend reflect on my face, even as relief courses through me. Ark doesn't know about the operation in the Ruins. *God, please keep her safe. Don't let him discover she's alive.*

"No," Ark continues. "The real reason we brought you here is to find out how connected Ari might be to this Callypso." He casually points to the hologram of Callypso that's still projected into the air.

"She's not connected at all," I say, even as I wonder if Ark will believe a word I'm speaking. "Callypso and her pirates are dangerous. If Ari's alive, as you claim, there's no way she would be caught up with them."

Ark looks at Mandeville, who's studying a handheld screen.

"According to these readings, she's telling the truth," Mandeville says.

My brow furrows. "What?"

"The chair you're sitting in." Ark nods at it. "It connects with your band to work as a lie detector. Impressive, is it not?"

I jump up.

Ark shakes his head. "No, no, Bria. Sit."

I hesitate, then think of all the people Ark will hurt if I don't obey. I sink back into the chair.

"Good." Ark stands and stalks toward me. "Now, are you confident Ari wouldn't work with Callypso if Ari thought Callypso might be able to free you?"

My throat thickens. "She wouldn't." The lie whispers through my closed airway, my heart slamming into my chest.

"Lie," Mandeville says.

Ark leans against the table mere feet away from me. "Bria. Why would you lie to me after knowing we can tell?" He clicks his tongue. "I thought you were smarter than that."

My mind reels. Ari's working with Eryndale. But I can't let Ark know that. Not at the risk of giving away more information than I intend to. Whoever his leak is within Eryndale, it appears the person hasn't told Ark *about* Eryndale. No doubt as a self-protection measure. Still, I refuse to be the one who gives Ark any intel about the refuge city.

Plus, I'm not sure Ari *wouldn't* work with Callypso.

"Callypso has her own people," I say. "She wouldn't trust Ari."

Ark turns to Mandeville.

"Truth," Mandeville says.

Ark leans toward me. "True as that might be, we both know that sometimes powerful people choose to use those they don't trust in order to accomplish their purpose. Don't we?"

I swallow hard but don't respond.

Ark stands to his full height. "That's all, Bria. Thank you for your . . . help."

Somehow, I get to my feet and leave the room, but everything that just happened jumbles together in my mind.

What is Callypso trying to get from Talionis? Whatever it is, I'm confident it would be as dangerous in her hands as it is in Demetrius Ark's.

And what will happen to Ari?

The sky is now full of clouds and cold air whips past me as I exit the Technical Operations Building, bringing with it a blinding clarity. I need to get word to Ari. Warn her. Ark knows she's alive, which means she has to go dark.

Panic grips my chest, pulsing through me. Choking me.

How will I get word to her?

"Bria." Matthias jogs to catch up to me as I walk down the street. He passes me a wrapped sandwich. "Thought you should eat something. Be ready for the games tonight."

The games. I take the sandwich. "Right. Thanks." I walk again, my mind a whirling mess.

He keeps pace with me. "What's wrong?"

"Callypso has someone hacking into Talionis. Looking for something." I probably shouldn't be sharing any of this with Matthias, but I can't stop myself. I pull the zipper of my jacket up higher as another gust of wind rushes past. "Ark thinks Ari is the one helping her."

Matthias puts a hand on my arm to bring me to a stop. "Why would he think Ari is alive?"

It's quiet out. Everyone's prepping for the games and conserving energy. But I appreciate his care to not explicitly say *how does he know Ari is alive?*

I swallow the bitter taste of betrayal. "He heard from a 'reliable source' about her miraculous recovery."

Matthias rubs the back of his neck. "What's he going to do?"

"I don't know."

I start moving again, and Matthias joins me. A few minutes later, I find myself in front of the tailors' building. With sudden clarity, I face Matthias. "I need to talk to Kemena."

Before he can respond, Kemena comes out of the building pushing a hover-cart full of uniforms. I can tell the instant she catches sight of us. First, her expression is one of welcome. Then she frowns.

She guides the cart down the steps and pauses in front of us. "Walk with me while I make this delivery."

It's not a request, and I'm happy to comply. Kemena takes us down deserted back streets, and I activate the cloaking mechanism on my band. Even if Ark knows I'm using it like he knew how Nika, Ari, and I snuck into the secure room, at least it will keep our conversation secure.

I give Kemena a longer explanation of my meeting with Ark and Mandeville. By the time I finish, deep lines furrow her brow.

"I need to warn her," I say. "Tonight."

Kemena shakes her head. "No. It's too dangerous tonight with the games." She turns down another side street. "Plus, from what

I've overheard about the games, you'll be wiped by the time they're done." She pauses to look at me. "Not to mention, you'll be monitored more." She gives a pointed look at the new tech-laced uniforms.

All of her reasoning is sound, and Matthias agrees with her. But a desperation to save my friend pounds like another force inside of me.

I clench and unclench my hands. "I have to do something."

Kemena grabs one of my clenched fists. "You have to trust God, girl. This one is outside of your control. At least for now." She pushes the cart forward.

"I can talk to my uncle," Matthias says after a few beats of silence. "Maybe he can get word to Cai. Let him know."

"Yes," I agree.

We arrive at the back of the Recruits' Living Quarters. I turn off the cloaking feature.

"Just be careful," Kemena says. "Tonight's going to be rough."

I should ask her how she knows that, find out whatever information she can give me. But my mind is too consumed with the need to warn Ari.

We go our separate ways, with Matthias promising to try to talk to Andor. I guess trying is all he *can* do, but I need him to find a way. Even if it's difficult.

I head back to my room and force myself to eat my sandwich.

A longing for Cai's Bible wells up in me. I haven't had it since I was captured, but I desperately need the comfort and direction it provides.

Fear not, for I am with you . . . I will strengthen you . . . I will help you . . .

Parts of the verse Cai circled and wrote my name next to in his Bible spring to mind.

I set down my sandwich and drop my head into my hands. *God, please help me like You promise. Everything is falling apart, and I don't know how to keep my friends safe. Can people as evil as Ark and Callypso actually be stopped? Is it possible for good to win?*

The questions swirl in my mind, choking my thoughts, my prayers.

Again, more of the verse whispers through my turmoil. *Be not dismayed, for I am your God.*

The words are simple. A call to trust God and not succumb to my fears.

But all I want to do is *act.*

CHAPTER
SIXTY

I march to the staging area for the games with a swarm of recruits, cadets, and soldiers. The sun has set, but the sky still holds the final twinges of light before darkness falls completely. By the time everyone's briefed on what's happening in the games, it will be dark.

There are three different uniforms displayed in the crowd. Mine is black with a dark red stripe on my upper arm. There are also dark green uniforms and navy blue uniforms. But everyone else's uniform is one solid color, including those on my team. I'm the only one with a red stripe on my sleeve.

Strange.

A nervous energy pulses through the crowd, and an eerie silence consumes us. As though no one is willing to talk and voice their fears. Which is fine with me. I can't handle the hum of anxious conversation. Not with everything else swarming in my head and the fears I have for Ari and whatever terror this night holds.

The staging area is inside the Physical Training Arena. They're keeping whatever they've prepared for us in the Center hidden until the games begin.

As I enter the Physical Training Arena, I force myself to focus. As much as I want to help Ari, there's nothing I can do right now. I'm sure Ark intentionally told me everything he did today to sabotage my time in the games. And I won't give him the satisfaction of seeing me unable to function at the top of my abilities.

Soldiers inside the arena herd everyone into three different sections: Black Team Zone, Green Team Zone, and Blue Team Zone. All the training equipment has been moved to make for an open interior space.

When I move to join the ranks of the Black Team Zone, Sergeant Valarius stops me.

"You're one of the team leads." He gestures to the red stripe on my upper arm. "You'll be positioned in the front of your team with the other two teams' leads."

With that, he walks away, not giving me a chance to ask a single question. Or to deduce if Matthias talked to him.

A small, raised platform at the front of the Black Team Zone says *Black Team Lead*. My stomach clenches as the reality that I'll be in charge sinks in.

I take a deep breath, then mount the two steps to the top of the platform and face the balcony where a small contingency of Ark's most trusted advisors waits. A glance to my left reveals the other leads in front of rows of perfectly positioned teams of soldiers, cadets, and recruits.

The team lead for the Green Team, which is entirely soldiers, is Laban. His eyes are narrowed as he watches me. A tremor shakes me. I'm not sure what these games will hold, but I do know that Laban Meritas will do whatever it takes to bring me down.

The Blue Team is furthest away from my team. It appears to have the largest amount of cadets, but Hawthorne is the team lead. Dozens of recruits mingle with the cadets, and I catch sight of Asher, Marci, and a few others from the Resistance. Then my gaze locks on Matthias. An ache forms in my chest. I don't want to be on opposing teams, but there's nothing I can do about it.

"All at attention for our Commander, Demetrius Ark!" Colonel Valarius bellows from the balcony.

There's an audible *whoosh* as everyone in the room snaps to attention. Ark strides to the front of the platform. His uniform is perfectly pressed, and every hair is in place as he inspects the crowd before him.

After a long moment, he inclines his head. "At ease."

We all drop to the at-ease position simultaneously. Like the perfectly trained soldiers we are.

Ark rests his hands on the railing. "There have been many rumors stirring about the games tonight, and you have all been made aware of the importance of doing well in them. My soldiers know they will be greatly scrutinized as they go against recruits and cadets. And my recruits and cadets, you have been trained for this. You are ready to be tested." He focuses on first the Blue Team, then my team. "I am confident you will perform with excellence. You won't let me down, will you?"

"Sir, no sir!" The crowd of recruits and cadets chants.

And because Demetrius Ark's gaze doesn't leave me, I chant them as well. But every word is more difficult to swallow than a plate of slimy, overcooked mushrooms.

"Now." Ark paces to the left and away from me. "There's something vitally important I need to tell you before you're briefed on tonight's games." He sighs heavily, as though the weight of the world is on his shoulders.

What is he up to?

"My deepest desire has been to equip all of you to work with me to better the North American region. To work with you to create a better life for the survivors of the Demise." He rests a hand over his heart, his words rising with a passionate power.

The way the man can lie . . . it's almost impressive. I force myself to remain still and not fidget.

"Alas, there has been a change." He hangs his head. "And I am deeply distraught by the news I must now give."

He allows a pause to stretch over the room. Everyone here is well enough trained to know not to talk in the midst of the Commander's speech. But I sense the questions rising, the uncertainty of the team behind me as everyone waits for what Ark is going to say.

The news he's about to give that's *distressing* him so greatly.

I clench my jaw so hard pain radiates through my teeth. I know the news he's about to share. And I know it's not a change.

How many of these recruits will realize everything Ark's saying is a fabricated lie?

I'm sure Asher and the Resistance will be able to tell. But knowing something is a lie and stopping evil from winning . . . those are two very different things.

Ark slowly paces back across the platform, the click of his heels the only sound in the painful silence of the room. "There has been a rise of dissonance in my home country of Sitreea. And I fear that I need your help in order to prevent another devastating war for the people of my homeland." He braces his hands against the railing again. "In return for the training, education, and housing I have provided all of you, I will require your services not as recruits, but as soldiers."

His dark gaze rakes over the crowd in front of him. Colonel Valarius steps up to his left, with Major Vasco and Elva Trill flanking him on the right.

The message is clear.

This is not a request, and anyone who fails to acquiesce will be punished.

"Are you with me?" Ark asks.

"Always, Commander," Hawthorne shouts. "We'll follow you anywhere! Com-mander Ark! Com-mander Ark!"

Others take up the cry until the entire room is chanting their allegiance and support to Ark.

Soldiers. Recruits. Cadets.

So many consumed with following this evil man.

Even if someone shouts something against him, says they refuse, no one would hear it.

Still, in the deafening noise of the room, I shout, "No!"

But it's swallowed up by the hundreds given over to Demetrius Ark.

Ark raises his hands, silencing the chanting. "Thank you. I could not be more pleased with how far you've all come." He surveys the crowd. "You will be given more information and a timeline soon. But with this reality before us, the games tonight are even more vital than we first understood. They will, in fact, prepare you for our journey to Sitreea."

Does the man do anything but lie? How can he live with himself?

Ark shifts to Major Vasco. "Major, detail what our three teams will experience."

"Of course, sir." Major Vasco appraises the crowd. "Tonight will put to test your skills in warfare strategy in a way that is unlike what you have experienced prior to this. Each team will enter the Center from a different point. Green Team"—he gestures to Laban's team of soldiers—"will be the hunters. Their job throughout the games will be to find and capture enemy combatants, which is anyone who is not on the Green Team. They may choose to either shoot the enemy or take prisoners. Either way, anyone who is captured or shot with a training bullet by the hunters will be punished."

Ark whispers something to Colonel Valarius and Elva Trill, and it takes far more effort than it should for me to force my focus on Major Vasco. I need to be prepared for the games, for no other reason than to know how to lead the dozens of recruits and cadets on my team.

"Blue Team and Black Team, you will be attempting to find and retrieve a black box from the other team's camp. You will need to navigate through the Center, avoiding the hunters, capture the black box from your enemy, and return it to your own camp." He crosses his arms over his chest. "You'll also need to protect your own team's black box. For the first hour of the games, the hunters will not be authorized to enter either team's camp, but they will be free to roam everywhere else in the Center. After the first hour is up, if neither team has successfully retrieved their black box, the hunters will have free rein throughout the Center."

So, we'll need a defensive and offensive element to our strategy. Plus a potential pivot if we're unable to retrieve the box within an hour so the defensive teammates are ready for the hunters. I want to turn to assess who's on my team and figure out who should go where, but Major Vasco isn't finished with his briefing.

"You need to be prepared for war," he says, his deep voice resonating through the room. "And in war, there are times when you need to keep multiple objectives in mind. With this being the case, not only will you need to protect your black box and retrieve the other team's black box, you'll also have a list of targets you must destroy during the games before your team can win. The targets may be objects. Or people. Even if you retrieve the black box, you're not done until every target on your team's list has been eliminated. Until they've been eliminated, the other team has the opportunity to steal back their black box."

I release a slow breath. This is far more complicated and intense than I expected.

Major Vasco looks between my team and the Blue Team. "If you are captured or shot by the hunters, you fail. If your team does not retrieve the other team's black box, you fail. If your team's black box is captured and you're unable to retrieve it by the time the games end, you fail. If you do not eliminate all of your targets, you fail. Failure is not acceptable. Do you understand?"

"Yes, sir!" we all shout.

The problem is, failure is inevitable for one of our teams.

The Commander comes up next to Major Vasco. "Thank you, Major Vasco. Excellent briefing." His gaze drops to Laban's team. "Green Team, you already know the consequences of failure tonight if you do not achieve your full mission objectives."

Out of my peripheral vision, I catch sight of Laban clenching his fists.

"Yes, sir," the team of soldiers shouts the two words at a deafening volume.

"Then let the games begin." Ark's lips twist into a calculated smirk.

Each team is led to their entry point to the Center.

Sergeant Valarius leads my team as my mind scrambles to determine how we'll navigate this.

"You will have thirty minutes to prep your team before entry." Sergeant Valarius doesn't look at me as we walk to the Center. "As lead, your band has been equipped with intel on the various members of your team to help you strategize your plan. During that time, the hunters will be getting into position. Unlike you, they already know the course. They've been training in it. Do not underestimate them."

I nod. "Okay."

The one word is all I can manage, even though I have several questions I'd like to ask Andor. From whether or not he talked to Matthias about Ari, to if he's even supposed to be telling me this.

But none of it escapes my mouth. In part because I need to be focused. But also because I'm not sure I want the answers. Not yet.

Moments later, the Center looms before us. Its massive structure holds thousands of unknowns tonight. And I have to prep my team to enter.

"You have thirty minutes, starting now." Sergeant Valarius taps something on a handheld screen, and a timer above our entry point counts down.

I face my team. It's time to prepare.

CHAPTER
SIXTY-ONE

I notice several familiar faces on my team, including Storm, Kiwi, and Arwen, as well as some recruits I recognize from different warfare scenarios and a few I've seen working with the Resistance. My team doesn't have any cadets and very few high-ranking recruits. And I think we might have all of the youngest recruits left in the city.

It's like Ark *wants* my team to fail.

Although he's on the Blue Team, I can't stop myself from wishing for Matthias. I'd feel far more confident in our ability together than I do without him here.

Disappointment curls through me, but I shove it aside.

I only have twenty-nine minutes to prep my team for a very complicated mission.

We've all been given special contact lenses for the games, which everyone puts in. Some have more trouble than others.

While they're getting their lenses in, I take the first several minutes of our rapidly depleting time and divide my team into smaller groups of eight to twelve. Kiwi helps me review the information I have, and together we divide the team, noting any recruits or cadets who don't have weapons as a result of the combined course a few days ago. We have ten who are weaponless, three of them kids under twelve.

I divide the seven older weaponless recruits into different offensive groups, assigning them to navigation for their group. The three kids will stay back with the defensive groups, along with the six other kids under twelve who still have weapons.

I put two of those groups in position to defend our black box, which should be in our territory on the other side of our entrance.

Another group I assign to flank the left side of the territory and to do their best to get to the black box in the other camp. Then I map out routes for five other teams as well. I have a larger group than I'm used to working with, and as the time diminishes, my brain ricochets through different options that will allow each group the greatest amount of protection. And also give us the highest likelihood of completing our tasks.

Using the information about the recruits that was downloaded to my band, I select nine for the elimination tasks.

"You guys have the highest marks in weaponry training, stealth, and in hand-to-hand combat," I say to them. "But be careful. These objectives are likely traps as well."

They nod their understanding.

"I'm sending you the intel on the various targets," I say. "My recommendation would be to work in groups of three to find your targets and eliminate them."

"Yes, ma'am," the nine say simultaneously. Like good recruits of Talionis.

At least I'm performing this task as I'm supposed to. Otherwise, I have no doubt someone in the group in front of me would happily report me to Commander Ark for their own gain. I shake the thought aside and glance at the timer above me.

Seven minutes left.

"Dude," Kiwi says, eyes glued to his band. "The uniforms have tech." He grabs my arm and types a code into my band. An instant later, the band shows the location of every person on our team—all of us crowded together outside of the Center.

Kiwi's excited about the capabilities, but it just reminds me of how much Ark is monitoring.

Our lenses for the games are like the ones Ari stole for us when we were on the run as fugitives, but more advanced. They include an overlay that allows me to see a map of the Center and, with the new command Kiwi gave my band, it also indicates where my teammates are.

I blink twice to clear the overlay, and turn to the defensive groups, which include Storm and the eight other young recruits. "We have one hour before the hunters are allowed to enter our territory. But I'm not sure how long this will take." My gaze lingers on the kids, and I have to force my attention to the other recruits who will be with them. "If they're giving us that much time, the likelihood is that there are far more dangers inside than we anticipate."

I look at the group of eighteen in front of me. Letting my fears control me is out of the question, but I can't help but imagine what will happen if any of the kids are injured by the hunters.

I clear my throat. "The black box is of utmost priority to keep safe. But all of you matter as well. Do not take unnecessary risks to protect the black box. The Blue Team needs to complete their elimination targets as well, and I suspect they'll do what we're doing and divide their team in order to accomplish the various tasks in the games tonight. So, be careful and stay alert. Okay?"

I wait until I get nods from all of them.

Kyle, a guy I've added to the defensive group, is tall and broad. He's ranked high in hand-to-hand combat and is two levels below sniper in weaponry. He should be able to protect the kids.

"You'll be the defensive group lead once we're in there," I say to him.

He gives a curt nod. "Yes, ma'am."

"If you think you need to move the box, you may do so," I say. "But be careful to ensure you all have good cover, no matter where you're staging."

I shift my attention to the groups going for the black box, including the team that will be with me. "Our bands are synced, and we have a secure channel for the games. But make sure you keep the communication limited. We don't need distractions. Communicate vital intel only."

There's a chorus of agreements, then a beep behind me.

A glance back shows we have one minute left on the clock.

"All right." I pull my rifle into my hands, ready to enter. "Get ready. We don't know everything we're facing in there. This will not be easy."

I face the door, prepared to lead my team inside the Center.

"Yep," Arwen says, coming up next to me. "I mean, I guess they're preparing us for war." Her voice is quiet and waivers on the last word.

I grimace, but nod. Hopefully, I'll find something, some way, to keep these people from being taken across the ocean and being part of a battle none of us signed up for.

But right now, I just need to get them through these games.

Kiwi steps up to my other side. "Don't tell Asher, but there's no one else I trust more to lead me in there." His words are a whisper, but bring a strange amount of comfort.

"Same," Arwen agrees.

The three of us will be searching for the black box together, and their votes of confidence bolster my courage. Maybe we can do this. Our group is smaller than anyone else's, but I only want people I can trust working with me tonight.

"Black Team, prepare for entry." A mechanical voice chirps.

5, 4, 3, 2, 1.

Beep, beep, beep.

The door swings open.

"Let's move," I say.

We exit our zone and move through a long tunnel and into the Center.

They have completely redesigned the interior. I've been in this stadium-like arena before for evaluations. For those, they divided the space into sections for each training eval. There were physical training areas, weaponry and tech stations, and a huge enclosed cube for warfare scenarios.

But now, it's like entering another world. Although the Center is enclosed with a dome roof, it's like we're at the edge of a forest with rolling hills and narrow pathways visible through the dense trees.

The way they can transform places is astonishing and unnerving.

There's an open area at the end of the tunnel where I wait for the rest of my team. It takes a few minutes for everyone to get in, and once they're inside, I send each group on their way. I assign one defensive group the job of patrolling our area and finding any easy entry points, then go with the other two defensive teams—which include Storm and the other kids—to find our black box.

Arwen and Kiwi stay close by.

We easily locate the black box using the location finder on my band. It's out in the open, and Kyle picks it up.

"We'll find a place to hide it," he says. "And we'll camouflage ourselves nearby to maintain cover." He gives a discreet glance at the kids.

"Good plan," I say, pleased with how quickly he's taken control of the situation and his effort to protect the youngest members of our team.

I give Storm a quick hug, squeezing her tighter than necessary.

"We'll be okay," she says in my ear. "We've been trained too."

The words should bring some comfort, because she's right. But dread clings to me. I'm leaving these kids at the mercies of the hunters and those from the Blue Team who will attempt to gain access to an item the kids are supposed to be protecting.

Maybe I should stay.

"I'll take care of them," Kyle says. "You're a bit of legend, you know? If anyone can avoid the hunters and retrieve the black box for a team win, it's you."

"Thanks." Even as I say the word, it feels silly. But I don't know how else to respond. "Let's head out," I say to Arwen and Kiwi.

We exit our zone and head into the Center. With each step forward, it's less like a familiar building and more like enemy territory.

The three of us move in a triangle formation with me at the lead. I'm glad they're on my team.

Using my band, Kiwi and I programmed routes for each group

moving through the area, other than those tasked with eliminating our targets. They have to find the targets first.

So far, everyone appears to be following the route laid out for them.

I lead my group, all of us silent with our weapons in hand, alert for any signs of the hunters or the other team. Although with how big the Center is and the way it's been redesigned, I can't imagine we'll see the other team anytime soon.

An alert pops up in my retina display. Two names from my team, followed by the words *Eliminated by hunters.*

I grimace. We're barely into these games, and I'm already losing teammates. I can't protect everyone. Not with how spread out we are. But the sooner we can get the box and get it back to our zone, the safer everyone will be.

As long as the elimination team does their job.

We wind our way through the Center. Over old rubble. Navigating paths through the fake forest and over hills.

There are no signs of hunters on this path. But that doesn't mean they aren't around.

We crest a hill and move stealthily over the rough terrain. A branch breaks to the left. I put my fist in the air, bringing the others to a halt. I signal for Kiwi to look in the direction of the sound.

He lifts his sniper rifle and peers through the night vision scope. Then he fires off two shots, and there are thuds as the hunters fall to the ground. A quick search of the area reveals three more hunters, and we take them all out without being shot ourselves.

A ping sounds in the com unit in my ear, and the Commander Ark's voice stops me in my tracks.

"In a war, there are times when you can't trust even those in your own squad. In order to prepare for these types of scenarios, we have a twist for all of you." Ark pauses, and I tighten my hold on my rifle as I wait for him to continue. "On each team, there are two spies for another team. They know who they are, and they have their own objectives they must accomplish. They do not know who the other traitor is on their team, so they're functioning alone. But for all of you, the warning is clear: be careful who you trust."

A glance behind me at Arwen and Kiwi tells me they heard the message too. Which means it was an all-com alert.

I hesitate, ready to go back and check on Storm. But that won't accomplish anything of value. "Let's keep moving," I say to the others, but also to myself.

"What about the traitors?" Arwen asks.

"We don't know who they are," I say. "But I do know that if we worry about that, we'll never complete our mission."

Kiwi and Arwen nod, which encourages me a bit, and we continue our march forward. *What if one of them is a traitor?* The thought whispers through my mind, but I shove it aside. I have to trust someone out here, and I can't let fear dictate my actions.

The next several minutes pass quickly with us taking out two more hunters. We've been in the games for thirty-eight minutes now, according to the reader on my band.

Which means there are just twenty-two more minutes until the hunters have access to our base. Putting Storm and the other kids in even more danger.

A fence looms in front of us, demanding my focus. This wasn't on my map. Arwen finds a hole, and we slip through.

As soon as we're inside the fenced-in area, I look at my band to get a clearer picture of where we are, but see nothing. The green night vision tint of my contacts and all my retina displays disappears too.

"My contacts aren't working," Kiwi says.

"Mine either," Arwen says.

"It must be a dead zone," Kiwi says.

He's right, but surprise filters through me. With all of the additional tech enhancements in the uniforms and lenses, I didn't expect there to be any dead zones in the Center, but they must have programmed it this way.

It's strange to go through with no tech, but as we do, I register that we're not encountering anyone else.

For the several minutes we're in the dead zone, we don't see a single hunter or hear anything.

We exit the dead zone on the other side, crawling through another hole in another fence, and all of our stuff comes back on. The technology reboot is almost blinding, but I can see much clearer than I could a moment ago.

As we make our way across the treacherous terrain, over a river they've added and past different groups of hunters, we manage to stay safe and defend ourselves.

Which isn't true for everyone else. Several elimination alerts show in my retina display. Each one more concerning than the last, since I'm not sure if the eliminations are the result of one of the other teams, or the traitors in our midst.

FIFTY-NINE MINUTES HAVE PASSED IN THE GAMES, AND WE'VE GONE THROUGH three dead zones on our way to the other team's base.

Each time, there's no one else there. No hunters, no tech, no groups from the Blue Team. Nothing.

It's like they're intentionally avoiding those areas because they know their tech won't work.

The beginning of an idea filters through my mind, but rustling to my left grabs my attention.

I turn, lift my rifle and see a member of the Blue Team headed our way, weapon raised. I shoot him, and Kiwi takes out the other two with him in quick succession.

They drop to the ground.

Even though they're not dead since we're using training bullets, they're in pain because of what we just did. And something in my gut twists.

Ark's watching all of this like a sick game. He's calling it the games because he's entertained, and he's using it all to train us to do what he wants. Regardless of what we want.

And I don't know what to do about it.

I lead my group forward, my shoulders tensing more with each passing minute.

Hunters are waiting to enter my base.

I picture Laban prowling along the perimeter, waiting for his chance to slink in. To hurt me by hurting my team. And he knows he'll hurt me most by terrorizing Storm. More than by hunting for me.

I set my jaw. "We have to move faster," I hiss, more to myself than to Kiwi and Arwen.

Anxiety claws at me, and I pick up the pace. An alert notifies me that our elimination group has taken out another target.

Of the twelve targets we were given, our elimination group has hit seven of them. But they've also lost two people, which means two of the teams only have two people in them now.

Another positive is that our defensive teams have had no reason to alert me.

But we've lost several teammates from the other groups because of hunters and the Blue Team.

And I have no clue who the traitors are on our team. The thought breathes fresh life into the anxiety gnawing its way higher up my spine with each passing minute.

We enter another dead zone, and the tech goes black.

"I can't believe they have this many in here," Kiwi says.

"It's really weird," I agree. "But according to what I saw before we entered this zone, we're only five mics out from the Blue Team's base. And it looks like another one of our team's groups will enter around the same time from the west."

"But we'll still have to find the black box," Arwen says.

I nod, but a thought causes me to pause. "Before we exit this dead zone, let's do a quick sweep. We'll split up, see approximately how big the zone is, and see if there's anyone else in here."

Arwen gapes at me. "Why?"

I shift on my feet. "I have a weird hunch. We'll meet on the other side in a few minutes. From what we've experienced so far, these zones aren't that big."

"You got it, boss," Kiwi says. "I've learned to trust your hunches."

We split up, Arwen looking a little pale at the idea of navigating the space alone.

I take the path I've assigned myself, alert to any sound or movement.

But there's nothing.

No hunters have entered these zones the whole time we've been in here. Not once.

I round a boulder and come face-to-face with Asher.

He holds up a hand. "Hey."

Even though we're on opposite teams, I don't want to shoot him. We just came to a truce, and whatever happens next, I'll need the Resistance's help to defeat Ark. Thankfully, it seems Asher doesn't want to shoot me either.

"I'm surprised you're not heading to my base," I say.

"Gotta keep some good people around to patrol the perimeter." He cocks an eyebrow at me. "Clearly a smart move."

His right hand hovers near a pistol at his hip, and I don't release the grip on the rifle in my hand, even though it's not raised.

I gesture to the area around us. "This is weird, right?"

"That they have dead zones?" He nods. "Yeah, super weird."

"Have you noticed there aren't any hunters in them? At least we haven't seen any. The soldiers are avoiding the dead zones completely."

His hand drops away from his pistol. "I didn't realize that, but yeah, you're right. I've crossed through this one at least eight times on my patrol over the past hour. Nothing whenever I'm in here, but they're just about everywhere outside of it. Probably because in a few minutes, they'll be able to enter our bases, and I'm sure they're expecting to hit our weakest targets there."

My shoulder tense at the thought, and he offers me a strained smile.

"Maybe we can use this, though," he says. "I mean, I want to beat your team in these games, but I'm even more interested in hitting the soldiers with everything we can."

"This is something we can exploit," I say, letting some intensity into my words. "But not in the games."

His brow furrows. "Why not? We need to perform well. I mean, we're not shooting each other at the moment, but we *are* on different teams. Why shouldn't I use this weakness against the hunters in order to give my team an advantage?"

I shake my head emphatically as a bigger picture plan crystalizes in my mind. "No. The soldiers are avoiding any area without tech because they *rely* on their tech." I emphasize the word. "We can use that later. When it matters."

Even though this is a dead zone, I keep my words at a minimum, just in case there's some way they're monitoring us. Although from what I've seen, they don't even have drones overhead here.

Asher assesses me, then gives a single nod. "Okay. We'll talk about this later."

"Absolutely," I say.

He starts to move on.

"I got a couple other people in here," I say, making him pause. "Let them through, all right?"

He shrugs. "No promises."

With that, he slips away silently.

My brain races through possibilities now that I know there's a weakness with the soldiers I haven't realized before. And it makes my work in the games much harder.

I reconnect with Arwen and Kiwi, and the three of us cross the threshold into the Blue Team's territory.

An alarm chirps through the entire Center.

"Hunters, you may now enter all areas."

Wait. Were they not allowed to enter the dead zones? The question flies through my mind even as I work with Arwen and Kiwi to find the black box.

We'll have to intentionally travel through the dead zones on our way back to our base. Check to see if the plans forming in my mind could actually work.

Kiwi grabs my arm, stopping me in my tracks. Arwen halts next to me.

He points up. "The black box," he whispers.

I follow his gaze. The black box is nestled in the branches of a tree. Four members of the Blue Team patrol the area beneath the box, two guys and two girls.

I signal for Kiwi to take out the two biggest guys, while Arwen and I flank the smaller ones on the left. The two agree.

Kiwi holds his position for a minute while Arwen and I creep around to the left. We crouch down behind a thick boulder, as the two smaller guards move in our direction. Two shots crack through the air in quick succession. I don't even have to look to know Kiwi's taken out his targets.

The two girls whirl around, reaching for their weapons. Arwen and I rush them from behind, each of us tackling one. I quickly disarm the one girl, and seconds later Kiwi arrives to help Arwen disarm the other. Arwen and I secure them both with zip-ties while Kiwi retrieves the black box from the tree. He passes it to Arwen.

"Let's get out of here," I hiss.

Before we've gone ten steps, gunfire erupts from our right.

The three of us dive for cover behind a thick outcropping of bushes. Kiwi grunts.

I risk a glance back. "We need to keep moving."

Kiwi's breathing intensifies. "I won't be much help." He releases a low hiss of pain.

I glance over at him. He's cradling his right arm.

"These things might be training bullets, but my arm is numb. Not sure I'll be any good shooting my gun on our way back through."

"We'll cover you," I say, even as dread pulses in my stomach.

I was relying on Kiwi's skills more than I want to admit. Arwen and I are decent shots, but Kiwi can take out a target two thousand yards away.

"We should move," I say. "They saw where we went. They'll be coming for us."

Arwen grabs the black box, and we sneak out of the territory and back into the main area.

I use the map to determine where the dead zones are and to lead us through those as we head back to our base.

Team eliminations come through my alert every time we exit a dead zone and enter back into areas where our tech works.

Most of my team is down.

The three of us are among the fifteen left standing, and so far Storm is active. But Kiwi was right. He can still barely use his arm. The training bullets must be stronger than what we're used to experiencing. It's as though his arm has truly been shot. Even though there's no blood, he can barely move it, which makes having a sharp-shooter with me far less useful. Sweat beads on his forehead, and he leans on Arwen for support.

Guess Mandeville decided to make the bullets hurt more with these tech-laced uniforms rather than to protect those wearing them.

Another notification comes through my retina display. The elimination team hit all of their targets successfully. Although we've suffered many casualties, we've at least made it to this point. I just have to get the black box to the secure area at our base.

We cross back into the threshold of our team's zone, round a bend, and face a group of hunters. Guns poised. As though they were waiting for us.

"Well, look who it is." Laban sneers.

I aim my gun at him, but he has his gun pressed into Storm's back.

Her face is ashen, and her body quivers beneath Laban's hold.

"Don't hurt her," I plead.

Laban smiles, and my heart slams against my chest.

"Kyle was so helpful in guiding us right to where Storm would be."

Blood drains from my face. Kyle was a spy for the hunters. And I left him to protect Storm and the kids. How could I have been so foolish?

"I've been waiting for you," Laban continues. "Took you long enough to get here."

With that, he shoots Storm in the back.

She screams and falls to the ground. She stops moving.

I race toward her, and he shoots me three times.

The training bullets hit me, knocking the breath out of my lungs, but I keep rushing forward, even as I feel as though blood should be pouring out of me.

I reach Storm, but she's not breathing. I drop to the ground, adrenaline pushing aside my pain as I gently turn her over. Did he *kill* her?

She inhales deeply. Relief courses through me.

Laban lifts his pistol and whips me across the face, causing blood to flow this time.

It doesn't knock me out, and I turn and glare at him as my head and body pulse with pain.

"The games have concluded," Ark's voice echoes through the Center.

Lights come on, making it appear as though it's midday.

I squint against the intrusion, my breaths coming in painful and ragged bursts. "She's a kid," I say to Laban.

He leans into my face, his golden eyes flashing. "Who has to prepare for war. The little brat shouldn't have had her back turned. If she had been protected at all, maybe she could have stayed hidden."

He pats me roughly on the cheek he just pistol-whipped.

I hiss out a breath of pain, which brings a cruel smile to his lips.

"Then again," he says, "I guess we *did* have the advantage of Kyle."

I pull Storm close as silent tears course down her cheeks and look away from Laban.

It's too much for me to deal with. How could I be so *stupid* to continually put myself in positions where people can betray me?

First Elena. Then Shane. Now Kyle. Even though I barely know Kyle, the betrayal still stings. He may not have had a choice in whether or not he was a traitor, but he didn't have to sacrifice a *kid*.

The team scores come through, and although we eliminated all our targets and retrieved the black box, apparently the Blue Team got our black box all the way back to their secure zone. And suffered far fewer casualties.

Being in the dead zones kept the notification that they retrieved our box from coming through. Which means I made a mistake.

But I also found out more during these games than Ark intended.

Laban and his team stroll away, laughing and clapping one another on the back.

Arwen lowers Kiwi to the ground near us, and he gives me a sympathetic look filled with pain. Which means the excruciating pain Storm and I are currently experiencing will last a while longer.

Storm's cries grow louder, and I stroke her hair, careful to avoid where Laban shot her.

I glare at Laban's retreating back. They are going down.

I refuse to stand by and let these evil people win. And I'll die before I let them take Storm and force her into battle.

Before I can help Storm to her room, Ark summons all three teams back to the Physical Training Arena for a debrief.

Every step sends spikes of pain through my body. I hiss out a breath and support Storm the best I can as we enter the arena. Tears stream down her cheeks, but her sobs are choked. Probably because soldiers, cadets, and recruits swarm around us. Many are nursing invisible wounds.

Being shot with training bullets hurts normally, but this pain is on another level thanks to Mandeville's special suits.

Ark arrives and everyone snaps to attention. My breath catches as my hand rests against the bruise I'm sure is forming on my chest. Storm let's out a little yelp. Kiwi isn't even able to lift his arm into a salute.

"At ease," Ark says. He paces along the platform, eyes scanning the mob in front of him. "I will keep this brief since I know you all must be exhausted." He stops pacing in front of my team. "Black Team, you failed where the Green Team and Blue Team succeeded." Somehow his eyes soften, like he feels bad.

Chills sweep over my body.

"As much as it pains me, I'm afraid you will have to face consequence." Ark grabs the top rail and leans forward. "You will receive increased exercise regimes, more warfare scenarios, and additional time in the weaponry training complex."

A few soft gasps sound through the crowd.

"I know this seems harsh." He presses a hand over his heart. "But it is for your best. Everything must be done in order to prepare you for deployment to Sitreea. Tonight proved you're not yet ready." He strides to the center of the platform. "All of you will, in fact, need additional training over these next weeks. Give it your all. For me."

"Sir, yes, sir!" Everyone shouts.

The faintest smile tinges Ark's lips. "You're dismissed."

My body trembles, both from exhaustion and from anger. Ark is going to push every recruit to his or her breaking point. And he doesn't care.

CHAPTER
SIXTY-THREE

I follow the winding route I've mapped out for myself to get to the Resistance meeting taking place this evening. Asher got word to me about the meeting and, although we couldn't talk much, he expressed excitement to go over what we discovered in the games. The sky is dark and thick with clouds, and I tug my jacket zipper up higher. Early winter has grasped Talionis as tightly as Ark's hold on the lives of every person within the walls of the city.

It's been nine days since the games. Since my team lost.

Everything Ark promised has happened. The intensity and frequency of our trainings has increased to a frenzy. All to make sure we are ready in just a few weeks' time to go to Sitreea and fight Ark's battle.

There have been several briefings for all the recruits and cadets to prepare us for the journey to Sitreea. Trill spouts propaganda about how Commander Ark's plan will not only keep Sitreea from going to war with their neighbors but also bring about greater prosperity for his home country. Major Vasco and Colonel Valarius divide the recruits and cadets into units that center around specific skills and train the units for the various layers of attack planned.

Bomb squads. Sniper units. Stealth units for recruits excelling in recon. Tech groups.

But I know more than what the soldiers are telling the recruits.

We aren't preparing to defend Sitreea by battling with her neighbors. Each move we make will be seen as a direct attack on the bordering countries, which will bring about war and pave the way for Ark to sweep in and take control.

Not to mention, the targets set for elimination aren't enemies of the state like Ark wants the sniper units to believe. They are high-level members of the Sitreean government. Those who would stand in Ark's way if they were alive.

I round a corner and pause to check behind me. When I'm satisfied no one's tailing me, I continue forward.

An increased hysteria has taken over Talionis, with greater punishment for any person who speaks against what Ark is doing. A few recruits have openly expressed they aren't interested in leaving the North American region.

All three have since gone missing.

The only one I interacted with was Marci, but I recognized the others from prior meetings with the Resistance. And from what Kiwi told me, none of them are anywhere to be found. Silenced before they could poison others against Ark.

Leaves rustle to my left. I press myself against the building, searching for signs of anyone. Nothing.

Still, my heartbeat has found a new, much faster rhythm as I continue forward.

With all of my trainings, briefings, and the intensity that has taken over Talionis as the soldiers prepare the recruits for battle, there's been no time to get back out to the Ruins or down into the tunnels to Cai. But Matthias let me know he got word to Andor about the timeline until Day X, and Andor promised to talk to Cai.

I can only hope Cai is able to convince Eryndale leadership to *do* something. But the threat of a spy within their ranks makes everything so much more complicated.

Why would this person choose to betray Eryndale? It doesn't make sense.

But then, why does anyone choose to betray those who trust them?

Storm hasn't been the same since Kyle turned her over to Laban. She's jumpy. Fearful. I have to get her out of here.

Smuggling her to the Ruins is impossible with how closely we're both being watched. Not to mention, my schedule is chaotic, with soldiers waking me up at all hours of the night to train.

I'm barely getting enough sleep to function, and the danger of being away from my room if someone arrives to bring me to a training is too great.

I double back once more to make sure I'm not being followed, then enter a residential area. As I climb an old fire escape in the Lower Housing District, minutes away from meeting with the only people who seem ready to help, my mind jumps ahead to what I'll share. The good thing is, Asher is ready to do anything he can to stop Talionis.

Whispers from the Resistance have been that he's telling his people to lie low for now, because something is in the works.

I think he's referring to what I pointed out to him during the games.

I reach the top of the fire escape and crouch low to avoid being seen as I quickly cross the roof of the building. I come to the rooftop entrance into the old building and pause in the shadows, taking in the surrounding landscape.

The area is clear.

I rap on the door and wait. Seconds later, it cracks open, and Kiwi grins at me.

"Good to see you!" He opens the door wider and allows me in. "You're the last one we're expecting tonight."

"Am I late?" I ask as he locks the door behind me.

"Nope. Everyone else got here in scattered time slots. Asher gave you the last one." He scoops up a pack on the ground and leads me deeper into the building. "Not everyone could be here tonight—over half of the Resistance was scheduled with night exercises."

I nod, even though he's not looking at me, but don't respond. I'm too busy working on what to say that will convince everyone here to enact the plan I've concocted. A plan that isn't as sound as I would like. But it's all we have to work with.

There are forty to fifty people crammed into the room, and the low hum of conversation buzzes through the air.

When Kiwi and I enter and he closes the door, the conversations stop.

"Great, glad you're here," Asher says. "Let's get started. Bria, talk us through what we can do to get out of this nightmare."

My mouth gapes at how he's giving me control of the meeting, but I recover and plunge in. I quickly outline what I discovered in the games and talk about how the soldiers rely on their tech and avoid areas where they can't use it.

"And that's what we'll use against them," I say. "The best-case scenario has always been permanently stopping Demetrius Ark. But since I'm not sure how we'll be able to do so, this is what we can do to get as many out of here as possible."

Even as I say the words, I have to school my features to keep the disappointment with myself from leaking through. Getting some recruits out of Talionis feels like failure. Ark will move forward with his plans. Probably end up recapturing and punishing many recruits who escape. But like I just said, it seems to be the only option.

"Do you have a plan?" Asher asks.

"I do." I take a deep breath. "Because of the access Ark's given me, Kiwi and I have found some weaker tech points in the city. Over the past few days, I've been careful to take note of them." I nod to Kiwi. "Kiwi told me about a disarming device we could rework to disable some of those weaker tech points. The goal would be to strategically place the device so it can send out a virus that will disable the weak tech in the areas we tell it to. Then we'll take that route out of the city."

"What about the Wall?" Asher asks. "Isn't it on a separate grid entirely?"

Kiwi steps forward. "It is, but the guard towers have ways around the electrically-charged Wall. I'll forge a Wall guard's key card which will get us access to their route to the top of the Wall. Then we'll take the route down onto the other side. To freedom."

Kiwi and I only had a few minutes to discuss how I needed his help, and I'm impressed by what he's come up with. He and I talked about using the tunnels for part of this, but we both agreed it would be too much to coordinate and take too much time traveling. We need to move quickly once this starts.

"Sounds like a dangerous plan," a girl says.

A few others chime in their agreement.

"It is," I say. "But if we can create tech dead zones that become a route through the city, we'll have an advantage over the soldiers. They'll want to avoid them so they can stay in contact as they attempt to stop us. Use their tech to track us. But they won't be able to do any of that within our dead zones."

"Some might still come through," a guy in the back of the group says.

"Yes, some *will* come through," I say. "But their training has taught them that their tech is vital for success. Some will look for ways around the path we create for ourselves. And they won't know exactly where we are, because we'll create multiple paths we could take. It's how my friends and I escaped before. We created chaos through sabotage, and that kept them from discovering which route we were taking out of the city."

Asher crosses his arms over his chest. "I think it's a solid plan. But the sabotage will be harder now. They cracked down on what we can access after you guys escaped."

"With the way everything is amped up right now, I think the chaos of their tech going down will be enough to distract them," I say, hoping I'm right.

The discussion continues, and we flesh out our plan.

Asher tells everyone to be prepared for further details soon and to discreetly pass on the message *birds fly together* to everyone in the Resistance. Kiwi leans over to inform me that's the code phrase the Resistance agreed upon once an escape plan was in place. Since neither Matthias or Storm know the phrase, I'll make sure to tell them what's going on.

Asher dismisses the group, but asks me and Kiwi to wait.

Once everyone is gone, he turns his intense gaze on me. "The next step is planting the device, right?"

"Right," I agree.

"How will we get our hands on one so Kiwi can program in the virus?" Asher asks.

"Oh, I already got one." Kiwi opens the pack at his feet and pulls out an innocuous little box. "Reprogrammed it already too."

I raise my eyebrows, and Asher claps Kiwi on the back.

"You always impress me, my man." Asher takes the box Kiwi passes to him. "How does it work?"

"We just need to get it placed near the supercomputers in the secure wing of the Technical Operations Building," Kiwi says. "Which is easier said than done. That room is a fortress." He smirks. "But I have some tricks up my sleeve. As long as I know when Bria's going to place it, I can get her entry."

Before I can say anything, Asher's shaking his head. "No. I'll place it. Bria's being watched more than I am. Makes sense that I would be the one to do it."

"Are you sure?" I ask. "This is my idea, and it's risky."

"It's beyond risky," Kiwi agrees. "If they catch you, you'll be as gone as Marci, Peter, and Boden."

"Then let's not get caught," Asher says solemnly. He focuses on me. "When should I place it?"

The sudden change throws me off, but I recover. "My plan was to place it five days from now, assuming Kiwi could have the device prepped in time."

"Which I was," Kiwi says with a little bow that would have been comical any other time.

"So, Friday," Asher says.

I nod.

"Then Friday it is." Asher puts the device in his own pack. "Once it's in place, how long will we have to prep everyone to leave?"

"If you place the box out of the way, they shouldn't notice it," Kiwi says.

"That will give us time to work out the details and make sure everyone's ready," I say. "But I don't think we should wait long. According to the timeline Ark had Major Vasco show me, we have four weeks. But I suspect he plans to leave before then."

"The sooner we leave, the better, if you ask me," Kiwi says.

Asher gives a small smirk. "Can't help but agree. Bria, keep me updated on the plan as you iron things out. You're the best strategist we have, and I trust you to get my people out of here."

The words are the most generous Asher has offered me. But they come with a weight.

Once again, I'm responsible for keeping people safe. But this time, it's far more people than I've ever had to protect before.

I take in a stabilizing breath and agree.

I can barely sleep after I get back to my room from the meeting. So much rides on this plan. On me. If I fail, how many will die?

But if I don't act, then what? Most likely every person in the Resistance will die in the war Ark is starting in Sitreea.

It's the only option.

The next two days are filled with all-consuming trainings, with soldiers barking orders at a frenetic level. Since I've barely slept with my mind wrapped up in planning this mass exodus from Talionis, the trainings are even more grueling.

It's like every recruit is going through the Elite Recruit training regimen, and despite my training and skills, I'm feeling the effects of the mental, emotional, and physical stress.

The worst part is, I haven't had a chance to see, let alone talk to, Matthias or Kemena since the games.

But I will today.

A Sitreean delegation is arriving tonight, and I've been ordered to the tailors' to prepare, along with Matthias and several other key cadets. But no other recruits.

Kemena sent word to me that she would be helping me and Matthias with the first parts of our preparations while Sampta and Presidia worked with the other four cadets who are attending the dinner.

Which means I'll have a chance to finally talk to them.

I've sent both Kemena and Matthias messages that I missed them and that the games were unexpected. Hopefully it was enough to alert them to the fact that I need to talk to them. Plus, I need their help. I was able to let Storm know a plan is in place to get out of Talionis and to be alert. Even though I wasn't able to give her more details, I'm confident she'll be ready for whatever happens.

I weave through crowds of recruits making their way to eat an early dinner so they can be sent to the bunkers for the delegation's arrival. Although the delegation isn't expected until 1800 hours, Ark insists the recruits be hidden well in advance.

I envy them for the reprieve they'll experience tonight. Being in the bunkers is miserable, but at least they won't be put through night trainings. Or have to sit through a tense meal with delegates from Sitreea, all while Ark is watching with the eye of an eagle spying its prey. Ready to swoop in and gobble it up at the slightest misstep.

I enter the tailors' building, and I'm escorted by a soldier to a back room where Kemena and Matthias are waiting.

Once the soldier closes the door behind him, Matthias pulls me into a hug.

"I've missed you," he whispers into my hair.

I rest my head against his chest, listening to the beat of his heart. "I've missed you too."

"Y'all are cute," Kemena says. "But I don't think we have much time before the sisters will be here to take over your prep."

I pull back from Matthias, but he keeps his arm around me. "You're probably right," I say.

Kemena gestures to a chair. "Matthias, let me clean up your hair while Bria talks. Because I suspect she's got something to tell us."

Matthias gives me a gentle squeeze before taking a seat in the chair Kemena indicated. She picks up clippers and begins giving his short hair a fade.

"No buzz cut, huh?" Matthias asks.

"Not for a fancy dinner," Kemena says. "The sisters would die if their custom-tailored suits were worn by someone with such an *atrocious* haircut. Just ask them." Her voice is dry, and she pauses in cutting Matthias's hair to roll her eyes. Then she nods at me in the mirror. "This room isn't monitored. You can talk."

As an extra precaution, I enable the cloaking feature on my band. Then I dive into a quick explanation of what I discovered in the games and how I'm working with the Resistance to use it against Ark as a way for us to escape. The words come out rushed and jammed together, but coherent. I think.

By the time I'm done, Matthias looks almost angry, and Kemena's face is pinched.

I pace in the cramped room. The only sound for several moments is the buzzing coming from the clippers as Kemena finishes up Matthias's hair.

She turns them off once she's done and faces me. Something about her expression makes me tense.

"What?" I ask, the word sharper than it should be.

She tucks her braids behind her ear. "I heard something the other day. Didn't really make sense at the time, but the way it was said . . . just stayed with me, you know?"

I stop my pacing. "Okay . . ." I draw out the word, more uneasy with each second.

Matthias is scowling at his lap and hasn't turned from the mirror. I look at Kemena, not sure what to do with his suddenly sour mood.

"You can't go through with this, Bria," Kemena says the words softly, but there's an intensity to them I can't deny.

"Why?" I ask, unable to keep the defensive edge from my tone. "Do you want all of us to be shipped off for war with Sitreea?"

"Girl, that is not fair, and you know it," Kemena says in a tone that reminds me of my mom correcting me when I'm in trouble.

I drop my gaze. "But we have to fight. As soon as possible."

Her hand on my shoulder brings my eyes back up. She offers a small, understanding smile. "I know. But it can't be this." She holds up a palm to still my questions. "The soldiers talk in front of me. Pretty much don't see me while I'm working. And from what I've heard, Ark is playing you, girl."

I'm shaking my head even as the ring of truth in her words fights with my desperation to act. "No. I discovered the dead zone in the games. It's a weakness."

"It was intentional. Ark wanted you to find it." Kemena's voice becomes insistent. "I didn't understand before, but the soldiers were talking about orders to avoid tech dead zones during the games. To not enter unless they wanted to face severe punishment."

A wave of unbelief washes over me. "Because they wouldn't be able to use their tech. They rely on their tech. We'll take that away from them and get out of here. Once Asher plants the device in three days."

Kemena's lips press together. "It's too dangerous. You have to call it off."

I lift my hands in the air. "Anything we do against Ark is dangerous! But at least we can try to do *something*."

Matthias leaps to his feet. "Do you *want* to get yourself killed? You can't do this, Bria!"

I cross my arms over my chest, wishing for the protective armor uniforms I wear for some of the scenarios. "It's time to act."

He strides through the room until he's right in front of me. "Not if it will get you killed. And what will this plan accomplish, anyway? We escaped before. And we're right back where we started."

"Because Shane betrayed us," I say, anger rising. "And if I die fighting, it's worth it. We can't all stay silent just because we're afraid to speak against evil."

He steps back and blinks as though I slapped him. He exhales slowly. "We can't just escape, Bria. We'd be running. Not fighting. Ark needs to be stopped." His voice is measured now, but my anger still rages.

I step toward him. "And how are you going to do that, Matthias? By sitting by and *wishing* the bad guys away? Your mom knew she had to step up and fight against what Ark was doing!"

"What did that get her?" His voice cracks. "She's dead, and she didn't do a single thing to stop Ark's plans. Just left me alone to face my dad's fists and hatred."

Compassion for what he's lost wars with my frustration over his fears to step up and fight. "I'm sorry for what you went through. But come on. You know we have to act! Time is not on our side. And this is the one way we can at least get some kids out of here."

"It's not safe," Kemena says, breaking into our fight.

I forgot she was even in the room.

I pinch the bridge of my nose. "I thought of everyone in this place, at least you two would be in this with me."

"We want to stop Ark," Kemena says. "But Matthias is right. Ark needs to be *stopped*. We can't just escape. It won't be enough."

My fists tighten and my nails bite into my palms. "I have to try to protect the people I can. And the plan is already in motion. Asher is going to place the device in three days."

"Bria, you have to stop trying to do this all according to what you understand," Kemena insists. "I'm telling you, this is a trap. You have to trust God and the people He's put in your life. We wouldn't warn you away from this unless we were trying to save you from the trap Ark has laid out for you."

I rub my hands over my face and don't respond.

"Have you even prayed about this?" Kemena asks gently.

No. The answer to her question sticks in my throat like a rock.

"I have to at least try," I say.

Kemena's face falls, and I look away. I can't bear to see her disappointment, but she doesn't really get it. She's only been in Talionis for a little while. Hasn't been trained as a soldier. She doesn't know the lengths Ark will go to get what he wants. The lives he'll sacrifice.

And if there's a way for me to get recruits out of here so they aren't in his crosshairs, then I will.

God, help me do this.

"If you go through with this," Matthias says, breaking into my tormented thoughts, "we're done. I can't sit back while you throw away your life." His chin shudders. "I love you too much."

I put a wall around my emotions to keep from allowing the full impact of his words to strike my heart. "It's my life, Matthias. If I think it's worth this risk, I will take it."

For the second time in the thirty minutes we've been here, his face flinches like I slapped him.

But I don't stop. "So, I guess we're done."

Kemena's mouth drops open, and Matthias half falls back into the chair he vacated.

Before anyone can say another word, the door opens, and Sampta and Presidia walk in.

CHAPTER
SIXTY-FIVE

"The Commander wants to see you," Colonel Valarius says.

I choke back a groan, turn off the holographic table I was working with, and leave the warfare prep room.

During the dinner with the Sitreean delegation last night, I was distracted. Not sure how I couldn't be after the conversation—no, the fight—I had with Matthias and Kemena. I did talk more with Antonio, not that I can see a way for us to use him to stop Ark. But keeping that connection seems like a good idea. The best plan right now is to get as many out of here as possible. Even if Matthias and Kemena don't agree.

Still, I don't think I did anything that would warrant Ark being upset with me.

Not that it would take much to upset him.

I retrieve my rifle from the front of the Warfare Strategies Building and follow Colonel Valarius outside.

I've taken more solace in my trainings today than I should have. But if I don't let myself become completely engrossed in them so that they drive away all thoughts and emotions, I'll just be consumed by the far too logical words Kemena said last night about everything being a trap.

And the fact that I ended things with the one guy I care about more than anyone else. Not to mention the hurtful things I said.

I stare at the back of Colonel Valarius's head as I follow him through the streets of Talionis. He's done so much damage to his son, but despite all of that, Matthias has grown into a good man. A man I don't always agree with. But he tries to do what's right.

And I criticized him yesterday. Shoved him away. All because I didn't like what he said to me.

This morning in physical conditioning training, I had a brief opportunity to talk to Asher while we were completing a weight lifting circuit. I almost called off the plan. Told him there's been a development.

But I didn't.

Because I still want to believe that what we're planning could work. It makes sense.

You have to stop trying to do this all according to what you understand. Kemena's words crack through my mind like lightning. *Have you even prayed about this?*

Her words and questions have haunted me.

But the truth is, I'm not sure I *want* to ask God what to do. What if His answer is the same as Kemena's and Matthias's? What if He tells me to wait and not act?

And what if I listen and miss this one opportunity?

I square my shoulders and follow Colonel Valarius into the Main Headquarters Building.

No.

We have to go through with this plan. And I need to put on whatever show Ark needs to see so he doesn't suspect a single thing.

Colonel Valarius doesn't say a word to me as he leads me through the Main Headquarters Building and to one of the large conference rooms. I've been in these rooms several times since returning to Talionis and never once has it been a good experience.

Then again, when have I ever interacted with Demetrius Ark or any of his top officials other than Sergeant Valarius and had a *good experience?*

Colonel Valarius pauses outside the door to the conference room for so long that I finally look up at him.

He's staring at me through narrowed eyes. "I overheard my waste of a son tell my brother the two of you are over. Is that true?"

Anger, sadness, and frustration swirl through me and settle uncomfortably in my gut like a bad batch of gruel.

"Yes, sir," I bite out the words.

He doesn't respond.

I want to take out all of my emotions on him, scream at him for the way he's treated Matthias. But I swallow it back as he opens the door and gestures for me to enter.

I march into the room, my footsteps resounding with more force than necessary. I stop short.

A group of soldiers stands at the edges of the room, but that's not what snatches the air from my lungs.

Asher's bound, standing in the center of the room, his face bloody and swollen.

"Ah, Bria, I'm so thrilled you could join us," Commander Ark says smoothly.

My body comes to attention of its own accord, obeying the command to perform for these people I despise.

"At ease." Ark's sitting casually at the head of the conference room table to the left, one leg crossed over the other while he sips a cup of coffee.

As though Asher isn't even here. Like this is some little chat.

Ark sets his cup of coffee on the table and stands, slowly brushing his hands against his slacks. His dark eyes rise to meet mine, and the cool calculation there reminds me of other times I've faced him.

And lost.

Cade giving his life for me flashes through my mind. Why does this seem so similar? It's different. Ark hasn't brought Asher up before the entire crowd of recruits, cadets, and soldiers.

There's no chanting for Asher to die for his *betrayal*.

I'm not watching a friend sacrificially choose to die in my place.

But the feeling of imminent death . . . of more loss . . .

It takes my breath away.

My hands tremble from where they're clasped together behind my back.

Mere seconds pass, each one more suffocating than the last.

Ark prowls through the room, his half a dozen soldiers standing at the edges in perfect formation.

I meet Asher's eyes for the first time, and the resignation there does nothing to ease my rising panic. He's ready to take whatever punishment Ark is planning to dole out, but Asher won't betray me. Hasn't betrayed me, despite the beating he received.

But what happened? Why is he in this position? He wasn't supposed to plant the box until Friday. I saw him a few hours ago. Everything was fine.

He was laughing at a joke Kiwi cracked.

Nothing was out of place.

Plans were moving—

"You have become a great asset to our strategic planning, Bria," Ark breaks into my careening thoughts, nabbing my attention. "What do you think would be the proper response to a blatant act of sabotage that could weaken Talionis's infrastructure?"

"What do you mean, sir?" My pulse throbs in my throat so fiercely, I'm sure it's visible.

How could Ark have found out what we were planning?

Ark simply nods.

A blast sounds mere feet from me. Then another a fraction of a second later.

My ears ring.

Asher falls to the ground, lifeless.

I think I scream, but I can't hear it because of the ringing in my ears.

I sink to the ground, gaping at Asher.

Tears don't come.

Only horror.

Ark is saying something, but I can't make out the words. Even though Asher didn't give me up, Ark knows I was part of this. Deep within my gut, I'm sure of it. And this is his way of punishing me. Of showing me there's no way to defeat him.

I scrub my hands over my face, press my ears. Try to clear the ringing. Wipe the horrific scene from my mind. But even with my eyes closed, I still see Asher.

Colonel Valarius holsters his pistol, then grabs me by the scruff of my shirt and yanks me to my feet.

My knees wobble, not wanting to hold me up.

He shakes me.

My ears keep ringing, and the words in the room are muffled. Like I'm submerged under water.

Colonel Valarius smacks me across the face. Shakes me again.

It barely registers.

Someone puts a headset over my ears. White noise breaks through.

The ringing dissipates. Stops.

I don't want it to stop.

I don't want to hear whatever Ark's about to say.

Because the voice in my head is screaming.

Kemena was right. It was all a trap.

And because I chose to ignore her warning, an eighteen-year-old with so much promise is dead.

Colonel Valarius yanks off the headset, and Ark comes to stand in front of me until he fills my vision, hiding Asher's body.

Asher was the leader of the Resistance. What will happen to them now?

Ark nods at Colonel Valarius, and he steps away.

"Now, Bria," Ark says. "Thankfully, we discovered this heinous plan prior to it being accomplished. Catching him in the act of attempted sabotage, after all I've done for him. That pained me."

Catching him in the act . . . does that mean Asher moved up when he was planting the device? It must. But why?

"We're confident he had accomplices, but he refused to reveal who they were." Ark's jaw ticks. "But it has caused me to realize the severity of waiting too long to act." His face remains neutral, but hatred fills his eyes. "I've moved up the timeline for our journey to Sitreea. We'll leave in one week's time."

My mouth drops open. I can't stop it.

Ark's nostrils flare. "You'll work with Major Vasco to iron out any potential issues with my plans. Ensure all recruits are ready to leave." He shifts to look back at Asher. "I wouldn't want to see more lose their lives as a result of your . . . carelessness."

I drop my gaze to my feet. The numb shock from a moment ago rips away with the pain of a scab being torn off.

I squeeze my eyes shut, will myself not to cry. Not to break down.

"Do you understand, Bria?" Ark asks, the impatience in his voice an indicator that this isn't the first time he's asked.

"Yes, sir," I gasp out the words.

"Good."

He says more, but I can't hear it.

I could have stopped this. Called it off. Told Asher not to move forward.

I should have listened to Kemena. And Matthias.

But I didn't.

And now, Asher is dead.

God, what did I do?

What if I had prayed about this? What if I hadn't been so insistent on pushing forward?

Colonel Valarius shoves me toward the door, and I leave the room.

As I follow him back through the Main Headquarters Building, another thought breaks through my tormented questions and self-accusations.

Why did Asher change up the timeline for planting the device without telling me?

Did he tell Kiwi? Anyone?

Now that he's gone, will I ever find out?

CHAPTER
SIXTY-SIX

The rest of the day, various soldiers lead me through Talionis. No one leaves me alone. There's no way for me to get word to the Resistance of Asher's death.

Ark has isolated me as much as possible.

And it's my fault.

As Corporal Saylano leads me back to the Warfare Strategies Building, the deadness of the early winter around me seeps into my soul.

No leaves.

No flowers.

Everything that's not man-made is completely lifeless.

In one week, I'll be dragged across an ocean and into a war. A war where so many of the faces I see in this city will become as dead as the leaves crunching to dozens of pieces beneath my feet.

God, why would You let this happen? Why would You bring me so far only to let Ark win?

The events I've gone through have challenged my new faith. And I don't know how it will survive.

If God is so powerful that He can save me from sin and promise me eternal life, how could He allow evil to win in this world?

I enter the Warfare Strategies Building, and Corporal Saylano signs duty of me over to Major Vasco.

Major Vasco and I head to the staging room.

"We'll be running recruits through five different scenarios each today," Major Vasco says. "Each group will go through the scenarios that will best prepare them for their part in the Commander's plans." He pauses outside the door, his expression stoic. "I don't think I need to reinforce the importance of each recruit completing their scenarios without any trouble."

I swallow hard.

Does that mean he knows about the ways I've sabotaged the scenarios? Did they find the back door Kiwi's device opened for me?

Bitterness roils over me. Of course they did. Why would anything go well in this awful place?

"Understood, sir," I say.

I spend the next five hours putting stealth squads through several scenarios to prep them for Sitreea. It's mind-numbingly simple since I'm not attempting any form of sabotage.

Which means way too much time to think.

As I put squads through scenarios that include ones I went through with Nika, Ari, Cade, Shane, and Matthias, memories pound me. Bringing me back through the days, weeks, and months of my life since Talionis invaded my world.

Changed me.

The night I woke up in the forest to Storm's cries, thinking they belonged to my little brother.

Laban finding me awake and knocking me out. Chasing me when I tried to escape. When I broke his nose and created an enemy.

The terror of being a new recruit. Getting screamed at by soldiers.

Storm getting dragged away in order to punish me. Colonel Valarius sentencing me to the Ruins where I almost died.

Suffering through training as an Elite Recruit.

Ava dropping from the dead hang into the raging river. Drowning.

Cade getting shot while a crowd of brainwashed recruits cheered.

Elena and Shane's betrayals.

Nate's death at the hands of Talionis soldiers.

Running as fugitives and witnessing the horrific lengths Ark was willing to go to in order to get us back.

The frustration of finally arriving in Eryndale, only to have a new fight to prove we weren't spies for Talionis.

I wish I could go back to Derbe. Erase all the nightmares I've experienced. Undo the pain I've caused and the pain others have inflicted on me.

A beep rings through the staging room. The recruits in the scenarios I'm running have completed the intel-gathering mission in the heart of the Sitreean capital of Rome.

I program the next scenario to populate.

The recruits on the screens disappear as blackness engulfs them. The next scenario begins.

My mind once again drifts back.

Meeting Storm and then Cade, her fierce protector. Becoming friends with Nika and Ari. Training with Cai in the Ruins. Working with Damara to make sure Storm was well cared for.

Learning about God. Discovering His forgiveness and love.

Growing closer to Matthias and falling in love for the first time.

Laughing with my friends aboard *The Fearless Lady*. Making new friends with Catori, Davey, Nate, and Quwani.

Learning from Essie in Eryndale and meeting many amazing people in the refuge city.

Working with Kemena, Mom, Nika, Keesia, and Kiwi to smuggle kids out to the Ruins. Seeing those kids gain back a little of the childhood Ark stole.

Dozens of memories, moments, and people rush through my mind. Some bitter and painful. Others beautiful. Sweet.

I type the next commands for the scenario without focusing on them.

These fourteen months have felt like a lifetime of their own. And as much as it has hurt, as much as I wish I could forget the achingly painful experiences, erasing this year would mean cutting out some of the most incredible friendships and experiences of my life.

Kemena's words from weeks ago come back to me. *There are two options. Living in fear or embracing the fullness of what God has, despite the fear, despite the potential loss. Knowing that trusting Him and following His leading, wherever it may go, it's worth it. Even unto death.*

My faith is imperfect.

I've acted as though everything depended on me and on what I could do rather than trusting God, giving my fears to Him, and remembering He is in control. And He loves me.

I've allowed my circumstances to control me, rather than pressing forward and doing what I knew was right *despite* my circumstances.

Oh, God. Forgive me. You have been in all of this. Given me blessings despite the pain I've experienced. Please forgive me for not listening to Kemena's warning. For my part in Asher's death. A pang shoots through me. *Forgive me for not trusting You. For leaning on my own understanding. And for letting my fears control me rather than courageously doing what You call me to do. I don't know how to move forward, but I want to move forward trusting You. No matter what happens. Because I know for a fact that I can't do a single thing on my own.*

The scenario ends with a beep. It's the final one for this squad, which means it's time for my lunch break.

A new peace fills me. Different from the peace I felt when I accepted Jesus as my Savior. This peace is one of relinquishing control. Of not trying to be the one who saves the day. Of trusting God not just as my Savior, but as the One I'm trusting to lead my life.

"You're dismissed for lunch, Averton." Major Vasco says. He passes me a screen. "You can review the scenarios you'll be running recruits through after lunch. Be back at 1400 hours."

I take the screen. "Yes, sir."

A glance at my band tells me I have over an hour until I'm due back here. Enough time to find Matthias and apologize.

If he'll hear my apology.

How much have I ruined by trying to control everything?

"Averton." Major Vasco's voice stops me halfway down the hall. "Don't forget to sign in with your handler before leaving the building."

My stomach drops. I forgot I'm now being babysat by soldiers wherever I walk in the city. "Of course, sir."

I make my way to the front of the building, retrieve my rifle, and find Sergeant Valarius waiting outside.

He holds out a scanner, and I lift my band. "I'm your handler during your lunch break."

My stomach flips. "Okay."

"You won't be dining with the recruits today. Major Vasco said you need to review the next set of scenarios, so I'll be bringing you to a private dining area."

He walks, and I follow him. He doesn't seem to need a response to his statements, so I stay quiet.

Andor Valarius is someone Cai trusts. Someone who has been there for Matthias, even on really tough days. He terrifies me on many levels. He's someone I've been hesitant to fully trust.

But right now, he's also someone who might be able to help me.

Ask him about the day Laban beat you.

The thought is unbidden. Strange. And so outside of anything I even considered thinking about that I suddenly blurt, "Do you remember the day Laban beat me?"

His steps falter. He turns a corner down an alley, then stops.

He rounds on me. "Why?"

I swallow hard. "I, uh, just wondered." Well, that was epically lame. *Great job, Bria.* Why did I ask him? I hate thinking about that day. Almost dying at the hands of Laban's rage.

Andor frowns, causing the scar on his face to twist and make him appear far more menacing.

Yeah. This was a terrible topic to bring up.

"What do *you* remember about that day?" His voice is a low growl, but the question brings me up short.

I break eye contact. "Laban found me after a visit with Storm. Started beating me." I swallow. Talking about this is harder than I expected. "He would have killed me, but . . ." My eyes fly back up to Andor, who is still watching me. "Right before I blacked out, someone stopped him."

Now it's Andor's turn to look away. He rubs the back of his neck, just like Matthias does when he's uncomfortable.

"Was that . . . you?" I ask the question even as the reality of who my rescuer was that day slams into me.

"Didn't earn me any favors," he grumbles. "Not that Meritas and I were friends before it, anyway." He waves down the alley. "We should get you to lunch."

With that, he stalks down the alley. I'm frozen for a solid three seconds before I hurry to catch up to him.

"Why?" I ask the one-word question.

Andor picks up his pace. "Because some things aren't right. Which is why I connected with . . . our mutual friend."

Cai.

We pass a group of recruits heading to a training and lapse into silence. Soldiers bark orders like they do whenever a new wave of recruits comes into the city.

Now it's to spur recruits to train harder. Be better. And be ready to leave in a week. Not that Ark has announced that change yet.

But I know in my gut the change he told me about was solid intel.

Sergeant Valarius brings me to a building I've never been in before, leads me inside, and opens the door to a small room with a table. Sandwiches, chips, raw veggies with dip, and a glass of water wait for me.

Somewhere in our walk from Warfare Strategies to my *private dining area*, I decided to fully trust Andor Valarius.

It's dumb not to. As terrifying as he appears, he's warned me, worked with Cai. And saved my life.

"You'll eat and work in here." Andor pauses until we're both inside. "The room is cloaked. You'll have some privacy."

At his words, one thought rises to the surface. "Can you bring Matthias here?"

A line forms between his brows. "I don't believe you're authorized to have company."

I bite my cheek to keep from begging. Even though the room isn't monitored, Andor isn't someone who can be won over with an argument.

"But let me see what I can do," he says so quietly I almost miss it.

"Thank you." The words are barely out of my mouth before he's out of the room and closing the door.

I pick at my lunch as minutes tick by, barely tasting the food. My eyes stay trained on the door, and I ignore the screen I'm supposed to be using to prep for the next set of scenarios I'll be putting recruits through.

Fifteen minutes pass.

Maybe Andor can't bring Matthias here.

Or maybe Matthias doesn't want to see me. The thought makes swallowing the bite of sandwich in my mouth difficult. I wouldn't blame him if he doesn't want to see me. If he never wants to talk to me again.

Please, God, give me a chance to make this right. To at least apologize.

Another five minutes pass. Maybe I should have asked Andor to bring Kemena instead. I need to apologize to her too, and I'm confident she would have come. Even if she's upset with me.

But the one person I desperately want to see is Matthias.

I push my half-eaten lunch aside. Although I probably need all the calories for the rest of my day, my stomach is too tied in knots to force anything else down.

With a sigh, I grab the screen to work on the transport attack scenarios the bomb squads will go through after my lunch break.

The door opens.

The screen clatters to the table. As I stand, Matthias enters.

His face is guarded, and he only enters the room enough to close the door behind him before crossing his arms over his chest. "What do you want, Bria?"

"I, uh . . ." Words die in my mouth. What do I say to him?

"My uncle insisted you needed to talk to me about something. Even though I said I didn't care." His nostrils flare. "He *ordered* me to come see you. So, say what you need to say so I can leave."

I make a mental note to thank Andor for forcing Matthias to see me.

"I failed." I take a hesitant step toward him. "I didn't listen to you or Kemena. Didn't trust God. I thought I could do it all on my own."

Another step. "But I was wrong." I drop my head. "And because I didn't listen . . . Asher is dead." The word croaks out of my mouth.

"I heard," Matthias says. "They said it was a training accident. But the timing seemed too convenient." His words are careful, but not as harsh.

I look at him again. "He chose to move early. I don't know why. But if I had warned him, maybe he'd still be alive."

Matthias runs a hand over his hair. "I doubt you could have convinced Asher. If he thought the plan was solid, he was going to act."

My eyes burn from unshed tears, and my feet are frozen in place. The gap between us might as well be a thousand miles. But Matthias offering any words of comfort . . . it's more than I deserve.

I force myself to say the rest of what I need to say. "Not listening to you wasn't the worst thing I did."

His jaw twitches.

"I said things to you I deeply regret." I twist my hands together, willing him to listen. To believe me. "I spoke cruel, hurtful words. Took personal information you trusted me with and tried to use it against you." I force my feet forward another step. Two steps. "You asked what I want."

My heart pounds in my chest. The amount of vulnerability the next words will take terrifies me more than facing Ark this morning.

Matthias's face is still masked, but something in his blue eyes looks almost hopeful.

And it's enough to give me the courage to say what I need to say. "I want *you*, Matthias." My voice breaks. A tear leaks out of my eye. "I don't know if you can ever forgive me for what I did. For what I said to you." I take a shaky breath. "But if you can give me another chance, I want you. I love you."

His arms drop to his sides, then he closes the distance between us. He takes my face in his hands, and the love in his eyes takes my breath away.

"I love you too." His thumb strokes my cheek. "And I forgive you."

I fall into his arms.

His heart beats steadily against my ear, and I melt into his embrace as his strong arms wrap around me. I squeeze my eyes shut. *Thank You, God.*

He pulls back. "Can you forgive me?"

I give him a questioning look. "What do you mean?"

"I've let fears control me too, Bria. We both know it. It comes out differently for me—in silence rather than rash action. But I don't want to keep living that way." He tucks a curl behind my ear. "You are one of the bravest people I have ever known. And I want to be a man who will always stand by your side. Fight for those who can't fight for themselves, and willingly speak up for what is right." He rests his forehead against mine. "I can't do it on my own. But with God's help, I will be strong and courageous and trust Him to lead us. No matter how fierce the enemy we face." He pulls back to look me in the eye. "For a long time, I've known this is what God was calling me to do. To trust Him and not live according to my fears. And I'm ready to do so. Not trusting God has impacted how I've treated you. Please forgive me." Now it's his voice that breaks.

I put my hand on his cheek. "Of course I forgive you."

He smiles one of his Matthias-sized smiles. My stomach flips. How could such an evil place bring me to such an amazing guy?

Thank You, God. Again, the prayer whispers from my heart.

Matthias slowly steps back and takes my hand in his. "So. How will we stop Ark before he takes everyone to Sitreea in a month?"

The seriousness of what's before us settles over me. "Actually, we only have a week."

I quickly run Matthias through what I learned today and share the updated timeline.

His mouth presses into a thin line, and he squares his shoulders. "Then we have work to do."

The rest of my lunch break goes by in a blur. Matthias stays, and we talk through various options for how to stop Ark. With every passing minute, it becomes clear we need way more help.

I barely take time to review the scenarios I'll be operating after my lunch. Since I've run so many scenarios, I'm hoping I'll be able to get through the last three hours of my scheduled scenario operating with no major issues.

Plus, finding a way to stop Ark is way more important than any disciplinary actions I might receive for not performing at an optimal level.

When Andor arrives at the end of my break to take me back to Warfare Strategies, Matthias and I ask for his help in calling together a meeting.

"We need as many people involved as possible," I say. "Anyone we can trust, even a little, who doesn't want Ark succeeding."

"Right," Matthias says. "Maybe we could set the meeting up in the tunnels with Cai. Sneak in key people from the Resistance. And radio the scouts we trust too."

Andor has stood impassively as we've raced through our practiced speech. "Everyone is scrambling to prep for departure next week."

"I think we can use that to mask recruit movements after hours," I say.

He inclines his head. "I suppose."

"Will you help us?" Matthias asks.

Andor doesn't respond for several seconds. Each one that ticks by makes me wonder if trusting him this much was a mistake.

After all, he's served under Demetrius Ark for many years without ever going to the lengths we're asking of him now.

He inhales deeply. "All right." He scoops the screen off the table and enters a code to view a secure schedule. "There's an overnight training run that begins at 2200 hours. We'll schedule the meeting to run from 2300 to 0100 hours." He logs out of the schedule, wipes the history, then passes the screen back to me. "I'll communicate with Cai to have a meeting location set by the time you're done in Warfare Strategies this afternoon. We won't want to use his normal space in case there's a leak. Keep an eye out for a secure message."

I nod. "Thank you."

He holds up a hand. "Don't thank me yet. This is a massive risk. And I don't know which recruits you want there." He points between me and Matthias. "You two will have to figure that out."

"We will," Matthias says. "Bria and I put together a list of those we connected to in the Resistance. If we can at least get a few of them there tonight, that will be enough for us to loop them into the plan so they can spread the word."

Andor doesn't look pleased with the idea, but he doesn't argue. "It's time for you to head back over," he says to me.

I hesitate, hating the idea of going forward with my training as normal when what I want to do is work with Matthias to tell others about the meeting tonight.

Matthias picks up my hand and squeezes it. "I've got this. The longer they think you're doing everything they want you to, the more of a chance we have of pulling off this meeting."

"You're right." I blow out a slow breath, give Matthias's hand a squeeze back, then follow Andor from the room.

I get through the bomb squad scenarios without too many mishaps—although there are a few times when I'm as surprised as the recruits going through the scenarios by something that happens. Which wouldn't have been the case had I actually reviewed all the details Major Vasco provided me for the scenarios.

He doesn't seem pleased with me when I leave, but he also doesn't issue any disciplinary action since I didn't utterly fail.

"I expect you to perform better when you're back here tomorrow," he says.

"Yes, sir," I say.

With that, he dismisses me.

I walk as quickly as I can without drawing attention to the front of the building, retrieve my rifle, and exit into the cold evening. For the first time today, no soldiers are waiting to escort me.

It's already 1800 hours, which means most recruits will be at the Dining Hall.

My band pings with a secure message.

Andor came through.

We have a meeting location deep within the bunkers of Talionis, but away from the tunnels Cai's been working in. And Cai and Ari coordinated with the Wild Dogs and Azarias. They'll join via a secure holo-link, as will Nika, Mom, and Keesia.

My heart skips a beat. Now I just need to make it through dinner and my nighttime chores while also working on an attack plan to present to those who will be in the meeting tonight. And figure out a way to apologize to those I need to.

I ARRIVE AT THE BUNKER THIRTY MINUTES EARLY WITH NO ISSUES. As I suspected, the stress of preparing to leave has the soldiers wound tight. Since many recruits were out and heading to overnight trainings and ops, I walked through most of the city without anyone noticing me.

Still, I backtracked a few times to make sure I wasn't being followed or monitored by a drone.

I wait outside the bunker for a few minutes, observing the area. It's unusually quiet. No movement. No soldiers or recruits.

Makes sense why Andor chose this location.

I leave the cover of the bush I was hiding behind and slip into the dark tunnel that leads into the underground of Talionis. I jog through, using a small torch to light my way.

Since I'm early, I don't encounter anyone else, and before long, I pass through the doorway into the wide, open space of a bunker.

Cai sits with his back against the far wall of the dimly lit room, a small smile on his face as I enter. "I suspected you would arrive early, Bria."

I cross the room, and Cai stands.

"Tell me what's been going on," he says.

Words pour out of my mouth, tripping over one another as I attempt to express to Cai everything that's happened. He doesn't stop me. Just takes it all in. Nods occasionally. Listens.

By the time I'm done, others are arriving. First Matthias, then members of the Resistance.

Andor arrives a few minutes after 2300 hours. "I did a sweep of the perimeter and activated cloaking technology. We should be secure for the duration of the meeting." He reports each word to Cai, as though Cai is the higher-ranking officer.

Several members of the Resistance eye Andor warily.

"What is he doing here?" Arwen asks me, her eyes wide.

"We can trust him," I say quickly.

"If you say so," she says.

Cai clears his throat, and everyone goes silent. "Thank you for taking the risk to join us here tonight." His astute gaze sweeps the crowd before him. "If you choose to stay, I guarantee you will face many more dangers. Before we go into details about why we've called this meeting, I want each of you to know you have a choice." His words carry in the silence in the room. "If anyone here doesn't want to stay, or isn't sure they're ready for the risks we're about to take, you are welcome to leave. The rest of us will not ridicule you. But it is vital that no one feels forced into what is happening next." He pauses and no one makes a sound. "What we are doing holds the potential of great reward. But it is a very high risk. One that could mean the loss of life."

"If we don't do something, we're all going to lose our lives in Ark's war anyway," Kiwi interjects.

Several murmur their agreement.

Cai nods slowly. "That is true. Still. No one should be forced to enter any battle they are unwilling to fight. Although Ark is preparing to send you to war, we will *not* force you to join us. Many of us here serve a God who gives us free will," Cai says. "The power to *choose* what we will do. Although evil men and women will always attempt to steal that choice, we will not."

The power of choice is something I never thought of before Talionis. But as Cai's words settle over the room, the reality that he's allowing everyone here to choose—even though we need all the help we can get—is sobering.

Ark and his soldiers stole our choice. Demanded we do all they want, or pay the consequences. But Cai won't do the same. And I'm glad to be standing alongside my uncle in this battle.

A few people choose to leave.

"Sergeant Valarius will escort you back to your rooms and ensure you don't meet with any issues," Cai says.

Andor ushers the small group from the room. A tendril of anxiety weaves it's way through me, but I push it aside. Nothing was revealed so far, so even if they *did* report the meeting, they wouldn't have any real intel to share. Not to mention, Andor is going with them. He'll intimidate them into silence.

Once they're gone, Cai leads the rest of us through a secret door and into another room that's half the size of the bunker. A wall of screens fills the far side of the room, and this area is more well-lit than the bunker.

As everyone crowds into the space, Cai messages the scouts.

Once the last recruit enters, I secure the door.

A few moments later, a hologram flickers to life. So many faces I recognize. Ari, Bryson, Azarias, Malachi, Retro, Jordyn, Isaac, Thaddeus, Davey, Catori, Micah, and Quwani are all there. A lump forms in my throat. I miss them so much.

The door to the bunker opens again. I reach for my gun. No one else should be arriving.

Nika and Mom crawl through the opening.

"Girl, I know you're not pointing that thing at me," Nika says.

I drop my weapon and greet them. "What about the kids?"

"Keesia's watching them," Nika says. "They're all asleep, anyway."

"Okay," Cai says. "This is everyone." He waves me to the front of the group. "Bria, we're ready for you."

I hesitate, suddenly unsure of what to say. Despite mentally rehearsing this moment a dozen times in the hours leading up to it.

Mom gives me a quick hug. "You've got this."

Emotions slap at me again. Having my mom here right now . . . it's more than I ever could have asked for.

Taking a fortifying breath, I go to the front of the room.

My friends in the hologram wave at me, and I smile back.

"Glad to see you're in one piece," Retro says. "Especially since we ain't there to have your back."

I shake my head at him, even as his brothers both shush him. Retro doesn't seem to mind.

"I missed you guys too," I say.

I quickly introduce those I trust on the outside of Talionis with those I trust in the Resistance. Then I share about what really happened this morning with Asher.

The members of the Resistance have various expressions—some angry, others afraid—but one emotion echoes across all of their faces: the pain of loss. Something I understand far too well.

I focus on Kemena. "Asher changed the timeline for our plan, and I don't know why. But I do know that if I had listened to some wise counsel, I might have been able to keep what happened from happening." I pause, searching for the right words. Unsure if they even exist. "Please forgive me." I keep my gaze trained on Kemena. "I've been acting out of fear, trying to keep everyone safe on my own rather than trusting God. And trusting those He placed in my life."

I forgive you. Kemena mouths the words with a soft smile.

Relief floods through me.

"I wish Ash was still with us," Kiwi says. "But I doubt you coulda convinced him to stop. The guy was set on that mission. He moved it up because he was afraid we were waiting too long to act."

Kiwi's words so echo Matthias's that some of my guilt eases.

"I still wish I had tried," I say. "Warning Asher was my responsibility. What he would have done with the intel was his responsibility." I swallow hard, wishing I had more words to convey how sorry I am over Asher's death.

Andor enters the room, and I force myself to continue forward.

"But the reality is that we *do* need to act. Not just to escape Talionis. We need to stop Demetrius Ark." I make eye contact with several of the thirty or so people in the room and with my friends watching from the hologram. "And we only have six days to do so."

The room erupts in murmurs and questions about the changed timeline.

Andor steps up next to me. "I can confirm Bria's timeline. Ark moved deployment up. He's becoming more paranoid each day."

Fear flashes across the faces of several recruits.

"I can't go to war," one girl whimpers.

"We don't want *anyone* to go to war," I say emphatically. "Which is why we need to stop Ark."

"How?" Azarias asks. "Do you have a plan?"

I shrug one shoulder. "Sort of. But I need your help." Waving my arm, I encompass those on the hologram and those in the room. "I need all of your help. I can't take down Ark alone. But I know many of you. We all have different skills. Different strengths. Together, maybe we can stop him."

We spend the rest of the time working on our plan, which we'll begin enacting thirty-six hours from now.

I work with Cai to divide everyone into smaller groups who will handle various ops around the city.

From bombing key targets to sabotaging resources, some of the plans are very much like what we did to escape Talionis months ago. But on a much higher scale.

I roam through the space, offering help wherever I can and answering questions.

Mom and Thaddeus work over a secure hologram connection to map out various paths throughout the underground tunnels, the Ruins, and the city. The tunnels will allow groups to get to key targets in the city undetected, and Kemena will lead the group smuggling any kids and more vulnerable recruits out to the Ruins.

Ari, Bryson, Isaac, and Kiwi talk tech with one another, discussing options for disabling the Wall. Instead of creating tech dead zones, they talk about ways to hack into the tech the soldiers use and turn it against them.

Azarias and Cai strategize how Eryndale Scouts will infiltrate the city once the Wall is down. Although the leak within Eryndale is still active, they determine the best chance at success will be to bring everyone they have available. We need a show of force to stop Ark, which means taking on the risk of alerting the enemy to what we're planning.

But we decide not to let all the scouts—other than the trusted group present—know about the attack until the last possible moment.

Hopefully by then, enough will be happening to keep Ark and his soldiers occupied and unable to communicate with their spy.

Arwen and a few others who are munitions experts are tasked with the job of setting the explosives in the morning. They'll be targeting every building recruits have been training in, as well as trying to take down part of the Center, with the goal of disrupting as much as possible in the heart of Talionis. Since it's under the highest level of surveillance, the Main Headquarters Building will be the last one they hit. Hopefully the cacophony of the other buildings going up in flames will be enough of a distraction so the munitions squad can take down the main hub of Talionis. It will be a risk—even with the distractions we plan to set. But we can't leave Ark's headquarters standing.

Andor promises to get them what they need, and Mom and Thaddeus walk them through the routes they'll take—some through back alleys in the city, but most through the tunnels.

Once the various groups have finished their planning, everyone gathers together again. I share as much intel as I can about what I've learned while in the strange position Ark has placed me in.

"I've also had dinners with the Sitreean delegates more than once," I say. "There's one man, the Minister of Defense, who I think might be an ally." I quickly share more about my interactions with Antonio and his cool demeanor toward Ark.

Andor interjects that he's also noticed the man doesn't seem fully supportive of what Sitreea believes Ark is doing in Talionis. He shares that Ark and the Minister of Defense have a complicated history.

"We could use that," Azarias says. He focuses on me. "Could you get word to him? Send a message?"

I look at Kiwi and Ari. "Could you guys help me with that?"

They agree. The two of them turn to Bryson and Isaac and start talking through various options, using tech terms that make my brain spin.

Cai holds up a hand to silence them. "Excellent. You four will get Bria what she needs to send the message. We'll have to be cryptic in the message in case it's intercepted." He looks at me. "Since you're the one who has connected with him, you'll need to be in place for his arrival so you can fully brief him."

I agree.

"Still doesn't seem like we have enough to stop Ark," a guy from the Resistance says.

Silence descends, and I stare at him, not sure how to respond.

"May I say something?" Catori asks.

"Of course," I say.

"This is not the first time I've faced an enemy that feels unstoppable." Her face takes on a faraway look, and Micah puts his hand on her shoulder. "But one thing I have seen over and over again is that God is able to work—whether with many or with few—to stop evil. He did it through small groups in the Bible, like with Jonathan and his armor-bearer, or Gideon with his three hundred. And He's done it in my life too. Even though we are outnumbered, my encouragement to all of us is to remember that God is stronger than the enemy we face."

The passion in her words sends a jolt of courage through me.

"She's right." Matthias steps up next to me. "I have let my own fears become so large that I was afraid to stand up and speak. Afraid of what might happen. But not anymore. Together, let's fight. Whether we win or lose, at least we will know we have taken our place to stand against evil."

I reach for Matthias's hand, pride swelling through me.

Some in the room and on the hologram don't believe in God, and they don't seem nearly as encouraged by what Matthias and Catori said as the rest of us. But everyone gathered is prepared to do whatever it takes to stop Demetrius Ark.

After we map out some additional details, Cai calls the meeting to a close.

Andor sends out the recruits in small groups to keep things as secretive as possible.

"Could I get a minute with Bria and Nika?" Ari asks before the hologram is shut off.

Azarias and Cai agree, but before Azarias can walk away Kemena asks for a private channel with him. I've never heard her quite so . . . vulnerable. As curious as I am about what Ari wants to share with me and Nika, I'm equally curious about what Kemena's about to say to Azarias. Although, I'm pretty sure I already know. She loves him, and with everything going on I'm sure she needs a chance to tell him.

After Nika, Ari, and I say goodbye to some of our other friends, the three of us are left alone.

"Isaac and I finished decrypting Ark's secret files," Ari says without preamble. "And it's bad."

"What have you found?" Nika asks.

"It's all notes on his top men and women." Ari pauses. "He's manipulated almost all of them into the positions they're in."

Nika and I exchange a look.

"But how would they not have realized that?" I ask. "I mean, I don't like Ark's top people, but they're not stupid."

"Ark staged events to keep himself from being implicated. He was careful. But the things he did in order to ensure their loyalty . . . it's horrible. Do we leak the information?"

I squeeze the bridge of my nose, exhaustion washing over me.

"Even if Ark did manipulate his top people to get them to do what he wants, at this point, they're completely invested in his cause. I doubt they'd believe the intel."

"Yeah, Bria's right," Nika agrees. "Not to mention, we have a solid plan for moving forward. This could just cause increased complications."

"Have you briefed anyone else?" I ask.

Ari nods. "Isaac and I shared the information with Azarias and Cai yesterday. They weren't sure how useful it would be either."

"Then let's set it aside," I say. "At least for now."

The three of us say our goodbyes.

Tomorrow, everyone will begin setting things in motion for the attack that will start rolling out in thirty-four hours.

Andor calls for me to join the final group about to leave, and I say goodbye to my friends, mom, and uncle.

Instead of going back through the city, Kiwi, Arwen, and I use the tunnels to the secret entrances to our rooms.

Before we go our separate ways, with Arwen and Kiwi heading to the Recruits' Living Quarters and me heading to my room, Kiwi and I agree to meet up before breakfast. We'll connect remotely with Ari and Isaac, and the four of us will send the com to Antonio.

As I drop into my bed, a mix of exhaustion and excitement washes over me. We might be a smaller group than those loyal to Talionis, but together, we've created a powerful plan.

And we might be able to stop them from carrying out their schemes.

The plan will utilize multiple group efforts: tech, sabotage, and an outright battle line established by the Eryndale Scouts making entry once the tech team dismantles the Wall.

It's a good plan. One I couldn't have come up with on my own.

Plus, although no one brought it up tonight, I'm sure my dad, Hosea, and Kassre have been working on their plan to break through an old tunnel too. Maybe it'll be ready by the time we kick things off here.

A shiver goes over me.

Ark is brilliant. Insane. And willing to do whatever it takes to win. Even going so far as to manipulate those closest to him into doing whatever he tells them to.

Can such a terrifying evil ever be stopped?

Please, God. Help our plan to work.

CHAPTER
SIXTY-EIGHT

Beep! Beep! Beep!

The alarm blares through my room. I sit straight up in bed. My heart hammers in my chest, and my eyes are gritty from lack of sleep.

I feel like I just fell asleep minutes ago, but the adrenaline coursing through my body is enough to jolt me fully awake.

I poke at my band until the alarm shuts off. The time catches my eye.

0430.

An hour and a half earlier than what I set my alarm for.

I swing my legs over the side of my bed. What's going on?

My band *pings*, and a secure message pops up from Kiwi.

Timing changed. We need to get the message sent now. Meet at designated location.

A thousand questions leap to my mind, but I reply with a simple, *Okay. Be there in five.*

I tug on my boots, thankful I was too tired to change out of my uniform after the meeting last night. Then I program my band to show me as sleeping in my room. After grabbing my jacket from a hook, I stride to the door, picking up my rifle on the way.

The door is locked.

Panic sends goose bumps over me.

My door hasn't been locked since I first arrived. Why is it locked now?

The tunnels will take way longer to get to the meeting location, and it sounds like I need to meet Kiwi as soon as possible.

I release a slow breath and send another secure message to Kiwi. *My door is locked.*

After a few seconds, I hear a click.

Try it now, Kiwi's message comes through.

I try the door, and it opens this time.

Cameras are on a loop. You're clear for the next three minutes.

I ease into the empty hallway, on an even higher level of alert.

Something is very wrong.

Why would Kiwi change the timing, and why was my door locked?

I creep through the hallways of the Main Headquarters Building, not encountering anyone. I pick up my pace. The timing of all of this is too . . . perfect.

It's like Ark knows something is up. But he couldn't. Right?

As I near the exit to the building, I pause. Inhale. Exhale.

Whether Ark knows something or not, I have to move forward and trust the rest of my team to do the same. There's no other choice. I slip out of the building into the thick darkness of early morning.

The streets are quieter than they've been for days, and every rustle of leaves and creak of old buildings sounds like an explosion to my hyperaware ears.

One team will raid the weaponry complex later today and distribute weapons to all of us for the full attack later tonight.

I wish I had something right now. Even though my rifle only has training bullets, I hold it in my hands at the ready rather than leave it on my back.

I round the final bend to the alley near the Physical Training Arena where Kiwi and I planned to meet.

It's cloaked in shadows, and there's no movement.

I creep into the darkness. "Kiwi," I hiss. "Where are you?"

No response.

I move deeper into the alley, wishing for night vision lenses or a torch. Anything to force the shadows to reveal their secrets.

An overflowing dumpster blocks my view, the stench lessened by the cold winter weather. But not by much. I carefully step around it.

Someone stands.

I bend and, with a low kick, sweep their feet out from under them. I jump on top of them, and pin their arms to the ground.

"It's me," Kiwi wheezes.

The moon pokes out from behind the cloud covering, giving me enough light to make out Kiwi's face.

I release him, and he eases to a sitting position. He taps a screen to give us a low light.

"Why didn't you answer when I said your name?" I ask more harshly than I need to.

He pulls a tech device from his ear. "I was decoding a message from Ari."

"What's going on? Why did you move up our meeting time?"

He pulls a small twig from his hair. "*Everything* has been moved up." He shifts his screen to show me a new timeline. "After the meeting last night, an undercover team arrived at the scout camp. Azarias and Thaddeus had been waiting for them, I guess."

A branch cracks behind us. I shut off the screen and motion for Kiwi to stay quiet. He opens his mouth anyway, and I press my hand against it to silence him.

Someone comes around the dumpster. I release my hand from Kiwi's mouth, preparing to attack.

"Hi, Matthias," Kiwi says slightly above a whisper.

Kiwi turns his screen back on, illuminating Matthias's face.

Matthias raises his eyebrows at me. "Why do I feel like I was about to get flipped onto my backside?"

I almost smile, but the gravity of the situation is too much. "Wait. What are you doing here?"

"Kiwi told me to come." Matthias nods at him. "But didn't say why."

Kiwi pushes a couple buttons on his screen. "I've activated a jamming signal on Bria's band, and on this." He hands Matthias a thin bracelet-type device. "It's untraceable and it'll disrupt any video feeds or audio surveillance." He gets to his feet. "We should walk and talk."

Matthias slips the device onto his wrist, and he and I exchange a glance.

"Do you know what this is about?" he asks me.

I shake my head. "Not really. Just that our timeline has been moved up."

Kiwi leads us toward the empty Physical Training Arena. According to him, we can tap into a communication room in there to send our message.

"Why did the timing get moved up?" Matthias asks.

I'm half tempted to tell them to be quiet, but no one's around, and I want more answers to why we're doing this now.

Kiwi repeats what he told me. "Sounds like the undercover team that arrived at the scout camp has been planning an infiltration of Talionis. They made something that's supposed to help them get in." He shrugs as we approach a side entrance to the arena. "They didn't give me all the details, but apparently, they're ready to act first thing this morning. Don't want to wait until tomorrow because they're afraid of the leak."

Matthias and I exchange a look while Kiwi hacks the lock on the door and disables the alarm and cameras. Could it be my dad and the small group he's working with?

We slip inside. No one is in sight.

"What's their plan?" I ask, hoping I'm right about who the undercover team is.

"Don't know the full plan," Kiwi says. "They're keeping it really secretive. But Ari knows more, and she said it's a solid strategy."

We pause at a bend in the hallway, and Matthias checks to confirm the way is clear. He waves us forward.

"Are we sure everyone else can change their timeline?" Matthias asks.

Kiwi doesn't answer, and I glance over to see him reading something on his screen.

"Room is two doors down." He looks up. "Ari said they've gotten word to everyone they could."

We stop at the door, and Kiwi gets us inside. It's a full communication room, just like he said.

"Why do they have this in here?" I ask.

Kiwi shrugs. "Who knows? But at least they do. It's a good break for us. Much easier to sneak around here than the Technical Operations Building or Main Headquarters."

Good breaks right now seem *too* good to be true.

Kiwi settles himself at the main console and becomes engrossed in the tech. "I'll need twenty minutes to get us a secure channel."

"That's a long time to sit here and wait," I say.

Kiwi spears me with an annoyed look. "Anything less, and I won't be sure the message is delivered to the right person. Not to mention, we can't risk an unsecured message going out. Sergeant Valarius gave me everything I need to get through to the nearest Sitreean transport, but we still need to ensure the message is rerouted to the Minister of Defense."

I hold up my hands. "Sorry. Do what you need to do."

Kiwi nods once, then goes back to work.

"Maybe we should do a sweep of the hallways around here," Matthias suggests. "Make sure we don't have any unexpected company."

"Good idea," I say.

Kiwi doesn't respond, so Matthias and I tell him we'll be back in ten minutes and exit the room.

Once we're alone in the hallway, I turn to Matthias. "I think the undercover team is my dad, Hosea, and Kassre."

Matthias stops. "Really? Why?"

"My mom said they were working on a top secret plan with an old tunnel near the river that involved Bill and Paul and their guys." I chew my lower lip. "They were only bringing in people they trusted implicitly because of the leak and . . . I don't know. The timing seems right."

Matthias nods thoughtfully. "It does." He grins. "If Bill and Paul are involved, we'd better make sure we're ready *before* the scheduled time."

For a second, I'm not sure what he means. Then I remember how they started working on the DeFort's porch before their scheduled start time. Which, according to Kemena, wasn't unusual.

I smile back at Matthias, enjoying the memory. Then I wave a hand at the empty hallway. "We should split up for the sweep."

Matthias sighs. "I don't want to, but I know you're right."

He gives my arm a light squeeze, and we take different paths down the hall.

For the first few minutes, there's nothing along my search route. I round a corner into an area with private training rooms, and a noise catches my ear.

Grunts. The thud of something being hit.

Someone is in one of these rooms. Training or beating some-one up.

I'm not sure which.

I hesitate. Either way, I need to figure out what we might be dealing with. I creep forward.

The first two rooms are empty.

I slink up to the next door on the right. Peek inside.

Shane is beating a practice dummy with so much force, I think he might break it.

He throws a right hook at the dummy. An upper cut.

I can only see part of the side of his face, but he looks . . . haunted. I've worked out hard enough in an attempt to kill my personal demons. I know what it looks like.

Seeing him almost makes me sad. I miss the friendship I thought we had. But his betrayal brought us back to this place.

He spins and throws a roundhouse kick into the dummy's head.

I duck back into the hall, holding my breath.

Did he see me?

I press against the wall, wondering why I thought it was a good idea to watch him for any length of time. Shane is as well trained as I am. One of the best recruits to come out of Talionis.

He probably sensed me watching him.

Used the roundhouse kick as a discreet way to catch sight of whoever was lurking by the door.

It's what I would have done.

I tiptoe away from the door, heart racing. With everything about to happen, I can't get caught now. Not by Shane.

Not this soon.

I move faster. I need to get back to Kiwi. Hopefully Matthias is already there. Tell them Shane is here. That I might have compromised our position.

I round the corner and almost run into Shane.

Sweat drips down his forehead, and his eyes narrow at me. "Guess you didn't see there was another exit. Getting sloppy, Bria."

My heart skips a beat before rocketing forward. I have to take him down. I shift into a fighting stance, but Shane crosses his arms over his chest.

"What are you doing here?" he asks.

Even though I will likely lose this fight, I don't drop my guard. Shane is bigger than me. Knows all the moves I would make. But I still have to try.

"I can't tell you that," I say, trying to distract him as I determine the most surprising attack.

He drops his arms. "Is Ari really alive?" His voice is so soft, so vulnerable, that it hits me like he took a swing.

I blink and stand straighter. "Yes."

He rubs a hand over his short hair, eyes closed. "She was going to die. I knew she was going to die. That's why I left . . ." His voice trails off.

"Well, she didn't die," I say. "And she's part of the reason I'm here right now." I'm not sure why I say the words, but I let them linger in the air.

Shane hesitates, then steps aside and waves an arm down the hallway. "Then continue on."

My mouth drops open. "What?"

He shrugs. "If Ari is alive and if you're working with her, the last thing I want is to give her another reason to hate me. I did enough already."

The self-loathing in his voice catches me.

He's serious.

I take a hesitant step forward, keeping as much distance between the two of us as the hallway will allow. "How do I know you won't come after me or tell the soldiers I'm here as soon as I leave?"

We stare each other for three full seconds before he responds.

"I guess you don't. Haven't exactly given you a reason to trust my word." He juts his jaw toward a door on the opposite side of the hall from the room he was in. "Those rooms are equipped with interrogation locking capabilities. They'll seal for whatever amount of time you set. Lock me in one."

"How do I know you won't override it?"

"Once the lock is set, the only person who can override it is an officer." He shrugs. "I don't have a high enough rank."

I hesitate for a fraction of a second. "Okay."

He uses his band to unlock the door, then programs the locking time for an hour. "If it's set for any longer, someone will look for me. It'll be hard to explain why I'm in here."

"Fine." Nervous energy zaps through my veins.

He enters the room, starts closing the door, then pauses. "Good luck with whatever it is you're trying to do."

Before I can respond, he closes the door with a *thud*.

The lock clicks in place and a red *Occupied* light flashes over the doorway, counting down the interrogation time.

I try the handle, and it releases a low *chirp*. A small panel by the doorknob reads *Sergeant clearance or above required to break set interrogation time.*

Shane wasn't lying.

But if he's here, who knows who else might be. Or who might show up. I race down the hall.

No one else is around, and before long, I'm back at the room where Matthias and I left Kiwi.

I stare at the closed door for a long moment, confused emotions fighting their way through me.

What just happened?

Did Shane—the guy who betrayed me and my friends, the reason we're all in this position—just *help* me?

I give myself a subtle shake. He might have let me go, but we need to get out of here as soon as possible. Because one interaction does not mean the guy is trustworthy.

I slip into the room, and Matthias and Kiwi whirl to face me.

"Where have you been?" Kiwi asks.

"Shane's here," I blurt out. "He let me go. Locked himself in an interrogation room for an hour. We gotta go." The words are scrambled.

Matthias and Kiwi gape at me. Kiwi recovers first, and pulls up camera feeds of the interrogation rooms.

Shane's where I left him, sitting on the floor in the far corner of the room, head resting on his bent knees. The timer on the room shows fifty-five minutes remaining.

Before I can share more of what happened, Kiwi spins around. "He's not going anywhere for a bit." He leans forward. "I sent the com, and we got word back."

"Already?" I ask.

Kiwi waves at the screen. "Read it yourself."

I step closer, taking in the messages on the screen.

Ark is preparing to attack Sitreea with a secret military force. Many are in danger. Come immediately.

—Bria

Antonio's response is time-stamped only a few minutes after Kiwi's sent. *Message received. I expected more was going on in Talionis. I'll be there with reinforcements in two hours. Meet me at the Main Head-quarters transportation dock.*

I read it twice. "He's coming."

Matthias gives me a grin. "Yup. Great call, Bria. We have a chance."

The words settle in my heart.

We really might have a chance.

As the thought flits through my mind, so does the reality of what I'll need to do. Getting to the Main Headquarters transportation dock will be nearly impossible.

"We need to send word," I say. "I'll need help—and a lot of distractions—if I'm going to get to the transportation dock in two hours."

Kiwi gives me his two-finger salute. "Already on it."

The three of us clear the room and slip out into the early morning darkness.

Once we're back in the alley where we met up, Kiwi outlines how he's arranged a weapon drop pickup for me thirty minutes from now, and he's also informed my mom about the update, since she's the one who's mapping out the attacks from a base in the Ruins.

"Arwen is heading up the bomb squad. She'll use the tunnel entrance to your room in the Main Headquarters Building to set off a controlled explosion a little deeper into the building. It should provide enough chaos so you can slip up to the dock," Kiwi says. "And your mom said she's getting Ari to send you the updated timeline for the targets so you can confirm everything."

As though Ari heard him, a message from her pops up on my band. The first message I've had from her in a long time.

I open it and frown. "It's encrypted."

"Let me see." Kiwi reaches for the band.

I stretch my arm toward him.

"Impressive encryption," he murmurs. After a minute, he releases my arm. "There you go."

I open the holographic map, noting the new timeline Mom is recommending for bombing each target. It's almost identical to our plan last night, except now the Main Headquarters Building will be hit before the Center bombing. And it will be a controlled explosion, like Kiwi said. Not an all-out takedown of the building. Which means it will be much more dangerous. Instead of planting the bombs in the tunnels beneath the structure and running before the explosion, they'll have to sneak into the Main Headquarters Building.

Arwen's team and the two other bomb squads have all confirmed they are a go.

According to the notes on the map, the bombing will begin at 0715.

"This looks fine," I say. "But I think we could make a few adjustments." I recommend small tweaks that will mean two more small targets are attacked before the Main Headquarters Building, with the goal of providing as much protection as possible for Arwen and her squad. Kiwi relays everything to Ari.

Within minutes, Mom sends an updated map including the new targets.

Her trust in my recommendations warms my heart a bit. I force myself to stay focused. Every minute counts.

But when this is over, maybe Mom and I will get to work together again.

BAM!

The explosion rocks the ground, spilling additional garbage over the side of the dumpster.

Matthias grabs me.

Kiwi types on his screen. "We need to get out of here. Sounds like Arwen's group has started on their part of the plan."

I shake my head. "No. It's too early." I check my band and confirm the time is only 0603 hours. I point to the notes on my band that show the bombing isn't set to begin until 0715. "Plus, we just adjusted the targets."

Kiwi's movements freeze. "Then what was that?"

"Let's go find out," Matthias says.

CHAPTER

SIXTY-NINE

We barely make it four feet before sirens blare throughout the city and on Kiwi's and my bands.

Wall breached. Prepare for enemy attack. Wall breached. Prepare for enemy attack.

"Did the attack start?" I ask as the three of us pick up our pace.

"No," Kiwi says, face buried in the screen even as we run through the alley.

He stumbles on a rock, and Matthias and I catch him before he falls.

He looks up. "That wasn't any of our people."

Soldiers, cadets, and recruits stream out of buildings. Recruits are being directed to weaponry stations to gear up for the attack. Bright lights glare from every point, making it look like mid-day, even though the sun still hasn't risen.

A frantic energy pulses around us.

And I feel it pulsing through *me*.

What's going on? If that wasn't us, who was it?

The three of us use the opportunity to grab weapons from one of the stations. But when I check the ammunition on the rifle and pistols, I find training bullets.

"Is this a test?" I whisper to Matthias.

He straps a pistol to his ankle while keeping his attention on the chaos growing around us in the dark morning. "I don't think so. Soldiers are too panicked."

Soldiers herd recruits to different zones throughout the city, while some are forced to board a transport to go to the front lines.

The three of us slip into a crowd heading away from the front lines.

Some recruits are crying. Others are zapped by soldiers and forced forward.

Before the transport takes off toward the front lines, the ground rumbles.

A hundred mechanical horses gallop into the city. I've only seen mechanical horses in Eryndale, and the sight is stunning. They move like real horses. Their riders lean over the horses necks, driving them at full speed. Their metal bodies glint in the glaring lights of the city.

They draw closer and the lead rider is illuminated.

Callypso.

Her metal-studded hair whips behind her, her face smeared with black warpaint. One hand holds the reins of her horse, while the other wields a submachine gun.

Seconds later, one of her pirates fires a rocket launcher. The transport erupts, knocking back everyone within fifty yards of it. Even from this distance, the heat of the flames warms my skin.

Why are they here?

But the why matters less than the fact that we can use this as a distraction.

I whirl toward Kiwi. "Send a message to everyone. Tell them to start attacking now, but to stay clear of Callypso and her pirates."

The woman's dreadlocks whirl about her head as she shoots down anyone in her way. She's not here to liberate the teens.

Despite the rush of soldiers attacking them, Callypso and a few of her pirates force their way into the Technical Operations Building.

I'm sure we should be worried about whatever it is she's here for. But right now, we need to take advantage of the opportunity afforded us.

A young recruit screams as one of Callypso's pirates barrels toward her. I fire my rifle. The training bullet finds its mark and the pirate veers away.

I race toward the girl, Matthias on my heels, both of us firing at the enemies swarming around us.

By the time we reach her, she's huddled on the ground, sobbing.

"We have to get her to safety!" I shout to Matthias over the roar of the battle.

Matthias shoots at a pirate, pivots and fires two shots at a soldier. "Let's move then!"

It takes a minute, but we're able to get the girl, who can't be more than thirteen, to stand. We gather three other young recruits on our path to the Educational Building, herding them along with us to safety. As we bring them up the steps of the building, a young soldier plants himself in our path.

Matthias and I both raise our weapons, but the guy holds his hands up. "Don't shoot!"

A flash of recognition hits me.

This is the soldier who allowed me, Storm and Quincy to get safely through the Kill Zone months ago. Rafael Cruz.

"Wait," I say to Matthias.

Matthias listens, but there's a question in his eyes and his gun doesn't waver from where it's aimed at Rafael's chest.

Rafael closes the distance between us. "I don't want to be part of this." He gestures to the battle. "I never signed up to go to war."

An explosion cracks through the air, as though to emphasize his point.

"Please. Let me help you."

Before Matthias or I can respond, Rafael shoves me to the left. He fires three shots. I huddle over the kids as Matthias joins Rafael in pushing back soldiers coming to force us into the fight.

Another explosion hits, drawing the soldiers focus.

I pull the kids into the building, and Matthias and Rafael join me an instant later.

Other recruits cower inside.

"Thanks for your help back there," Matthias says to Rafael.

Rafael doesn't so much as nod. "Let me help you. Please." He repeats his earlier plea.

I look at Matthias and he nods.

"Fine," I say. "Get as many of these recruits to the back of the building as you can. Someone will meet you there and tell you what to do next."

Rafael doesn't question a word. He moves into action, encouraging the recruits to follow him to safely. Although many of them eye him warily, they all follow. Including the kids we pulled from outside.

I send a quick message to Kiwi telling him to send Kemena with a crew to meet Rafael at the hidden tunnel entrance in the Educational Building to help him with the kids and recruits he's protecting.

Trusting a Talionis soldier is dangerous, but Kemena won't let him get away with anything. She's well-trained as a scout, and she'll protect those kids at any cost.

Plus, at this point the uprising against Ark has begun.

Rafael won't have an opportunity to betray us more. Whatever happens today, we are taking our stand.

Defense Minister is arriving early, Kiwi's encrypted message flashes on my band. *He'll be here in thirty minutes.*

I show Matthias.

"We better hurry then," he says.

We exit the Educational Building and re-enter the fight, using the confusion to get back to where we left Kiwi. The rising sun highlights the smoky haze of the city.

We round a bend, leap over a fallen pirate. Kiwi's only a few yards away, crouched in a small alcove as he types away at his screen.

An explosion in the Technical Operations Building rattles the ground, shaking everything around us.

Callypso emerges from the smoking tech building with two of her pirates, a pack over her shoulders.

She whistles loudly, mounts her mechanical horse.

It rears up. And with it, so does my fear. Callypso has what she's been hunting for. Whatever it is, she's more dangerous now than ever before.

"We can't let her escape," I say more to myself than Matthias.

Before I can do anything, her eyes connect with mine, like she knew I was watching her.

Chills race over my skin at her evil smile. She races back the way she came.

Her pirates who survived follow, but there are far fewer than she entered with. Still, even the riderless mechanical horses follow Callypso, leaving none behind.

The triumphant look in her eyes . . . whatever she just retrieved, it was worth it to her to lose over half of her men and women in the fight.

"Girl, we need to move." Nika's voice behind me causes me to spin around.

"What are you doing here?" I ask.

"Can't leave you to handle this stuff on your own. Plus, I've been bored out of my mind strategizing in the Ruins. And the kids, as cute as they are, were driving me crazy. It's time to get in on this action." She lifts a rifle and shoots at a soldier coming toward us.

The three of us close the distance to Kiwi. He mutters something about needing Arwen to redirect and target the Main Headquarters Building now as he types on his screen.

Once the message is sent, his gaze locks with Matthias. "Matthias. I need your help."

"With what?" Matthias asks.

"We need to project a holographic message out to all the recruits." Kiwi types on his screen as he talks. "Let them know it's time to take a stand."

"Okay . . ." Matthias draws out the word.

"You need to tell them from your family home." Kiwi finally looks up from his screen. "You're Colonel Keenan Valarius's son. If you say it, they'll hear you."

Matthias's Adam's apple bobs up and down as he swallows. Sweat beads his forehead.

Nika, Kiwi, and I all wait for him to respond. The conversation I overheard between Matthias and Cai comes to mind. This is reminiscent of what his mom did. Taking a stand by verbally denouncing Ark and calling others to fight.

I reach over and take his hand. He squeezes it so hard one of my knuckles cracks. I squeeze back.

He clears his throat. "Okay." He looks between me and Nika. "Will you guys be okay getting to the dock?"

We nod. He hesitates, then releases my hand and looks at Kiwi. "Let's do it."

Fierce pride rises up in me as Matthias and Kiwi jog away. This is Matthias's moment to speak, and he's doing it.

Nika and I race in the opposite direction of the guys, toward the Main Headquarters Building.

The streets of Talionis are in chaos. Soldiers, recruits, and cadets rush around like ants whose home has been flooded. Debris and chunks of buildings clutter every visible path. My eyes burn from the smoke in the air.

Three more explosions blast through the city in quick succession.

Nika and I sneak into a side entrance of the Main Headquarters Building. No one's in sight. Alarms blare.

A quick check of my band confirms what I suspected. Arwen bombed the western portion of the building where my room was. Protocol would dictate the rest of the building be evacuated.

Despite needing to shift course, she successfully attacked the building. I make a note to thank her later. It would be nearly impossible for me and Nika to get to the transportation dock if her bomb hadn't triggered the evacuation.

Without a word, Nika and I race to the lift. In less than a minute, we're at the top level.

Screens in the hallway to the dock show camera footage of what's happening around the city.

The hallway is empty, and Nika and I silently agree to slow down. We have another ten minutes before Antonio is set to arrive.

"It's working," Nika says, awe in her voice.

I can't find words to respond. Callypso's attack might have been unexpected, but everyone was ready to use it to aid our cause.

Recruits are fighting with soldiers throughout the city. Eryndale

Scouts are charging through the Ruins, closing in on the city limits and taking down the few soldiers brave enough to enter the Ruins to try to stop them.

There's a gaping hole in the wall.

The Transportation Dock has multiple fires blazing, hindering the transports not disabled from taking off.

My band buzzes an instant before a holographic message shoots out of it.

Matthias is standing in his father's home office, in front of a large desk cluttered with screens and papers. Behind him is a family portrait of a young Matthias and his parents. No one is smiling.

The camera zooms in on Matthias's face. His jaw is set in determination, hands fisted at his sides. "My name is Matthias Valarius. Son of Colonel Keenan Valarius. Everything you've been told is a lie. Demetrius Ark is a manipulator seeking to use you for his own agenda. He doesn't care if you live or die. He's an evil man that must be stopped." The fire and passion in his words is almost otherworldly. Like he's found a strength outside of himself. "You do not need to be a part of his plans. You have a choice. Now is the time to take your stand. Let's fight!"

The message cuts out.

"Don't think I've ever heard him so passionate," Nika says. "If I wasn't already in this battle, he'd have convinced me."

I open my mouth to agree, but my eye catches on a screen across from me.

Arwen's planting a bomb under the side steps of the Weaponry Training Complex. Two recruits with her keep watch as she crawls partway under the steps to settle the device in place. Something feels off. Maybe because I know there are too many soldiers nearby after the early evacuation of the Main Headquarters Building. Plus the fact that she should have been able to plant the bomb using the underground tunnels. My heart pounds in my chest like I just ran a race. Why did she deviate? What happened?

The recruits with her yell, panic masking their faces.

"Oh no." I put my hand to my mouth as five soldiers surround them, led by Corporal Sidon.

Arwen doesn't stop what she's doing, even as Corporal Sidon shouts at her, gun trained on her back.

Nika and I watch in horror.

The soldiers bind the hands of the two recruits with Arwen, hauling them away from the building.

If the attacks had gone according to plan, if they hadn't been rushed because I needed her to evacuate the Main Headquarters Building early . . .

Corporal Sidon grabs Arwen's leg, and yanks her out from under the steps. Arwen kicks his knee. He stumbles back. With a look of determination etching her face, she presses a button on her band, then races away from the building.

Corporal Sidon recovers, raises his rifle, and fires. Arwen crumbles to the ground.

A small cry escapes me.

The light on the bomb flashes. Corporal Sidon's eyes widen.

An explosion erupts. The video feed cuts off.

Pain rips through me and tears burn my eyes.

I pinch the bridge of my nose, desperately wishing I could undo the last minute. Bring Arwen back.

But I can't. Just like I can't bring back Cade or Ava.

Another friend. Gone.

My band beeps, signaling the transport's arrival time.

"We need to go," Nika says, voice choked.

I nod.

The two of us jog the rest of the way down the hallway as a flood of emotions washes over me. I can't let the sacrifices of so many be in vain.

We have to win.

I use the code Kiwi sent me to access the rooftop dock.

Nika and I step outside.

"Ah, yes," Ark says. "You were right, Ryder. Here she is."

I stop short.

Ark is standing with a dozen soldiers and his most trusted advisors: Colonel Valarius, Mandeville, Elva Trill, Major Vasco. And the Sitreean Minister of Defense, Antonio.

No.

Ark's sharp gaze snaps to Nika, surprise lighting his eyes. "Now I can't say I ever thought I'd see you again, Nika." His lip curls. "I do hate having my orders disobeyed, but the look on both of your faces right now . . . it eases the pain." He gestures to Antonio. "Bria, let me more properly introduce my comrade: Ryder Tendivi."

"You're working with him," I state the obvious, unable to stop myself.

Antonio—Ryder—inclines his head. "It is as you see. I really thought the nerve agent I slipped into your drink would deter you from trusting anyone in the delegation." He focuses on Ark. "But you were right, Demetrius. She really does want to believe people see the world as she does."

"Indeed. Thinks everyone should follow her morality, just like Chaplain Antonio at the academy," Ark says.

The two of them laugh, and my blood curdles.

Not only is Ryder working with Ark. He tried to poison me. Almost *killed* me.

How could I have fallen into this trap?

Ryder grows serious. "There are other Sitreean transports not far from Talionis airspace. I'd hate to see them witness what's happening here before you have time to clean it up."

As though to emphasize his point, a bomb goes off nearby, shaking the building.

Ark claps him on the shoulder. "I appreciate your concern, Ryder. But it's well in hand. We'll have everyone ready for deployment within twenty-four hours."

"What? Why did you move it up again?" I ask, unable to stop myself.

How is Ark still planning to leave and attack Sitreea after everything that happened today? And *sooner* than we thought?

Ark's dark eyes find mine, the calculated cruelty within their depths sends goosebumps over my body. "I suppose it doesn't matter if you know. You'll be sentenced to death soon enough."

Chills claim every inch of my body, but I remain silent. He's baiting me, but others are fighting. All hope isn't lost yet.

Ark continues. "Ryder informed me of a new treaty and defensive agreement the Chancellor of Sitreea is working on negotiating. Once it's in place, it will make my job much harder." His eyes narrow. "So we'll attack by week's end. Whether the recruits are ready or not."

"You won't win," Nika says, staring defiantly at Ark and his soldiers.

Ark snaps his fingers, and Colonel Valarius hands him a holographic display. "Let's see about that, shall we?" Ark turns it on.

The hologram erupts from the device. A feed of Eryndale Scouts in the Ruins, led by Lorenzo. Thaddeus, Gabe, and a handful of other scouts who were tasked with heading to the site where Mom and Keesia are protecting the kids and running the operations.

Nika gasps and clutches my hand.

Chills coat my entire body.

Nika and I squeeze each other's hands so tightly I can't feel my fingers, but I don't let go.

"Now, Gabe," Ark says into a com device in his ear.

The feed shows Gabe signaling.

A unit of soldiers bursts from the shadows of a broken-down pre-Demise building and attacks the Eryndale Scouts.

Gabe was the leak in Eryndale.

I drop to my knees, the breath leaking from my lungs as I watch friends being led into a trap. And there's nothing I can do.

Lorenzo fights off multiple soldiers at once, firing two guns until they're out of bullets. He chucks the weapons at an oncoming soldier, hitting her in the head. Another solider closes in. He lands an uppercut on the soldier's jaw that sends the man to the ground. Two more come at him from either side. He does a low sweep with his leg, taking out the one on the right. Lorenzo crouches into a fighting stance, preparing to strike the soldier coming from his left.

Before he can make a move, a female soldier shoots him in the back.

A sob catches in my throat. Lorenzo and I might not have always seen eye to eye, but he was a good man.

Within moments of Lorenzo's death, the fight is over. Several scouts are injured. Others bound. A few . . . dead.

Ark turns on another hologram to show the soldiers attacking different teams of scouts outside of Talionis. Gabe gave away all of their positions.

We're going to fail.

Ark is going to win.

And he doesn't care who has to die.

By some miracle, no one enters the site where Mom, Keesia, and the kids are. At least not yet.

Soldiers activate more holograms, and suddenly, the multiple battlefronts are projected across the rooftop.

Tears burn the backs of my eyes as I witness the tides of the battle turn.

Recruits are rounded up by soldiers.

Some are shot when they run.

Everything is too wide of a camera angle for me to identify those who are shot or tell if they're dead or if the soldiers are using training bullets.

My breath comes in ragged bursts.

Maybe this isn't real. Maybe it's all a simulation.

I leap to my feet. Race to the edge of the roof.

"What are you doing?" Colonel Valarius shouts.

"Let her be," Ark says calmly.

Too calm.

Before I reach the edge of the roof, I know I'll see more of what the holograms showed.

But I can't stop myself.

I skid to a stop at the low wall. Look out over the city.

Fires consume several buildings, but soldiers work to contain them.

The small teams we created less than twenty-four hours ago, those who all vowed to do what they could to stop Demetrius Ark, are being rounded up by other soldiers.

And based on Gabe's act, my friends outside of the city are now surrounded by soldiers.

If they're not already dead.

Ark snaps his fingers. "Mandeville, project these images throughout the city. Let the rebels see what their resistance has done. Nothing."

Screens I didn't know were built into the buildings project the dismal images of our failure.

I drop my hands to the low wall, the smalls stones digging into my hands.

God, I tried. We tried. What did we do wrong?

Nika gasps, and I realize she's joined me.

"What do we do?" Nika's words are a breath. A broken, shattered breath.

"I don't—"

Release the files.

The thought pops into my head, stopping my words.

Nika stares at me. "What?"

Tell Ari to release the files. Again, the thought takes over my mind. Almost as though it's outside of me.

God, is that what I should do?

I chew on my lip, but I don't hear an audible voice from God that confirms I should take that action.

Still, I can't shake the thought from my mind.

A glance behind me reveals Ark laughing with the men and women of his inner circle. Which apparently includes Ryder. And Gabe.

He's prepared for every contingency. Knew we would do everything we could to stop him. Planted his spies . . . everywhere.

I face the surrendering Resistance in front of me. Lift my band,

and subtly type a message to Ari on the channel she opened up for me hours ago.

There's a chance Mandeville or another tech-savvy soldiers will intercept it. See what I'm telling Ari to do.

But it's a risk I have to take.

Besides, what is there to lose?

Nika shifts closer to me, giving me an extra burst of courage as I finish typing my message to Ari. Nika has no idea what I'm doing, but she's got my back.

Like she always has, even from the day we were first chained together in the transport that brought us to the city.

Whatever happens next, I'm glad my friend is here with me.

"Finish up, girl," Nika hisses. "Not sure what you're doing, but they're gonna come over any second."

I double-check my message, sensing Nika reading over my shoulder.

Release the information you and Isaac decoded. Project it onto the screens Mandeville is using if you can. Now.

I hit send.

Half a second later, a reply comes from Ari.

Of course I can.

Nika snorts lightly, and I shake my head.

"The girl is confident. Gotta give her that," Nika says.

"Bria, Nika," Ark calls over.

We turn, but don't move closer to the group staring at us.

"We'd best get you in position for your public trial in the Center. No sense waiting." His dark eyes narrow. "We have a schedule to keep."

Soldiers flank us, and Ark leads his entourage from the rooftop.

Nothing on the holograms change.

Maybe Ari was overly confident in her abilities.

Soldiers march Nika and me out of the building and into the chaos on the streets.

Chaos that is, unfortunately, dissipating.

We've done damage to Talionis. Buildings are marred, some still blazing. Soldiers even appear wounded—although I'm less confident that was us. Probably Callypso and her pirates.

But none of it was enough.

Laban's golden eyes catch mine from where he stands. Clutching Storm on the steps of the Educational Building. Rafael is in shackles at the bottom of the stairs, his lip bleeding.

"No." I bolt toward Laban, but the soldier on my right grabs me, quickly followed by the soldier on my left.

I try to pull away. Get to Storm. But their hold is too tight.

"Leave the kid alone," Nika shouts.

A soldier holding her slaps her across the face. "Don't you dare—"

"Greetings." Ari's image takes over all the holograms throughout the city, silencing the soldier and causing our party to stop.

"How is she in our system?" Ark snaps at Mandeville, who is already typing frantically on a screen.

"I'm not—"

"Get her out! Now!" Ark shouts.

"When we escaped," Ari says, "we took items from Commander Demetrius Ark's safe. Items he was desperate to get back. All were returned to him, save one. This one." She holds up a thick packet of files. "It was encrypted, but my team decoded the files."

"Turn it off!" Ark screams, inches from Mandeville's face.

"I'm trying sir. I don't know how she got—"

"I don't care how she got in. Just get. Her. Out." Ark's voice holds the threat of death.

I focus on what Ari's saying as the soldiers loosen their grip on my arms.

"These files hold proof that no one is here who hasn't been manipulated by Ark," Ari says.

Then she begins reading off names of Ark's top men and women. Along with information that details their personal lives. Ways Ark leveraged circumstances to make them loyal.

Ari names person after person, from Sampta and Presidia, to Elva Trill, Colonel Valarius, and Major Vasco.

She speaks quickly, giving short explanations for each person.

Sampta and Presidia were lied to. Told their designs would never make the Sitreean fashion circuit for political reasons. Ark promised them he'd get their designs the fame they deserved. Become world-renowned. If they worked for him first. But he was the reason they didn't make the fashion circuit. Ari details how Ark spread lies about the sisters. Scandal.

The whole time she shares the information, Ark becomes more and more unhinged as he yells for Mandeville to stop it.

"I need time!" Mandeville shouts back.

Ark shoots him in the leg. Mandeville gives a strangled cry as his body contorts in pain.

"Get it done before you bleed out," Ark says through clenched teeth.

The sisters emerge from the tailors' building, arms loaded with recruit uniforms.

"How could you?" Sampta shouts at Ark. "No amount of fashion could ever be powerful enough to make you worth following."

"And you. *Ryder.*" Presidia's voice cracks. "You were working with him?"

Before either of the men responds, the tailors drop their armloads of uniforms on the steps of the building, douse them with a liquid concoction I can't identify, and then each of them light a match. Together, they toss their matches onto the uniforms. Flames erupt. Seconds later, the blaze is raging. The sisters walk away arm-in-arm. Before they've gone five feet, the building housing their designs catches fire.

The soldiers surrounding me and Nika release their hold, some caught up in the display from Sampta and Presidia, others listening to Ari as she continues to share details.

I ease my way toward Storm, catching Nika's eye.

She nods, moving subtly in the opposite direction.

"Laban Meritas," Ari says, capturing my attention.

And Laban's.

His face flashes confusion, then anger.

But unlike the soldiers who don't seem to notice Nika and me slipping away, his hold on Storm tightens. She whimpers.

I step closer.

Ari continues, "Demetrius Ark ordered your wife and daughter murdered when you didn't extend your Sitreean military contract to continue serving under him. He made it appear as though someone within the Sitreean government was at fault, but it was all orchestrated by him. If you don't believe me, Ark says in his notes about you"—she pauses to pick up a paper and read it word for word—"'If Laban Meritas needs to be manipulated, ensure oranges or some citrus scent is in the room. The man associates it with the notification of the death of his wife and daughter. It will come in handy in the event his loyalty ever wavers.'"

"Shut! Her! Up!" Ark is screaming now.

"They were everything to me." Laban shoves Storm aside. "You lied to me." He rushes toward Ark, but Colonel Valarius and other soldiers still loyal to Ark surround their Commander.

I race to Storm, glancing back occasionally at the fight ensuing behind me.

Laban disarms two soldiers, then takes a blow to the side from a third who approached from behind.

I reach Storm, Nika right behind me.

I help Storm to her feet.

The three of us whirl around to face the fight.

Laban ducks a right hook from one of the soldier's guarding Ark, then raises his rifle and shoots two others. The gun clicks, empty. Several other soldiers in the area join Laban's attack as Ari continues reading off the evidence of Ark's manipulation. Laban and the soldiers with him overwhelm the group guarding Ark, leaving Laban a hole.

He slips past Ark's defenses and the two men face each other. Laban's holding a knife.

Ark glares at him.

Nika, Storm, and I stay frozen in place, unable to tear our eyes from the standoff twenty yards away, highlighted by the raging fire the tailors set.

Ari's voice continues echoing from the screens as she details how Ark hid Colonel Valarius's war crimes and used the intel to manipulate Andor into working for him. All so Ark wouldn't leak the intel and destroy Andor's parents' lives.

"Why?" Laban's shattered cry cracks through the air like the fire crackling behind them.

Ark's cold gaze doesn't waver. "Because I needed you to be ruthless. And you never would have been if they were alive. They made you weak."

Laban lets out a raw and desperate scream. Rushes Ark, knife raised.

Maybe Laban will stop—

A gunshot cuts through the air.

Laban drops. Ark holds the pistol that just took down one of his most loyal men.

I gape at the scene, my mind unable to process. Laban has tormented me since I was kidnapped. Now he's dead. But there's no relief.

Ark's eyes find mine. He raises the pistol.

"We need to get out of here," I say to Nika and Storm.

Storm grabs my hand, and the three of us run.

The pistol fires, but no one chases us. I glance back. Colonel Valarius and the soldiers loyal to Ark are overtaking the ones who attacked with Laban.

We round a bend.

Ari continues reading off more information, and everyone we pass is enraptured by it.

Some appear angry at Ari, talking about how they don't believe a word she says. Others stare in shock.

Major Vasco emerges from the Warfare Strategies Building, the scowl on his face thunderous. I duck down the narrow alleyway next to the building with Nika and Storm, all of us breathing hard. The alley is empty. We press our backs against the wall.

"Yes, sir," Major Vasco's voice drifts around the bend. "Send local Sitreean forces immediately."

His footsteps move away from us, cutting off whatever else he's saying. Nika and I exchange a look, and I see my questions reflected in her eyes. Is Major Vasco calling on the forces to help Ark? Or stop him?

Ari pauses what she's saying, grabbing our attention.

Someone off-screen says something unintelligible to her. She nods, then focuses on the camera again.

"I'm going to interrupt this message for something more important." Ari tucks a piece of blond hair behind her ear and types.

The image changes from Ari to show my dad.

CHAPTER
SEVENTY-ONE

Dad sits in the back compartment of a massive, drill-like machine, driving it forward. Bill and Paul stand to the left of Dad, working at a complex control panel. The head of the drill arm jerks upward. The tip spins so fast it's dizzying and rocks and debris drop to the ground, swept away almost immediately by the machine.

On the outside, Wade and Joey race back and forth on either side of the contraption, shouting instructions to the guys in the compartment.

All the men wear thick gloves, headgear, and goggles.

Darkness clings to the edges the video feed, interrupted only by the blinding spotlights the guys have set up to see their work. Fred adjusts the spotlights as the machine inches forward.

Kassre and Hosea stand back, away from the machine but at the ready. Movement in the shadows behind them catches my eye. I squint. Are there others with them?

The ground rumbles.

They're under the city.

As soon as the thought enters my mind, the video feed shifts to show the near-empty street outside of the Physical Training Arena. The change is so sudden I blink. Did Mandeville shut Ari down?

The street in front of the arena shudders, like it's gasping. Then it drops, creating a ramp.

Dad and the guys with him race out of the tunnel, a half-dozen others I don't recognize with them. The undercover team has arrived.

"The tunnel is open!" Dad shouts.

Ari changes the screen to display scouts rushing through the tunnels. Coming to help us. More than I realized were still safe.

Gabe's betrayal may have crippled the scouts, but it didn't destroy them.

I push away from the wall and look at Nika. "We need to use this distraction while we can."

"Agreed." Nika checks her ammo. "Ready to move when you are."

I turn to my young friend. "Storm, stay—"

She's shaking her head before I finish. "I'm fighting with you."

Her fierce determination keeps me from arguing. Plus, there's no time.

We need to act now.

The Wild Dogs and other Eryndale forces swarm through the tunnels. They're coming.

And they will find us fighting.

The screens cut off.

Mandeville and his team must have figured out how Ari was getting in, but it doesn't matter now.

The damage was done.

The three of us race back in the direction we just came from.

Matthias stands on the top of a small building next to the tailors' building. "If you want to fight, now is the time! You have a choice, recruits. Do not let Demetrius Ark take that from you!"

Another burst of pride swells within me as Matthias rallies the recruits.

Nika, Storm, and I near the group of soldiers surrounding Ark, and I'm stunned as recruits who I always saw as loyal to Ark rise up to fight alongside us. Maverick. Zadie. Even Fin. Until the swarm of those rushing through the city is more than I can count.

The sounds of battle deafen my ears as I fight the soldiers getting between us and Ark. In the cacophony, it's hard to know who is fighting with us and who's against us. I lead Storm and Nika toward the building Matthias was in, planning to attack from the side since a direct approach isn't working. It takes several minutes to travel the short distance, weaving around rubble and sidestepping those who are injured.

We finally arrive near the steps of the building. Matthias joins us.

Two soldiers aim their guns in our direction. The four of us leap behind a low wall. Bullets ping the other side.

There's a pause. We take turns poking our heads over and shooting back.

I don't want to kill anyone, but I also know the training bullets won't be enough to stop Ark and his loyal forces. Especially since the soldiers are now firing real bullets.

"I'm out of ammo," Nika says, dropping back behind the wall.

"Me too," I say.

A few moments later, Matthias and Storm's guns are empty as well.

It won't be long before one of the soldiers comes back here. My heart hammers in my chest.

I peek over the wall. Two soldiers are advancing, rifles pointed in our direction.

The female fires her gun as I drop below the wall. Chunks of rock spray over me.

Storm lets out a small yelp.

God, please help us.

A streak of movement to my left jerks my attention that way. Andor aims and fires a pistol three times.

Without looking, I'm confident he hit the soldiers advancing on us.

He closes the short distance to us, and removes two rifles from his back, a pistol from his shoulder holster, and another pistol from his belt. "These have real ammo."

Matthias, Nika, and I each grab a weapon, but I stop Storm from taking one.

"I need a gun, Bria." Storm reaches for the pistol again, her determined expression made less effective with the wobble in her voice.

"You'll be my lookout." I gently pull the pistol from her grasp and hand it to Nika.

Andor's com device chirps to life. "All loyal to the Commander, join forces at the Center," Colonel Valarius demands.

Matthias loads a bullet into the chamber of his gun. "We need to stop them before they get there."

We emerge from our hideout, guns poised. But the battle has shifted. No one's waiting for us.

Everyone's moving toward the Center.

Eryndale Scouts now mix with recruits as they attack soldiers. But it's not over yet. Even though we've had some success, the soldiers in Talionis still outnumber us.

And far less of them were won over by Ari's reveal than I had hoped.

I join the push toward the Center with Matthias, Nika, Storm, and Andor.

Smoke from the burning buildings clogs the air, masking our movements. And the movements of our enemies. No one is able to go very fast. With opposing groups scattered at various points between here and the Center, it takes several minutes to go a few yards.

Andor's presence, with his Talionis uniform, seems to confuse scouts and recruits alike, but he fights against every soldier who attacks with a tenacity that shows which side he's on.

A few soldiers join us when they see Andor. Though I'm thankful for their help, it makes knowing who to fight that much more confusing.

Five scouts surround Andor and the soldiers with him.

"He's with us!" I shout at them as I pass by through a cleared stretch of an alley. There's no time to stop and explain.

If we don't get to the Center in time, the soldiers will set up a Kill Zone with no escape route.

I clutch my pistol close to my chest, and take Storm's hand as we round a bend. The Center looms at the end of the street.

It will be too dangerous for Storm in there.

Nalani rushes in from a side street with a medic team. She drops down next to a recruit huddled near a wall ten feet away from us, and rips off the girl's sleeve to tend to a bullet wound on her shoulder.

"Storm, help Nalani, okay?" I say.

Storm hesitates. "I don't want to leave you."

Matthias and Nika are already several yards away, moving toward the Center with other recruits and scouts.

I kneel in front of Storm. "I have to go, but I'll do everything in my power to come back to you, okay?"

She nods.

"Nalani!" I shout to my friend.

She looks up from the girl she's helping.

"Can Storm help you?"

Nalani nods, waves Storm over, and then goes back to tending to the wounded girl.

I give Storm a quick squeeze, then take off after my friends.

The transports not destroyed in the bombing now swarm the air, but the battle is too fierce for the fighter pilots to attack. The crowd of soldiers mixed with recruits would mean too many losses for them.

A transport turns toward the Ruins.

Another transport blocks its path.

I stumble. Steady myself.

Then catch sight of the Sitreean symbol on the transport.

Major Vasco must have gotten through. And he must have been telling them to stop Ark.

"Well, you've ruined everything." Shay's voice behind me freezes my blood.

I turn slowly, eyes scanning the area.

The fight has moved beyond here. No one else is close enough to call for help.

I face Shay.

Two drones spin about her. The other drones are nowhere in sight.

Her gun hand is trained on me.

She cocks her head to the side. "Why do you always have to ruin everything?"

"Ark isn't worthy of your allegiance," I say, hoping I can implore her to change sides. "Think about everything they've done to us! They tore us from our families—"

"No." She aims two guns at me now. One from her mechanical arm, the other in her still-human hand. "They tore *you* from your family. My mother has wanted nothing to do with me for years. We both know it. The Commander gave me a *purpose*. And you've stolen it from me."

I drop my pistol and lift both hands. There's no way I'll get a shot off before she does. "You don't have a purpose here, Shay. You're as trapped as I am. To have a purpose you have to have a *choice*."

Her lip curls into a snarl. "Goodbye, Bria."

I release a slow breath. *Okay, God. Help them finish this. Please.*

Phew!

The sound zings past my ear.

My eyes fly open.

Shay drops to the ground, eyes staring lifelessly at the sky. Her drones spin, firing at the attacker. I dive for cover behind half-trampled bushes, searching for whoever saved my life.

Shane perches on a rooftop across the street, shooting a sniper rifle at the drones. "Run!" he screams, and I obey.

I take off in the direction Nika and Matthias went. To the Center. To finish this fight.

As I approach the Center, the noise from the battle is almost deafening. Scouts, recruits, and soldiers battle one another.

But what grabs my attention is Matthias in a hand-to-hand fight with his father near an entrance to the Center.

Both have discarded their weapons and grapple with one another.

I scoop up one of the pistols as I approach.

Colonel Valarius delivers a blow to Matthias's side. Matthias barely flinches. He throws a right hook into his dad's face.

Blood rushes out of Keenan Valarius's nose. He smiles wickedly. "At least you can throw a punch. Not that you're good for anything else."

Matthias winces as though the words hurt more than the blow

he just absorbed. He steps back, hands still poised to fight. His father wipes the blood from his nose.

I inch closer, trying to determine what to do. The pistol handle grows slick with my sweat.

"Ark took Mom from us, Dad," Matthias says, voice cracking. "How can you still serve him?"

Colonel Valarius steps toward Matthias. "Because *power* is more important than anything else. And the Commander offers more power than I could ever have obtained elsewhere. The losses are insignificant."

Matthias drops his hands.

Colonel Valarius pulls a small pistol. Points it at Matthias.

"No!" I race forward, firing the gun in my hand.

It clicks.

Empty.

Time slows. The sounds around me fade. All I can think of is keeping Matthias alive.

I just got him back.

I can't lose him.

Colonel Valarius shifts his attention to me. An evil smile gleams in his eyes.

The shot cracks through the air.

Matthias yells my name.

Pain slices through my side.

Blackness darkens the edges of my vision.

More gunfire.

Dozens of transports fill the sky. Soldiers descend.

Matthias drops to my side. Takes me in his arms.

I try to smile, but the darkness takes over.

CHAPTER
SEVENTY-TWO

I shift and wince as the pain in my side brings me fully awake. Bright lights pierce my vision, generating an immediate headache. I squint.

"Excellent." Nalani hovers over me, her face filling my vision. "Glad to see you waking up." She frowns. "You were shot, and you had some smoke inhalation, but I expected you to wake up hours ago."

I rub my eyes. "Sorry about that." I shift to sit and draw in a sharp breath.

Nalani gently presses me back down. "You'll need time to heal. But you'll make a full recovery."

She goes on about the medication she's using, but the words jumble in my brain. I try to ask how the battle ended, how many friends are gone, but before I can sleep overpowers me.

THE NEXT TIME I WAKE UP, I'M ALONE. THE PAIN IS MORE MANAGEABLE NOW, but the stark white walls of the infirmary in Talionis bring back far too many memories.

If I'm here, does that mean we lost?

There's a knock on my door. Before I can say a word, it opens.

Nika, Ari, and Matthias enter the room.

"Oh, good! You're up!" Ari exclaims. "There's so much to tell you."

"Girl, give her a minute," Nika says, rolling her eyes.

Matthias just studies me like he's trying to make sure I'm truly alive.

I smile at him. "Hi."

He crowds next to my bed, and Nika and Ari go quiet.

He takes my hand. "I was ready to let my father kill me." His blue eyes shine with unshed tears. "But I was not ready to lose you, Bria." He releases a broken breath. "Never do that to me again. Please."

I kiss his hand. "No promises." I bite my lip. "I really don't want to lose you either. And if your insane father is going to try to murder you, I will do whatever it takes to stop him."

"Well, that's not gonna happen," Ari interrupts.

"Shh!" Nika hisses. "Give them their moment!"

A laugh bubbles up out of me.

"See?" Ari says. "They're done."

Matthias grins, then shifts so our friends can come closer.

I don't let go of his hand, but desperation to know more washes over me. "Tell me what happened. Did Ark . . ." I can't finish the question.

Ari jumps in first, relaying how Sitreean forces arrived and worked with the scouts and recruits to overwhelm Ark and those who remained loyal to him. Major Vasco orchestrated the attack from Warfare Strategies. Between his aid in defeating Ark and the intel he's provided Sitreea through the scenarios Ark had him design, he's negotiated a reduced sentence.

Mandeville survived the gunshot wound to his leg. He's brokering a deal with Sitreea to leverage his tech ability and insights into Ark's plans in order to avoid a prison sentence. According to Nika, Mandeville's allegiance to Ark vanished after Ark shot him.

Colonel Valarius was killed when the Sitreean troops arrived, and Matthias seems almost . . . relieved.

My friends share about how the Sitreeans have arrested Ark along with his soldiers and are preparing to take them to Sitreea to be tried for their crimes. Elva Trill is claiming she was coerced into becoming Ark's personal propaganda specialist, but the Sitreean's aren't offering her any kind of plea deal. Which gives me additional confidence in the Sitreean government. Trill's lies have manipulated people long enough. I'm glad she'll be locked away.

"Gabe will be taken with them," Nika says. "It appears he was the only leak for Talionis within Eryndale. Ark promised him military power to control as much of the North American region as he wanted to, as long as Gabe provided good intel that served Ark's purposes."

"I was sure it was Reginald Finnigan," Ari says. "But apparently the guy is just annoying."

I smile, but focus on Matthias. "What about Andor?"

"He received a full pardon when Cai vouched for him," Matthias says. "He'll be staying back as part of a new Sitreean diplomatic program working with Eryndale to aid the North American region."

I lean my head against the headboard. We won. The reality doesn't fully sink in. Maybe because I'm still feeling the effects of the battle. Maybe because I was unconscious for the end.

Exhaustion washes in and I can't stop a yawn that cracks my jaw with its force. My eyes flutter shut. I pry them open.

Nalani walks in. Her eyes widen behind her glasses. "What are you guys doing? She needs to rest."

I open my mouth to protest, but it's stifled by another yawn. This time I can't stop my eyes from closing again. Not even when Matthias presses a kiss to my head before Nalani shoos him out of the room with Nika and Ari.

CRUNCHING SOUNDS GRATE AGAINST MY EARS, PULLING ME OUT OF THE blissfulness of sleep.

I keep my eyes shut, hoping it goes away.

The noise fades. Then another loud *crunch* shatters the quiet.

What is going on?

My eyes pop open to find Kiwi sitting in the chair in the corner of the room, munching on a carrot with one hand and working on a screen with the other. His legs are propped up and the screen rests on his knees.

"What are you doing?" I ask.

He gives a yelp. The carrot goes flying across the room and the screen clatters to the floor. He scoops it up. "You scared me."

"No kidding." I smirk and shift myself into a sitting position, feeling even better than I did the last time I woke up. "What are you doing?" I repeat the question.

"I had some work to do," he lifts up the screen, "so I figured I'd do it in here in case you woke up. Plus, Matthias needed to wash up before he started to stink." He gives me his two-finger salute. "Good to see you, boss."

I chuckle. "I'm not your boss, Kiwi."

He shrugs. "Course you are."

I shake my head but don't argue with him. "What kind of work were you doing?"

Kiwi sobers. "Preparing for the funeral."

A lump forms in my throat, but the door opens, keeping me from answering.

Ari walks in. Her eyes light up when she sees I'm awake, but dim quickly. "Are you okay?"

"I told her I was getting things ready for the funeral," Kiwi says.

"Oh." Ari releases a sigh, but gives Kiwi a soft smile.

"How many friends did we lose?" The words barely squeeze themselves past my thickening throat.

Ari steps closer and stops at the foot of my bed. "Arwen died, along with a seventeen other recruits. Several scouts are missing or dead. Including Lorenzo."

A tear squeezes past my defenses and rolls down my cheek. Lorenzo fought until the bitter end. It doesn't seem right that he won't share this victory with us. And Arwen. I don't want to close my eyes for fear of seeing Corporal Sidon shooting her in the back.

I force my focus onto what Ari's saying.

"We'll have a funeral for them in a few days." Ari gestures to

Kiwi. "Kiwi and I are helping put together a visual memorial for everyone we can." She offers a slight smile. "But the crew of *The Fearless Lady* and the Wild Dogs are all okay. So are your parents, Storm, Kemena, and Cai."

I nod, relief and pain at the losses burning the back of my eyes. The three of us stay silent for several minutes.

Matthias enters, Kemena and Nika right behind him. The room suddenly feels crowded, but I don't mind. It's so good to see everyone here. Alive.

Especially after what Ari shared.

Matthias maneuvers himself until he's right next to me. "How are you feeling?"

"Okay." I smile at him, then catch sight of Ari watching us.

I focus on her and she ducks her head. "Shane saved my life."

The words bring her head up. "He did?"

I nod and tell them what happened with Shay and how Shane took fire to save me. A single tear trails down Ari's cheek. She cared about Shane, but he betrayed her just like he did the rest of us.

"He received a full pardon." Ari twists my blanket in her hands, and the rest of us stay quiet. "Once he knew he wasn't going to jail, he found me. Begged me to forgive him and take him back." Ari falls silent.

I exchange a look with Nika, hoping she can give me a clue as to what happened. She shrugs, eyes wide.

I guess this is the first Ari's shared about this.

Kiwi's arms are crossed and he chews on his lower lip as he waits for Ari to continue.

When she doesn't, Kemena puts her hand on Ari's arm. "What did you say?"

"I told him I forgive him. But I can't trust him." Ari releases my blanket. She looks up and there's peace in her eyes. "When he knew there wasn't a future between us, he requested the opportunity to return to Sitreea and start a new life. He left yesterday."

I offer her a half-smile. I can't fully imagine what she's gone through, but I'm glad she made the choice she did.

Matthias is close enough for me to rest my head on his arm.

We've lost many friends, but I still have him. And my closest friends, my family, and Storm.

Somehow, we've all survived this nightmare.

We've risen above the darkness of Talionis and survived.

Thank You, God. I don't know what else to say but thank You. We couldn't have done this unless You were with us.

"Ow, ow, ow!" The cries from someone in another room crash through the moment.

"That's Quwani. Apparently she got a 'really bad' splinter when she hurdled an old fence in the Ruins." Ari shakes her head. "She is *not* a silent sufferer."

The six of us burst out laughing. It hurts to laugh, but I don't want to stop. I just want to enjoy the miracle of all that's happened.

THE NEXT TWO WEEKS PASSES IN A BLUR. I MEET WITH AN OFFICIAL FROM Sitreea, and she debriefs me on everything I know. All I've learned about what Ark was planning. My work with Major Vasco. The interactions I had with Ryder Tendivi. Everything.

We review dozens of scenarios, with her asking me detailed questions. Apparently all to confirm Major Vasco hasn't been lying to them. At first going over each scenario is painful. So many memories. So much pain. But by the time we're done I feel intense relief.

I'll never have to go through or put a recruit through a scenario again.

She records the meetings, drilling me with questions until I'm exhausted. But when we're done, she tells me my testimony will be enough to seal Demetrius Ark's fate. He'll never be free again.

The fact that he's still alive sits uneasy with me. The man is a ruthless manipulator, and I don't know that I fully believe the official's promises. But I don't argue.

For now, it's enough to know Talionis will no longer exist as a training ground for kidnapped teens to become soldiers.

A week after Ark's defeat, there's a city-wide funeral for those who died in the battle. It's a difficult and emotional day. But acknowledging their lives and the sacrifices each of them made in their deaths is cathartic. The list of names and faces is far longer than I wish it was, and every person is given their own moment in the service. Scouts. Recruits. Kids. We spend the entire day mourning the loss of each one.

A few days later, Max, Cade's older brother, and his team of scouts bring Storm's parents to Talionis to reunite with their daughter. It's a tearful and beautiful reunion and after spending time with Storm, her parents find me and thank me for taking care of their daughter.

I tell them Storm became like my little sister and helped encourage me in my lowest moments. And I share how Cade was there for her too. It only seems right for them to know the part he played in protecting Storm. And me.

Sitreea works with Eryndale to get all the teens returned to their homes and reunited with their families. Although there are several teens who aren't interested in going home. Some are even angry to be in a position where they're forced to return to places they hate.

Many of them run away to find their own life.

I'm reunited with my own parents and friends from Eryndale, and we work together to clean up Talionis.

Sitreea has given the city to Eryndale. Now that the Sitreeans know there are so many survivors in North America, they have decided to use Talionis as a consulate to communicate between Eryndale and the rest of the world. Andor has received the lead position, which seems to make him more uncomfortable than anything.

Cai handles the negotiations, which brings some relief. But the reality that Talionis won't be leveled and buried bothers me almost as much as Ark still being alive.

I hate what this city stood for. But maybe it will change.

Cai promises me it will be used for good, and there are few people I trust more in the world than my uncle.

Matthias and I take every opportunity we can to spend time together as the weeks rush by, but it's not nearly as often as I'd like.

And then, it's time for me to go home.

Back to Derbe.

I SIT ON THE BEACH AND LOOK OUT OVER THE WATER IN THE BAY, BROUGHT back to a time before Talionis. To a time when I tried to outswim my memories. To forget about the pain and guilt of Ezri's death.

Retro and Kiwi let out whoops and splash water at Nika and Ari. I laugh as the girls yell at them, then slosh through the water toward them. Retro's eyes widen, then he races away, followed closely by Kiwi. Eli and Zeke jump up and down at the edge of the shore, shouting for the guys to run faster.

It's early spring and the water is freezing, but my friends insisted on swimming since today is unseasonably warm. And my little brothers are loving the chance to play in the ocean with everyone.

Jaxon and Lencie are a bit further down the beach chatting with Quwani and a couple members of the Wild Dogs. It's surreal watching all my worlds collide, but reuniting with my friends from Derbe has been wonderful. I'm thankful they were spared the horror of Talionis. Lencie wouldn't have survived with her condition.

Matthias plops down on the beach next to me, putting an arm around my shoulders. "I'm glad we were all able to come see what Derbe is like before we head back to Eryndale."

I lean into him. "Me too."

My friends and I will officially join the Wild Dogs in two weeks' time in coordinated effort with the crew of *The Fearless Lady*. Callypso recovered the Apex Hunter, a high-tech weapon from Talionis, and she's on the move through the region, taking over towns and destroying anyone in her way. As much as my parents and Kemena aren't thrilled that Nika and I will be back in harm's way, they understand.

And now that Kemena and Azarias are reunited, I suspect a wedding isn't far in the future.

Levi, Azarias's adopted son, certainly expects it.

Matthias and I fall into a peaceful silence as the shouts and splashing from our friends and my little brothers fill the early afternoon. Eli and Zeke love having everyone around. Thankfully, they'll be returning to Eryndale with me. My parents decided to move back to the refuge city with us.

Thaddeus has talked Mom into working with the cartography unit in Eryndale again. And Dad will be busy as well. Since they're convinced they're the reason Talionis was defeated, Bill and Paul are creating an "old guys" unit. Dad, Hosea, and Kassre joined, no questions asked.

My aunt has been released from custody in Eryndale and she's being escorted to Talionis to reunite with Cai. Which means I don't have to see her. I almost feel bad at how relieved I am that she won't be in Eryndale when I arrive in a few days. She sent me a letter apologizing for betraying me. I'm no longer bitter about what she did, but I doubt I'll be able to trust her anytime soon. She and Cai are the most mismatched couple I've ever seen. But hopefully they'll figure out a way forward as Cai takes over running Talionis.

Zeke let's out a burst of laughter as Kiwi lets the twins tackle him into the waves. I smile and rest my head on Matthias's shoulder, more at peace on this beach than I've been in years.

The waves lap at the shore, but they don't chant my name anymore.

The monster is dead.

The darkness of my past no longer haunts me. I still miss Ezri. Losing him was more painful than I could ever fully express. The pain of his death and the deaths of so many friends will be forever etched in my heart.

But God allowed me to walk this dark road so that I could find Him. So I could see I couldn't do it all myself.

And He made me stronger. Better.

I found Him *through* my pain.

And it was worth it.

There is still evil to fight. Callypso. The Raiders. Probably more than I realize at this moment. But I will fight. And I'll do it alongside those I trust. And whatever I do, I'm going to follow God's leading above all else and be a woman who stands courageously against every enemy.

"Hey guys, gather around," Malachi calls to us.

Matthias and I stand and join him as our friends come in from the water.

The seriousness in his expression leaves me uneasy.

"We heard from Sitreea," Malachi says. "Ark orchestrated an escape upon his return. He's being hunted, and he doesn't have the resources to return to Talionis and finish what he started, but we wanted you guys to know."

The words send a solemn blanket over our group.

Malachi claps his hands, as though to dispel the tension he created with his news. "And Mrs. Averton said to tell you guys lunch is ready." He winks at us. "Eat the good food while you can. Retro always angers Eryndale's chefs so much they don't pack us the best portions for our trips."

"Hey!" Retro puts a hand over his heart like he's been wounded. "That's not fair."

Everyone laughs, then traipses through the forest back to my house.

Matthias tugs me to the water. "I just want one second alone with you," he whispers as our friends disappear into the trees.

I tuck my hand into his, and we walk to the edge of the shore. He pulls me into his arms, and I rest my head against his chest as we stare out at the water. The waves lap at our feet.

Matthias turns toward me, his bright blue eyes shining in the sun. All traces of Talionis have vanished from his appearance—from the bruises his father inflicted to the military haircut. His face is full and healthy, and his dark curls are trimmed close to his head.

He tucks a hair behind my ear. "I love you, Bria Averton. Even though we faced evil, I'm glad we faced it together. Glad I have you in my life to face whatever else may come."

I trace the chain of the necklace he still wears. "I love you too, Matthias. God gave me a gift when He brought you into my life."

The smile he gives me warms my heart.

A bell rings in the distance, signaling dinner is being served.

Matthias takes my hand and turns away from the water. I give the waves one final glance. My goodbye.

I turn and walk with Matthias toward the forest. A thrill of excitement washes over me and I squeeze Matthias's hand.

We're entering a new life. There will be challenges, but I have a peace and settledness now that I never had before.

God, I can't wait to see what You will do.

FREE DOWNLOAD
LABAN'S UNTOLD ORIGIN STORY

Every villain has a story. Discover the tragedy and choices that shaped Laban, one of the fiercest antagonist in the Talionis Series. Download your FREE copy of *Shattered Ashes* below!

SPREAD THE WORD

I hope you enjoyed this epic conclusion to the Talionis Series!

Thank you for journeying through all four books of the Talionis Series with Bria and her friends. After every battle, every loss, every triumph—your dedication to seeing Bria's story through to the end means the world to me. And now, I have an invitation for you.

If these stories have impacted you—if you've found hope in these pages—I'd love for you to become what we call a "Triple Threat" against the darkness.

WHAT IS TRIPLE THREAT?

When you take action with us, we call this Triple Threat because by taking these three steps, you become a threat against the darkness and a fellow comrade-in-arms in our mission to spread the hope that Jesus Christ offers to all.

1. PRAY FOR US

Prayer is powerful. We would love your prayers for the furtherance of our mission to share the gospel and the abundant life in Jesus Christ through these adventure stories.

2. LEAVE A REVIEW

Reviews are essential. When someone decides to read a book, they give one of their most valuable commodities—their time. Leaving a review on Goodreads and/or Amazon will give new readers confidence that these books are worth their time.

3. SHARE THESE STORIES

Sharing is vital. If you loved these stories, please help us spread them! A recommendation from a friend goes a long way. You can help by sending a text or email, posting on social media, and/or having a conversation with someone you feel would love these adventures.

As my thanks for joining this mission, everyone who completes all three Triple Threat actions can download a free printable Map of Talionis!

Scan below to join our mission and claim your Talionis Map.

Together, we're spreading light in dark places.
Thank you again for reading,
C.J. Milacci

ABOUT THE AUTHOR

C.J. Milacci is the author of the Talionis series, a multi-award-winning young adult sci-fi dystopian series. She is passionate about empowering teens and young adults through her inspiring stories and engaging speaking events. Her stories and talks seek to bring hope, healing, and the message that each person has a unique, God-given purpose. She's passionate about crafting stories of good overcoming evil, finding hope in the midst of seemingly hopeless circumstances, and true acceptance. Find out more on her website at cjmilacci.com.

ALSO BY C.J. MILACCI

THE TALIONIS SERIES

Recruit of Talionis (Book 1)

Fugitive of Talionis (Book 2)

Enemy of Talionis (Book 3)

Captive of Talionis (Book 4)

A TALIONIS SERIES COMPANION NOVEL

Abandoned Shores

ACKNOWLEDGMENTS

Wow. After years of writing and plotting and planning, it is a strange thing to come to the end of a series. And it is certainly not something I could have ever done on my own. Every bit of this series has come together by God's grace and with the help of an amazing team of people.

I couldn't begin listing those who have helped me without first thanking my Lord and Savior, Jesus Christ. You have made this possible. Truly You do take the weak and lowly and use them to magnify Your amazing strength. Thank You for creating this story with me, teaching me as I wrote it, and allowing me to see You through all the messiest and hardest moments. My life would have no meaning without You. All I am is Yours. I love You!

There are countless people who have encouraged me, helped me, and are responsible for making this story better. To thank them all by name and in detail would take many pages, so I'll keep this short for now.

My amazing parents who have cheered me on from day one. Mom, thank you for reading this story from its messiest version up through its final version, and encouraging me every step of the way. Especially when I'm second guessing everything (sorry that happened so much!). Dad, thank you for being so excited for this book and for being one of my biggest fans. In a world where not everyone gets even one good parent, I am beyond blessed to have the two of you as my mom and dad.

Ani, the best little sister I could ever ask for, who has been an instrumental part in bringing this book to life. This book would not be what it is without you. Thank you for the hours you've spent brainstorming with me, the countless projects you help me with, and for the beautiful formatting job you did for this book. And thank you for joining me in this adventure. Two really are better than one, and I thank God for you every day.

My talented and amazing beta readers. Katie Robles, Katie Briggs, Bella Raine, Ani, and Mom. Your feedback, encouragement, and insights helped strengthen this book and make it so much better.

My incredible extended family. To have cousins, aunts and uncles, and nieces and nephews who are so supportive and excited about what I'm doing and my stories—it is a priceless gift. I couldn't imagine having a better hype crew than all of you. Love you guys!

Karyne Norton, my fabulous friend who is on this author journey with me. Thank you for regular texts, brainstorms, and idea sharing. Having you in this with me is such a blessing. I wish Arizona wasn't so far from Pennsylvania!

Becca Wierwille, my outstanding editor. You helped hone this story, make it so much stronger, and wrangle all my ridiculous commas. Thank you!

Emilie Haney, my cover designer, who has created each cover for this series. Thank you for making beautiful covers for me!

Chris Pearce, my proofreader, who can catch the littlest of mistakes. Thank you for cleaning this up and for loving the story.

To my readers. There are over half a million words in the Talionis Series (and that's not including these long acknowledgments!). Thank you for being here with me for every word. Every twist and turn. Every exciting win, and each devastating loss. Thank you for loving my stories, emailing me, and coming to see me at events. I write these books for you. My prayer is that this series, Bria's story, would give you the courage to boldly live out *your* story. God has a purpose for your life, a plan He wants to unfold day by day. May you embrace it with everything you have. Following after Jesus is the greatest life you will ever experience.

And to my Kickstarter backers who made all this possible and helped bring this book to life in ways I never imagined, thank you. You all made this project an amazing experience, and I'm honored that you chose to be a part of this. Without further ado, here's the list of Kickstarter backers (in order of when they backed):

Dad & Mom, Lee Anne Womack, Z.R. McCormick, Karah Little, Giselle Trejo, Micah Madden, Josiah DeGraaf, Elyssa Rose, Kelly Jo Wilson, MadiJoy, Chad Abbs, A.C. Williams, Rachael, Jacey Veltman, Olivia Ramos Fusaro, Laurie Christine, Sara Belle, Maria Jacques, Jessica Gwyn, Heiko Koenig, Aunt Kelly, Bella Raine, Elizabeth Collins, Marcy B, Elliana and Josiah Seyller, Gabby Peters, Mindy Hite, Elizabeth Grace, Patty R, Aunt Michelle & Uncle Dave, Peter DeHaan, Zachary Dale, Lily Moriah, Andrew Milacci, Jerry Paradise, Keith & Becky Woods, Jennifer Dyer, Rebecca Washburn, Jacob H Joseph, Jeremiah Friedli, Karyne Norton, Emelyn Petcaugh, Kenneth Ost, Joelle DiAntonio, Sarah Beckman, Charmagne Kaushal, Matt & Sarah Scales, A. Hope Dexter, Naomi Sowell, Chuck and Hannah Chandler, Becca Wierwille, RuthAnna Miller, Emilee Stoltzfus, Janet DiAntonio, Chris, Erin Dydek, Grace Harris, Aunt Judy and Uncle Gene, Harold van Bolhuis, Jonas, Remington Cloutier, Josh and Tori Bair, E.A. Hendryx, Maria Broome, Hannah Summers, Jane Penderwick, Jill, David Holzborn, The Schreiner Family, Camy Tang, Abigail B., Kristyn Brendle, Emily Hutnyak, S.D. Smith, Eddie Joo, Mahina, Amy, Christen Krumm, Celeste Richardson, Sarah Summers, Christa Stoltzfus, Dan Daetz, Caleb Jefferies, Angela Miles, Katie Robles, Katherine Briggs, Krystina Roupe, April, Jake Stoddard, Chelsea Rich, Cayla Belser, Pamela Hart, Wolf & Glacier & Remus & Toa, Becky Sorensen, Kevin, Ethan Eshleman, Kristin Flanagan, Connie Hendryx, Emmy, Erica Martin, Candace Kade, Elisha Snowdon, Alicia Jacques, Rachael Ritchey, Jeremy Jacques, Nicole O'Meara, Kathy Brasby, Lance and Angie Emma, Z.S. Diamanti, Susan Macias, Marc Anthony Salas, Brandon Wilborn, Alan D Simcik, Suzie Anne, Ellis K. Popa of Ellis Kaye Creates, Steven A. Guglich, Taylor Belser Yinger, Uncle Paul & Aunt Linda, Abigail Jefferies, Andrew Jefferies, Taylor S Newport, Sam Monach, Pat Zab, Shanon M. Brown, Daniel Martinez, Author Given Hoffman, Jennifer Arndt, Chase Meadows, Katherine Malloy, Uncle Fred & Aunt Tommie, Jennifer Benoit, Benjamin J. Wright, Doug Erling, Scott Minor, Natalya Cerebe, Rob and Jewell Rowlands, Alexandra Corrsin, Abigail Beyer, Leticia, Ashley, Kristin

Cooney, A.C. Hilleson, Michele Collauto, Zach and Bridgette Huebener, The Foster Family, H.M. Hershberger, M. Weedin, LMSradio/Podbean, Melanie Lehman, Kristi Lay, Thomas Umstattd Jr., Meagan Myhren-Bennett, Riley Lynch, Liz Jacques, Lily Martin, Naresa McRwray-Williams, Deb McGuire, Hattie Larrison

www.ingramcontent.com/pod-product-compliance
Lightning Source LLC
Chambersburg PA
CBHW061534190726
48289CB00004B/1044